Brio

Chris Cross

HADLEIGH HOUSE
PUBLISHING

Hadleigh House Publishing
Minneapolis, MN
www.hadleighhouse.com

Cover design by Alisha Perkins

ISBN-978-1-7357738-5-8
ISBN-978-1-7357738-6-5 (ebook)

LCCN: 2021917297

FOR MOM 'N' DAD,
TO WHOM I OWE ABSOLUTELY EVERYTHING—
FOR TYLER,
FOR BEING MY BACKREST—
AND FOR CAT,
WHO ALWAYS SAID, "KEEP GOING!"

THE EARTH HAS ITS MUSIC FOR THOSE WHO WILL LISTEN,
ITS BRIGHT VARIATIONS FOREVER ABOUND.
WITH ALL OF THE WONDERS THAT GOD HAS BEQUEATHED US,
THERE IS NOTHING THAT THRILLS LIKE THE MAGIC OF SOUND.

—REGINALD V. HOLMES—

IT IS NOT HARD TO FIND THE TRUTH;
WHAT IS HARD IS NOT TO RUN AWAY FROM IT
ONCE YOU HAVE FOUND IT.

—ÉTIENNE GILSON—

Chapter One

THE NOBODY

Jay flipped his mattress over, yanked up every loose floorboard, searched behind his dresser a hundred times, shook out his rumpled bedcovers, and tore through the musty feathers inside his pillow before he forced himself to admit the awful truth: It was *gone*. He'd lost it.

He was dead.

Jay dove down to check under the bed again, wanting to curse and to whisper a desperate prayer at the same time. He wound up saying something between a prayer and a curse—something so sour it would've made even the most sweet-tempered old lady slap his filthy mouth clean off his face.

"Blast the blessed Seraphs! Where is it?" Jay hissed, kicking through dirty clothes on the floor. Somebody was bound to realize it was missing at some point. And when they did, it wouldn't be long before they looked for him.

So dead.

Desperate, Jay rifled through the dresser drawers again when he heard the dull sound of a gong tolling across town. He counted the *ba-bong*s as they rang through his window, his stomach shrinking:

One. Two. Three. Four. Five. Six. Seven. Silence.

Seven o'clock. Late. *Very* late.

Bandersnatches!

Abandoning the search, Jay scrambled to get ready—stumbling into his trousers, diving into his shirt, tangling his suspenders, pulling his vest on inside out, losing precious seconds hunting for his cap—and, stuffing his feet into mismatched boots, he unlocked the flap door in the floor and blitzed from his loft down the stairs.

Jay skipped the last few steps and stumbled onto the shop floor, shutting his eyes tight and bracing for his custodian's shouts—

But they didn't come.

The shop was empty.

Weird. Mr. Douse was normally at work long before the birds tumbled out of their nests to catch their wormy breakfast. He was never late.

Jay peered around. On the counter, fresh news bulletins lay beside a steaming mug. At the back, molten candle wax bubbled inside iron crucibles, ready for dipping. All that was missing was the candlemaker himself.

Whew. Jay figured Mr. Douse would be all set 'n' waiting to give him a lecture, but maybe the old man had stepped out. *Excellent*.

Jay snatched up an apple from a basket behind the counter, biting a large chomp out of it as he tiptoed toward the front door—

"Well now," said a deep, raspy voice. "If it isn't my truant lamplighter."

Aw, nuts.

Cheeks full, Jay whirled around to find the back door of the shop swung wide open. From the workroom beyond came a man who looked like a scruffy bear fresh out of hibernation, with the foul mood to match. Under his wild beard he had a scarred, pockmarked face, and his mouth turned down in a perpetual scowl. As he lumbered forward, he scraped a whittling knife over a chunk of hardened wax.

"All the town lamps were dark after sundown yesterday," said Mr. Douse, his eyes fixed on the wax in his hands. "That's not like you, missing a shift."

Jay swallowed the apple with a loud *gulp*. He hesitated.

"I got stuck up a tree."

Flecks of wax cascaded to the floor as Mr. Douse continued to carve, the knife spinning deftly in his fingers. Then his gaze slid upward.

Jay squirmed under the old man's hard look. Heck, it was the truth. Jay had only just started to make his rounds with the lamps when one of *them* had shown up.

Jay had panicked when he'd spotted it. He'd hightailed it up the nearest tree without thinking, praying it wouldn't sense him. After an hour of drifting about, it finally ghosted away—

And that's right when Jay had been spotted by the grove workers, who'd accused him of scrumping. Jay hadn't scrumped in his life!

Well, okay, he had filched a few nuts from the groves on occasion, though only ones on the ground, which didn't count. But since Jay didn't dare tell them the real reason he'd climbed the tree, the grove workers had dragged him off and given him an earful about stealing and trespassing. After that, Jay had bolted, never giving the lamps another thought.

But that was a bit much to explain right now.

As the silence spun itself into a thick discomfort, Mr. Douse sighed.

"I won't drag the truth from you." He set down the knife and his wax carving. "That's not what we have to talk about anyway."

Wuh-oh.

Jay watched Mr. Douse pull something out from beneath the bulletins. As soon as Jay saw it, the stone weight in his stomach increased by a few bricks.

"Now I understand why you started locking the door when you're in your room," said Mr. Douse, pinching the scandalous item in his fingers.

Jay said nothing, his voice blocked by a knot of dread in his throat. The thing he'd hunted for all morning, which he was positive he'd lost: *There it was* in Mr. Douse's hand. The old man held it as if it were utterly criminal, equal to a blood-crusted knife or a sack of stolen gold:

A small children's book, with a bright cover and crisp pages.

Jay choked down the knot, avoiding Mr. Douse's eyes. "That isn't—"

"Isn't what?" Mr. Douse cut in, an edge in his voice. "You saying this *isn't* a book from Mr. Barnes' shop? 'Cause we both know it is. My question is, how come you had it hidden under your mattress?"

Jay shuffled, stalling. "That's . . . uh . . . actually, funny story—"

Mr. Douse raised a hand to stop him. "You know you can't tell a lie worth a Whit. Be honest. When did you nick it?"

"I didn't *nick* it. Borrowed it, more like—"

"Julian." The old man's look was as flat and sharp as his knife.

Jay's mouth twisted in guilt. No point in lying. "On my day off."

Mr. Douse's eyes narrowed. He threw the book down with a *thwack*.

"I was just curious!" said Jay, trying to head off the storm. "That's all!"

"Julian—"

"I was gonna put it back, honest—right after I finish it—"

"*Julian—*"

9

"Okay, *okay*, I'll go now and return it, if that's what you want—"

Mr. Douse unleashed a hurricane.

"That's not the problem!" he snapped. "What d'you think would've happened if you were caught? You are on probation!"

That last word struck like a swift hand slapping Jay's cheek. He flinched.

The old man spat. "If the town council knew about this, it wouldn't've ended with a tongue-lashing. A one-way ticket back to the reformatory— that's what they'd've given you. Here I thought you never wanted to go there again." His face hardened. "Do you?"

Jay let the torrent of reprimands blow over him, not sure what to say.

But, c'mon, it was just a *book*. Jay had seen the grubby copy sitting in Old Man Barnes' book shop, begging to be picked up. It was called *Legends of the Muses*. Flipping through it, Jay had found stories about the Musicians—folks who could summon muses, the spirits of nature and harmony, for all kinds of things. With muses, Musicians could spark fire, control water, even vanish like smoke. Jay especially liked the tales of the Crafter, the most powerful Musician of all.

Something about those stories had made Jay curious, so he'd grabbed the book. But he hadn't stolen it. Just borrowed.

Mr. Douse laid a palm on Jay's shoulder.

"Listen. You're a decent kid. But you've got to stop this. Nicking things, I mean—oh, don't look so insulted. I know you. As your custodian, it's my job to look after you, and I only want to keep you out of trouble. Understand?"

Jay frowned. Him 'n' trouble were on too good of terms to break it off so easily. But Jay kept his mouth shut and nodded.

Mr. Douse *hmph*ed and picked up his mug from the table. "Here's how we'll handle this," he said. "I'll go to Barnes and pay for the book. I'll hand it over to you only when you've shown you've earned it. How's that?"

That sounded more than fair. Jay's spirits brightened a little.

"But first, you'll face punishment for pinching it," added Mr. Douse, tugging Jay's rising spirits back down. The old man swished the dregs of his mug. "Let's see. How should I discipline you?"

Jay shot him a hopeful grin. "Give me a warning and let me off easy?"

The old man acted like Jay hadn't even spoken. "The streetlamps in the main square could use a good scrubbing," he thought aloud.

Jay groaned in protest. Those lamps were the worst. They were huge, always covered in grime and smoke and all the nasty things that birds and other critters left behind. It'd take half the day to clean them.

"I suppose we can work out something else," Mr. Douse went on. "I hear the river fishermen would love help. Sorting the fish, swabbing the guts, that sort of thing."

Jay grimaced, imagining mopping up slimy fish muck. "D'you want me to refill the lamps after I've cleaned them?"

Mr. Douse's knowing smile was plain irritating. "That'd be helpful. Next time, think twice before shirking work." He jerked his thumb toward the book. "And don't let me catch you 'borrowing' more books, got it?"

He disappeared into the back room.

Jay scuffed his feet. At least Mr. Douse wouldn't snitch on him. But next time Jay brought borrowed books home, he'd have to find a better hiding place. And he'd do as he was told: He wouldn't let Mr. Douse catch him again.

The candlemaker returned, carrying a metal can of lamp oil. Mr. Douse set the can down and held his fist over Jay's palm.

"Here." He released a trickle of coins from his hand. "For last month."

Jay clutched his wages and slid them into his vest pocket.

"Only use as much oil as you need," added Mr. Douse. "And try not to get into any funny business around town today, you hear?"

Jay reached for the oil can. "I won't."

Mr. Douse raised an eyebrow. "The last time you said that, I found you scraped up under a collapsed pile of crates. And what about the time before that, when you got those welts and—?"

"I *won't*."

"All right," said Mr. Douse, relenting. The old man sat, shaking open the bulletins.

"Listen, Julian," he said, "I know you've had a rough start for a boy your age. But if you want to make something of yourself, the important thing to do right now is work hard and keep yourself well out of—"

Loud footsteps interrupted him. Mr. Douse glanced up over the bulletins, then sighed in surrender. Jay had already snatched up the oil can and his apple and had made his escape: clear, free, and out the front door.

"—trouble," the candlemaker finished, resuming his reading.

HANGMAN'S RUN

Jay bolted from the candle shop, taking the ladder and a rag from the back shed before making his way into the dusty town of Hazeldenn. He bit down on the apple stuffed in his mouth, trying not to dwell on Mr. Douse's scolding.

It was blazing frustrating. Jay had tried to get that book the honest way, saving up his wages and everything—but when he went to buy it, Old Man Barnes had refused to sell it to him. The cranky bookseller was convinced Jay had pickpocketed the money, and he said selling the book to him was just as bad as having him steal it. He'd shooed Jay from his shop.

So, an hour later, Jay had snuck back into the store, slipped the book inside his vest, and slinked out without the bookseller seeing him. Borrowing it for a couple days seemed harmless enough. That way, Barnes didn't have to sell it to him, and Jay still got to read it. What was wrong with that?

Jay munched the apple, frowning at his reflection in the gleam of the oil bucket. To the natives of Hazeldenn, what you saw was what you got. In Jay's case, he looked an awful lot like somebody who shouldn't be left alone without supervision. He'd been told that he had the smirk of a trickster and the eyes of a troublemaker—the perfect face for a wanted poster. The fact that Jay's face had once been on wanted posters didn't help.

Being an outlaw in another life meant not many of these straight-laced country folks understood his sense of humor, either (tie the shoe-

13

laces of a sleeping watchman to his chair *one time*, and everybody goes flying off the handle). And they didn't always appreciate his gestures of goodwill (he'd never meant to knock the head off that statue of the town founder, honest; he'd only been trying to get an empty bird's nest off it). But he wasn't a delinquent anymore. He'd been on probation for half a year already. By now folks should've trusted that he'd buy his own book.

And besides, of all the people in Hazeldenn qualified to read a book about muses and Musicians, *he* should've been number one on the list . . .

Jay stopped the thought, then shoved it away. No use thinking such things.

He hurried along familiar roads, passing chattering ladies, tired grove workers, patrolling watchmen. Though it was the loneliest place in the southwest frontier of Merideyin, Hazeldenn was like any other town in one way: Everybody pretended to mind their own business, all the while being very interested in what everybody else was up to.

Jay's ears picked up the street's idle gossip. Most talked about dull town business: the hazelnut harvest, the autumn weather, what the councilors were up to. But some were talking about bigger things—like if the sickness across Merideyin would ever be cured, if the Nightcreepers were real, if war was coming. The jabbering filled the street with a noisy current, and Jay drifted along the chatter all the way to the town square.

The square was crowded with folks trying to finish shopping. From every corner of the square came the sound of jingling bells as people swept out of stores, the doors hardly shutting before fresh customers entered.

And lining the perimeter of the square's shops were the lamps Jay had to clean. The lamps were stained by smoke and char; the glass panes were plastered with feathers and bird droppings. "Gross" didn't cover it.

Jay cut around the crowd. The faster he started, faster he'd be done. He set the ladder against a lamppost and climbed, fighting his gag reflex—

"—*told* you, no!" somebody nearby snapped. "Now get out of here!"

Above the crowd, Jay caught sight of a red-haired girl with a fair, freckled complexion standing behind the news bulletin stand. She wore an eyepatch over one eye, and her face was red with anger.

Jay smirked, leaning on the ladder. Ah, Lina. Cecilina Kindle was the town's resident spitfire, with a fuse shorter than the dead wick of a melted candle. Who could've put her in such a mood?

As soon as Jay saw who it was, his smile fell. Several boys stood around Lina. Five were thickset and wore matching dumb expressions; the sixth, however, was a tan, well-built blonde boy with a handsome, shrewd face.

Jay's gut knotted. It was the Jackal Gang, Hazeldenn's homegrown thugs. And the blonde guy was the worst of 'em all.

Braxson Gripps, the "Grinning Jackal" of Hazeldenn and leader of the Jackal Gang, made a show of inspecting his fingernails while Lina fumed.

"—not going to tell you again," she said. "Leave my stand!"

"Not until you say *yes*," said Brax.

Lina glared at him, holding out one of her bulletins. "I have other things to do today. And every day after, for that matter."

Brax laughed and whipped the bulletin from her hands.

"Such as?" he said. "It's just a turn around the town, Miss Cecilina. That's all I'm asking. It's not like any other fellow's gonna offer to step out with you, right?"

Lina turned away, hiding her eyepatch.

Jay watched from above, frowning.

Lina snatched the bulletin from Brax. "*Harmony Monument renovations underway!*" she called out. "*Memorial site closed to public!*"

"C'mon, Miss Cecilina," said Brax. "Why won't you?"

"*New cases of outbreak confirmed! Quarantine in effect!*"

"I'm asking nicely, aren't I?"

"*Airships grounded by record storm!*"

Brax's smirk faded. Jay saw Brax nod to one of his cronies. The guy nodded back, then bumped the stand with his hip, sending bulletins flying. Lina cried out as they splashed into the mud.

"Oh!" said Brax with an almost convincing gasp. He smacked his goon on the arm. "You moron! Look what you did!"

"Whoops," said the goon, a few seconds too slow.

Brax picked up a mucky bulletin. "I'm so sorry, Miss Cecilina. I don't think anybody's going to want to buy these now." He turned an unrepentant smile on her. "I'll have my boys clean these up. And to make it up to you, I'll treat you. You can go around the town with me! What d'you—?"

"One bulletin, please."

Brax and his gang turned and stared. Jay slipped up and snatched the mud-smeared bulletin from Brax's fingers, fishing five Whits from his pocket.

"Thanks," Jay told Lina, handing her the coins. Putting himself between the stand and Brax, Jay opened the bulletin at its centerfold.

"Hey!" said one of Brax's ferret-faced followers. "Get lost!"

"*Ugly weasel protests arrival of dashing hero!*" Jay called out, pretending to read from the bulletin. "What a great headline."

The ferrety guy blinked, confused.

"*Thickskulled bum-wipes get a kick out of bothering girls!*" Jay shouted. "That's so wrong."

Brax's minions bristled, catching on. A burly, bovine chump, who must've had a cow somewhere in his ancestry, stepped forward. "Hey now. You got a smart mouth, don'cha?"

Jay squinted at an imaginary headline. "Oh, here's a good one: *Against all odds, big dumb ox learns human speech!*"

Probably by accident, one of the other Jackal Gang kids laughed. The ox in question smacked the guy before turning back to Jay, snorting in rage.

"I'mma pound you 'til you're flat!"

The guy started to charge, but he skidded to a stop when Brax stepped forward, wearing a cool sneer.

"If it isn't the Nobody," said Brax. "What d'you think you're doing?"

Jay glued his gaze to the tiny print. "It's called 'reading.'"

Brax snorted. "No, what d'you think you're doing *here?* You've butted into a discussion I was having with this little lady of mine." He winked at Lina, then cracked his knuckles. "I oughta teach you better manners."

Jay didn't react. He scanned a few actual headlines, not absorbing them: LATEST WAVE OF MERIDEYIN'S EPIDEMIC CONTAINED, FOR NOW and NEW SIGHTINGS OF "NIGHTCREEPERS" DISMISSED BY AUTHORITIES.

"Lucky for you, I'm feeling generous," Brax went on. "I'll give you one chance to scram." He shooed Jay. "Don't you have work to do?"

Jay looked up. "If you're feeling so generous," he said, tilting his head toward the ruined bulletins, "why don't you pay for all those?"

In the corner of his eye, Jay saw Lina smile.

The cool look returned to Brax's face. "Think you're funny, huh?" he said. "Do the math, funny man. You got no friends, no class . . . what's that add up to?" He lifted a hand, his fingertips meeting his thumb. "*Zero*."

Jay held the bully's gaze. Brax's sneer grew.

"Did I hit a nerve? I thought you'd be used to hearing that by now." Brax leaned in, uttering a cruel litany. "You're nobody. Nothing. Worthless."

Jay refused to answer him. They were only words.

"Moron. Freak."

Empty words.

"*Outlaw*."

Jay flinched. The word sizzled in his ears, hot and awful.

"I'm *not*," he said before he could stop himself.

Brax smirked in triumph. "Sure. Says the Quickstep Kid."

Jay felt a hot flush of shame. That wasn't his name. Not anymore.

Brax flicked Jay's forehead with a finger. Hard. *Ow*.

"Get it through your skull, Nobody," said Brax. "A loser like you who ran with stinking outlaws belongs in the dung heap." He spat at Jay's boots.

Jay ground his teeth. Brax knew nothing. *Nothing*.

He was trying so hard to find a comeback he almost didn't hear it.

Grrrr.

Jay twitched. It was a growl, but not from any natural beast. It was sweet and dangerous, soft and deep—and it was coming from someplace nearby.

Jay froze in horror. One of *them*.

Here? Now?

He closed his eyes and pretended he hadn't sensed it. At the same time, he silently pleaded: *Stay away—stay away*.

A soft hand landed on Jay's shoulder. He opened his eyes. It was Lina.

"If Jay belongs in the dung heap, I'd hate to imagine the foul place *you* belong, Braxson," Lina snapped. She turned to Jay and hissed, "Go."

Spooked by the strange, growling voice, Jay was perfectly happy to slip away—but Brax blocked his path.

"Oh, we can't let him go—right, boys?"

Brax's lips peeled back in a nasty, grimacing smile. The famous grin of the Grinning Jackal had emerged at last. Warning bells rang in Jay's ears.

"Fellas, you've seen the trouble this reformatory rat has caused," said Brax, sending glances to the rest of his gang. "Shouldn't we stop him?"

As two of Brax's goons rushed him, Jay's street instincts kicked in. Jay tossed up his bulletin; distracted, they didn't see Jay duck and sweep out his leg. One goon stumbled over it into the other guy, sending them both toppling.

Jay had only just gotten upright when the bovine chump and the ferret-faced kid dove for him. Sidestepping, Jay spun away from the larger boy's charge, throwing his weight against his back. The ferrety kid yelped as his much larger companion barreled into him, sending them both into the mud.

Jay dusted his hands while Brax's gang lay groaning on the ground. Poor little jackals. They should've known not to mess with an ex-outlaw.

GRRR.

Jay's breath caught. The strange growling snarled again, louder this time. The voice was powerful, beautiful . . . and closer.

Jay went cold. He had to get out of here—fast—before it found him.

"Gotcha!" said Brax as he grabbed Jay from behind. Jay thrashed, but too late; he was trapped by Brax's hold.

"Get up, you idiots!" he barked at his gang. The others stumbled to their feet as Brax wrenched Jay's arms at a painful angle. He turned to Lina.

"Believe me, Miss Cecilina, I'm happy to help," said Brax. "Why, we all saw how this delinquent started harassing you." His grin sharpened. "Just look at what he did to your bulletins! I can bring him to the watchmen and have them take care of him for you, if you want. Just say the word."

Jay swung his legs to kick at Brax. Was that the story he was gonna spin? Blast it! He didn't have time for this nonsense.

Jay scanned the square, hoping to catch the eye of an adult. But nobody saw. Aw, heck—even if they did see, would they care about what was really going on? Why were adults always so blind to these things?

Jay tried to kick Brax again, missing his shins.

GRRRROWR!

Jay gasped. The strange voice growled so loudly it made his ears buzz.

It was close—so close that Jay was positive it would find him any second. As Brax and Lina faced off, Jay looked wildly around, searching.

Seconds dripped by like cold syrup. Jay felt his surroundings shift, like all sound was gently muted to a hum.

Then, at last, he spotted it, shining like a beacon of prismatic color against a grayscale world. Chills of dread fluttered up Jay's spine.

A muse stepped out among the townsfolk with regal poise. The music spirit had taken the form of a great wild cat: its radiant fur rippled along its body, and its whiskers twitched with curiosity. Its entire being thrummed with mysterious, melodious energy, captivating and terrifying.

Jay trembled to his core. He recognized it. It was the same muse that'd shown up the day before, the one he'd dodged by climbing up a tree.

He glanced around. All the townsfolk in the square were going about their everyday business, oblivious to the strange, powerful being in the square with them. Even though the music spirit was standing right in the open, nobody reacted to it. Their eyes passed over the muse as if it weren't there.

Which wasn't surprising. Jay had yet to meet anybody in Hazeldenn who could see or hear muses. The folks around here weren't like him.

The muse ignored the humans around it, too, not interested in them—but as it drew near the bulletin stand, it paused, ears erect. Jay swallowed a scream. Of all the lousy times, why'd a muse have to come out *now?*

Jay held his breath, praying: *Don't notice me—please don't—*

The muse turned in Jay's direction, as if it could hear him sweating. After an eternity, it started off again, the sound of its footfalls growing softer, its voice going quiet. Then its presence faded entirely.

Jay exhaled a shuddery breath. It was gone.

Unfortunately, Brax still had him in a tight grip.

"*Say the word*, Miss Cecilina," Brax was insisting, drumming his fingers on Jay's forehead. "You know the one I mean."

Neither Brax nor Lina had budged—but then Lina met Jay's gaze.

"Fine!" Lina snapped. "*Yes.* I'll go out with you. Now put him down!"

Brax grinned, dropping Jay. Once Jay was free, Lina stamped off.

On the ground, Jay rubbed his sore armpits and glowered.

Don't, his sensible side pleaded. *Not worth it—walk away—*

Not gonna happen, Jay answered himself stubbornly. He rose, catching Brax's sleeve before he could follow Lina.

"I challenge you," Jay blurted.

Brax turned toward him. "Excuse me?"

"You heard me. I challenge you."

Brax yanked his sleeve from Jay's grip. "You're serious. You wanna go against me?"

Jay nodded. "A Hangman's Run from the Gallows Yard. Fifteen minutes. If I win, you leave Lina alone—and you pay for those bulletins you ruined."

Brax's grin turned vicious. He cracked his knuckles.

"Fine. Fifteen minutes. And *when* I win, be prepared to hurt."

∞

Practically every kid in Hazeldenn showed up to watch. In the Gallows Yard, the Jackal Gang kept an eye out for any adults who might break up the fun. Boys hoisted themselves up into the hazel trees. Girls flocked together and demanded front-row places, as ladies deserved. The rest fell to shoving or kicking to get a better view. Brax and Jay hovered at the starting line.

"When this is over," said Brax, grinning widely, "I'm gonna feed you your own shirt. Can't wait to watch you choke."

The crowd's *Oohs* chorused across the yard.

"Rules," said one of Brax's goons, a giant with curly hair. "Follow the course, get the flag, and bring it here." He pointed to the long-abandoned gallows platform, standing in the middle of a large plot of goopy mud. "Use shortcuts 'n' you're disqualy-uh-fied. Touch the other guy 'n' you're disqualy-uh-fied. You beat him, you punish him. May the best man win."

"I intend to," said Brax. The Jackal Gang all laughed.

Jay threw his cap off to the side, trying to hide his nerves. Had he really challenged Brax to a Hangman's Run? Was he out of his mind? Brax had run this obstacle course a million times, and he'd *never* been beaten.

Brax stepped up beside him. "It's over, Nobody," he said as he fell into a running stance. "I'll tear you to pieces."

The predatory glee in his voice made Jay want to shudder. Torn to pieces! Gee, that sounded swell. Why in blazes was he even doing this?

. . . Oh, right. The bulletins. Lina.

Jay lowered himself into a sprinting position.

"Ready," said the giant, "set—"

"Hullo, Miss Cecilina!" Brax cried out, waving to the side.

"*Go!*"

Jay's eyes flashed toward where Brax was waving—and saw too late that Lina wasn't actually there. Brax dashed off at full throttle.

Cursing himself for getting tricked, Jay stumbled into a run. The jeers of the crowd followed him as he headed into the first leg of the course: the hazelnut groves. Jay sprinted after Brax, who was already out of sight.

Some grove workers shouted at him. "Hey! You're not allowed here!"

Jay darted around trees, bumping ladders. He winced when he heard yelps and baskets of harvested nuts tumbling to the ground behind him.

Jay caught up to Brax at the next stage of the course: the old town wall. The jerk was waiting casually by the pile of stones.

"Gotta keep up," he jeered. "Are you even trying?"

Brax spun around and vaulted onto the wall with an effortless leap. He waved playfully at Jay, then jumped down to the far side.

Jay scrambled over the wall after him. The instant he landed on the wall's other side, he went rigid, realizing where he was: Widow Tinner's backyard. Widow Tinner was famous for the none-too-friendly animals she kept.

"You finally made it," said Brax.

Jay's eyes flashed to the other end of the backyard, where Brax was standing by a row of kennels. His fingers rested on the kennels' master latch.

Jay's eyes widened. "You've *got* to be kiddi—"

Before Jay could finish, Brax released the latch and darted off, right as the kennel gates opened. Jay pressed against the wall as Widow Tinner's critters were set loose: a gaggle of geese, all zeroing in on him.

Jay yelped. In a heartbeat, he flew across the yard, getting angry pecks from the geese before he shot over the fence.

Jay's momentum carried him down the street until he reached the dead-end alley where Brax had disappeared. There at the end of the alley was the flag: a scrap of red cloth, tied to a rusty gutter spout.

Brax had slowed down, not noticing Jay. Jay darted up behind him. In seconds, he caught up to Brax—then he was *passing* him —

Just before he grabbed the flag, something solid punched Jay in the ribs. Jay staggered at the blow.

"Nice try," said Brax. He snatched the flag.

Jay stared in outrage. "You can't—against the rules—!"

Brax grinned with malice. "What rules?"

Then, instead of following the course back out the alley, Brax opened the back door of the nearest shop, slipping through.

Jay choked on a protest. Now Brax was taking a shortcut!

The injustice pushed Jay to his feet. He chased Brax into the shop. "HEY."

Jay froze. The moment he burst inside, he found himself face-to-chest with a colossus dressed in a bloodstained apron, bearing a gory meat cleaver.

"What're yer doin' in my shop?" said the butcher.

Jay gulped. Somehow, Brax had avoided the butcher's eyes. Jay watched as the jerk bounded around the counter and out the front door. *Son of a jackal.*

"Get out!" the butcher yelled, raising his knife.

Jay's feet were already moving. He jumped away from the butcher and flew up the shop's back stairs. The butcher's shouts followed Jay all the way until Jay found his exit, tumbling out an open second-floor window.

He landed on the slanted rooftop beyond, catching himself before he slid down the shingles. Regaining his feet, he searched for Brax.

There. Brax was running below. The red flag flapped in his fist.

Jay ran, darting with nimble feet along the apex of the building to the edge of the rooftop. He jumped down onto a balcony with a laundry rope strung next to it, sporting clean butcher's aprons and pairs of underpants. The rope ran to a pulley on the opposite building.

Jay hopped onto the balcony. He grabbed the rope tightly in both hands.

His brain told him, *This is a terrible idea.*

Telling his brain to stuff it, Jay held his breath and pushed off, zip-lining to the opposite building. A high-pitched yelp escaped him as he gained speed—aprons and underpants went flying—"*Oof!*"

Jay smacked into the wall, losing his grip on the rope. He fell into a compost heap below, which caught him with a disgusting squelch.

Jay staggered up, rotting compost dripping from his hair and clothes.

Ignoring looks from passersby, he shook off what gunk he could and ran as fast as his feet would go to the Gallows Yard.

As he rounded the last corner, Jay saw the cheering horde of town kids. Brax was waiting for him at the far side of the yard, his grin stretching wide. He hadn't climbed up the gallows platform, so he technically hadn't won yet—but the jerk was already savoring his victory.

"All right, Nobody. I'll give you one last chance," he called. He stepped over the mud patch and pinched the red flag in his fingertips, flapping it in Jay's direction. "C'mere. Try to take it. Let's see who's faster."

Brax waved the flag at Jay before he started to climb the platform steps at a tortoise pace, earning a laugh from the crowd.

Sweat and compost ooze ran down Jay's neck. He couldn't possibly catch Brax—he'd humiliate himself by trying. How could he win now?

Brax reached the third step. "Looks like me and my little lady will have a nice afternoon together!" he called out. "Right after I thrash you!"

The words made Jay seize up. If Brax won—if he left Jay in tiny pieces here—then he'd go back and torment Lina. No way could Jay let that happen.

He would not let that happen.

ROOOWL!

A majestic, musical roar filled the Hangman's Yard, sending a gust of wind that shook leaves from the hazel trees.

Panic squeezed the air from Jay's lungs. For a split second, he'd let down his guard, exposing his will. And the muse had heard.

Bandersnatches.

Jay saw a flash of motion from the edge of his vision. He turned and saw the wildcat muse jump right over the heads of the watching kids. It landed with a graceful arch of its back, claws extended, standing between Jay and the gallows platform.

Every nerve in Jay's body sparked with panic. The music spirit growled, scrunching its feline face, sinking into an attack position—

And then the muse clawed the ground with playful movements, its long tail twitching and flicking. Its growl softened to a melodic purr, and it stared at Jay with bright eyes, waiting.

Jay wanted to groan. The muse knew exactly what Jay was, all right.

It wasn't going to leave until it got what it wanted.

And it wanted him to *play*.

Laughter came at Jay from all sides. Jay looked up to see Brax acting out a pantomime of him, bugging out his eyes and letting his mouth hang open like a halfwit. Nobody was looking at the muse.

With everybody's eyes on Brax, Jay hissed at the music spirit.

"*Shoo!*" he ordered under his breath. "Go away!"

The muse's eyes were dazzling like smoldering sapphires. It growled at him, insulted, impatient.

"Okay!" Jay hissed. "*Just once.* Then you leave me alone, got it?"

The muse purred, its tail lashing the air in excitement.

Jay's eyes flickered to Brax. "Fine," he whispered. "Let's play."

He hated muses—and he'd sworn years ago that he'd never have anything to do with them ever again—but this was an exception.

This was for Lina.

Jay took a breath, concentrating. He pressed his fingertips together and snapped.

The instant the snap cracked from Jay's fingers, the muse purred, arching its back in delight—then it was off, following Jay's will. It dashed across the yard toward Brax, jumping on his shoulders like a housecat pouncing on a mouse . . . and then it bounded away with a happy, satisfied yowl, shimmering out of sight.

Brax never saw it. With a yelp, he stumbled and lost his footing—

Jay didn't think. He rushed forward, snatching the red flag from Brax, and scrambled up the steps right as Brax tumbled face-first into the mud.

SPLAT!

Everyone stared between Jay on the platform and Brax eating muck, as if they couldn't believe what had happened.

Then somebody snickered. It might have been an innocent sneeze for all Jay knew, but it was enough to get everyone else started. The crowd erupted, turning on Brax in a blink. They laughed even harder when Brax stumbled to his feet, howling in disgust as he tried to wipe the muck off his clothes.

Nerves bounced in Jay's stomach. Jumping from the platform, he jogged over to the rest of the Jackal Gang. "Pay up," he said, holding his hand out.

The Jackal Gang shuffled in place, looking stupid and angry.

"We'll get you for this!" the giant spat. The rest of the Jackal Gang dug into their pockets, fishing out coins. Then, after tossing the coins at Jay, they tucked tail and ran off. Brax ran too, jeers following him all the way.

Jay gazed at the hard-won coins in relief. That'd been close. Most of his encounters with muses ended much, much, *much* worse—usually with him all banged up and in trouble up to his eyeballs. By some miracle, he'd sent the muse on its way without destroying anything. Heck, it'd even helped him beat Brax.

Hopefully it wouldn't come back anytime soon.

Jay left the Gallows Yard and wandered through the tumult of the main roads toward Lina's family's shop, Kindle News Press. The money the Jackal Gang had thrown at him wasn't enough to pay for all the wasted bulletins, he knew—so Jay added in a bit from the wages he'd gotten from Mr. Douse to cover the difference. He shoved the coins under the door.

There. That'd do it. Jay smiled, wandering off. Sweet victory.

The raw odor of sloppy mud came to his nose a little too late.

Before Jay could register the stench, he was grabbed from behind. Brax's rank breath moistened the back of his neck.

"Where d'you think *you're* going, Nobody?"

Jay winced. He was in trouble.

Chapter Three

THE JINX

*E*ven before the duel started, Ark was certain who the winner would be.

In the center of Echostrait's most isolated courtyard, the opponents stood twenty paces apart. On one side, a tall blonde girl smirked with confidence, wearing her blue, ankle-length talaris coat buttoned all the way up. Facing her was a pimple-faced girl, her talaris buttoned halfway, her hand nervously clutching a reed flute. Both girls stood within a ring of eager spectators.

Perched in the branches of a nearby oak, Ark sat unobserved above the scene, frowning as he squinted over the rims of his spectacles. He wasn't exactly bothered that they were having a music duel—but the fact that their little contest was disturbing his peaceful ditching . . . yes, that was irritating.

He had planned it so carefully, too. Bad dreams had plagued him again last night, so between breakfast and the first bell Ark had slipped away from the students heading to class, removed his talaris so he wouldn't be so easy to spot, and sneaked to the courtyard. From there he'd climbed up to his favorite tree branch, ready to compose some fresh music. But with this ruckus, he couldn't concentrate long enough to write a single note.

Stupid rotten luck.

The courtyard hushed. Sensing the start of the match, Ark sat up and closed his eyes, shutting off his sight and opening his ears.

At once the world around him transformed from one of light and color into one of sound. The creak of the branches told him the direction of the breeze; the crunch of gravel revealed where the two duelers had positioned themselves. The rest of the courtyard took shape around him through the offbeat coordination of a dozen sounds: whispering, shuffling, humming, knocking, coughing, squeaking, fluttering, snapping, clacking—

And through it all, Ark could feel countless muses nearby, drifting along with ever-changing harmony. Even with his eyes closed, Ark heard their telltale Resonance all too clearly. Some thrummed with a heavy bass rumble; others gave off a delicate reedy whisper or a shivery jingling. Still others sang with a bold, brassy blare. A good number were now drawn to the courtyard, circling around the Musicians in curious anticipation.

Ark opened his eyes again right as the blonde girl called out: "Virelai!"

The air shimmered, and a muse appeared at her side, answering the summons. It looked like a white crane, its outline flickering like lightning.

Then the blonde girl began to sing a cantus, her voice filling the courtyard. The white crane flew up with a keening cry, matching her song. It dove toward the pimply girl and pumped its wings, creating a furious blast of wind.

The pimpled girl's shoes slid along the pebbles as the wind buffeted her, but she held her ground. When the wind passed, Pimples lifted her reedy flute to her lips, piping out a shrill stream of stinging notes.

As she played, another muse entered the duel, taking the form of a swarm of golden bees. The bees roared forward. Blondie yelped as the bees droned around her. The white crane flew over to defend her, flapping its wings against the swarm. At once the bees dispersed.

The yard went silent, as if the world had taken a breath and wouldn't let it out. Each of the girls waited for the other to make a move.

Then Blondie shifted ever so slightly. She drew her arm behind her, shaking her wrist. A slender bracelet slid down from beneath her sleeve.

Ark frowned. He strained his eyes, studying her.

By then Blondie had opened her mouth and was chanting a new cantus in a confident voice. The white crane began to circle above them, spiraling higher and higher, its feathers flickering. Pimples, along with the rest of the students in the yard, stared up at the crane with watchful eyes—

And that's when Ark saw Blondie shake her bracelet with a sharp flick.

Faster than Ark could blink, a muse in the form of a black snake manifested inside Blondie's shadow. It slithered straight over to Pimples' feet. No one else saw it, not even Pimples: Everyone was still staring up at the crane, which had gone into another steep dive. Pimples raised her flute—

Before she could play anything, the snake muse wrapped itself around her legs, pulling her off balance. Pimples wobbled with a startled yelp— and the crane blasted her with a thunderous gale, hitting her dead on.

Pimples flew off her feet with a wail. She rolled twice in a backward somersault before flopping hard on her stomach, her flute knocked from her grasp. Like that, it was over.

Onlookers cheered or groaned in sympathy. Blondie laughed in triumph.

Ark's frown deepened. Fetching his coat off a branch, he jumped to the ground, wandering over.

Most of the spectators surrounded Blondie, fawning over her. Ark kept his talaris draped over his arm as he stooped low, picking up Pimples' flute. Then he walked up and offered her a hand.

Pimples stared at his hand, repulsed. An ugly, misshapen scar marred the back of Ark's left hand, jagged and discolored. He quickly withdrew it, hiding it in his sleeve and holding her flute out with the other.

"You couldn't have won," Ark told her. "She cheated."

Pimples' eyes widened as she took her flute. "Cheated?" she squawked.

Everyone stopped jabbering. Blondie spun around.

"What did you say?" she said.

Ark stopped a sigh. He hadn't meant to make a scene.

"It was pretty obvious," he told Blondie, adjusting his spectacles. "You illegally summoned a second muse. That's the textbook example of cheating."

"Hey!" a kid snapped. "Show some respect. That's Odetta!"

Ark turned to him. "Who?"

The boy scoffed. "Odetta Krump, idiot. Daughter of the famous Maestran Krump. She's already got her own patron muse!"

Ark glanced from the boy to Odetta. The girl stared down at him with a smug look, waiting for him to be impressed.

Ark didn't give her the satisfaction. "You still cheated," he said, pointing to Odetta's wrist. "Your bracelet. There are bells sewn all over it. You used a tonus to call another muse to trip your opponent. Simple, but effective."

Odetta was too late to hide her bracelet from view. Pimples looked at her in disbelief. Several others began whispering.

Odetta's eyes ignited with anger. "What's your name?"

Ark hesitated.

"Won't tell me?" said Odetta. She leveled a hand at the top of Ark's head, taking in his height. "Maybe I'll just call you Shorty."

A few bystanders sniggered. Odetta pressed the advantage.

"So, *Shorty*—you've got guts, insulting me. But I didn't cheat—I'm just better than she is. You're clearly too much of a little newbie to know anything."

A trickle of irritation chilled Ark's insides, but he held his composure.

"I know exactly what I saw," he said. "You're nothing but a bully."

Odetta pressed a hand to her chest in feigned offense.

"I didn't bully anyone!" Odetta glanced at Pimples. "Finny said she could beat me in a contest. She bet me this." From her talaris, Odetta drew out a bejeweled, antique pendant. "She lost. Now it's mine."

"No, you *took* it!" the girl, Finny, said. "My grandma gave me that!"

Odetta ignored her. She turned to Ark, wearing the same greedy look as a gluttonous spider who'd ensnared another victim in her web. Before Ark could stop her, Odetta plucked the spectacles from his face.

"You want these back, huh?" she said, holding them beyond Ark's reach. "Too bad. This is what you get for falsely accusing me."

"Make him jump!" someone called from the side. Smirking, Odetta held Ark's spectacles even higher. Everyone laughed.

Ark refused to jump. Odetta's smirk grew a million times more annoying.

"Tell you what: I'll make a bet with you, too," she said. She hummed softly; the white crane muse appeared at her side at once.

"This is Virelai, my patron," Odetta said, stroking the crane's neck.

"Beat us in a duel, and I'll give your spectacles back. Lose, and they're mine." Odetta waved Ark forward. "C'mon, Shorty! Show me what you've got."

Ark kept his face flat. "I won't challenge you."

Odetta's eyebrows shot up. "Too scared to face me, huh?"

The group's whispers grew into mocking chitters. Ark ignored them.

Odetta barked a scornful laugh. "You really are pathetic, aren't you?" She tossed her hair. "Well, at least you know your place. Fine. I'll change the deal. I'll return your spectacles—*if* you apologize." She pointed to the ground. "Kneel. Take back what you said. Then they're yours."

"Yeah, on your knees, Shorty!" said the boy from Odetta's class, jeering. "That shouldn't be too hard. You're close enough to the ground already!"

They all laughed at Ark again. Ark's mouth fought a scowl. He really wished they would stop pointing out his height. Or lack thereof.

Odetta waited for him to obey her. Before Ark could tell her to go stuff her head in a furnace, Finny crashed to her knees instead, bowing low.

"I'm sorry!" she blurted. "You didn't cheat. You'd never cheat. You're much better than me!" She looked up. "Now can I have my pendant back?"

Odetta's mouth shriveled in disgust. "I didn't say I'd accept *your* apology, Finny," she spat, twirling the pendant's chain around her fingers. "Maybe if I keep this, it'll teach you not to challenge your superiors."

Finny lowered her head, hiding tears.

Ark felt the tide of icy anger inside him rise until it burst in a glacial flood.

"You're *not* her superior," he spat out.

The chittering whispers hushed. Ark's squint sharpened to a glare.

"You take advantage of others," he said. "You have no respect for your fellow Musicians. You're not worthy of Virelai or the musical arts."

Everyone gasped. Pimples stared at him, awed.

Odetta blinked at him in shock—and then her expression hardened. With a twist of her hand, she broke his spectacles along the bridge.

"Whoops," she said, a sadistic light glowing in her eyes. "I'm only getting started, Shorty. I'll teach you a lesson you won't forget!"

Ark's squinting glare turned stony. He couldn't say which part ticked him off most: being called short, watching her torment an underclassman, or hearing her say she would teach him a lesson. *Him.*

"What now?" said Odetta. "Are you gonna cry?"

Ark finally let himself scowl. He cleared his throat with a gentle cough. "*Vivvo legnno.*"

His cantus was soft, but clear. Odetta tensed, not expecting it. Everyone else around them waited, holding their breath.

A few heartbeats passed, and nothing happened. Odetta relaxed.

"What?" she sneered. "Is that all you—*aaaiiieee!*"

Odetta's words broke off with a shriek as something covered in green leaves reached down and wrapped around her middle, plucking her into the air. The onlookers staggered backward, staring up in amazement. The muse Virelai squawked and pumped its wings, unable to intervene.

The old muse dwelling in the oak tree Ark had been sitting in earlier had responded to his cantus. The tree's branches had coiled around Odetta's waist and lifted her off the ground. Odetta's shriek grew shrill as the tree swung her back and forth like a giant blonde pendulum.

Ark watched, his expression neutral. "*Cessura,*" he chanted at length.

At once, the tree muse obeyed. The branches released Odetta, depositing her on the ground, where she landed with a yelp. The old tree returned to its age-old posture with a groan, sending down a shower of leaves.

Ark stepped up to Odetta, offering her a hand. She slapped it aside, shooting him a glare of outrage as she pushed herself up to her feet.

"How dare you!" she snapped. "Who do you think you are?"

Ark sent her an even look. Without a word, he took up his talaris. As he slid the coat on, Odetta's eyes bugged out. The bystanders started jabbering:

"What the—!"

"A *white* talaris?"

Ark gave his talaris's collar a final tug. His coat wasn't blue, like a regular student's; it was white, with a twelve-point star on the sleeves.

"Y-You're an Adept?" stammered Pimples, pointing to the insignia.

"Great gavotte! He's Arkalin Encore!" someone said, recognizing him.

Jaws dropped. Everyone slid away to a respectful distance. Ark sighed.

"So," he said to Pimples. "Finny, right?"

Finny nodded. Ark plucked the pendant from Odetta's stiff grasp.

"If this is so important, take better care of it," he said, handing it to her.

Finny took the pendant, her eyes never leaving Ark's face.

"And *you*, Odetta—" Ark added, ready to give the upperclassman the payback she richly deserved—but sadly, he was interrupted.

"Adept Encore!" a page called out, hurrying across the courtyard.

Ark resisted the urge to hang his head. He'd been found. *Frigits.*

The page, out of breath, handed Ark an envelope. "Looked all over for you!" he panted. "The Maestran wants you! Right away!"

Ark frowned as he cracked open the envelope and skimmed its contents. He stifled a groan. So much for enjoying some time to himself.

"Let's go, then," said Ark, stuffing the envelope into his pocket. He turned to Odetta, holding out his hand once more.

"I'll have my spectacles back now, thanks."

∞

From one end of the lane to the other, students paused to stare as Ark walked past, chattering curiously after him. After all, it was rare to see Arkalin Encore, the Principal Adept of Echostrait and the top-ranking student of the entire school, out in broad daylight as if he were just one among the many other happy-go-lucky students.

With one glance, though, it was clear Ark wasn't feeling happy *or* lucky.

"Frigits . . . *frigits*," he cursed, holding the pieces of his spectacles. The frames were broken beyond repair; he'd have to ask for new ones. Again.

Ark sighed. He stuffed the lenses inside his coat, angry that he'd broken his own rule: *Leave other people alone.* He should never have gotten involved. Still grumbling, Ark made his way toward the Maestran's office.

Ark kept a few paces ahead of his escort, glancing around the campus. When he'd first come to Echostrait as a scrawny eight-year-old, his breath had caught in his lungs as he walked past the school's antiquated buildings, dying to know what secrets of music he'd learn inside them. The climbing walls and crested rooftops stretched on forever, so beautiful that Ark had been convinced it was a mirage and would vanish when he got too close.

Now, after living here for seven years, the only word that came to Ark's mind to describe Echostrait was "labyrinth." The Maestran's office stood in the center, while the primary school, the advanced school, the assembly halls, and the myriad libraries, dormitories, archives, and courtyards spilled out shambolically in other directions, squished together without any sense of design or order. Though a bit odd and old, Echostrait had a refined character passed on from their Musician ancestors.

Time had marched on since the golden age of Musicians—but at least in Echostrait, it was impossible not to hear the voices of muses around every corner or to feel the comforting harmonies of music imbued in every wall.

As he strode ahead of his escort along the paved arteries of the campus, Ark spied Echostrait's inhabitants hurrying in constant circulation. Eager pages gushed about on errands. Students shed their blue talarises and basked in the sunshine while their instructors gave practical demonstrations on playing instruments, singing canti, and writing scores. Many muses drifted nearby, wearing their preferred forms: birds, beasts, plants, insects—even spiraling whirlwinds or flickering flames. Echostrait's pulse was maintained by the flow of all these people, one heart of music still beating in Merideyin.

With each step, the corner of the summons envelope poked Ark through his pocket like an admonishing finger. Dread corroded holes in his stomach. What could the Maestran want with him?

He glanced down to his left hand, glaring at his scar. His rotten luck just couldn't leave him alone for once, could it?

A burst of laughter made Ark pause in his tracks. His escort bumped into him from behind.

"Adept Encore?" said the page. "Anything wrong?"

Ark didn't say anything. Off to the side in the shade of trees, one class was practicing how to call upon muses with instruments, looking like a common orchestra as they sat in rows with violins, horns, flutes, reeds, and drums. A cluster of students in the back were goofing off.

Ark stared in envy at the jovial group for another long second—but then he squashed the feeling and broke his gaze, dutifully continuing forward.

As he walked into the administration building, Ark stayed out of the way of passing instructors and their muses. After climbing a stairway and passing several conference rooms, he came to the reception hall outside of the Maestran's private office, leading to a pair of enormous double doors at the hall's far end.

There, a dark, curly-haired woman barely in her twenties was hovering by the doors, one ear close to the crack. She hugged a bright red folder stuffed with papers. As Ark approached, she glanced up.

"Encore!" she squeaked, startled. "You're here!"

Ark joined her, not surprised to have caught her eavesdropping. "Nice to see you too, Capricci," he said. He pulled out the envelope with his summons. "The Maestran asked for me. I had a rushed walk from the courtyard."

She studied him. Judging only by her yellow talaris, some might have thought Xyla Capricci was just one of Maestran Pandoura's assistants—but more than a few people knew she was also the Maestran's niece. She was nice enough, but she was a shameless busybody, too.

"The courtyard? *Ah.*" Xyla smiled. "Gaffing off there again, were you?"

Ark frowned. "No. I saw some students having an unfair duel—"

"While you were gaffing off," Xyla inserted.

"—and so I sorted it out," he finished. "What are you doing here?"

Xyla lifted a finger to her lips.

"Aunt Toni's having a chat," she said. "I was asked to wait outside."

Ark listened. He could hear the Maestran's sonorant voice beyond the doorway. He wondered who she was talking to.

"Fix your collar," said Xyla. "What happened to your spectacles?"

Ark straightened his shirt, avoiding her stare. "They're broken."

"You broke them? Again?" Xyla sighed. "Jinx."

Ark scowled, unconsciously tugging his left sleeve over his scarred hand. "I'm not a jinx!"

She shook her head. "Not *a* jinx. *The* Jinx. Honestly, Encore, you've got the lousiest luck of anyone I've ever—"

Before she could finish, a nasty *crash!* and furious shouting exploded beyond the double doors. Ark and Xyla both jumped.

"Aunt Toni?" cried Xyla, rushing over to the doors.

"Wait, Capricci!" cried Ark. Thinking fast, he put two fingers in his mouth and blew a sharp whistle.

At his tonus, a muse rose out of the floor, one in the form of a dark, slithery creature from the ocean depths. It wrapped its sinuous tentacle arms around Xyla's waist and pulled.

Xyla cried out and dropped her folder as the muse tugged her backward to safety. A split-second later, the doors flew open and slammed the wall, making the windows rattle.

Spooked, the muse shrank away, sinking invisibly back into the floor. Ark dove to catch Xyla. She thanked him, collecting all the papers that had fallen from her folder.

"—waited long enough!" someone snarled, charging out the doors. "Absolutely insulting—perfect waste of time!"

As the shouter came into the hallway, Ark and Xyla retreated a few more steps. Ark knew at a glance that the woman wasn't from Echostrait. In fact, except for the muse laying across her shoulders like a stole—a small, black-furred fox—she didn't look like a Musician at all. She had a slender face and pinned-up curls of hair. She wore a fine blue waistcoat buttoned over her dress, and her skirts had so much fabric that they swished around her with each movement. Velvet gloves covered her hands, and makeup tinted her cheeks and lips. She was quite beautiful, except for her shouting.

The Maestran appeared in the doorway. Maestran Antonia Pandoura was chancellor of the school, held in awe (and fear) by her students. With her tall, broad frame and commanding voice, she was the single-most imposing Musician Ark had ever met—but Ark was close enough to her to know she was kind and hid plenty of humor behind her keen stare.

"My apologies, Lady Vielle," Maestran Pandoura was saying to the stranger. "I am certain he was only delayed, but I know he will soon— ah!" she exclaimed when she saw Ark. "Here you are, Encore."

The other lady's eyes locked onto Ark with an offended look, as if he were a scampering mouse. Her fox muse slipped off her shoulders and stared hard at Ark, flattening its ears.

"Encore?" the lady repeated, incredulous. "*This* is *him?*"

"It is indeed," said the Maestran.

The lady's skeptical expression didn't waver. Ark returned her sour look.

"Instead of glowering at him, Callie," spoke a new voice, "you could try saying hello."

Ark turned to the doorway again, surprised to see a regal young man exiting the Maestran's office. He had slicked-back hair and wore a well-tailored suit and shiny polished shoes. In his hand he carried a leather-bound case, scuffed from age. A muse—a tiny crested bluebird—sat on the man's shoulder, its keen little eyes staring. Ark tried not to stare back.

"Hello," said the man, extending a hand. "I'm Sir Dulcian Mandore." He gestured to the bluebird. "And this is Trillo, my patron. Pleased to meet you."

The man smiled with such unaffected kindness that Ark found himself smiling back. "The pleasure's mine, sir."

He glanced down and saw again the black leather case the man was holding. The case bore a golden crest that Ark didn't recognize: a blazing lantern, flanked by a pair of feathery wings. Ark was surprised to see a chain dangling from the case's ebony handle up to the man's arm. Whatever was inside had to be valuable; why else would he have it chained to his wrist?

"We've traveled a long way to get here," said Sir Mandore, gesturing to the lady. "We're looking forward to working with you."

Ark's gaze rose again. What?

The lady scoffed. Maestran Pandoura quickly spoke up.

"Well," she said, gesturing toward her office. "Now that we're all here, Lady Vielle, perhaps you would like to continue our discussion?"

"No!" the lady spat. "He can't be Arkalin Encore. He *can't!*" She whipped her head over her shoulder. "Mara! We're leaving!"

Ark noticed only then that a third stranger trailed behind them. The woman was so plain that Ark wouldn't have seen her at all if the angry lady hadn't called to her. She hid behind a curtain of mousey brown hair, hunching over as if attempting to make herself disappear into the floor. In her hands she held a small tinkerbit device, her fingers tracing the machine's many buttons.

The lady caught up the hem of her substantial skirts with a huff.

"Good day!" she spat like a curse. "Let's go, Fiore!"

She stormed off with the fox muse running after her, yipping all the way. The mousey woman followed.

Everyone stood in stunned surprise. At length, Sir Mandore cleared his throat, breaking the silence.

"Please excuse her, Maestran," he said, embarrassed. "I'll, ah, I'll talk to her. Thank you for your time. We'll speak again soon."

Bowing, the man turned and left, his bluebird latched to his shoulder.

Once the young man had gone, Ark glanced at Maestran Pandoura. She was staring after them with grim eyes, but before long, she released a sigh.

"That was interesting," she said with a mild smile. "Please, come in."

Chapter Four

JURY DUTIES

Still recovering from the bizarre encounter in the hallway, Ark stepped into Maestran Pandoura's office. There wasn't much inside—only a few bookcases, a musty old portrait of the school's founder, and a desk with an imposing pile of papers stacked haphazardly. The Maestran's patron muse—a sleek-finned fish with jewel-bright scales—was swimming along the ceiling, humming serenely and trailing tiny lustrous bubbles that floated in the air. The only thing out of place in her office was a broken chair, its fragments scattered in a corner of the room.

"What happened?" said Xyla, spying the wreckage.

"Ah," said the Maestran, sighing. "Lady Vielle has quite a temper."

Ark stared. Quite a *violent* temper.

"Who were those people?" he asked.

Maestran Pandoura slid into a chair. "That was Sir Dulcian Mandore and Lady Calliope Vielle. And the other woman was Miss Mara Fipple." Without elaborating, she nodded to the broken chair. "Encore, would you be so kind?"

Ark stepped up and surveyed the chair pieces, thinking through the cantus he wanted to use. "*Restaurro,*" he chanted, his voice low and steady.

A spot on the floor began to glow. A muse in the form of a tree—short and supple, with emerald leaves—grew from the glowing spot. Its skinny branches stretched out, sweeping up chair fragments. As the muse worked, Ark closed his eyes, listening to the creaking of wood knitting itself back together. When he opened his eyes, the muse was gone and the chair was as good as new.

"Thank you," said the Maestran. "Impeccable technique."

Ark returned the chair to its place.

"I may need a tonic," the Maestran added, smoothing her hair. "Our lively guests have strained my nerves . . . but, enough. Xyla, dear, did you bring what I asked from student records?"

Xyla nodded, handing over the large red folder. Ark eyed it suspiciously.

"Excuse me, Maestran," he said, "but may I ask why I'm here?"

Maestran Pandoura turned to Xyla.

"That will be all, dear."

Xyla nodded, sending Ark a furtive wink before retreating to the hallway. Once Xyla exited, the Maestran rose from her chair, glancing to the ceiling.

"Kithara," she called.

Hearing its name, the fish muse swam to the Maestran, hovering level with the woman's face. Maestran Pandoura smiled.

"*Sordinno*," she chanted.

At once, Kithara swam through the air in figure eights, trailing a dense stream of bubbles. The bubbles began to join, forming one giant iridescent globe, which continued to grow larger. Ark felt the pressure in his ears tighten as Kithara's bubble stretched over him; soon it pushed against the walls and corners of the room, muffling the sound.

Maestran Pandoura hummed in satisfaction.

"There," she said. "Now our conversation will be private. Have a seat."

At that, Ark felt even more uneasy. Nevertheless, he sat.

The Maestran studied him. "No need to be perturbed, Encore. I actually have good news for you." She reached for her letter pile and lifted the one on top, handing it to him.

Ark took the letter, holding it close to his nose and squinting as he read:

—FROM THE DESK OF J. F. LUTHIER, GRAND MAESTRAN—

To Maestran Antonia Pandoura, Chancellor of Echostrait
Dear Madam:

The Maestrans Council has reviewed and approved your request on behalf of Mr. Encore. We will send our Conservatory's finest to accompany him on his task. We wish him all the best.

Kind Regards,

Johann F. Luthier,

Ark read the letter twice. "I don't understand."

The Maestran smiled. She lifted her hand toward her office doors. "You asked a moment ago about the individuals who had just been in my office. They are from the Royal Conservatory."

Ark looked up at her in surprise. The Royal Conservatory was the heart of all Musicians' affairs in Merideyin. The Grand Maestran, Johann Luthier, was the Royal Conservatory's current director, with the national Maestrans Council beneath him. Ark had dreamed of going there ever since he was little.

"I had expected Lady Vielle and Sir Mandore to explain, but since they have stepped away, I shall do so," the Maestran added. She spoke her next words slowly, giving each one weight. "They are to be your jurors."

Ark blinked. "My jurors?"

"For your formal jury mission," the Maestran continued, suppressing a smile. "I petitioned the Maestrans Council on your behalf. I needed their approval first, seeing as you would be graduating and completing your certification requirements years ahead of schedule. The Grand Maestran has been very accommodating of your circumstances."

The letter fell from Ark's hands back onto the Maestran's desk. A surge of excitement swelled in his chest. "Are you serious?"

The Maestran finally let herself smile.

Ark's own smile stretched from ear to ear. *His jury mission!* He couldn't believe it. Students who were preparing to graduate and become certified Musicians took on an official assignment first—observed by jurors—to prove their skills in the real world. If he completed his jury mission successfully, he'd no longer be a student; he'd be a full-fledged Musician. He'd be free to leave Echostrait—free to hold his head high again—*free!*

"Once you formally accept, you will no longer be under my authority—you will answer directly to your jurors," Maestran Pandoura went on. "Sir Mandore and Lady Vielle already have a mission in mind for you . . ."

Ark was only half-listening. He was so happy he almost jumped out of his chair and gave a loud *whoop* of joy.

". . . which, as I'm sure you know, can involve anything from evaluating a commoner's musical potential to performing a muse patronage ceremony. Exorcizing dischords is also a common task, so do keep on your toes."

Dischords.

With that word, Ark's smile dropped off his face. His blood went cold.

Maestran Pandoura didn't notice. "Regardless of what lies ahead," she said as she lifted another sheet of paper from her desk, "I'm positive you will do fine. Now, if I could please have your signature on this form—"

"I'm sorry, Maestran Pandoura," Ark interrupted.

She looked up. Ark tried not to meet her gaze.

"I appreciate everything you've done—truly—but I can't accept."

The Maestran regarded him. "Why ever not?"

It took Ark a full seven seconds to respond.

"I'm not ready," he said at length.

That was a lie. He had spent countless days studying musical theory in the library, had practiced different canti and tonai well into the night, and had perfected his summoning techniques for more than a year—all for his chance at a jury mission. He was more than ready.

But he couldn't tell the Maestran the truth. Even now, after so many years, he was afraid to open that wound, terrified that his terrible secret would be known . . . though he'd have to face it eventually if he were ever to become a Musician. But he wasn't ready for that.

Ark's eyes wandered down toward his left hand. Seeing the scar brought his mind to a distant place. Soon he was no longer standing in the Maestran's office: He was reliving his oldest nightmare, the images flickering unbidden behind his eyes:

The moonless night—the winter forest—the terrible Beast—

As the dark memories flashed through his head, a voice from somewhere deep inside rose up, echoing between his ears:

You are a disappointment.

His scar throbbed with a dull ache. Ark blinked away the sting in his eyes, trying not to change his expression in front of the Maestran.

Meanwhile, Maestran Pandoura was eyeing him. "You are not ready?"

Ark pinched his mouth shut and nodded.

Skepticism flashed across the Maestran's face. She took another sip from her glass, then pulled out the red folder Xyla had given her earlier.

"When I finally received approval from the Grand Maestran, I glanced over your student records," said Maestran Pandoura, opening the folder. "Do you know what I found inside?"

Ark's chest clenched. "What?"

The Maestran pulled out the sheaf of papers within. "Shall we take a look?" She shuffled through, singling out a page. "Here is a report detailing your rather memorable prank on Instructor Strumb."

Ark stared at her, stunned she would bring that up. "Strumb was a bully! He used to terrorize his students!"

"Duly noted, Encore. However, using muses to make the man cluck and strut like a chicken in front of his class is not how we had ever planned to address his lacking teaching skills." She glanced his way. "Oh, don't give me that look. You can't pretend it wasn't you—there were witnesses. They told me the exact cantus you used to pull it off."

Ark stifled a snort.

"Let's see, what else?" She flipped through more pages from his folder, finding a thick stack of pink slips. "All these 'absent without permission' notes are from this past academic year alone."

Ark scuffed his boot on the floor. He didn't ditch class to be lazy. He only skipped because studying by himself at his own pace was better than wasting time at lectures. His instructors were probably annoyed that he still got top grades on his assignments without coming to class.

The Maestran kept going. "Here's more," she said, pulling out several pages. "These reports come from Instructor Hemiola."

Ark cringed. Instructor Hemiola was the advisor for the Adepts, in charge of their dormitory and their extended curriculum.

"According to Hemiola, when she has asked the other Adepts to partner up with you for a project, the universal reply has been that you are, and I quote"—she traced a finger down the page—"'impossible to get along with,' and they 'refuse to work with you.'"

Seething, Ark didn't trust himself to say anything. He and the other Adepts could not and *would* not get along. As the top ten Musicians in the school, Adepts took special courses and were granted exclusive privileges. The other Adepts had come from well-to-do families who'd put them in private music lessons early on, giving them a jump-start on their training.

But Ark had come to Echostrait with only the clothes on his back, without a Whit to his name. Still, ever since he'd started here, it'd been obvious that Ark's musical gifts were on a different level. During his first year, while his classmates learned how to play basic scales, read simple scores, and call minor muses, Ark had tackled advanced musical forms, mastered multiple instruments, and summoned all kinds of muses on his own. He was named an Adept at the end of his first year. Later, when he'd started to outperform even the older Adepts, Maestran Pandoura had named him the Principal Adept, a title given to the number-one student in Echostrait.

That decision hadn't made Ark popular. To the rest of the Adepts, the fact that Ark had been set above them was galling. Resentful, they'd tried to make his life miserable ever since: insulting him, isolating him, tearing him down.

Ark got back at them by continuing to get the best scores on exams and all Adept challenges. That was the sweetest kind of revenge.

Maestran Pandoura returned the condemning papers to the red folder and looked Ark in the eye. "Do you know what all this tells me?"

Ark felt a flush fan across his face. "Maestran Pandoura, ma'am, I—"

The Maestran held up her hand. Ark fell silent.

"It tells me you *are* ready for your jury mission," she went on.

Ark squinted at her, surprised.

"Your technique is flawless, your instinct is incomparable, and your skill is second to none," she continued. "You are bored in your classes, which is why you've been skipping them. You are more serious than the other Adepts, which is why they don't enjoy working with you. You even managed to perform a cantus that ex-Instructor Strumb was not prepared to counter. In short, you're an outstanding young Musician who deserves to prove himself."

Ark's flush darkened to a blush.

The Maestran gestured to the walls around them. "As much as it humbles me to admit, this school doesn't have much more to teach you." She glanced his way. "And while I would happily take you on as one of my assistants, I sense you don't want to remain in Echostrait for the long term."

Ark was smart enough not to agree out loud.

Maestran Pandoura sat back in her chair, reaching for her glass. "Your jury mission is a grand opportunity, Encore. Considering your jurors were sent by the Grand Maestran, it would be smart to take this chance to show them exactly what you're made of."

Ark kept his face blank. "You're saying I should try to impress them?"

The Maestran nodded. "An endorsement from the Royal Conservatory could serve you well. Especially back home."

Her remarks were simple on the surface, but Ark immediately sensed her deeper meaning. Maestran Pandoura had been present when Ark's father, Tristen de Cani, had dropped off his son at Echostrait. She had overheard the man's last words:

You're no longer a de Cani. You're no son of mine.

She knew he couldn't go home, not until he redeemed himself in his father's eyes. If he succeeded in this jury mission, which was sponsored by the Grand Maestran . . . well, that would change things. It would change everything.

If he succeeded.

Ark felt the unlucky scar on his hand twinge. Of course, passing his jury mission was no guarantee. What if his jurors *did* ask him to take care of a dischord? What if he froze? What if his rotten luck got in the way? What if he failed?

He'd be sent back to Echostrait in shame.

He'd lose the de Cani family name forever.

And his father would never call him "son" again.

Ark cast the thought from his mind. No. He *would* succeed. He'd perform every task perfectly, without error. And if—no, *when* Lady Vielle and Sir Mandore gave him his certification, his father would return for him. He'd have a home again. He would be Arkalin de Cani once more.

Finally, Ark nodded. "I accept."

"Glad to hear it," said the Maestran, pleased. "Just sign the form."

Ark plucked a pen from her desk and scratched his name along the bottom of the paper.

"I'm sure you will learn the details of your mission soon," the Maestran added. "In the meantime, I will inform your instructors, so you do not have to return to class."

When he'd finished signing, Maestran Pandoura rose and walked with him toward the door.

"*Senzza sorrdino*," she chanted. Above, Kithara stretched her fins; the giant bubble dissolved, releasing the soundproofing. Ark's ears popped.

"Thank you, Encore," said the Maestran. "Good day."

The door shut behind him with a definitive *click*.

Ark stood staring at the double doors, dazed . . . and then it all sank in. This was it. No more classes or assignments. No more stupid pranks from the other Adepts. His jury mission had begun.

Great gavotte, he hoped he didn't screw it up.

With that cheerful thought hanging over him like an omen, Ark turned and started off—

Another person was in his way, standing in the middle of the hall.

Ark stumbled to a halt. It was the timid, mousey woman who'd been with Sir Mandore and Lady Vielle. She hunched, clutching the same mechanical device in her hands, staring at him with moon-bright eyes.

"Ah, hello," said Ark. "You're Miss Fipple, right?"

She nodded.

"Nice to meet you," said Ark. "Did you need to see the Maestran?"

The woman raised a finger to her lips, flashing him a sharp look. Ark's mouth clopped shut.

Without a word, Miss Fipple held up her device, punching buttons with expert speed. A tiny ream of paper unfurled from the top of the machine. When she was done, she tore off the strip and handed it to Ark.

Bewildered, Ark took the slip of paper, holding it close so he could study the tiny message she'd typed:

DO NOT GO

Ark looked up at her, not sure what to make of her or the message. "Don't go?" he said, confused.

Miss Fipple nodded with a single jerk of her chin.

"Why not?" he asked.

Miss Fipple punched the buttons on her device again, and the ream of paper unfurled a new message. She tore it off, handed it to Ark—and without waiting for him to look, she walked away, vanishing from the hall like a ghost.

Ark studied her message, more flummoxed than before:

$$1 = A$$
$$5 \times 5 \mid 11 + 4 \mid 37 - 16$$
$$39 / 3 \mid 14 - 13 \mid 17 + 8$$
$$9 \times 9 \mid -7 + 12 \mid 35 / 5 \mid 42 - 24 \mid 2 + 3 \mid 60 / 3$$
$$11 - 2 \mid 19 + 1$$

She'd written in code? What for?

He had no answer to that. But his curiosity was piqued, so he worked through the simple mathematic formulas one at a time, taking a moment to mentally transcribe each answer to the corresponding letter in the alphabet.

"*You . . . may . . . regret . . . it,*" he said slowly aloud, translating.

He glanced up, as if the empty spot where she'd once stood would help explain. Regret what? Was it to do with his jury mission? What had he just signed up for?

The doors behind him opened so suddenly that Ark jumped.

"Encore?" said Maestran Pandoura. "You're still here?"

Ark's lips parted, but he couldn't think of anything to say. He was still trying to make sense of the bizarre encounter when he felt the Maestran's gaze settle on him, waiting for an explanation he wasn't sure how to give.

"Is something wrong?" the Maestran asked.

Ark glanced down at the papers in his hands. Miss Fipple had clearly been waiting for him. She'd come back on her own to catch him at exactly the right moment, all for the sake of giving him a warning:

Do not go. You may regret it.

Ark hesitated. He could tell Maestran Pandoura. But if he did, she might want to put his mission on hold if she believed there was cause for concern.

And he'd be stuck in Echostrait, waiting for his next chance at a jury mission—which might not come for a while.

Well. He *might* regret going on his jury mission. But he'd *definitely* regret getting left behind and missing his chance.

The mental debate took only a few seconds. Ark gripped the slips of paper in his hand a little tighter, hiding them in his sleeves.

"I thought I had a question about my jury mission, but I figured it out." He nodded respectfully. "Thank you, Maestran."

He tried to act natural as he walked away.

"Encore," called the Maestran, "one moment."

Ark stiffened. He tried to keep his face blank as he spun around.

"Don't think I didn't notice," she said, her expression indecipherable.

Ark gulped. Had she realized he was holding something back?

But Maestran Pandoura's face softened with a knowing smile.

"Go put in a rush order for new spectacles," she told him. "We can't have you squinting during your mission."

With that she slipped back into her chambers, still smiling.

Chapter Five

SPOOK STORIES

*H*anging upside down from the town gate where Brax and the Jackal Gang had strung him up by the ankles, Jay wondered if he had pushed the whole thing with the Hangman's Run a bit too far.

The world was strange, upside down. Tangled tree limbs reached down into the sky, sweeping at the clouds like brooms clearing out cobwebs. Jay might've enjoyed the new perspective if his ankles didn't hurt so much.

Throb throb throb went his ankles. *Pound pound pound* went his head. Jay clenched his stomach and threw out his arms, trying to swing. The town gate was made of two log posts and a signboard with chipping paint:

WELCOME TO HAZELDENN
THE NUT CAPITAL OF MERIDEYIN!

If he built up enough momentum, Jay figured he could swing to a post and escape Brax's snare of vengeance. He lost count of how many times he swung. Closer now . . . closer . . . almost got it—

"*Hey!*"

Distracted, Jay fumbled, smacking his face against the gate post. *Ow.*

Blinking away stars, he spied someone running toward him. Lina Kindle raced up, then slowed to a walk.

Jay winced. Of all the people to see him strung up like an idiot.

"Some kids were saying a poor, dumb creature was trapped out here," said Lina. She gave him a glance-over. "Guess they were telling the truth."

Jay—hair standing on end, trousers drooping past his knees, still reeking of compost muck—cringed. He hoped he wouldn't throw up in humiliation.

"So," said Lina, shielding her eyes, "is this the part where I rescue you?"

Jay tried to smile. A rescue would be nice. "Please?"

Lina crossed her arms. "And why should I? You're the one who stirred up a ruckus at my bulletin stand."

Jay's mouth fell open against gravity. "But—but Brax—!"

"Ah, right. Brax. But if you hadn't stuck your nose where it didn't belong, you wouldn't've become his punching dummy."

Jay frowned. Well, yeah, okay—that part had been less than helpful.

Lina eyed him. "He gave you a black eye, huh?"

Gingerly tracing his bruise, Jay recalled the solid fist that had put it there.

"I could've taken him."

Lina snorted. "Face it. You couldn't take him even in a fair fight. It was a fluke you beat him in the Hangman's Run."

Jay frowned. He couldn't exactly deny it.

"I only just heard about it," said Lina. "How did you win, anyway?"

In a blink, Jay remembered the muse—the wildcat with amber fur.

"Brax . . . tripped going to the finish," he fudged. "I got the flag as he fell."

"He fell?"

Jay nodded. "In the mud."

"The mud?" said Lina.

Nod.

"Face first?"

Nod.

Lina said nothing. Then she doubled over in laughter.

"What I would've given to see the look on that jerk's face!" she said.

Jay's ankles throbbed out of sync with his pounding head, but he was too relieved by Lina's laughter to care. He laughed along with her.

Lina's giggles finally died. "All right, I suppose your meddling did keep the Grinning Jerk of Hazeldenn away from me all afternoon. I owe you." She grinned. "Hang on."

Jay swayed in the breeze. *Hang on.* Right. Very funny.

Lina loosened the rope's knot. Before he knew it, Jay was falling.

"Oof!"

"Can you walk?" asked Lina.

Jay yanked the rope off his feet, testing his ankles. "I'm fine."

Lina offered him a hand. Jay took it. "Thanks."

Once he was up, Lina reached out and flicked his forehead. Jay yelped.

"Don't forget this," she said, stuffing his cap on his head. Her stare met his. "By the way, Brax was out of line with what he said. About you, I mean. If he talks that way again, I'll soak him in the ink from Ma's printer."

A soft smile reached Lina's face. Jay smiled back.

"And listen," she went on, "I appreciate that you cared to help, but next time, stay back. I can handle Brax well enough, one way or another." She stared him in the eye. "Don't go jumping into fights you can't win. Okay? Stop trying to be someone you're not."

With those words, Lina crushed the last bit of good feeling in Jay's chest like a ripe berry she'd smushed between her fingertips.

"Besides," added Lina, nodding down the road, "it seems you'll have enough of your own troubles soon. *Real* soon."

Jay spun around. He spied a familiar shape lumbering toward them like a grumpy bear.

Jay gulped. Mr. Douse looked furious—but he'd be forgiving. Right?

∞

Wrong. *So* wrong.

Jay's next day began alongside the river fishermen, who gladly handed him a mop and a pail and set him to work. By the time he finished swabbing up all the gooey, grimy guts, Jay swore he would never eat a fish again.

And that was only the first of the punishments Mr. Douse had in store. After Jay's tuck-n'-tumble with Brax, a handful of grove keepers, Widow Tinner, and the butcher came around, complaining how Jay had trespassed and caused a terrible fuss. To mollify them, Mr. Douse lent Jay out to do whatever chores they asked. Jay went all over town—washing what was filthy, fixing what was broken, plucking what was overgrown.

The fact that Brax shared *none* of the blame or the punishment stirred the grit in Jay's gizzard, but he still did as he was told.

Two days after the Hangman's Run incident, as the morning sun climbed toward noon, Jay was still hard at it, this time mucking out Widow Tinner's goose shed. As he shoveled out soiled straw and foul droppings, Jay couldn't help but hear the echo of Lina's words, chasing him wherever he went:

Stop trying to be someone you're not.

Jay threw a shovelful of muck, trying to shrug off what Lina had said. But then Brax's voice chimed in, gnawing at him like vicious teeth:

Zero. Nobody. Outlaw.

Jay tried not to sink deeper into his glum mood. He knew that's what most folks thought about him. When people glanced his way, they never saw *him*—only the inky sketch of his face from his old wanted posters.

Outlaw.

But that wasn't who he was anymore. He'd gotten away from the city of Fairdown Falls—away from the Capo, his old boss—away from the life he'd been born into.

When he was little, Jay had lived with the Capo and the Staccato Gang because, according to the Capo, his folks had owed them a huge debt. Jay had no idea how his parents had gotten tangled up with the Staccatos, no clue why they owed the Capo so much money; the only hints the Capo ever gave were that his father was a failed Musician with a strong temper and his mother was a lonely club singer with a weak heart. His dad had disappeared mysteriously after Jay was born, and his mom had died before Jay was old enough to walk. Their debt had outlived them both. The Capo had trained Jay up as a thief so Jay could pay back his parents' debt. He wasn't proud of it, but he *had* been pretty good— good enough to earn his own nickname, the Quickstep Kid, when he was eight.

Back then, Jay didn't think about what he did as being wrong. It was enough to have a place to sleep, food to eat, a boss to follow.

But that was all before he'd found Windfalle. Before he'd realized what his ability to see muses meant. Before he'd seen the Capo's true colors.

A monk's kind smile . . . a muse in a tree . . . a building in flames.

Jay squashed the memories before they could fully come to life in his mind, but he still felt a sickening twist in his gut. After what happened at Windfalle, he'd fled from the Capo and the Staccatos. He'd practically begged the city watchmen to arrest him. The watchmen were happy to send him to Blackmine Reformatory for Wayward Boys. After he'd done his time, Jay had been picked up by Mr. Douse, who'd taken the reformatory's commission to be Jay's custodian during his probation. The rest was history.

Even so, Jay couldn't forget what had happened—and he knew the Capo wouldn't forget, either. Thankfully, all the Staccatos were in Fairdown Falls, on the opposite side of the country. The Capo had a long reach, but Jay figured he was safe in Hazeldenn, so deep in the backwoods that even mapmakers forgot to put it on their maps.

Still, there were times Jay caught himself jumping at shadows, expecting to see the Capo staring him down from the darkness.

Jay shuddered. He scooped more muck into the wheelbarrow, forcing his thoughts to change direction. He couldn't change what people thought of him, and his outlaw past still haunted him—but that didn't mean his life was over. If he kept his chin up and finished his probation, he could start fresh.

Jay considered the possibilities. Maybe he could learn to mix elixirs as an alchemist or build devices as a tinkerbit mechanic. Why not? Maybe he could join the International Research Society, exploring all corners of the world. He could be an officer in the Queen's Cabinet of Justice.

Or maybe, just maybe, he could be something else . . . someone who practiced musical arts.

Stop trying to be someone you're not.

Jay's shovel caught a snag on the ground, jerking him from his thoughts. He straightened up, gulping down the bitter tang crawling up his throat.

Him? A Musician?

No use thinking such things.

Jay set the shovel against the goose pen and heaved the full wheelbarrow, glancing up at the darkening sky. A storm was coming.

"Hi, Jay!"

Startled, Jay skidded in the mud, the wheelbarrow nearly toppling over.

"Colton," said Jay to the visitor, "don't sneak up on folks like that. The last thing I want is to dump this all over myself."

"Sorry!" said Colton, not sounding sorry at all. Colton Kindle—Lina's nine-year-old brother, with bright red hair and an apple-dumpling grin—stood beaming. Colton's friends were with him, too: Gabe, Jed, and Owen, all leaning on the fence.

"Where've you been at?" said Colton. "You haven't been around the candle shop much. You made Mr. Douse real mad, huh?"

Jay sighed. For some reason, Colton always wanted to know everything Jay was up to. Sometimes the kid would follow Jay around, jabbering his ear off. Normally, Jay didn't mind. Colton was kind of an annoying kid, but it wasn't a bad kind of annoying. Today, though, Jay wasn't in the mood.

He turned to Colton, about to tell him and his friends to get on home—until he saw something on Colton's face. "What the heck is that?" asked Jay, pointing to a bruise on Colton's cheek.

Colton kicked the fence. "Nothing," he said, trying to sound tough.

Jay gave the small boys a hard look. Jed cracked.

"After school, Lee Mackaroy called Trudy Primple an ugly cow!" he blurted. "So Colt told him to apologize!"

Jay looked at Colton. "You got into a scrape over that?"

Colton shrugged. "He wouldn't apologize."

Jay forced down a grin. Part of him wanted to pat Colton on the back. On the other hand, it probably wasn't good to praise him for fighting.

"That's no good," said Jay. "You shouldn't go getting into fights with other kids, even if they're jerks."

Gabe snorted. "Like you're one to talk," he said, pointing at Jay's eye.

Jay reached for his face. His black eye from Brax hadn't faded yet. "Me getting into a scuffle is different," said Jay.

"Oh yeah?" said Gabe. "How?"

Pretending he hadn't heard the question, Jay hefted the wheelbarrow, dumping another load of muck.

A far rumble stirred the air. Above them, the dark clouds grew nearer.

Sensing the turn in the weather, Jay hurried on while Colton and the other boys watched him.

"*Oh!*" said Colton. "Guess what, guess what, guess *what?*"

Jay shoveled on. "You got a new girlfriend?"

The boys all gagged in disgust. Jay smirked.

"Yuck, no!" said Colton. "I get to go to Harvestide this year!"

Jay glanced his way. "Don't you go every year?"

"Well, yeah—but *this* year I get to stay up late!" said Colton. "I'll get to see all the dancing and games and fun stuff!"

"Good for you."

"You gonna set out the Harvestide lanterns soon, Jay?" asked Owen.

Jay sighed. That was a chore he wasn't looking forward to. For Harvestide, the folks of Hazeldenn celebrated the end of the hazelnut harvest and honored their deceased loved ones. They lit candles at family graves, and then from sundown to sunup they enjoyed dances and partied the night away. As a candlemaker, Mr. Douse loved Harvestide because it was the best time for his business. Specialty candles were in high demand.

As the lamplighter, Jay didn't love it so much. He was the one who had to light all the special Harvestide lanterns. It was a ton of extra work.

"My sister won't stop talking about Harvestide," said Colton in a grumble. "Ma says Lina gets to stay up all night if she wants. But I can't stay up past midnight, which is *so* unfair—"

Jay's ears perked at once. "Is Lina going with someone?" he asked, his mind flashing to Brax. Hopefully that jerk had been leaving her alone.

Colton rolled his eyes. "Don't know, don't care. But if you wanna go, you need about fifty baths first. You stink!" He plugged his nose.

The boys laughed. Jay's irritation flared into mischief.

"I'll be sure to remember that," he said, keeping a straight face. "And *you* should remember to watch out for dischords that night."

The kids' laughter died at once.

"Dischords?" repeated Colton, puzzled.

"Wait—you don't know about dischords?" said Jay with mock surprise, leaning on his shovel.

Colton and the others shook their heads.

"Then I should warn you," said Jay. "Dischords—they're nasty things. They always hang out in the dark. They hide under beds and inside wells 'cause they can get ahold of their victims real easy from those places." Jay shoveled more into the wheelbarrow. "There'll be plenty of dark places for 'em to hide during Harvestide."

A flicker of surprise and uneasy curiosity flashed across the kids' faces.

"What do dischords look like?" asked Gabe.

Jay shrugged. "Heck if I know."

Gabe snorted. "If you haven't seen one, how d'you know they're real?"

"'Cause dischords aren't supposed to be seen," said Jay, his voice going even softer. "Dischords can only be *heard*."

The chubby boy's eyes went wide. Colton and the others chittered.

"They say the sound of a dischord is the most wonderful, horrible thing you'll ever hear," Jay went on, drawing them in. "You won't know where it's coming from, but it'll sound so strange that you'll want to follow it. That's how the dischord will lure you away until you're all alone."

"You're making that up!" said Jed, but he didn't sound sure.

Jay shrugged. "I'm only telling you what I've heard."

"So, *then* what happens?" asked Owen, clinging to the fence.

Jay sent them a wary glance. "You really want to know?"

"No!" said Colton in a squeak. "I don't wanna hear any more!"

Jay hid an impish grin. Too easy. Of course, once upon a time, tales of dischords had given him the shivers, too. Jay could remember those times—standing at the back of a crowd of kids, listening to a kind man in monk robes rattle on about dischords in a low, chilling voice.

The memory sent a pang through Jay like a snapping string. He used to love stopping by Windfalle to hear Brother Elfenbein entertain the orphans in his care with such stories. Jay's favorite was about how the demon Din, the King of Discord, had brought a legion of dischords into the world—and how the first Crafter, against all odds, had defeated him. For a time, Jay had been so scared of Din and dischords that he used to shield himself with the anointing water and sacred herbs he'd filched from Brother Elfenbein's sanctuary cupboards, hoping to ward them off.

"As soon as you're alone, the sound you hear will start to change," continued Jay, waggling his fingers. "The soft, pretty noise you followed before will turn into something horrible. The only chance you'll have is to stop yourself from listening—plug your ears, scream—but it's more likely you won't be able to do even that. You'll be surrounded by howls and shrieks and all the scary sounds from your nightmares."

"Stop it, Jay!" cried Colton. The other boys sank further behind the fence.

"And then," said Jay, in the creepiest voice he could muster, "once you step into the shadows where the dischord is waiting, it'll get ahold of you.

It'll sneak into your ears, it'll slither up your nose, it'll ooze through your eyeballs . . . and by the time you realize it, it'll be *too late*—!"

Jay should've been prepared to duck. As he spoke, Colton scooped up a mound of mud from the ground and threw it at Jay's face.

At once Colton and the others fell over laughing. Jay gripped his shovel, pushing the spade deep into the mud and hauling out a huge shovelful of mud.

"Just remember, Colton," he said, "*you* started it."

Colton and the other boys stopped laughing. Half a second later, they roared as Jay slung mud at them. Then they dove down to grab clumps of dirt to throw back. It was a filthy free-for-all. Showers of mud flew. The geese went wild. Jay laughed with the smaller boys, until—

"*What are you doing to my yard?*"

Jay stopped mid-throw. Wuh-oh.

A squat old woman emerged from the house. Widow Tinner took one look at her yard and squawked in outrage.

The boys on the far side of the fence disappeared, leaving dust clouds in their wake. Jay was trapped as Widow Tinner yelled, her cheeks puffed like an angry chipmunk. At length, the woman smacked him upside the head and told him to clean it up, grumbling as she returned inside her house. Jay sighed, grabbing the shovel to fill in the holes they'd all made.

"Is she gone?"

Jay saw Colton's carrot-top head pop up from behind the fence. He actually had the nerve to look sheepish.

"She's gone," said Jay. He shot a thumbs-up. "Thanks for that backup."

Colton looked so remorseful that Jay couldn't hold a grudge.

"Don't worry about it," Jay muttered, flicking away glops of mud from his clothes. "Look, I've gotta finish up here. See you 'round—"

"I'll help!" said Colton brightly. "Lemme help!"

Colton hopped the fence and grabbed the shovel from Jay, patching up all the holes. Seeing no reason to stop him, Jay left him to it, dumping the last load from the wheelbarrow.

Jay had only just wiped off the grime from his hands when something cold and wet landed with a *splot* on his shoulder. His eyes rose toward the gathering clouds. They had expanded from a flat dark haze to a dark billowing mess. From somewhere above, a rumbling pulsed through the sky.

Beside him, Colton shivered.

"I'd better get home," he said. Before he left, he faced Jay again. "Sorry I ran off before. I shouldn't have let you take the blame by yourself."

Jay ruffled the nine-year-old's hair. "I told you not to worry about it, dummy." He pushed Colton playfully away. "Now get away from me. You reek like swamp."

"You're the one covered in muck!" Colton retorted.

"Just get going. And be sure to watch out for dischords."

Colton shuddered. "I will." He grinned. "Thanks, Jay. You're a good guy."

He bolted off. Jay smiled. As he returned the shovel and wheelbarrow to Widow Tinner's shed, he whistled loudly to himself, for the moment no longer able to hear Lina's or Brax's voices in his mind.

Chapter Six

UNEXPECTED DELIVERY

Soon the rain started to fall steadily, so Jay picked up the pace. He'd just finished stuffing the wheelbarrow back in Widow Tinner's shed when Colton came dashing up again, running into him at full speed.

Jay almost toppled over. "Colton! What the heck?"

Colton flailed at the sky. "*Look!*"

Jay tilted his head, a hand on his cap. From the heart of the storm, a sky schooner appeared—a long-bodied air vessel, sailing in the air. Its large oblong balloon was tethered to the boat by crisscrossed rigging. The thrumming of high-powered engines grew louder as the vessel approached, banking against the clouds.

"Mail!" cried Colton, grinning.

Jay squinted against raindrops, studying the ship. The stern was trailing a black line of smoke even darker than the clouds, and the wing-sails were straining against the high-altitude breeze. The vessel was losing altitude, heading in the direction of the nearest body of water: Hazel Lake.

"C'mon!" yelped Colton, running off. Jay followed him, dashing through the hammering rain.

By the time Jay and Colton had come to the docks, a crowd of townsfolk was already swamping the banks. Holding Colton's shoulder, Jay guided them both through the crowd for a better view.

After making its splash landing, the ship bobbed across the lake through the misty rain toward the docks, accompanied by some quacking ducks that swam in cautious ranks alongside the enormous vessel. Workers on deck darted back and forth, guiding the boat in. It didn't look much different than any other boat—except for the aero-propellers sticking out near the stern, the smoking engines sizzling with steam, the wing-sails stretching above their heads, and the glass-enclosed navigation deck on the prow. The captain, wearing a peaked cap and a pair of goggles, approached the side of the ship, greeting the drenched crowd.

"Rough skies, Captain?" somebody called up.

The captain grunted. "Storm caught us by surprise. But we made it."

That was all the man spared for small talk. The ship's crew got to work, fetching up the post for Hazeldenn. The crowd pushed forward, impatient for their long-awaited letters and parcels. The crew sorted and distributed the mail under the shelter of the wing sails. Soon the whole dock was caught up in a noisy exchange as people shoved to and fro, trying to shield their envelopes and packages from the rain.

As the mail delivery went on, Jay caught sight of a couple fellows hopping down onto the dock, wearing identical top hats and long coats. These men began setting up portable billboards alongside the boat. Each billboard displayed headlines from dozens of national bulletins, with short excerpts and a price pinned beneath them. At the far end of the billboards, the men set up a tiny sandwich board bearing fancy lettering: *Curtiss & Felixson Dispatch Co. (Proof of License Available Upon Request).*

While waiting for their turn for mail, most of the crowd read the news merchants' billboards. Jay turned to the closest one, scanning headlines: HARMONY MONUMENT RENOVATIONS DELAYED, VISITS PROHIBITED; EASTIRN REFORMERS CUT MILITARY SPENDING, BOLSTER EDUCATION BUDGET; MERIDEYIN'S MINISTER OF MEDICINE CALLS OUTBREAKS "ALARMING"; and SOUTHIN TRIBES VOICE CONCERN OVER WYSTIA'S NEW TERRITORIAL MAPS.

None of those reports looked particularly interesting, so Jay scooted along to read the next billboard. This one had a few ink illustrations pinned up beside the headlines, which were all printed in gaudy, eye-catching letters: WHAT IS HER MAJESTY WEARING? 8 NEW TRENDS FOR THE SEASON; MIDNIGHT K'NAPPER STRIKES AGAIN! ANOTHER VICTIM MISSING; ARE "NIGHTCREEPER" SIGHTINGS IN MERIDEYIN A SIGN OF THE END TIMES?; and WYNNFIELD TIMBERCATS FAVORED TO MAKE PLAYOFFS.

The only thing worth reading there was the sports pages. Jay looked for the price of the story, then whistled in dismay when he saw it: C.120.

He checked his pockets. Sifting through the extras—a couple of spark stones, a candle stub, some string—he gathered the money he had on him: half a Mark, two Clinks, nine Whits. Fifty-four. Not enough.

As Jay stashed his coins away, Colton poked his arm.

"What's *impasse* mean?" he asked.

Jay shrugged. "No idea. Where'd you see it?"

Colton pointed to a headline: NURTHICA AND WYSTIA REACH IM-PASSE—PEACE NEGOTIATIONS STALLED.

Colton squeezed up next to him and read the excerpt of the story aloud, stumbling over only a few words as he sounded them out:

"'Following the . . . *ee-nish-ee-ay-shun* of the latest North-West cease-fire, General Wolfram of Nurthica and Chairman Xenocrates of Wystia still refuse to . . . *ack-wee-yes* to peace terms.'" Colton frowned. "I don't get it."

Jay didn't really get it, either. From the little Jay could figure, there was some foulness going on between other countries. The nations of Sedrinel were like kids on the street. Some were bullies, going around throwing punches at smaller ones out of some cruel impulse to prove they were better. Then the other nations stepped up to fight back, while more timid ones on the fringe tried to stop the struggle. People were on edge, just waiting for someone to start kicking dirt.

Jay felt the chill of the rain seep through his skin. He rubbed his arms to get rid of the goosebumps, glancing at the men sorting letters and parcels. Perhaps he should go pick up the mail for Mr. Douse; it wouldn't do the old man any good to come out in this chill.

Shoes squelching, Jay headed toward a crewmember with a mail sack.

"Got anything for Bert Douse?" he asked.

The mailman lifted his head. "Come again?"

"*Albert Douse*," Jay shouted over the rain.

The mailman sifted through his sack, peering at what he had left. By the time he pulled something from it, Jay was shivering.

"One here for Douse's Candleworks," the mailman said, handing him a crumpled blue envelope.

Jay slinked his way back up the dock, studying the envelope. There was no recipient name. Huh.

"What is it?" asked Colton, who'd found his way to Jay's side again.

Jay shrugged, then smirked. "Maybe a love letter for Mr. Douse."

Colton made a gagging noise, and Jay grinned. It was more likely the latest letter from one of Mr. Douse's foreign friends; the old man had pen pals from all over the world. Jay flipped the envelope over to check the return address.

His grin vanished. Shock froze his lungs, filling his chest with ice.

On the back flap of the envelope, where the return address should have been, the sender had drawn something very small, something nobody else would've recognized:

A scarlet butterfly.

Jay couldn't breathe. The butterfly.

It was the Capo's mark.

As the thought sank in, a snake of dread wriggled out of the ice in his chest; it coiled around his heart and squeezed tight, making each thump painful. Frantic thoughts pounded through him:

It's from her—she's found me—blessed Seraphs, she's found me.

"What's wrong?" asked Colton. He peered at the envelope.

"Colton," said Jay, his voice stern, "get on home."

Colton frowned up at him. "I wanna stay with you!"

Jay rounded on him. "Get outta here already!"

The words came out sharper than he'd meant. Colton shot Jay a hurt look, then scampered away. Jay watched the small boy until he was out of view—then he took off. He pushed his way through the lingering crowd and ran, blitzing down the road. At the town gate, Jay took a sharp turn off the path and into the trees. When he was sure he was far from prying eyes, Jay stopped, ducking under the heavy boughs of a large spruce.

Jay wiped rain from his eyes and examined the blue envelope. Then, hands shaking, he tore into it and yanked out the piece of paper inside.

The page was blank.

Most people would've figured it was some joke if they'd been mailed a blank piece of paper. But Jay knew this was no joke.

He dove into his pocket, pulling out his candle stub and spark stones. He struck the stones together, lighting the wick and setting the candle on the ground. Holding the paper in both hands, he set it over the dancing flame. For several eternal seconds, nothing happened.

And then, as the sharp heat of the candle flame licked the page, words slowly appeared across the top:

BRIO

Hello, Quickstep.

Jay's heart thudded at the base of his ribs like a stone hitting the bottom of an empty well. *Quickstep.*

He moved the paper back and forth over the flame, careful not to singe it or let too much smoke cloud the surface. At last, the invisible message revealed itself with the candle's heat:

I've known where you've been for some time now. You didn't even try to cover your tracks. Didn't I teach you better?

Jay clenched his jaw. She *would* say something like that. He could hear her disparaging tone in his head as he read on:

I have not forgotten what you did. You betrayed me. You tried to leave the gang. I can't let you get away with that. You should be grateful I let you enjoy your freedom these past few years—but playtime is over. You have a debt to pay, and I will collect every last whit.

Jay scowled. His time of "freedom" had been spent between jail, a reformatory, and probation.

Here is your choice, Quickstep.
Come back to the gang—or pay back the rest of your debt by midnight on Wintertide Eve, plus interest. Don't bother trying to run again. If you don't pay, someone else will. Don't make the same mistake you made at Windfalle. I'll be waiting for you.

Jay fell back against the tree, shivering.

Three years.

Three years since Jay had last set eyes on the Capo. Three years since he'd escaped the Staccato Gang. Three years since he'd rebuilt a life from the scraps of his past.

And, just like that, it had all come crashing down again. She knew where he was. Even from the other side of the country, he couldn't escape her.

Jay dipped the corner of the letter in the candle flame, the paper curling and crackling as the hungry fire chewed it to ash. As he stared at the flame, he began to relive old memories.

Flames against the sky—so much screaming—

Jay shook his head. He didn't want to remember.

But the memory came unbidden, painfully sharp:

Ragged screams pierced the night—Jay pushed and shoved against the fleeing people, his body jostled every which way—this wasn't the plan—everything had gone wrong, so wrong—

The memory was too cruel. Jay's chest hurt. He couldn't swallow.

The Capo was a silhouette against the chaos, watching the blaze burn out of control—tears streamed down Jay's cheeks as the sanctuary was consumed by the vicious inferno—no, no—

"No," Jay whispered, cringing against the memories.

He screamed for some muse, any muse, to help—but none answered him—the flames rose higher, higher, higher—

"No!" Jay screamed aloud, his eyes snapping open.

Squee!

Jay jumped at the sound of a soft, melodic squeak. He glanced down, heart pounding.

A small muse—one that looked like a tiny silver field mouse, with a tufted tail and intelligent green eyes—was crouched hardly two paces away from where Jay sat. Jay had been so lost in the past that he hadn't even heard it approach. The music spirit was sitting on its hind legs with its front paws tucked against its chest, watching Jay with bright intensity.

Jay felt something in his chest harden to an ugly lump.

"Go away, you rotten muse!" he hollered, flinging his arms to chase it away.

The mouse muse tilted its head. *Squee?* it squeaked again.

"I've got nothing for you!" Jay roared, leaping to his feet. "Leave me *alone!*"

Spooked, the muse scampered off, vanishing into thin air. The woods went shivery silent.

Jay trembled in the sudden quiet. He had to get out of here before other muses sensed him.

Jay hurried off, chattering as he dwelled on his dilemma. The rest of his parents' debt, in full. Plus interest. By Wintertide Eve.

Impossible. His folks had borrowed half a million Medallions from the Capo. Jay didn't know why his foul-tempered father and feeble-hearted mother had needed that kind of cash in the first place; all he knew was he had to pay it back himself. In all the years he'd worked for the Capo, pulling all kinds of robberies and scams, he'd barely managed to pay back a fifth of it. He'd be an old man before he earned enough money to cover the debt. And Wintertide Eve was, what, three weeks away? How was he supposed to get his hands on hundreds of thousands of Medallions by then?

The Capo wasn't really giving him a choice. Paying off the debt by that deadline was hopeless.

But he couldn't go crawling back to the Staccatos. He didn't want to be the Quickstep Kid again—always hungry, always putting his guard up, always having to avoid being snatched by watchmen or getting the fluff beaten out of him by a rival gang.

If you don't pay, someone else will.

Jay shook the threat from his mind and continued onto the road, staring out at Hazeldenn. The town hunched under the downpour, the smoke heavy from the chimneys and the windows alight. In every direction, the hazel groves showed off their best colors, their nutty scent smothered by the smell of the storm. After living here a whole year, it all felt so familiar.

But he should've known the Capo would find him, no matter how deep in the boonies he tried to hide.

I'll be waiting for you.

Feeling the chill numb his bones, Jay hurried back through the lonely streets. Even before he reached the candle shop, he'd made his decision.

He had to run.

Chapter Seven

FAREWELL PRESENT

*A*rk ran as fast as his legs would go, his talaris flapping behind him. He'd lost track of time. The clock tower in the middle of Echostrait's campus had just chimed a quarter past four—he'd been told to report to the train station at half past five—which left him almost no time to pack.

It'd been his own fault, really. A few days had passed since Maestran Pandoura had told him of his jury mission. But every time he found an opportunity to put his suitcase together, one thought had stopped him:

Do not go. You may regret it.

Ark kept coming back to his strange encounter with the timid Miss Mara Fipple, her coded message swirling in his thoughts. But he hadn't seen the woman since she'd left him outside the Maestran's office, so he hadn't been able to ask her what she'd meant.

In the meantime, Ark's imagination had run wild with theories. Maybe she was trying to tell him that whatever assignment they were on would be so awful that he'd be better off staying in Echostrait. Maybe she'd wanted to warn him about Lady Vielle and Sir Mandore, his jurors. Maybe she wanted him to know that wherever they were headed wasn't a nice place.

Ark frowned. He had no answers, and he was out of time—so he swallowed his frustration and ran on, heading to the Adepts' residence hall.

Ark was out of breath by the time he reached the dormitory. At the front doors, he checked to make sure the coast was clear, then he raced up the main stairs toward the boys' wing. Perhaps, he considered hopefully as he darted past closed doors, perhaps he would be able to get in, pack, and get out without having to deal with any of them.

Ark stole silently down the corridor, whipping around the corner—

And nearly careened into a group of people crowded outside his room.

"Whoa! Watch it, Encore!" said one of them. "What's your rush?"

Ark steadied himself. He should have known the other Adepts weren't going to make his departure easy.

"I'm in a hurry, Saregama," said Ark to the boy who'd addressed him.

Adept Saregama gave Ark a not-so-playful pat on the head. "Oh, right! You're leaving on your *jury mission* today, aren't you?"

Ark almost cursed aloud. Of course they had found out.

"What will you be doing?" added Saregama in mock curiosity. "Playing lackey to some Conservatory snobs? *Exciting*."

The other Adepts chuckled. Ark didn't.

"Your jealousy is touching," he muttered. "What do you want?"

Saregama shared glances with the other boys.

"Us, jealous? Of *you*?" spat one of them with a hard laugh.

Ark smirked. "Wow. Jealous *and* in denial."

All the other Adepts scowled—except Saregama, who snorted a laugh.

"Don't flatter yourself, Encore," he said. "Maestran Pandoura's only sending you because you're her special pet. It doesn't change the fact that you're a disfigured little *jinx*."

Saregama's eyes drifted toward Ark's scarred hand.

Ark's smirk fell. He didn't have time for this.

"*Vienni damme*," he chanted softly.

Ark wasn't sure what muse his cantus would attract, but seconds later, the air hummed around him. A brutish muse with a bull's face and four curved horns appeared next to him, beating the floor with its hooves.

The other Adepts drew back a step.

Ark smiled inwardly. He wasn't Principal Adept for nothing.

"Hey now, don't ruin the mood," said Saregama, raising his hands in surrender. "We only came to give you a proper send-off."

"Is that so." Ark didn't buy that for an instant.

"Sure," said Saregama. "We even have a farewell present for you." His grin turned rotten. "We left it in your room."

Ark's chest went tight. His room. He'd left his notebook in there.

"Move, Saregama," said Ark, feeling his insides go cold.

Saregama blocked Ark's path. "Won't you guess what we got you?"

"Let me through."

"Not until you guess."

"An airship, a Medallion, and the Crafter," Ark spat. "Now *move*."

"Wrong!" said Saregama. "Try again!"

The Adepts snickered.

Ark's scowl broke free, his temper dropping to below freezing. He didn't like to call on muses in direct confrontations. The golden platitude that the instructors hammered into their students' brains was one Ark generally agreed to follow: *Do not summon muses if you don't have to.*

But his notebook was at stake.

Ark drew in a deep breath. "*Diffendimmi!*"

A heartbeat later, the four-horned muse, still at his side, charged with a thunderous bellow down the corridor. Saregama and the other Adepts were sent crashing into the walls, cringing as the muse stormed away.

His path clear, Ark slipped into his room—and froze, staring.

His wardrobe had been ransacked, and all his dresser drawers had been dumped out. His bookshelf had been stripped, and most of his books lay strewn across the floor, many with pages torn from their covers. An enormous heap of trash was left on his bed, soiling his covers. Someone had even taken ink and smeared foul insults on the walls in dripping letters.

"Have a nice trip," said Saregama. He'd recovered from Ark's attack, standing at Ark's shoulder. "Hope you fail!"

Ark slammed the door as they all broke into callous laughter, their footsteps fading down the corridor.

Ark scowled. Creeps.

Then he turned and dove into the mess, searching every corner. He couldn't believe he hadn't taken his notebook with him.

At last, he felt his fingertips brush against it, hidden under the soil of a broken flowerpot. Ark tossed the ruined plant aside and gripped his notebook, inspecting. It looked unscathed. Thank goodness.

He flipped the notebook open and scanned the pages. Ark could have rewritten the notes from scratch, if he'd needed to—but there was something else in his notebook that Ark couldn't afford to lose.

Ark flipped the pages along the edge of his thumb, letting the notebook fall open to the inside back cover. Pressed there was a separate, coarser piece of paper that bore the sketch of a woman holding an infant on her lap. Under the sketch was rough handwriting:

SONYA, 1867
FROM TRISTEN WITH LOVE

The sketch was one of Ark's most precious belongings: a picture of his mother, drawn by his father. He'd stolen it from his father's things just before he'd been sent to Echostrait. It was the only thing Ark still possessed that connected him to his parents.

Ark could barely remember a time when his family had lived in a house. After his mother died, Ark's father had turned nomadic, dragging his son all over the country for work. Ark rarely slept in the same bed twice. He didn't mind; that was all Ark had ever really known. So long as his father was near, Ark felt secure.

As Ark studied the sketch, an unrelated memory washed through him.

He was six years old. Ark and his father were crouched in the straw on the back of a rickety wagon, sharing a threadbare blanket. Ark was supposed to be asleep, but he peeked at his father through the slits of his eyelids, watching him. Tristen de Cani was holding an engraved silver ring hanging from a chain around his neck, his gaze distant and hollow. When the man realized his son was only pretending to be asleep, he pulled Ark into his lap and stroked his hair, singing a lullaby in a rough voice.

Adieu, adieu, ma luciole
La nuit est presque terminée
Les étoiles se fondent dans le soleil . . .

The memory faded, and Ark felt a pang in his chest. Ark hadn't lived in a house for most of his life, but he'd always had a home. Home was with his father.

But Ark hadn't been home in years.

Ark flipped the sketch over. He read the hastily scribbled note on the back, as he'd done a million times before:

REMEMBER WHY YOU FIGHT

The words put a lump in Ark's throat. He clenched his scarred hand into a fist as echoes of the past pounded through him:

You're no longer a de Cani. You're no son of mine.

You are a disappointment.

Ark closed his notebook. He couldn't face the memory now.

He glanced around his ruined room. There was no time to clean it up, so Ark dragged his suitcase out from underneath his bed and plowed through the mess, digging out his essentials from the floor.

Packing took all of ten minutes. Before he left, Ark paused, compelled to take one final glance out his window. His hackles rose as he spied Saregama and the other Adepts exit the dorm right below him, all laughing together.

Ark glared at them. Maybe he could exact his vengeance before leaving. Throwing all their book bags under a running faucet would take about three minutes. Putting shoe polish on their doorknobs would take a minute—two minutes, tops. That left a couple of minutes to dump their underwear out the window and make a clean getaway.

Ark shook off the temptation. No. He was better than them.

Sighing, he forced himself to swallow the sourness of not getting even. He turned away from the window, seizing his suitcase.

"*Chiusso,*" he chanted in an undertone.

As he walked out of the room, a muse shut the door behind him, turning the lock in a final farewell.

Chapter Eight

FORTES SOLI, FORTIORES UNA

*A*s Ark exited the dorm, someone called to him.

"Need a hand, Encore?"

Ark glanced up. Xyla Capricci was standing by the dorm gate.

"Aunt Toni asked if I could see you off," she said. "Let me take that."

She grabbed Ark's suitcase before he could protest.

Ark followed Xyla along Echostrait's tree-lined thoroughfare. The wind accompanied them down the street; a fleet-footed muse chased the breeze between them, the tails of their coats whip around their legs.

Meanwhile Xyla kept shooting him glances, wearing a goofy smile.

"I hope your face freezes like that," Ark muttered. He was still grouchy over the mess the other Adepts had left in his room.

She grinned. "Better that than have a face like yours."

Xyla, one; Ark, zero. With a grunt, Ark stole his suitcase back from her.

"Aw, did I make you mad, Mr. Pouty?" said Xyla, poking his cheek.

Ark leaned away. "Goodbye, Capricci."

"I'm only trying to keep your spirits up."

"I prefer my glum spirits, thanks."

"The grumpy routine is getting old," Xyla told him, not unkindly. "The Grand Maestran *himself* gave you his blessing to go on your jury mission years ahead of schedule! Don't you realize what an honor that is?"

"Of course I do!" Ark snapped.

"Then why are you acting like you've been kicked in the duff?"

Ark frowned. He wasn't being fair to Xyla. Not wanting to bring up what the other Adepts had done, he mentioned something else bothering him.

"I haven't been outside of Echostrait in a while," he answered at length.

"Oh?" said Xyla, her tone changing. "How long?"

"Not since I was eight."

Xyla's eyebrows shot upward. "How old are you now?"

"Fifteen."

Her eyes went wide. "Seven years?"

"Remarkable math skills you've got there, Capricci."

Xyla elbowed him. "Let me get this straight. You haven't been outside of Echostrait, *not once*, since you were eight years old?"

Ark shook his head. Xyla stared at him, scandalized.

"What about your family?" she pressed. "Don't you visit them?"

Ark froze. The innocent question swirled inside him like a sharp, cold draft that roused the embers of a dying fire. He didn't like it.

"That's not possible," he said in a controlled voice.

Xyla's eyes softened. "I'm so sorry. I didn't know." She squeezed his shoulder. "You know, I'm an orphan too—"

Ark pulled away. "I'm not an orphan. My father's alive. I just don't know where he is. He's been out of touch."

In a heartbeat, Ark wished he could take back what he'd said. Xyla didn't seem offended, at least—but she looked curious, which was worse.

"When did you last hear from your father?"

Ark shrugged. "Not for a while." *Not since I was eight.*

Xyla's gaze was unreadable. "That's . . . ," she said, not finishing the thought. Instead, she said quietly, "You must miss him."

Ark said nothing, staring at his shoelaces.

A bell sounded across the campus, pealing the top of the hour. Xyla gave him a push. "Hurry, you'll be late!"

They soon came to the train station. As they walked through the entrance, Ark looked around. The building's north side was open to allow trains to enter along the water-lined tracks. From above, sunlight shone through glass panels along the ceiling. This was where draft beasts who hauled the trains rested and fueled up between journeys—the source of the fetid odor of manure in the air. Thankfully, Ark had made it in time. No train had arrived yet.

As he set down his suitcase, his eyes were drawn toward the western wall of the station. It had been painted over in a grand mural, the colors so bright and the details so precise that Ark couldn't help but stare. Elaborate designs led his eyes to two iconic figures in the exact center. One was a woman in a black talaris; the other was a winged, humanesque figure in flowing robes. Together they held up a shining lamp, looking profoundly heroic.

Ark knew who the figures were. The woman was the first Crafter, and the winged one was Brio. They were the two greatest heroes in Sedrinel's history.

The story played through Ark's head.

Long ago, Din, the King of Discord, had nearly consumed Sedrinel with his cruel, callous reign. He used profane arts to bring dischords, the antitheses of muses, into the world. He sent his disciples, the Dischordians, to conquer every land in his name. He was, in a word, evil.

Though Din and his brood of dischords were terrible, there was already another power in the world, benevolent and wise: muses. The greatest muse of all—Brio, an ancient being of harmony—sought to save Sedrinel from Din's malice. Brio chose a young woman whose spirit reflected his own to fight alongside him. The great muse became her patron and graced her with knowledge, teaching her how to call upon muses and summon their creative power. Brio then gave her a title by which the rest of the world would know her: *Crafter*, the mortal entrusted with the immortal gift of music.

Together Brio and the Crafter found others willing to fight Din, and they passed the musical arts on to them. With muses on their side, the Crafter and the first Musicians banished many dischords and routed the Dischordians. In the end, the Crafter and Brio faced Din alone, fighting him head on. Din was defeated, and Sedrinel was saved.

The rest was history. The Crafter and her fellow Musicians traveled to every corner of Sedrinel, exorcising dischords and teaching others who could detect muses how to summon them. Then, when the Crafter's final days came, Brio took a common musical instrument and marked it with his power, declaring that the one who could hear his call and play his instrument would be his next Crafter.

The first Crafter passed on. Sedrinel mourned. But eventually, someone else took up Brio's instrument, inheriting Brio's patronage and the Crafter title. That's the way it had gone for centuries.

But that had been a long, long time ago.

Ark would have happily studied the mural a few minutes more, but Xyla pulled him from his art-gazing.

"Well, this is where I leave you," said Xyla, patting Ark's back. "Just remember, you're a good Musician—so no matter what horrors your jurors put you through, you can handle it." She grinned. "Probably."

Ark's mouth went dry. "Thanks a lot."

"I'm kidding," she said. "You'll do fine. We're all rooting for you!"

Xyla shot him a double thumbs-up—and with that, she walked away.

Ark watched until Xyla disappeared through the doors, then he looked around, wondering when his jurors would arrive. His gaze was drawn toward the mural again, seeing something he hadn't noticed before. Along the bottom was an inscription in gold lettering:

FORTES SOLI, FORTIORES UNA

Ark stared at the words, pondering them. Minutes slipped past.

"Do you normally wear spectacles, Adept Encore?" a voice asked.

Ark jumped. Sir Dulcian Mandore had walked up silently next to him. The man wore a dark green talaris with the emblem of the Royal Conservatory on the back—a capital R with a line crossing through it from top to bottom, entwined with red and gold roses. He was carrying the same black leather case in his hand, with a chain dangling from his wrist to the handle. Trillo, his bluebird muse, was perched on his shoulder, its bright feathers glimmering.

"I didn't mean to startle you," he said. "It's good to see you."

It sounded like the man genuinely meant it. Ark bowed his head. "Thank you, Sir Mandore. It's an honor to be traveling with you."

Sir Mandore smiled. "Call me Dulcian." The man glanced at the station mural. "Do you know what it means?" he asked.

Ark followed Dulcian's gesture toward the inscription along the base of the wall: *Fortes Soli, Fortiores Una.*

"*Strong alone, stronger as one,*" said Ark, translating it.

Dulcian hummed, nodding in approval. "The motto of the First Crafter. How wise those words are." He gazed at the rest of the mural. "It's so easy to get lost in the study and practice of it that we can quickly forget how marvelous it all is. Music, I mean. Those words speak perfectly to the heart of all musical arts: We must listen to each other and work together as one. When we can do that, we create true harmony, which the malice of discord cannot possibly overcome."

Ark listened, not sure how to respond. He'd never thought of it that way before. To him, music was a skill to master, an ability to use—and something he could do just fine alone.

Dulcian stepped off. Ark grabbed his suitcase and trailed behind him.

"We haven't had the opportunity to get to know you yet," said Dulcian. "Before we head off, perhaps you could indulge us with introductions."

Ark realized Dulcian was leading him across the station toward two other people already waiting. One of them was his other juror, Lady Vielle. She had a dark green talaris like Dulcian's. Fiero, her black fox muse, crouched by her ankles, its bushy tail sweeping the floor.

The meek Miss Fipple was there too, wearing a brown talaris. Ark had suspected, but the brown talaris confirmed it: She wasn't a Musician, just an Aphonian—someone who could see muses but who possessed no musical talent. Ark wasn't surprised to see the woman holding her strange mechanical device, absently pressing buttons.

Dulcian swept an arm behind Ark to guide him forward. "Adept Encore, I'd like you to meet Lady Calliope Vielle—"

"*Don't* call me Calliope!" Lady Vielle interrupted. She raised her chin at Ark. "And it's 'Lady Vielle' to you. Call me Calliope and you'll regret it."

Ark sent her an even gaze. Then he bowed.

"I wouldn't dare, Lady Vielle," he replied, deadpanning.

Lady Vielle stared at him. She smiled thinly.

"Anxious to please, aren't you?" she said. "I was afraid we'd have a rebellious brat along for the ride. Perhaps you won't be as insufferable as I'd imagined."

Ark smiled back. Her compliment—insult—insultiment?—didn't faze him. "Thank you, ma'am."

"To be clear," she went on, her tone masking a dangerous edge, "if you *do* become insufferable or disobey orders, I'll give you a failing jury report."

Her smile went sharp. Ark's own smile fell from his face.

"Determining his report isn't just up to you," Dulcian chimed in. He sent Ark a kind look. "Don't mind Callie. She's an acquired taste. If you get past her sour glares and acrid words, she can be quite sweet."

Callie shot him a glare. Dulcian winked back.

While Callie turned her wrath on Dulcian, Miss Fipple shuffled up to him. She held out her hand for Ark to shake, saying nothing.

"Miss Mara Fipple," he said aloud. He took her limp hand for one second before dropping it. Her fingers were like ice.

Miss Fipple's pale eyes studied him. Ark didn't know why, but he wanted to get off on the right foot with Miss Fipple. She'd done it in a strange way, but she had tried to warn him privately: *Do not go. You may regret it.*

He suspected she'd been trying to warn him about his jurors. Callie and Dulcian were probably . . . interesting to work with.

"Thank you for trying to warn me," he whispered, tilting his head toward the other two. "I'll keep on my toes around them."

Miss Fipple continued to stare at him.

"Stop gawping, Mara," barked Callie. Mara dropped her gaze.

"All right, then—that's introductions out of the way," said Dulcian cheerfully. "Perhaps now we should take this opportunity to explain what our assignment is and what Adept Encore's duties will entail."

Ark straightened, bracing himself. This was it. No matter how tough or unpleasant it might be, there was no turning back now.

Dulcian noticed his posture change. He smiled. "Relax. As far as jury missions go, the task is quite simple. The Grand Maestran is sending us as his representatives to conduct a Crafter evaluation."

That was the last thing Ark expected to hear. "A what?"

"A Crafter evaluation," repeated Dulcian. "Every so often, the Maestrans Council sends Musicians from the Royal Conservatory to test a candidate. Since it's your jury mission, we'll have you administer the evaluation and make sure everything goes smoothly." Dulcian paused. "You seem surprised."

Ark wasn't sure *surprised* was the right word. His immediate response was relief. It flowed through his limbs like a cool, refreshing breeze.

They weren't going out to hunt dischords. He wouldn't have to face his worst nightmare. *Yes!*

But hearing Dulcian say they were instead hunting for a new Crafter didn't exactly put him at ease.

"I guess I didn't realize anyone believed a new Crafter could still show up someday," Ark admitted. "How long has the Royal Conservatory been conducting these evaluations?"

"Ever since the last Crafter passed on," said Dulcian.

Ark's eyes widened. The last Crafter died more than two centuries ago, and no Crafter had been appointed since. Instead, Maestran Councils had been formed in each nation to handle Musician-related affairs across the globe, with Grand Maestrans elected to run them.

"If you want to know more, you should ask Mara," said Dulcian, gesturing to Miss Fipple. "Mara is the Royal Conservatory's resident expert on the Crafter. She's overseen these evaluations for . . . how long, Mara?"

At the question, Mara lifted her eyes and started counting on her fingers, then switched to her calculation device, punching at buttons.

"A long time, it seems," Dulcian answered without waiting for her. "She's come to ensure the evaluation is done correctly and to confirm whether the candidate passes." He turned to her. "Want to take it from here?"

Mara obliged, lowering her device.

"The Royal Conservatory has tested hundreds of candidates over the years," she said. Her voice was weak and breathy, exactly what Ark had expected her to sound like. "Candidates through the centuries have shown exceptional musical ability and a natural affinity with muses. However, with the Crafter evaluation, they all failed."

Ark considered that. "Our candidate must be a great Musician," he murmured. "Who are they?"

Callie scoffed with a bitter laugh. Dulcian sent her a sideways glance.

"We actually don't know who the candidate is yet," he admitted. "But we received a tip that they're living in the frontier of Merideyin. The tip came from a confidential but highly trusted source, so we can't ignore it."

Ark frowned. Dulcian's explanation should have satisfied him. But one more thought bothered him.

Dulcian could tell. "What's on your mind?"

Ark hesitated.

"What's the point?" he finally asked. "I know Crafters were important a long time ago, but times have changed. Why go looking for a Crafter when each country has its own Grand Maestran now? Does it even matter?"

Before Dulcian could respond, Callie cut in.

"Of course it doesn't!" she said. "This is all a waste of time. But you don't get to complain. You are only here to follow orders—and here's mine: Stay out of the way and don't make this more exasperating than it already is!"

"Callie!" said Dulcian sharply.

Callie scowled and stalked off toward the tracks, Fiero padding behind her. But she'd said enough. Ark felt his face burning. Maybe he should have taken Mara's warning more seriously.

Dulcian spoke again.

"You have a point, Adept Encore," he said. "The Grand Maestrans of Sedrinel are all excellent Musicians and capable governors. Crafters have all but faded into history. So why does it matter?"

Dulcian's gaze traveled. Ark followed his glance to the station mural, where the icons of the First Crafter and Brio stared back at them.

"The Crafter isn't just some Maestran with higher political authority," said Dulcian. "They are living instruments of Brio's power, capable of things no Maestran can dream of. In the past, Crafters always inspired unity through their leadership—and whenever people started to go astray, Crafters always stood against dissonant forces to guide Sedrinel back to harmony."

His expression went grim. "Since the last Crafter passed, many have lost interest in the musical arts. Fewer people can see muses today than ever before, and even those with aptitude for music choose not to pursue it. Musicians have forgotten the purpose of their art, summoning muses for academic study or their own amusement rather than to serve and defend. Without a Crafter to inspire us, challenge us, fight for us—without someone to remind Musicians what their gifts are for—the very fabric of the musical world will someday unravel to nothing."

Dulcian glanced back to Ark so suddenly it made Ark stiffen.

"That's why the evaluation matters," said Dulcian. "Nothing may come of it this time, or the next, or the next. But for the sake of all Musicians in future generations, the Royal Conservatory will remain steadfast in searching for the Crafter, even if it takes another hundred years to find one."

Ark had no idea how to respond. Clearly Dulcian felt strongly about the Crafter, as misguided as his views may have been. Ark didn't want to challenge the man's beliefs, though, so he changed the subject.

"All right," he said. "What do I do?"

Dulcian's smile returned.

"As I mentioned before, we'll let you conduct the evaluation with the candidate since it's your jury mission," he said. "We'll also rely on your help to make sure *this* gets there safely. It's the centerpiece of the evaluation."

He held up the case that was chained to his wrist. Ark saw the unfamiliar crest adorning it, the winged golden lantern.

Dulcian reached into his talaris sleeve and pulled out a key, unlocking the case and opening the lid. Ark leaned forward to peer inside. He gasped.

Inside the case, cushioned by emerald green velvet, was . . . a piece of junk.

Ark couldn't think of a more delicate way to put it. It was a violin—just an ordinary, beat-up violin that had clearly seen better days. The violin's wooden body was ivory white, its surface scuffed and scored. A long, slender piece of weathered ebony was fixed along the center, with five strings held taut to its surface by tarnished silver screws. Resting next to it was a thin bow laced end to end with frayed horsehair.

"Is that . . . ?" said Ark.

"Yes," said Dulcian. "Brio's instrument. Not very impressive at first sight, is it?" He traced a finger delicately over the violin's hollow end. "But even so this is an ancient, powerful, and *very* important relic. 'Priceless' doesn't begin to cover it. Hence the extra security." He shook the wrist that bore the chain attaching him to the violin's case.

"The candidate has to play *that*?" said Ark. It didn't look like the violin was capable of making any sound, not in the shape it was in.

Dulcian nodded. "To be eligible to receive the Crafter title, the candidate must first play the instrument. If they pass the evaluation, they'll need to perform one final ritual at the Royal Conservatory for Brio's patronage to be official. But no one has gotten to that stage in two hundred years, so I am not certain of the details." He glanced Mara's way. "Do you know?"

But Mara wasn't paying attention. She was fiddling with her calculations device.

"Anyway, it's not important," said Dulcian, sending Ark a reassuring smile. "All you need to do for your jury mission is stay sharp and perform admirably." He winked. "No pressure."

That made Ark laugh. Dulcian shut and locked the leather case, then guided Ark to the tracks, joining Callie and Mara just as their train arrived.

The conductor blew a shrill whistle, signaling the draft beast to halt. Then the train crew swarmed out and crawled over the train like ants on a fallen apple, making their checks: testing the couplers, loading luggage, refilling the tender feed for the draft beast. The beast itself—a gargantuan pachyderm with blunted tusks and legs the size of tree trunks—sat on its haunches for a well-deserved break, munching on its feed to refuel.

"This is it," said Dulcian to Ark. "Are you ready to depart?"

Ark nodded to be polite. He didn't know how he felt anymore. But he grabbed his bag and went to the train, climbing aboard.

"Whoa," he breathed aloud.

The luxury of the car was excessive. It was lit by crystal lamps along the walls. A table with a vase of flowers stood between a cushy lounge chair and a small travel bed. Along the wall, a cabinet had been stocked with snacks.

Ark stepped further in, setting down his suitcase. Well, his jurors certainly knew how to travel in style. He didn't know how his jury mission would turn out—but having his own private, first-class train car was a sweet perk. If only Saregama and the other Adepts could see him now.

He searched the snack cabinet and seized a few honey biscuits, munching them as he settled into the lounge chair. He could get used to this.

"—can't get rid of him fast enough!"

At the voice, Ark went dead still. He glanced behind him and found a window cracked open. He went over to it, peeking around the curtain.

Just outside, Callie stood in the gap between the train cars. She held Fiero in her arms and glared at Dulcian. Dulcian himself was stone-faced as he sat on the car's coupler. Trillo hopped on his head, tweeting anxiously.

"—strapping us with a scrawny runt who looks like he'd faint the instant he saw a dischord!" Callie was saying. "What was Luthier thinking?"

Ark tightened his jaw. Who was she was calling a scrawny runt?

Dulcian was staring at the leather case in his lap, his fingers idly tracing its golden crest. "I can only guess what Luthier was thinking," he said. "I'm sure he wanted to help us draw some good out of our disgrace."

Ark started. *Disgrace?*

"Some good?" sneered Callie. "He's a teenager! He's good for nothing!"

Dulcian looked up. "Unlike you, I reviewed his file. Arkalin's father is Tristen de Cani—as in *the* de Cani clan. They have famous dischord exorcists on every branch of their family tree."

"He's a de Cani?" said Callie, surprised. "Why does he go by Encore?"

"I couldn't say. But when Luthier told us Arkalin was involved with this assignment, I'd originally thought we'd be evaluating *him* as the Crafter candidate. The boy's exam scores are off the charts."

Callie smirked without humor. "Too bad we can't choose a Crafter solely by test results. Then we wouldn't have to waste our time with this trip."

"My point is, Arkalin is a virtuoso," said Dulcian. "He's also respectful, attentive . . . we could have been punished with worse." He tried a smile on her. "Tell me I'm wrong."

"You're wrong," Callie spat. "We used to be the best agents the Royal Conservatory had. We've faced down dozens of criminals, commoners and Dischordians alike. And now we've been reduced to babysitting. I can't think of a worse punishment."

"Be that as it may," said Dulcian patiently, "this is our chance to redeem ourselves. Succeed, and we're back on real missions. Fail, and it's job hunting for the both of us. No more missions—ever."

At his words, Callie's face twisted like she'd swallowed poison.

"So," Dulcian continued, "you could attempt to finish this with your usual dedication and grace, and *not* your usual caustic charm." He sent her a pointed glance. "And you could at least try to be civil to our young Adept. All his hopes must be riding on this."

"As are ours," Callie groaned. Her eyes flickered toward the car window. Ark ducked out of sight, cringing. Had she spotted him eavesdropping?

He didn't hear any immediate shouts of outrage, so after a few deep breaths, Ark chanced peering over the window's edge.

". . . galling enough as it is without having a brat in our way," Callie was grumbling. It seemed she hadn't seen Ark. She faced Dulcian. "Do you know what really irritates me?"

"Everything?" inserted Dulcian.

Callie ignored him. "We're facing our worst plague of dischords in ages," she said, starting to pace. "Nature is out of balance. Sickness is spreading, despite quarantines. Dischords have even been spotted wandering in the open—commoners are calling them Nightcrawlers—"

"Nightcreepers," corrected Dulcian. "That's what their bulletins say."

"The point is," she said over him, "our fellow agents have all been sent out to fight dischords and defend commoners. Every second we waste being suspended means we leave others to suffer—others who actually need our help. But Luthier is still making us do this one last worthless task. How could he be so heartless?"

At length, Dulcian reached out and took her hand, stopping her pacing.

"Maybe that's the point," said Dulcian. "Maybe our real punishment all along has been knowing exactly what's going on but not being allowed to help."

Callie closed her eyes, looking pained by his words. Dulcian gently brushed his thumb across her knuckles.

"We deserve this, Callie," he said, staring up at her. "We didn't follow orders with that last mission. We have to face the consequences." He paused, then added, "It may be awkward, humiliating, frustrating. But we will survive this last assignment. Because you're right: We are the best team Luthier has. You and me." He squeezed her hand. "We'll fight another day."

Callie's eyes snapped open. She jerked her hand out of his.

"You sicken me," she hissed. "We didn't follow orders on that mission, but we did the right thing. And the only reason we were suspended was because *you* cowered to the will of the Council like a whipped dog! Don't try to make it sound like they were right!" She waved him away. "We're done here. I'm going aboard, and *no one* will disturb me until we reach our destination. Am I clear?"

Ark could almost feel the hurt radiating from Dulcian.

"You're positively transpicuous," he said, rising to his feet. "Excuse me."

Ark turned from the window. Eager as he was to understand what his jurors were talking about, he felt he'd overheard too much. His jurors were not who he thought they were. For them, this assignment was a punishment. And bringing Ark along was part of that punishment.

Ark didn't know whether to feel insulted or disappointed. His rotten luck had struck again, landing him with suspended jurors on a worthless mission. At least Saregama and the other Adepts couldn't see him right now.

Not sure what to do, Ark dared to glance out the window again. He didn't see Callie or Dulcian anywhere this time; instead, his eyes caught the station mural and the golden inscription.

Fortes Soli, Fortiores Una. Strong alone, stronger as one.

Ark replayed Callie's harsh words to Dulcian in his mind. So much for being "stronger together."

A quiet sound made him spin around. Ark saw something on the floor of the car: a slip of paper, just inside the door. It was another message, printed in the familiar type from Mara's calculations device:

LAST CHANCE
LEAVE NOW

Ark pulled open the car door, hoping to catch Mara walking away. But no one was there.

He stood on the threshold of the train car. Maybe he should listen to Mara. Maybe he should step off after everything he'd overheard.

Or maybe he should see the jury mission through to the end. Show them he wasn't a disappointment anymore. Prove he was a true de Cani.

Before Ark could decide, the conductor cracked his whip in the air, rousing the draft beast. As the train pulled out of the station, Ark exhaled a shaky breath he hadn't realized he'd been holding. He wasn't a Designist—he didn't follow religion—but without thinking, he said a wordless prayer that this duffed-up jury mission would go smoothly and that he could be done as soon as possible.

Chapter Nine

CANDLES AND GRAVES

Thank the Design, Jay's time of extra-special punishments was over.

The sun made its mid-morning debut over the rooftops as Jay followed his ordinary route through Hazeldenn, making his routine check of the town's lamps. As he went, he spied folks chatting nonstop over their juiciest gossip:

"—all a hoax, that Nightcreepers nonsense. Just some stunt—"

"—you hear? Wystia's planning another assault. Looks like their peace meeting with Nurthica is officially off—"

"—droughts in the west, floods in the south, fires in the east—"

"—in quarantine. Not enough medics. How is it spreading?"

Jay heard it all as he walked the streets—but there was something else on his mind, something that had nothing to do with Hazeldenn's idle chatter.

I'll be waiting for you.

The Capo's ominous letter hung over him like a noose, her threats ready to choke him. If he didn't settle his parents' debt by Wintertide Eve, the Staccatos would chase him down. Since he had no money, the Capo would make him rejoin the gang until he paid back the debt through thieving. And to make him go, she might lash out against the people around him here.

Mr. Douse. Colton. Lina.

Don't make the same mistake you made at Windfalle.

Jay set his jaw. He had to leave, disappear, run far from Hazeldenn—before people he cared about got hurt because of him.

Jay finished checking the last lamp and started back, thinking about where he should run. Out of the country would be safest. The tropical archipelagos of Southin were an easy choice, a quick boat ride away. The cities of Eastir sounded even better: lots of people, lots of buildings, lots of ways to hide. Nurthica was way too cold most of the year, so that option was out. And he'd take no chances traveling in Wystia, even with the ceasefire. But it didn't matter where he went, so long as he got beyond the Capo's reach for good.

Jay tromped into the candle shop. Inside he found his custodian sitting at the table, reading the bulletins. Above him were racks of cooling Harvestide candles, dangling like colorful icicles.

"You're back," said Mr. Douse. He gestured toward a plate of hazelnut rolls. "Eat up. Today's inventory day."

Jay pulled up a chair. "D'you know how fast somebody could travel between here and Fairdown Falls?" he asked.

Mr. Douse brushed crumbs from his beard. "Why d'you wanna know?"

Jay shrugged as casually as possible.

Mr. Douse folded his hands on his stomach. "Dunno. I've never visited the capital. Though you could probably ask some train men about it soon."

Jay perked at the words. What did that mean?

Before he could ask, his stomach made a pitiful gurgle. Mr. Douse snorted and tossed a roll to him. Jay caught it, whispered grace, then began eating.

"So," said Jay, spewing crumbs, "wha' d'you mean?"

Mr. Douse glanced up from the bulletins. "What's that?"

Jay spoke between bites. "Train men. I could ask them?"

"Oh." The man nodded. "Just something I heard from Barney Weston. He'd heard it from Iva Primple, who'd heard Tom Mackaroy on the council say we've got visitors from the capital coming."

Jay choked in surprise, coughing on crumbs.

"Chew your food, don't inhale it," chided Mr. Douse, patting Jay's back.

Jay struggled to clear his windpipe, panic stabbing his heart. He'd only just gotten the Capo's message, and now *visitors from the capital* were on their way? Had to be the Capo's thugs, coming to collect him. Who else from the capital would bother coming out to Hazeldenn?

"When's it coming in?" Jay asked.

"The train? Day after tomorrow. That is, if Barney's not full of malarkey."

Jay couldn't taste the bread in his mouth. The day after Harvestide. Three days, counting today. *Bandersnatches.*

"What's wrong?" asked Mr. Douse, eyeing him.

Jay managed to shake his head. "Nothing."

Mr. Douse shuffled his bulletins. "Well, if you're finished, go wash."

Jay stuffed the last piece of hazelnut roll into his mouth, snagging a few more rolls as he made his way out the back door.

Outside, Jay headed straight to the rain barrel. He peeked around to make sure Mr. Douse hadn't followed—then he knelt and reached behind the barrel. His bundle was still there: an extra shirt wrapped around some money and food that'd keep awhile. He added the rolls to his stash.

Three days. Jay cursed again. He'd wanted more time to prepare. He was still a delinquent on probation, after all; if he were caught trying to run, he'd be sent straight back to the reformatory. Still, it'd be better to get going now with half a plan than stick around just to get nabbed by the Staccatos.

Jay stared down at his dark reflection in the rain barrel. Under his cap, the face that stared back at him was grim, resolute.

"Sorry, Mr. Douse," he murmured.

A guilty weight settled in Jay's chest. He thrust his hands into the rain barrel and rinsed, trying to wash the sensation away.

∞

Jay helped Mr. Douse take inventory, and then the candlemaker went out for some Harvestide business, leaving Jay to wait on customers.

"And don't even *think* about trucking off and getting into mischief," the old man had added, giving Jay a look before he'd gone.

Jay sat on the shop stool for a good ten minutes, just in case Mr. Douse returned unexpectedly. When he was sure the old man would be out for a good while, Jay figured it was safe to slip upstairs and finish packing. Tonight was the night. No time to waste.

Just as he was about to head upstairs, the bell above the shop door jangled.

"Looks like you've started to gather dust," greeted a friendly voice.

Jay jumped in surprise, stumbling as the stool tumbled out from under him. Lina Kindle laughed from the doorway, stepping up to the counter.

"I, uh, meant to do that," said Jay, righting himself.

"Right." She hoisted herself onto the counter. "Slow afternoon?"

Jay hummed. Normally he'd be fine with having Lina drop in—but all he could think about was everything he needed to do before tonight.

"Did you need something?" he asked, drumming his fingers.

Lina slapped a few Clinks on the counter. "Harvestide candles, please!"

Jay pulled out the most colorful candles they had in stock, wrapping them in paper so they wouldn't break. As he passed them to her, Lina reached for his hands, holding them in hers. Jay almost dropped her purchase.

"Say, would you go to the cemetery with me?" she added, taking the candles. "My family hasn't gone yet. I don't like going alone."

Jay blinked.

"Don't be dense, Jay," she said. "It's almost Harvestide!"

Jay finally got what she was saying. Right. Folks around here traditionally left candles and mementos at the graves of loved ones a few days leading up to Harvestide as part of the celebration.

"So?" said Lina. "Can you come?"

Jay chewed his lip. He remembered Mr. Douse's warning. Besides, he had more important things to do than tag along with Lina to a graveyard.

"Please?" said Lina, smiling softly.

A minute later, Jay was following Lina outside.

The town was busy. Dozens of people raced helter-skelter, hoisting banners and unraveling garlands. Jay fought the uneasiness in his chest and tried to act casual.

"So," he said, "what're you looking forward to at Harvestide?"

Lina shrugged. "It's the same every year, isn't it? Same speeches, same contests—same, same, same."

"Mm-hmm." Jay was half-listening, watching out for Mr. Douse in case he came strolling down the street.

"But, y'know," said Lina, turning her head shyly, "I was wondering—about Harvestide—that is, if you wanted to—with me—"

"What?" said Jay, not following.

Lina met his gaze with her good eye. "Wanna go together?"

Jay stopped walking so fast he almost stumbled. Did she just ask what he *thought* she asked?

Lina's cheeks were pink. Jay felt his own face grow warm, wishing he were someplace less public. But there was only one answer he could give her.

Lina looked at him, hopeful, nervous, waiting. Jay cleared his throat.

"Sure," he heard himself squeak.

It took two seconds for Jay's brain to catch up to what his mouth had said—but by then it was too late to take it back. Lina beamed at him, practically skipping as they continued down the street. Jay cursed his stupid mouth with every step. If all went as planned, he wouldn't be anywhere near Hazeldenn by Harvestide. He couldn't go to a festival. What was he thinking?

He was still trying to figure out how to rewind the past few minutes when they arrived at a quiet field. Jay saw dozens of graves, marked with simple stones. Most of them had bright-colored candles on top like vibrant jewels.

As they entered the cemetery, Lina latched onto Jay's arm.

"Libby Newcottage said she saw a ghost out here," she explained softly. "She said she saw a shadow standing by the graves—and then it drifted away into the woods." Lina shuddered. "I'm getting goosebumps!"

Jay was getting goosebumps too—but his had nothing to do with ghost stories. A weird crackle blitzed across his skin as Lina clung tighter.

"Maybe Libby didn't meet a ghost out here at all," said Jay, trying to sound reassuring. "Maybe it was a muse."

Lina glanced around the graveyard. "I hadn't thought of that. A muse would be way better than a ghost." She smiled, her face brightening. "D'you think there could be any muses here now?"

Jay shook his head. "There aren't any."

Lina looked unconvinced. "How would you know?"

Jay shrugged off the question.

"C'mon, this way," said Lina. Jay followed her around the graves until she came to a stop at a headstone. It read CECIL WARREN KINDLE.

"Orange was Pa's favorite color," said Lina as she opened her package of candles. She knelt and placed a bright orange one on the headstone.

"From all of us, Pa," she murmured in a voice almost too soft to hear.

Feeling like he was intruding, Jay gazed out over the many burial mounds, listening to the lonely sound of rattling grass and rustling leaves. He didn't hear a ghost or a muse anywhere, but with all the graves surrounding him, Jay couldn't help but feel they weren't quite alone.

He removed his cap.

"Dust and ashes, yield to earth—and may souls departed find their way to the Restful Shore," he said, reciting a prayer Brother Elfenbein used to say. The words left a honey-sweet taste on his tongue.

After Jay made the Designist sign of blessing, he saw Lina staring at him.

"Sorry," said Jay, slipping his cap on. "Should've asked."

"No, it's fine," said Lina. Her smile was pretty, but sad. "I liked it."

Everything fell quiet. Lina stood, blinking away a tear in her eye.

Jay coughed. "Listen, Lina. About Harvestide—I don't think—"

But she started speaking too.

"Here," Lina added, pulling out another candle, a blue one. "Anyone you'd like to leave a candle for? I'm sure Pa won't mind sharing his stone."

She grabbed Jay's hand and placed the candle across his palm.

"Go on," she said.

Not wanting to disappoint her, Jay closed his eyes. He thought of his parents first, but he didn't really know them—so instead he thought of Brother Elfenbein. Jay could still picture the monk's welcoming smile. He could still hear echoes of the man's belly laughter and his old sandals slapping the sanctuary floor as he walked. Jay smiled at the memories.

But then his brain conjured up another person without his permission: a woman, hauntingly beautiful, surrounded by a halo of flames.

Jay's chest twisted. A flash of old, bitter anger shot through his heart.

"Hullo?" came Lina's voice in his ears. "You okay?"

Jay's eyes opened. He glanced down to his hand. He had clenched his fist without realizing it, snapping the blue candle in two.

Jay hid the candle from view, glancing over to Lina. She was staring at him, puzzled, expectant. Mortified, Jay scrambled for an explanation.

"I was just thinking about—well, ghosts. D'you think there could be some around us right now?"

As soon as he'd said the words, Jay wished he could've stuffed them away again. Lina shot him a glare.

"Don't make fun of me!" she said, punching Jay's arm—the same arm she'd been clinging to a minute ago.

"Stop!" Jay yelped. "I didn't mean—!"

"Lina! Jay!"

At the call, Lina stopped. Jay peeked around his raised arms. From the edge of the graveyard, Colton approached at a skipping run.

"I just heard the greatest thing!" said Colton. "Wanna hear?"

Lina rolled her eyes. "If you're gonna say you and your friends saw a *dischord* again . . . ," she sighed. She gave Jay a sour look. "I guess I have you to thank for telling him about that. D'you know how many times he's asked me to check for dischords under his bed since you told him that story?"

Jay gulped. He should've escaped when he'd had the chance.

"It's not about dischords!" Colton cut in. "It's about a train!"

Lina and Jay both turned to him. "What train?" they said at the same time.

"A train's coming! Right now!" cried Colton. "Wanna go see it?"

Jay stiffened.

"What d'you mean, 'right now'?" he asked.

"It's almost here!" said Colton, flashing an excited grin. "I heard from Owen, who heard from some grove keepers that they saw the train coming toward the station not long ago. You wanna see it too, don't you?"

A steady stream of curses ran through Jay's head. The train was already here? It couldn't be here. It was too soon, way too soon!

"Sure!" said Lina, grinning as she turned to Jay. "Let's go!"

Jay felt a swell of panic climbing in his throat. He swallowed it down.

"Actually," he said, "I think I'd better get back to the shop—"

"Oh, c'mon, don't be like that," said Lina.

"Hurry!" said Colton, grabbing Jay's wrist and tugging impatiently. Lina hooked an elbow around Jay's other arm, and before Jay could come up with a reasonable excuse, they dragged him from the cemetery to see the train.

Chapter Ten

TROUBLE WITH GRAVITY

Jay struggled to break free from Lina's and Colton's grips as they dragged him along through the hazel trees. Slithering out of others' grasp had been one of his specialties when he was the Quickstep Kid—but Jay was long out of practice, and the Kindle siblings were surprisingly strong. And strong-willed. With every step, they deflected his objections.

"I don't think this is a good idea—"

"Sure it is!" said Colton. "When's the last time a train came here?"

"Seriously, I shouldn't go—"

"It'll be *fine*," said Lina, laughing.

No use. Jay felt his dread crawl into his throat as they arrived at the train station. The stationhouse itself was right on the edge of town limits. There was one humble bench on the platform, a shed with sacks of stale feed for draft beasts, and a lone lamppost that Jay never had to light.

Jay, Lina, and Colton all came to a stop. They didn't have a choice. Word must've spread about the train's arrival; practically half the town had turned up to get a look, milling around the tracks, gawking at the train.

"Wow!" said Colton. "It's big!"

Jay gaped. The cars were twice as tall as he was. The draft beast hauling the thing—a runner-class pachyderm with huge ears and a snaky nose—would've made a bear look teensy. *Big* was an understatement.

Through a window of the nearest train car, Jay saw a flicker of movement from within: one of the passengers, glancing out toward the crowd.

A *woman*.

A buzz of alarm filled Jay's head. He'd never considered it 'til now, but what if the Capo *herself* had come here to fetch him?

Jay gulped. If he'd had any sense, he'd fling Lina and Colton off and run, not stopping until Hazeldenn was smaller than a speck of dust behind him. But panic had turned his legs to stone.

The buzz between his ears grew into a drone, like agitated bees that drowned out every noise—until Colton's voice broke through.

"—gonna go closer!"

The nine-year-old took off, ducking around the grown-ups.

"Good idea!" said Lina. "C'mon!"

"I don't—" Jay began.

Lina didn't let him finish, latching onto his arm and hauling him along.

"It's packed!" Jay protested.

Lina pointed. Jay followed her gesture to the stationhouse roof.

Before Jay could turn down the idea, Lina squeezed herself against him and pulled him along, breaking free from the crowd as they came around to the back side of the building. Lina stopped at the drainpipe.

"Gimme a boost," she ordered, tapping his arm.

Jay stared up. "You wanna climb up *there*?"

"Where else're we gonna be able to see anything?"

Jay leveled his gaze at her. "Lina, that roof looks like it'd collapse if somebody sneezes at it."

"Then don't sneeze." Her eyes turned impatient. "C'mon."

Jay sighed, then held his hands out one on top of the other, palms up. Lina stepped on them, then his shoulder, his head—*ow*—and scrambled up on the roof. Jay grabbed the drainpipe and shimmied up after her, trying not to think about how the roof groaned under his weight.

"Yay!" Lina cheered, clapping in delight. "We've got the best view!"

She settled herself upright on the apex of the roof. Jay opted to lean forward on his stomach and stay low on the far side, away from where the train was parked, in case he needed to duck down out of sight. He kept his eyes fixed on the train car, the one with the woman inside, like it would disappear if he blinked.

If it was the Capo, what would he do?

His heart thudded in his chest. In some expanse of his mind, Jay watched it unfold: the train car door opening, and then *her* stepping out—a beautiful face, cinnamon-colored hair, smoldering umber eyes, a ruthless smile.

"... d'you suppose it is?" said Lina.

Jay only caught the end of her question. "On the train?" *Not the Capo. Please not the Capo.* He blurted the first ridiculous thing he could think of. "Southin royalty."

Lina giggled. "Southin doesn't have royalty. It has tribes."

"Nurthican royalty, then."

Lina shook her head. "Nurthica's a military state, Jay."

"Wystian royalty."

"Don't you know about Wystian democracy?"

Fed up, Jay spat, "Then who do *you* think's on board?"

Lina shrugged. "Somebody boring. Governor's men, or land hunters. It would be neat if they were Musicians, though."

Jay looked at her in surprise.

"I've never seen any real Musicians before," she went on. Lina smiled. "Wouldn't it be a treat to see one call some music spirits out? Not like *I* could see the muses, but still!"

Against his will, Jay felt his cheeks burning. "You think so?"

"Sure!" Lina turned her smile on him. "Wouldn't you like to meet one?"

An innocent question, but it was sharp enough to pull Jay back to reality. He shifted uncomfortably, making the roof beneath them groan.

She's not talking about you.

Jay swallowed. That's right. He *wasn't* a Musician.

"Yeah," he mumbled. "Sure."

"Oh!" said Lina, not hearing him. "Here they come!"

Jay followed where she was pointing, seeing the door of the middle car swing open. His heart climbed into his throat—

Then the great tangle of dread in his chest unraveled, and all the tension in his limbs melted away.

It wasn't the Capo. And he could tell at a glance the woman passenger wasn't with the Staccatos, either. He was so relieved he laughed.

"What's funny?" asked Lina.

Jay didn't answer. He offered silent, steady *Thank you*s to the Design as he pushed himself up, sitting beside Lina.

"Who d'you suppose she is?" Lina added.

Jay shrugged. No clue—it wasn't the Capo, that's all he cared about—but the more he looked at the strange passenger, the more curious he became. The lady wore a showy dress, a long green coat, and a pair of high-heeled boots. A small black fox with long ears trailed at her heels. The lady stared around, grimacing like she'd come to the worst place on earth.

"I'm getting a closer look," said Jay.

"Be careful," said Lina as he went down the sloping shingles to the edge of the roof, just above the open platform. Just as Jay was starting to wonder if the lady was the only passenger, other car doors opened. Another woman came out; she had a sallow face, stringy hair, and a long brown coat. She stared at the crowd, looking apprehensive.

"Say," said Lina from behind him, "there's a kid!"

Jay's eyes shifted. A short boy had stepped off the train onto the platform. The most Jay could see of his pale face was a pair of spectacles on his nose. The guy's yellow hair was a nest, the ends sticking out in odd places. He wore a coat that reached his ankles, except his was white.

Not long after the boy came down, a final passenger disembarked. The man wore a green coat like the first lady and carried a black case stamped with a golden crest. A bird with blue feathers was perched on his head. He glanced at all the townsfolk in fascination, wearing a winsome smile.

"Oh, my," said Lina, a smile in her voice. "Who's that?"

Jay smirked. "You mean the guy with the bird?"

Lina blinked at him, bemused. "Bird?"

The grin left Jay's face. He turned back around. The bird was sitting right there on top of the man's head, impossible for her to miss—unless . . .

Unless the bird wasn't a bird.

Jay leaned out to get another look. The blue bird and the black fox trailing the lady's high heels . . . nobody else was looking at them. Like they couldn't see them.

Muses.

Jay eyed the strangers on the platform, suspicious. If the fox and the bird were muses, these strangers were probably . . .

Julian.

Jay's mental stream cut off.

Who said that?

He glanced back at Lina, but she was studying the strangers. Jay scanned the crowd below, searching. Nobody was looking up at him.

Jay rubbed the inside of his ears. Maybe he'd just imagined it.

But then, before his imagination could make up an explanation for what he'd just heard, something below him started to sing.

Jay went still, goosebumps racing up and down his skin. The jabbering villagers, the groaning eaves of the roof beneath him, now sounded distorted, as if he'd been dunked underwater. The strange singing evolved, engulfing him with perfect, impossible music. It sounded like a hundred voices raised in seamless harmony, like a thousand crystal bells ringing across the air. All at once the music felt as alive as the sunrise, as gentle as moonlight.

Jay drew in a breath, mesmerized—

Julian.

Jay twitched. Who *said* that? Who was calling his name?

He clung to the edge of the roof, feeling lightheaded.

"Jay!" Lina's voice crashed over him like a cold waterfall. "You okay?"

Jay winced. "*Shh,*" he hissed, his head spinning. He searched hungrily for the source of the perfect music. Wherever the source, it was close.

Below, the visitors moved closer to the edge of the stationhouse, gathering just underneath him. Jay's gaze flew over them, studying their faces, their coats, their luggage.

"Jay, come away from there! It's dangerous!"

But Jay couldn't hear Lina anymore. The perfect music sang in absolute majesty, and Jay searched for it like a man dying of thirst who knew a river was near. Jay leaned past the edge of the roof as far as he could.

CRACK.

Jay jolted. The sound of snapping wood jerked him out of his daze. The perfect music cut off in his ears as sharply as a lid closing shut. Jay tried to scramble backward to safety.

CRA-KACK!

In a blink, the wooden roof supports beneath him broke, leaving nothing but empty space. For one gasp, Jay hung suspended in the air—

And then the irrevocable pull of gravity found him, taking him down.

"*Jay!*" Lina screamed.

Her cry caused the people below to turn their startled faces upward. They gasped, pointed—but too late. Jay plummeted toward the person right below him on the platform.

WHOMPH!

Jay didn't dare open his eyes. He was afraid to see what was broken.

The ground underneath him heaved.

"*Get—off—me.*"

Huh?

Jay blinked. Hardly a hand's-span away from his face was another one. Two sharp blue eyes were staring at him through spectacles.

A second later, Jay rolled off the boy who'd broken his fall. He gaped, disoriented, his ears ringing.

For another second, everybody was frozen—then people rushed forward. Next thing he knew, Jay was being helped up by the man from the train, who clutched his black case under one arm.

"Encore!" the man called to the other boy. "Great gavotte, are you okay?"

"...'M fine," the bespectacled boy said. The man exhaled in relief.

Just then Lina came up and grabbed Jay, squeezing him as if she thought he'd fly away. "Tell me you're okay!"

"Lina, you're hurting me—"

"I *told* you to be careful!" she yelled, close to tears. "You idiot—could've broken your neck!"

"I'm okay!" he insisted, trying to calm her. "No broken necks. See?"

Lina tried to pat his clothes free of debris, without success. "Jay," she said, her voice shaking, "that was a huge fall. You're sure you're—?"

"Out of my way!" someone barked.

The green-clad lady from the train shoved Lina aside, bearing down on Jay with rage. Her black fox was snarling in equal fury.

"You!" she barked, pushing Jay against the stationhouse wall. "You could have killed one of us!"

Her words sent a hush rippling through the onlookers.

"Well?" said the scary lady. "Don't you have something to say?"

Jay tried to say he was sorry, but his throat was stuck. He felt everybody's stares stabbing into him from all sides. Finally, Jay forced a cough.

"Uh ... welcome to Hazeldenn?"

Chapter Eleven.

NUTTER VILLAGE

*T*he only luck Ark ever had was the rotten kind.

Blinking away stars, Ark pushed himself up to his feet. People were jabbering all around him. Some called for a medic, others for a watchman—and others stood by like it was all some kind of show.

A few strides away, Callie was chewing out Ark's squasher. She'd pushed the boy up against the wall in outrage, as if she'd nearly been crushed. The boy himself—a filthy scarecrow of a kid, dusted with splinters and roof debris—fought to pull free.

"I will not say it again!" spat Callie. "Apologize this instant!"

"I'm sorry, I'm *sorry!*" Scarecrow sputtered. "Leggo!"

A girl with red hair and a patch over her left eye jumped into the fray. "It's not like he fell on purpose! Can't you see that?"

Callie gave the girl a disdainful glance-over. She pointed to the girl's eye patch. "You are hardly the one to talk about seeing clearly."

The girl's mouth dropped open.

"Callie," Dulcian hissed, stepping in. "That was uncalled for."

"You take that back!" Scarecrow demanded.

Ark watched their altercation, annoyed. They were squabbling like toddlers on a playground. Someone had to play grownup.

He looked up at the roof. "*Rippari comme nuuovo,*" he chanted.

Ark listened, waiting. A local muse came hopping across the station floor, taking the form of a large purple frog. The frog gave a *croak*—and morphed into a small army of little purple frogs, which all moved speedily.

They snatched up wood bits and fallen shingles with their long tongues and hopped up to the roof, setting the broken pieces back in place and sealing them in with sparkly yellow saliva.

The bystanders sent up gasps. Ark wondered what they were seeing. Most of them probably just saw wood and debris magically weaving back together.

Soon the hole in the roof was gone. The job done, the army of little purple frogs morphed back into the single large frog. Then it hopped away.

The applause and cries of wonder were gratifying. Even Scarecrow gaped with a look of unguarded awe.

"What the—?" the eye-patch girl exclaimed. "What just happened?"

Before Ark could reply, Callie snorted.

"Haven't you heard of muses before?" she said, crossing her arms.

Eye-Patch Girl's mouth fell open. "Wait. Just now—there was a muse?" she squeaked. "Does that mean . . . are you Musicians?"

Ark nodded. The girl's face broke into a smile. Beside her, the boy looked doubly stricken.

"Do it again!" some random bystander called out.

Others in the crowd cheered for more until Callie snapped, "Enough!"

The crowd blinked back at her. Feeling their stares, Ark was strongly reminded of a fantasy book he'd once found in Echostrait's library: *Darcy Harper and the Sorcerer of Nozz*, in which Darcy and his cat Otto were carried off by a winged horse to the land of Nozz, a strange country where it was summer all year long. The relevant part of the story in Ark's mind was when Darcy faced the Nozzlers for the first time, each baffled by the appearance of the other—except Ark wasn't baffled. Just uneasy.

Ark stood by, uncertain what he should be doing. Lady Vielle was muttering disagreeably under her breath. Dulcian hovered nearby, greeting some locals, while Mara melted into the background. Everyone else was whispering loudly, pointing between Ark, Scarecrow, and the roof.

"*A-CHOO!*"

Ark jumped as Scarecrow gave the loudest sneeze Ark had ever heard. The boy sniffed miserably and rubbed his hand along his nose.

"Bandersnatches!" he cursed.

Ark couldn't explain why, but he didn't feel angry. Instead he felt . . . well, sorry for him. He looked about Ark's age. At second glance, Ark could tell the boy was poorer and dirtier than everyone else, not even counting his extra layer of roof debris. Almost before he realized it himself, Ark stepped up to him.

"Here, hold on," he offered. "*Fressco.*"

At his call, another local muse—a cat with amber-yellow fur, large and feral-looking—prowled into sight. The cat sniffed at them both, and then it yowled. Its feline scream sent a twanging pulse through the air, blasting the last bits of shingle and roof from his clothes.

The boy yelped. The muse padded away and vanished.

"Bless you, by the way," said Ark, unfazed, cleaning his spectacles on his shirt. He offered the boy his hand. "Bygones?"

The boy raised his head so suddenly that Ark jumped. They met each other's gaze. Scarecrow scowled, and his light green eyes blazed as he shoved past Ark's extended hand. Ark staggered as the boy dashed off.

"Wait!" cried Eye-Patch Girl, hurrying after him.

Ark frowned. Any pity he'd felt for him vanished.

Dulcian came over with a worried look. "Are you all right?"

Ark wanted to laugh at the question. He also wanted to kick something. "If by 'all right' you mean I'm not a human pancake, then I'm just dandy."

Dulcian winced. "I'm sorry. We told Maestran Pandoura we'd keep you safe. But one hardly expects bodies to fall from the sky." He patted Ark on the shoulder. "At any rate, that was a good save. I'm amazed you were able to catch him."

Ark looked at him. "What?"

"I mean, if you hadn't, you wouldn't be standing right now," Dulcian went on, glancing toward the roof. "But you managed to slow his fall. Most impressive. What cantus did you use?"

Ark shook his head. "I didn't—"

But he was cut off as Callie stomped across the platform, clearing her throat. "The *person in charge*," she demanded. "Where are they?"

The crowd stared. Callie rubbed her temples with a long-suffering sigh.

"We are on business for the Royal Conservatory," she said. "We must meet with your mayor, or whoever runs this place. Where can we find them?"

As she spoke, Ark spied a man step through. He gave Callie and Dulcian a formal bow and Ark's hand a few wrist-dislocating shakes.

"Pleasure to meet you!" he said. "I'm Tom Mackaroy, Vice Councilor. 'Scuse the rabble. We're not used to seeing your kind in these parts." He gestured around. "Welcome to Hazeldenn—home of Merideyin's nuts!"

Ark squinted. *Merideyin's nuts?* Did this guy just admit that out loud?

Tom Mackaroy pointed toward a speck of buildings down the road. "Allow me to bring you to our head councilor. He'll be thrilled to meet you!"

The man held out his hand, inviting them along. Callie took off as if he'd kept them waiting on purpose. Dulcian followed serenely. Mara scurried.

Ark took up the rear, his mood sinking with each step. It was his first time outside of Echostrait in seven years—and so far, he had gotten crushed, been treated like some spectacle, and made a brand-new foe. All before supper.

What else could go wrong?

∞

After getting a closer look at Hazeldenn, Ark wished he hadn't asked.

All around was the most miserable landscape Ark had ever seen. Ugly hazel trees were everywhere, along with spiny stickleweed and fox-briar that poked through Ark's shoes. If there were such a thing as an underworld for punishing wicked souls, Ark was sure it looked just like this awful place.

His headache began after sneezing for the seventh time in a row. A perpetual stench and a haze of dust hung on the air. Ark had to use all his willpower not to plug his nose.

He wasn't sure why he was acting so polite, when everyone he saw behaved like crude boors. Even though he'd known their destination was along the wild frontier, Ark never anticipated seeing men wearing no shirts, women wearing trousers, and everyone around wearing a layer of sweat and grime. As if it were normal.

At the edge of the tangled groves of hazel trees, Mackaroy paused, raising his hand toward the town. "Welcome to the most charming little place in Merideyin!"

Ark stared. If Hazeldenn had ever been charming—which he found hard to believe—all its charm had long since worn off. The nest of little homes and quaint shops seemed to sag against each other as if barely able to hold themselves up. The whole place was like an heirloom clock that had broken down decades ago.

Thankfully, Ark noticed some improvement the further into town they went. At length, Mackaroy brought them to a town square paved with flat stones, bordered by streetlamps. The townsfolk here were hanging festive decorations and strings of lanterns. As Ark and the others crossed the square, he felt more than a few pairs of eyes turn to watch them.

Unaware of the attention they were gathering, Mackaroy led them to a large stone building, ushering them inside.

Ark's eyes adjusted slowly as they were led into a spacious room. A group of austere men sat around a table, looking full of their own importance. The man at the head of the table had a broad frame and a bulldog face.

"Tom, there you are!" he barked, biting down on a pipe. His eyes flickered toward Ark and the others. "Who're these people?"

"Visitors, sir," said Mackaroy. In a whisper, he added, "*Musicians.*"

The bulldog looked them over. "And why did you bring them here?"

The councilors chittered among themselves. Ark's mind flew back to the Darcy Harper story: This scene was straight from the chapter with the backwards-talking Grouslings of Nozz, when they asked Darcy *Are you friend or foe?*—or rather, *Foe or friend, you are?*

"This is Head Councilor Boden Gripps," said Mackaroy, introducing the bulldog.

Dulcian stepped forward. "A pleasure to meet you. I am Sir Dulcian Mandore. I hope this isn't an intrusion—"

"It is," said Gripps curtly. "State your business and be quick."

On Dulcian's head, Trillo chirped in disapproval, but Dulcian kept his smile. From his talaris, he retrieved an envelope with a purple wax seal.

"This missive from Grand Maestran Luthier explains our purpose," he said, holding the envelope out for the head councilor to take. "In sum, we've come to meet the young Musician living in your town—"

"Sorry," said Gripps, not taking the missive. "Can't help you. Good day."

Dulcian faltered. "I beg your pardon?"

"You've come to the wrong place," said Gripps. "Besides, I don't need outsiders 'round here causing trouble. You're not welcome." He glanced at Mackaroy. "Get them on their way, Tom."

The room felt thick with awkward silence. While Dulcian grasped for a polite response, Callie elbowed him aside.

"Are you refusing to let us stay?" she asked.

The bulldog matched her gaze. "I am head councilor here—appointed by Her Majesty's regional governor and loyal servant of the crown," he growled. "You should at least address me as *sir*."

Callie narrowed her eyes. "Mr. Gripps, *sir*," she said, barely keeping her tone civil, "we have business here that we must complete. You can't tell us to leave when we've only just arrived!"

"This is my town—so yes, I can," Gripps snapped. He gestured to his fellows. "We're finalizing important details for our Harvestide celebration tomorrow. The last thing we need is outsiders like you wasting our time." He took a draw from his pipe. "Get along, girlie. The men are talking."

Callie stared at the man with such venom that a whole flowerbed would have withered under her glare. Fiero began to growl; soon the whole room trembled with inclement energy. The windows creaked. The wooden floorboards shivered.

Dulcian reached out and touched Callie's arm. A few tense moments later, she stepped back and Fiero's growls hushed.

"Do excuse us, Mr. Gripps," said Dulcian, intervening. "But perhaps we may reach a compromise. If you will allow us just a few hours, we can meet with the Musician, finish our business, and—"

"Like I said, we can't help you," said Gripps, waving Dulcian away. "If that's the reason you're here, you came a long way for nothing. There aren't any Musicians in Hazeldenn."

Ark blinked as if the man had just said *There aren't any legs on a fish*. The statement was obvious ... so obvious, in fact, that Ark was caught off guard. Of course there weren't Musicians here. If there had been, those people at the station wouldn't have been so amazed by his cantus.

But as the realization settled in, Ark's stomach squeezed in dread. If there wasn't a Musician here, they couldn't do a Crafter evaluation. So what had just become of his jury mission?

Mara stepped forward. As unimposing as she was, she somehow made everyone hush. "We must be sure, Mr. Gripps," she said, her watery gaze intent. "Could you be mistaken?"

"Don't you think I'd know if a Musician were in Hazeldenn?" Gripps barked. "As I said, you've come to the wrong place."

Mara shared a look with Dulcian and Callie, all of them at a loss for words. Ark's stomach twisted in knots. He couldn't bear the thought of having come all this way just to go back to Echostrait.

Gripps jabbed his thumb toward the door. "Now, unless you have some other absurd request to make—"

Before he could finish, the door to the council room swung open. An imperious woman with blonde hair came rushing in, stalking straight up to the head councilor's seat.

"Boden!" she snapped. "What do you think you are doing?"

Gripps gaped at her, his bulldog jowls quivering. The other councilors sank in their seats.

Ark studied her. The woman sported a hat with so many ornaments and feathers that it looked like she was wearing an enormous bird's nest.

Gripps finally found his voice. "Eliza, how many times do I have to tell you that you can't burst in during council business!"

The woman ignored him, turning to face Ark and the others. "Mrs. Eliza Gripps, at your service!" she declared. "Delighted to meet you!"

She gave each of them a hearty handshake. Ark must have looked stunned when she took his hand because she laughed.

"Oh, don't be startled, dear!" Mrs. Gripps told him. "I may be the head councilor's wife, but I don't bite!" she turned to the others. "I am the chair of the Hazeldenn welcoming committee, but I'd only just received word that your train had arrived. I've sent other committee members to handle your lodging and luggage."

"You have a place for us to stay?" said Callie.

"Yes!" said Mrs. Gripps. "We don't have accommodations for proper draft beasts in our town, so I sent your train to the nearest waystation to trade out beasts. But we couldn't let you stay at a filthy waystation. Until your train returns, we will host you here!"

"Eliza!" the head councilor barked. Mrs. Gripps snapped her head in his direction, her gaze narrowing like a disapproving cat's.

"We would *never* send such *distinguished* guests from the *capital* away like they were *unwelcome*," she said with biting emphasis. "Would we?"

The bulldog sank in his chair like he'd been whipped.

"Now then," said Mrs. Gripps with a smile, adjusting her hat, "I have a festival committee meeting within the hour, so please allow me to lead you all to the stay-inn house. I'll make sure you're comfortable." She glanced at the councilors. "Excuse us, gentlemen."

After a short walk, Mrs. Gripps brought them to a building with closed shutters, a crooked front door, and birds' nests stuffing up the chimney. A dingy sign said THE LITTLE NUTSHELL STAY-INN HOUSE & SCRATCH KITCHEN.

Ark peered at The Little Nutshell. If this was where they were meant to stay, he'd rather sleep in the stationhouse. Or a ditch.

The door gave a tired creak as Mrs. Gripps led them inside. Their luggage was waiting for them in the lobby, along with a servile old woman who gaped at Ark and the others like they were a mirage.

"Mrs. Pembrooke will take it from here," Mrs. Gripps told them. "I will see you all tomorrow morning for breakfast! In the meantime, please don't hesitate to ask Mrs. Pembrook for anything you may need. Ta!"

She departed, the feathers on her hat bobbing with every step. Once she'd gone, the innkeeper gestured to their luggage, pointed to the stairs, mumbled something incoherent about supper, and then tromped away.

"Well," said Dulcian, "she either said supper will be hen and biscuits—or in ten minutes." He passed Ark's suitcase to him. "Whichever it is, we might as well freshen up."

Ark took his suitcase from Dulcian, but he didn't make for the stairs. He pulled at his talaris collar, not sure how to ask the question in his head.

Dulcian had good intuition. "You're worried about what this turn of events means for your jury mission," he said. Ark nodded.

Callie drew up next to him, Fiero trailing at her ankles. "I wondered the same thing," she said, looking expectantly at Mara. "Well?"

Mara seemed to shrink under their stares. "W-We have to determine whether the information we received about a candidate in Hazeldenn was somehow scrambled or whether our informant was mistaken."

"And in the meantime, Grand Maestran Luthier will probably expect us to stay put," said Dulcian. He stared at the case chained to his wrist, holding Brio's instrument—then he looked up and sent Ark an encouraging smile. "Don't worry. As your jurors, Callie and I will make sure you'll have another chance. In the meantime, let us handle things."

That wasn't exactly reassuring. Still, no point in waiting for a better answer.

Ark hefted his suitcase and headed up the stairs to the second floor, escaping into the first empty room he found. He shut the door behind him with a sigh.

Alone. Finally.

"Frigits," he swore. He dropped his suitcase and sat on the bed, sending up a cloud of dust. He coughed, cringing against the twinge in his skull.

Stupid rotten headache. Stupid rotten dust. Stupid rotten luck.

Ark stared at the floorboards, taking inventory. After spending days traveling across the country, there was no reason to come here in the first place—and now his jury mission was pretty much canceled. Xyla had been right all along: he really *was* the Jinx.

Ark scowled. Having his jury mission postponed due to misinformation was bad enough—but something else was eating at him that had nothing to do with his mission.

It was the moment when the stationhouse roof collapsed and Scarecrow had fallen on him. Despite Dulcian's belief that Ark had used a music skill to intervene at the last second, Ark knew the truth: he'd panicked. He hadn't even had the presence of mind to jump out of the way, much less call for a muse to save himself.

At least he and the boy had walked away more or less unscathed, so it had all worked out . . . *this* time. But now a heavy feeling of doubt was pulling Ark down, like a sodden cloak thrown over his shoulders. Being an Adept in school meant nothing if he was so inept in the field.

How would he ever earn the right to call himself a de Cani again if he couldn't use his skills when they mattered most?

He could feel the scar on his hand throb. *You are a disappointment,* his father's voice reminded him, echoing between his ears.

Ark sighed. "I know," he whispered back to his empty room.

Hunger clawed his stomach like an impatient beast, but the thought of sitting through dinner with his jurors made him lose his appetite. Not sure what to do with himself, he stepped over to look out the window.

He wasn't prepared to see Scarecrow below him. But there he was, standing under the streetlamp right outside the stay-inn house, reaching up with a long pole to light it. Soon a halo of firelight bathed the barren street corner with a warm yellow glow, and the boy moved on.

A frown pulled at Ark's mouth as he watched the boy walk away. Hopefully the two of them wouldn't have to cross paths ever again.

Ark started to turn from the window—but then his eyes caught sight of a flicker of motion and color. He stopped and stared.

Several muses—a silver one like a mouse, a blue one like a lizard, and a glittery orange one that looked like a mass of fireflies—wandered into the open in the boy's wake. They paused under the streetlamp, then continued down the street, all in the same direction.

Ark watched the muses until they vanished from sight, curious. He hadn't heard of muses acting that way before. If he didn't know better, Ark would have thought they were following Scarecrow.

A seed of suspicion landed in the back of his mind, taking root. *Could it be . . . ?*

Before the thought could grow any further, Ark weeded it out and tossed it away. Impossible. The head councilor had already said there weren't Musicians here.

Ark pulled away from the window and plopped down on the bed, kicking off his boots and stretching across the mattress. He stared against the darkness, counting the twinging pulses of his headache until it dulled and he at last drifted into sleep.

Chapter Twelve

LESSONS

*W*ith a gasp, Ark wrenched himself from his nightmare. He took deep breaths, then blinked up at the cobwebby ceiling.

Where . . . ?

Ark sat up, squinting at the unfamiliar room bathed in sunlight. Slowly, it came back to him: Hazeldenn. Village of nutters. Right.

Mumbling curses against mornings, Ark finger-combed his hair and got out of bed. After he'd changed clothes and slid his spectacles on, he headed down to The Little Nutshell's dining room.

"Good morning, Arkalin," greeted Dulcian. He, Mara, and Callie sat at a table, eating breakfast. Mrs. Gripps was also there.

"Yes, good morning!" she echoed. "Please join us, dear boy!"

Ark sat beside her, trying not to gape at her hat. It featured baubles, lace, and a huge taxidermied bird with gaping glass eyes, its wings stretched out over her ears and its tail feathers drooping behind her head.

He tore his eyes away from the dead bird and watched as Dulcian poured him a cup of something hot from a teapot.

"Beautiful day, isn't it?" said Dulcian, handing Ark the cup. Trillo chirped merrily from his shoulder, fluffing himself up.

"Do keep your morning cheer in check, Dulcian," grumbled Callie, clutching a mug in both hands like a lifeline. Fiero gave a grumpy snuff in agreement.

The door to the kitchen opened. Mrs. Pembrooke emerged, delivering a plate with a tower of griddle cakes drizzled in hazel syrup.

More awake, Ark realized how hungry he was. He had half devoured his meal before he realized Mrs. Gripps was talking to him.

"—were telling me about *you* earlier, my boy," she was saying. "You are an Adept, they said. What does that mean?"

Both Mrs. Gripps and the bird on her hat were watching him with the same wide, unblinking stare. Ark almost choked on his griddle cakes.

Thankfully, Dulcian intercepted the question. "An Adept is a virtuoso, you could say. Adept Encore is one of the most skilled Musicians his age."

Mrs. Gripps' feline smile widened. "Well, that settles it!"

Ark swallowed. Settled what?

Mrs. Gripps grabbed Ark's elbow. "I'm on the school curriculum enrichment committee. Our school children have half a day of lessons before Harvestide celebrations begin. It would be marvelous if you could perform for them!"

Ark blinked. "Excuse me?"

"Oh, you know—a show!" she said. "Won't you share some of the tricks you know? It would be such a treat!"

"Why not?" said Dulcian before Ark had a chance to decline. "Adept Encore is supposed to be on his jury mission right now, demonstrating his skills. We could all go watch."

The griddle cakes in Ark's stomach turned sour. Watch? Him? *Now?*

What kind of demo was he supposed to give?

Before he could answer the question, Callie shook her head.

"We have information to follow up on, remember?" she told Dulcian. "You and I need to contact the Grand Maestran about our next orders."

"Then perhaps Mara can accompany Arkalin to the schoolhouse, and we'll join them afterward," said Dulcian. "Yes?"

Mara nodded, saying nothing.

"Splendid!" said Mrs. Gripps. "Shall we?"

She swept Ark up from his chair so fast that Ark didn't even get to eat his last bite of breakfast. In a blink, they were out the door. Mara trailed behind him like a shuffling shadow.

As they returned to Hazeldenn's dusty roads, Ark almost couldn't believe it was the same town. Since yesterday, buildings had been festooned with so many wreaths and garlands that it was hard to spot the town beneath the trimmings. The streets were packed with people selling holiday trinkets, chatting merrily to one another, and hanging last-minute decorations.

Mrs. Gripps took up the role of tour guide, telling them about the splendid holiday festivities that would begin that evening, pointing out the splendid decorations, and praising the splendid weather. Ark started to keep a tally of how many times she used the word *splendid*. Five, six, seven . . .

Ark had made sixteen *splendid* mental tallies by the time they came to the schoolhouse—which wasn't a proper house at all. It was an open-air pavilion at the edge of the town square, with students all sitting in rows.

Ark squinted at the group as they approached. The students were of various ages. At the front, Ark spied a girl with red hair—Eye-Patch Girl, from the train station yesterday—dutifully following the recitation, though she was one of the few paying attention. In the middle rows, a cluster of other girls chatted blithely. A pair of boys five rows up were having a belching contest. In the very last row, a teenaged version of Mr. Gripps with a smug face and sandy hair—the head councilor's son, no doubt about it—sat with his feet on his desk, surrounded by a cohort of other older boys.

Ark was amazed. They wanted him to give a demo to this unruly bunch?

Another thought put a double knot in Ark's stomach. He scanned the faces of the students, and slowly, the knot loosened. Scarecrow wasn't here. *Whew.*

"Please welcome Adept Arkalin Encore," Mrs. Gripps said. "He's here to give you a music lesson. Isn't that splendid?"

Ark sighed. *Seventeen*, he thought, ticking off another tally mark.

Mrs. Gripps guided Ark to the front of the pavilion. He felt stares all around, sizing him up. Mara remained in the back, watching mutely.

Mrs. Gripps turned to him. "Adept Encore, I need to discuss some things with Miss Cooper—curriculum committee business, you know. For now, the class is yours!"

With that, Mrs. Gripps adjusted her hat, latched arms with the teacher, and floated away—leaving Ark alone in front of fifty or so expectant faces.

Ark took a deep, steadying breath. He wouldn't be intimidated. He was the Principal Adept of Echostrait. He could handle giving a demo.

"All right, then—" he began.

"Can you fly?" A pudgy boy in the second row blurted the question.

"Uh—" said Ark, startled, "—no."

"Can *she* fly?" the kid asked again, pointing toward Mara with his thumb.

"Musicians can't fly," said Ark, waving the kid down. "Now, then—"

The class started speaking at once:

"Can a muse turn you immortal?"

"When a baby laughs for the first time, is a muse born?"

"If you catch a muse by the tail, is it true it has to grant you a wish?"

"Ohh-kay!" Ark yelled. They ignored him, shouting over each other. One girl with curly pigtails even stood on her chair to get Ark's attention.

"Are there any muses here right now?" she shouted above everyone.

Her question hushed the class. Ark closed his eyes and opened his ears, stretching his senses.

"Yes," said Ark at length. "I can sense about ten of them."

The class broke into excited chitters.

"Yeah right!" came a loud voice from the back row, cutting off the chatter.

Ark turned to the boy. It was Head Councilor Gripps' son. He still sat with his feet on the desk in front of him, sending Ark a challenging look.

"It's true," said Ark. "There are muses all around you."

"Then how come we can't see 'em?" inserted another boy. He sat next to the head councilor's son, chewing a shoot of stickleweed the same way a cow chewed cud. "You a liar or just some kinda freak?"

The class went twitchy quiet.

"I'm neither," said Ark, keeping his voice level. "I'm a Musician."

Before Stickleweed Boy or the head councilor's son could retort, Eye-Patch Girl raised a hand.

"Can you tell us more about muses?" she said, diverting the conversation. A murmur of agreement rose through the class.

Ark coughed to clear his throat. Muses. Simple question. Good.

"Muses have been around for as long as humans have—possibly longer," he began, thinking about how muses were defined in his textbooks. "They're the incarnate manifestations of incorporeal creative forces."

Some blinked at him, already lost. A few mouthed the words *incorporeal* and *incarnate* to themselves like they were from a foreign language.

"So muses are, well, they're spirits, kind of," Ark continued. "No two muses are alike. The true extent of their power is a mystery, but their job is to inspire creativity and protect the flow of nature. You've likely passed a muse in a field or a forest without realizing it."

That sent a gasp of amazement through the class.

"Muses interact with humans in a few ways," Ark went on, pacing. "Muses inspire creativity in nature—bringing out different colors, shapes, smells, and more—and they sometimes inspire creativity in people, too. If you've ever had an idea just pop into your head that caused you to make something, it's possible a muse inspired you."

Excited whispers ran through the pavilion.

"Muses also guard us," said Ark. "As I mentioned, a muse's job is to watch over the natural world—including people. Muses are beings of pure harmony and are friends to humans. When danger comes our way, a muse's instinct is to protect us, if it is in their power."

The class remained quiet, as if humbled by the thought.

"Commoners—that is, non-Musicians—don't really notice muses," Ark continued. "Most commoners don't ever see a muse their whole life. But there are some who are more sensitive to a muse's presence. They have what's called musical potential—and if they strengthen that ability, they can learn to see muses and become true Musicians."

"Could you show us how to see muses?" blurted a little boy with carrot-red hair from the front row. "Teach us! Teach us!"

His words became an eager chant across the pavilion.

"I can't," said Ark over them. "Even if you had musical potential, it'd take years of study for you to become aware enough to sense muses."

"How long did it take you to learn?" asked Carrot-Top.

"It's different for me," said Ark. "I've always been able to see them."

The class gaped at him with newfound awe.

"I'm what's called a natural," Ark explained. "About half of all Musicians today are those already born with the ability to see muses."

"What's it like?" asked another student. "To see muses all the time?"

Ark faltered. He'd never thought about it. Their presence was as familiar to him as the rise and fall of each breath. To explain would be like trying to explain to a blind man the ephemeral sparkle of a falling star or the prismatic radiance of a rainbow.

"It's a great honor," was all he could say.

"Muses, music, *blah blah blah*," one of the boys in the back interrupted. "Muses are boring. So're you. Tell us something interesting already."

"Yeah," Stickleweed Boy chimed in. "Tell us about dischords."

The class fell into a prickly silence. Carrot-Top shrank into his chair, as if spooked by the topic. From the back, Mara shifted, watching in silence.

"Dischords are the opposite of muses," said Ark, frowning. "If you're lucky, you'll never run into one. That's all I'll say."

At that, the head councilor's son spoke up.

"Aw, c'mon, don't hold out on us," he said, his tone mocking. "Give it to us straight. Dischords are more powerful than muses, aren't they? And they'll grant you any wish." He snapped his fingers. "Fortune. Fame. Prestige."

Ice bled into Ark's veins. He heard the chill enter his voice.

"First of all, no—dischords are not more powerful than muses," said Ark, sending the boy a cold look. "Dischords are predatory entities. They exist to dominate and destroy. If you were ever unfortunate enough to become possessed by a dischord, it wouldn't obey you. It would control you. It'd take hold of you, feeding off you until you wasted away—"

"Oh no!" the head councilor's son gasped sarcastically. "The horror!"

Soon the boy was jerking in his chair with his eyes rolled back into his head, acting like he was possessed. The gang of boys around him laughed.

"Give us a break," the head councilor's son said through the snickering, leaning back in his chair. "Your spook stories aren't scaring anyone. Who actually believes in dischords anymore? I don't."

"Then you're an idiot," Ark spat before he could stop himself. "Dis-chords are real. And dischord possession isn't a joke."

The class gasped. From the back, Mara was frowning at him. Perhaps she didn't like how he was handling things.

Ark didn't care. He wouldn't suffer morons.

The head councilor's son kept his smug expression, but his eyes flashed with irritation. "Easy there, music freak. Keep it up, and I'll let my father know you're being disrespectful."

"Would you shut up, Brax?" Eye-Patch Girl snapped. She turned in her seat to shoot him a glare. "Keep it up, and I'll tell your mother how rude you're being to Adept Encore!"

The class jeered. Brax's gang went quiet. Eye-Patch Girl sent Ark an encouraging look. "Please continue, Adept Encore."

Ark smiled gratefully at her.

"Sure," he said. "I'll show you how a Musician summons muses."

At that, everyone—even Brax—sat up straighter in their seats.

"Musicians can interact with muses and borrow their creative power," he said, picking up his teaching voice. "These arts have evolved across the nations over time into various musical forms."

He reached down and grabbed a lonely hazelnut from the ground, holding it in his palm. Ark focused inward, concentrating—and then he drew in his lips and blew a loud, trilling whistle.

After a moderate pause, one of the muses that had been floating near the main square swept over on a rush of wind. It looked like a hawk, with crimson feathers. With a keening cry, the muse plucked up the hazelnut in its shining talons and flew to the rafters of the pavilion.

Shouts of awe rose up.

"The hazelnut flew!"

"I think I saw the muse!"

"I didn't see anything!"

"I just used a tonus," said Ark over the chatter. "With tonai, a Mu-sician calls a muse with a sustained vocal tone, like whistling—or a per-cussive tone, like snapping or clapping. Musicians can also perform tonai with musical instruments, like flutes or drums. However a tonus is per-formed, a muse listens through it to follow a Musician's will."

He whistled again and held his hand out. The hawk muse soared down from the rafters and opened its talons, dropping the hazelnut on Ark's palm before flying off with a flap of crimson feathers. The class cried out again.

"The nut appeared again!"

"I'm *sure* I saw something—"

"It's magic!"

Ark let the nut drop to the ground. "It's not magic. It's music."

Eye-Patch Girl raised her hand. "How do you remember music forms?"

"Good question," said Ark. He went to the blackboard, taking a piece of chalk. "Musicians have different writing systems to record how to perform tonai and canti. The written version of a tonus or cantus is called a score."

On the board he drew a base of five circles, each one drawn inside the next in concentric rings. Then he drew symbols across the score, using the lines and spaces between them to mark each one.

"This is a Western-style score," he said. "The circle is the base—and these symbols represent different pitches and patterns. Any Musician who knows how to read this notation would be able to perform it. Observe."

Ark went over to the teacher's desk and fetched a book. He opened the book and laid it flat on Eye-Patch Girl's desk. Finally, he put his hands on the desktop and drummed out the rhythm he'd written on the score.

The class held its breath. Soon a new muse emerged, one like a fierce, tiny whirlwind. The muse swept up the book, its strong winds tearing the pages right out—and then the muse folded the loose pages into tiny kites, sending them flying around like paper birds. The class laughed, thrilled.

The only student not amused was the head councilor's son. Brax smacked away the kites flying around his head; then, fed up, he stood from his seat. Six other boys rose with him. They left together, brushing past Mara and heading into the town square.

Ark watched them go. Good riddance.

He drummed on the desk again. The whirlwind muse swept up all the pages, flattened them out and slid them inside the covers, repairing them.

"By combining the right patterns with the right focus," Ark finished, "a Musician can tell a muse how they want to shape the space and objects around him—just like I did with this book." He held up the book and flipped the pages out from beneath his thumb, as good as new. "See?"

The students clapped, delighted. Eye-Patch Girl was grinning in her seat, absolutely captivated. Even Mara looked impressed.

Ark smiled. He was starting to feel pretty good, until something in his line of vision snagged his attention. Past the excitable students, Ark caught sight of a figure wandering the town square.

Scarecrow had made quite an impression on Ark already, falling on top of him yesterday—so it was easy for Ark to recognize him, even from a distance. Scarecrow was making his steady way along, carrying a ladder on his shoulder. Every so often he set the ladder down and climbed up to inspect the strings of festive lanterns hanging above the crowd.

Ark looked away—and realized he wasn't the only person watching. Brax, now loitering in the town square with his gang, was following Scarecrow's movements too. He wore a disturbing grin on his face: the grimace of someone who liked causing pain.

"Uh, where was I?" Ark finally spoke, breaking his gaze. *Leave other people alone*, he told himself. "Right. Canti." He picked up where he left off. "The other basic form Musicians practice is canti. A cantus is—"

"Hey, look!"

One student pointed to the square. Everyone looked.

Ark followed their stares. As Ark and the rest of the class watched, Brax and his gang walked up to Scarecrow, circling him. Then Brax cuffed an arm around Scarecrow's neck, dragging him off behind a nearby building.

The class broke into chaos. Forgetting Ark's lesson, the students left their chairs and hurried to where Brax and Scarecrow had gone. Poor Mara was dragged off by the tide of kids who shoved her along with them.

Stunned, Ark followed as the chanting began:

"Fight! Fight! Fight!"

Ark tried pushing his way through the crowd, peering over everyone's shoulders to look.

Scarecrow had managed to escape Brax's headlock, but it was clear he was outmatched. Brax threw a punch. Scarecrow ducked—but then one of Brax's friends kicked him. Scarecrow stumbled.

"Not again," someone near Ark groaned.

Ark turned to the speaker. It was Eye-Patch Girl.

Ark edged closer to her. "What's his problem?"

"You mean Brax?" said Eye-Patch Girl, her expression sour. "He's just a jerk. He's always picking fights." She shifted her gaze to Scarecrow, sighing. "And he's the only one who always picks back."

Ark watched the spectacle. Brax had dragged Scarecrow over to a water pump. Then Brax stuck his foot in the pump's drain, kicking mucky water in Scarecrow's face over and over. Scarecrow sputtered.

Brax's friends egged their leader on. The crowd cheered. From across the crowd, Mara stood biting her lip.

Ark frowned. He and Mara should probably step in now, right?

At the same time, he really didn't want to. *Leave other people alone.* But if this kept going . . .

Ark was still trying to decide what to do when he heard it:

SNAP!

Ark flinched. He raised a hand to his head, feeling the echoes of the sound prickling against his skull.

. . . What was *that?*

An instant later, an inhuman voice screamed past him. Ark stared in shock as a muse—the amber wildcat, which he'd summoned at the train station yesterday—yowled and dove into the mucky water in the pump's drain basin. It splashed water up in Brax's face before leaping away.

Brax staggered, spitting water from his mouth. Seizing the moment, Scarecrow pulled away, taking a new defensive pose.

Ark's head spun. What the gavotte just happened?

His eyes quickly found Mara's. She was staring intently at him from across the mob, looking startled. *Was that you?* her gaze seemed to ask.

So Mara had seen it too. Ark shook his head. *Wasn't me.*

Ark scanned the yard, baffled. He hadn't called the muse. Based on Mara's reaction, she hadn't either. Had it come out on its own?

Ark rejected the thought at once. No. He'd *heard* it. Someone out here had used a tonus—crudely, but effectively. He was sure of it.

Which meant—

Which meant there was another Musician here.

The realization landed in Ark's brain like a ten-ton boulder. Could there be a Musician in this dinky town after all? But who?

Before he could work that out, Mara materialized beside him.

"Adept Encore!" she started, eyes wide.

"Go get Dulcian and Callie," said Ark, cutting her off. "Hurry!"

It probably wasn't appropriate for Ark to give Mara orders, but Mara hurried off without protest. Ark turned his attention back to the fight, trying to determine who among them was a Musician.

Brax was already at it again, knocking Scarecrow around.

"Jeez, this is dull," said Brax, faking a yawn. "I thought an outlaw dog like you would know a few more tricks. Maybe I can teach you to *beg.*"

His gang laughed at the remark. Scarecrow blanched, like he was about to be sick; then his face darkened in anger. Brax flashed his teeth in a nasty grin.

And then it happened again:

SNAP!

Not long after Ark heard the tonus, another muse—one in the shape of an enormous boar with curling tusks—came running out from a cluster of hazel trees, squealing in rage. The boar hit Brax squarely in the side, running right over him—and half a heartbeat later, it was gone.

Brax grunted as he fell. The crowd, who clearly hadn't seen or heard the muse, murmured in confusion.

Ark cursed, looking around. There was definitely a Musician out here, trying to help Scarecrow. They could use tonai, at least on instinct. But whoever it was didn't seem to know what they were doing.

Brax recovered. He charged Scarecrow, catching him in a full-on tackle—then Brax flipped him like a stuffed dummy. Scarecrow landed hard on his back with a wheeze, unable to take a full breath.

"Knock it off, Brax!" Eye-Patch Girl hollered.

Brax was having too much fun to pay her any attention, but her shouts were enough to spur Ark to action. He had to stop this. Now.

Though some part of him was certain he would regret it later, Ark set his jaw and stepped out into the open space. The crowd hushed.

Brax's grin widened. "Gotta problem, Mr. Fancy Musician?" Brax jeered. He gestured between himself and Scarecrow. "We're just having an honest tussle. What're you gonna do? Fly paper kites at me?"

Ark put on a stiff smile.

"You didn't let me finish my lesson," he said. He stepped next to the water pump, turning to the spectators.

"As I was saying earlier," Ark spoke in his best teacher voice, "the other musical form is a cantus. It may sound like singing, but it's really a Musician telling a muse what to do through the vocal patterns they recognize best."

The crowd went silent, stunned. Brax raised a derisive eyebrow.

"Is he serious?" he scoffed. His gang snorted.

"If you change the way a cantus is sung, different muses will respond with different effects," Ark went on, grabbing the water pump's handle. "That's why Musicians can perform many variations of the same cantus. Observe."

Ark pushed the handle down several times, pumping out a stream of fresh water from the spout. The water poured freely into the drain basin.

"*Aguisimmo!*" Ark chanted fiercely, his voice loud and crisp.

A muse like a bright blue lizard manifested beside him. It splashed into the water Ark had pumped out. The water surrounded the lizard's body like a rippling barrier; then the lizard gushed forth in a watery burst. Brax howled as the muse splashed him, soaking him completely.

"You'll pay for that!" Brax snarled at Ark.

Ark smiled calmly. He lowered his voice, chanting the same cantus softly and slowly, with a different melody than before:

"*Agguissimmo.*"

Another muse—a fluffy weasel that looked as soft as a sunrise—came out. The weasel zigzagged over the water at Brax's feet. The water froze into solid ice just before Brax's foot touched down. His boot skidded— Brax yelped, his feet slipping—and then he fell with a crash.

The crowd changed its loyalties. Everyone started laughing at Brax. Some of them cheered with whoops and whistles.

Ark caught Eye-Patch Girl looking at him and nodded at her. She nodded back, smiling with newborn admiration.

Then Eye-Patch Girl's relief turned into alarm. "Look out!" she cried.

Ark whipped around, but too late. Brax was already back on his feet and practically on top of him, his face red with rage, his fist coming for him—

SNAP!

The tonus sent a shiver through Ark. He gasped.

Three muses—the amber wildcat, the boar, and the crimson hawk Ark had summoned during the lesson—all appeared, stirring a gust of wind. The muses roared, their voices blending in uncanny harmony.

Their roar knocked Brax backward before his fist could connect. He staggered onto the ice, his feet going in opposite directions.

The crowd groaned as Brax fell in an unplanned split. He whimpered, drawing his knees to his chest. Brax's friends hurried to help him up, leading him away.

Ark didn't relish the victory. That tonus had come from right behind him.

He spun around—

Scarecrow lay there in the dirt, sprawled on his side. His hand was slightly raised, his fingertips pressed together. He stared straight at the three muses, his expression a blend of dread and disgust.

Ark went numb. No. No way. Not possible.

Not *him.*

Before Ark could reconcile the denials in his head with the proof before his eyes, he was surrounded, the crowd of kids praising him and asking a million questions.

Ark tried unsuccessfully to extricate himself from the mob. Eventually the group dispersed, and Ark returned to where Scarecrow had just been.

Gone.

Ark stared in disbelief at the empty space. *Frigits frigits frigits!*

"Adept Encore!"

Ark glanced up to see Callie and Mara. Dulcian was hurrying behind them, his black case hitting his leg with each step.

"We were on hold to speak with the Grand Maestran," said Callie sourly. "What happened?"

"Mara says you found a Musician," added Dulcian. "Who?"

Ark babbled. "It was Scarecrow—I mean, that boy—the one from the train station. The kid who fell on me!"

"*Him?*" Callie squawked.

Ark told them about the fight. When he finished, Dulcian sent Ark an even look. "Are you certain? Did you witness him perform a music skill?"

Ark nodded. The skepticism left their faces.

"So there was a Musician here all along," said Callie.

"A Musician who, for whatever reason, is keeping his gifts to himself," said Dulcian. "I suppose we have an evaluation to carry out after all. Now we just have to find where he's gone."

Chapter Thirteen

HARVESTIDE

"Are you up there?" called Mr. Douse from the shop floor below.

Still pressing a damp cloth to the bruises on his ribs, Jay rolled off his bed and staggered to the stairs of his loft. He shot his custodian a grumpy look.

At the foot of the stairs, Mr. Douse arched a shaggy eyebrow. "Should I be wondering where those contusions came from, or should I just assume Braxson Gripps beat the stuffing out of you again?"

Jay's frown curdled into a sour scowl. Mr. Douse sighed.

"We're gonna have a talk about that later. Get a shirt on," he said, tugging on his own sleeves. "Harvestide can't start if the lanterns aren't lit. Hop to it."

Jay wasn't about to *hop* anywhere. He scuffed across his room, pulled on a clean shirt, slid his cap on, and plodded down the stairs.

"That's the spirit," said Mr. Douse. "Got something for you."

Jay was confused as Mr. Douse dropped a colorful beaded bracelet into his hands—the kind of thing girls around Hazeldenn liked to wear.

"Thanks," said Jay, staring at the bracelet. "You, uh, shouldn't have?"

"It's not for *you*," chided Mr. Douse. "You're taking Miss Kindle around the festival tonight, remember?"

Jay hadn't forgotten—but he hadn't known he was supposed to give her something. He nodded, stashing the bracelet away.

"Show her a nice time. Be a gentleman," the old man added. "Let's go."

Jay was soon shuffling after his custodian through the festive streets with the ladder and lantern pole, trying not to run over happy holiday-goers.

Harvestide was here, and the excitement that'd consumed Hazeldenn for the past week was at its peak. Everywhere Jay turned, there was color, laughter, and tasty smells. Everybody was decked out in their holiday best and sharing smiles in all directions, already having a grand time.

Except the lamplighter. Jay was *not* having a grand time.

Since getting thrashed by Brax that afternoon, a foul mood had infected him like a nasty cold. Jay had tried not to let it bother him so much. He had bigger things to worry about—like ghosting away from Hazeldenn without getting caught, before the Capo found him again.

He didn't have time to imagine how stupid he must've looked, lying sore and pathetic in the dirt.

He couldn't think about the sappy smile Lina had given that Musician after he'd gone and interfered, either.

And he flat-out *refused* to think about how he'd called muses for help.

Jay didn't know what'd come over him. Brax had started kicking the snot out of him . . . and before Jay knew it, he was using the one and only music trick he knew to get muses to defend him.

But when Jay had seen those three muses rush in—stopping Brax just before he'd punched the Musician kid's lights out, unleashing Jay's will—Jay's thoughts had flashed to Windfalle, and he'd finally come to his senses. He'd stopped himself immediately.

Even now the thought of what might've happened if he'd lost control made his stomach twist in disgust. He should never call for a muse again. *Ever.*

Not after what he'd done.

"Hurry up, Julian!" called Mr. Douse. "Don't keep Miss Kindle waiting."

Jay grunted a reply. Lina probably wouldn't want to step out with him tonight anyway, not after his epic humiliation. He just wanted to go home.

The town square was swarming with people by the time they arrived. Jay eventually found space to set up his ladder. A cheer went up when the first lantern was aglow. Soon the square glittered with dots of suspended light, the lanterns shining like sparkling dew caught in a spider's web.

"Almost done," said Mr. Douse, nodding to the last unlit lantern. "Make sure you return the ladder after this."

"Yeah, yeah," said Jay. "Got it."

"And your curfew is midnight, don't forget," added Mr. Douse.

"I *got* it," Jay grumbled. The old man sure knew how to nag.

"Everything all right up there?" asked another voice from below.

Jay was about to respond with another grumpy remark—but when he glanced down, he chomped his tongue in surprise.

Lina was below, wearing a green festival dress and a matching green eyepatch. Her red hair shone, framing her face and shoulders. She looked like a million gold Medallions.

"Miss Kindle, you look lovely this evening," said Mr. Douse, a rare smile under his mustache. He glanced toward Jay. "Well?"

Jay gulped. He wanted to say something—that she glowed even without the lantern light. But all he could manage was, "I—ah—you—nice."

Lina beamed, smoothing her skirts.

Jay slid down the ladder, dusted himself off, then pulled the beaded bracelet from his vest.

"Aw!" she said, taking the bracelet. "That's so sweet."

"For you," said Jay in a squeak. Mr. Douse shook his head, sighing.

"It's sad that Harvestide will be over after tonight," said Lina. She turned the bracelet over in her fingers, spinning the beads on the string. "At least the Musicians will be staying here awhile longer."

Jay didn't trust himself to say anything. He'd be happy if the Musicians left. Especially that blonde kid. When he'd stepped in the middle of Jay and Brax's fight, he'd been all, *Look at me, I'm better than you*—and then he'd made Brax look like a total nincompoop. Like it was nothing.

Yep. Jay would be perfectly happy if he never saw him again.

"It sure is something that they came to town, huh?" added Lina. "Y'know the one who was at school earlier—Adept Encore—I heard he's one of the best Musicians his age in the whole nation. Incredible, isn't it?"

Jay clenched his jaw. Yeah. Incredible.

"I mean, he's incredible anyway," she went on, beaming—what the heck was she getting so flustery for?—"but he doesn't act like what he does is a big deal at all. Makes you wish we had a Musician living here."

Jay pretended not to hear her.

"Say, Jay," she asked, "d'you think he could join us?"

Jay glanced up. "Who d'you mean?"

"Adept Encore," said Lina. "Maybe we could find him and ask if he'd like to come around the festival with us. What do you say?"

Something hot and nasty flared through Jay.

"I say forget it," he spat.

Lina stopped fiddling with her bracelet. "How come? It'd be fun."

"How could having a stuck-up skriff like him tag along possibly be fun?" said Jay before he could stop himself. "Just 'cause everybody thinks he's amazing doesn't mean *I* have to kiss the dirt he walks on."

"Didn't you see what he did?" said Lina. "Adept Encore *is* amazing."

Jay snorted. "'Cause he can sing a few songs? Oh, sure, real amazing."

"How would you know?" Lina snapped. "You're not a Musician!"

Jay could barely hear her over the roar in his ears.

"Hey," said Mr. Douse, trying to intervene. "You kids calm down—"

"You know what?" said Lina, red-faced. "I'll bet you're just upset that he saved you. That's what's got you all mad, isn't it?"

Jay stared at her, mouth open. Then the avalanche of rage roared down.

"He did not save me!" Jay yelled.

"Yes, he did!" she yelled back. "You're being so stupid!"

"*Stupid?*" Jay hollered. Some corner of his mind whispered, *Yeah, you kind of are*—but he shoved the thought away. "Well, if that guy is so blazing fantastic, why the heck d'you need someone stupid like me around for?" He waved his hand at her. "Go on. You two have a grand time!"

Jay flinched as something smacked him in the face. Lina had thrown the bracelet back at him, the beaded missile hitting its mark dead on. Lina's angry expression crumpled, a tear falling from her eye.

"You're such a jerk!" she fumed. She whirled around and dashed off.

In a daze, Jay bent over and retrieved Lina's bracelet from the ground, stunned at himself. Then he glanced over and saw Mr. Douse giving him one of the most disappointed looks Jay had ever seen.

"So much for being a gentleman," the old man grumbled. He took up the ladder and lantern pole, heading toward the candle shop.

"Aw, *blast* it," Jay hissed. What kind of jerk was he, taking out his sour mood on Lina? What in blazes was he thinking?

He had to catch up to her. Say sorry. Before it was too late.

Jay clenched the bracelet, stuffing it back in his pocket before he took off after Lina, running fast.

Dusk had settled in, and all across Hazeldenn familiar sights had been transformed by the radiance of lanterns. Jay blitzed along the crowded streets, shoving through people as he chased the flash of Lina's green dress, farther and farther ahead of him.

Soon Jay stumbled onto the town green, a wide-open field flanked by hazel groves on all sides. Out here, Harvestide was in full swing. Girls cheered each other on in the dances. Boys crowded around to watch hand-to-hand matches. Everywhere people were eating, drinking, laughing, and dancing together, looking like they hadn't a care in the world.

Jay scanned the huge crowd in despair. Where'd she gone?

"Lina!" he cried, cupping his hands around his mouth. His voice was swallowed by the festival. No matter where he looked, he didn't see Lina.

Desperate, Jay shouted even louder.

"I'm sorry!" he hollered. "I'm sorry, Lina!"

A hand landed on Jay's arm. Jay spun around, hopeful.

"Lina—?"

Not Lina.

The blonde Musician kid stood there, holding Jay's arm. His long white coat was rumpled, and his spectacles sat crookedly on his nose. He looked like he'd fought through the crowds to get to him.

Jay couldn't stop a sour glare. "What the heck do you want?"

The Musician returned Jay's glare. "Believe me, this has nothing to do with what I *want*," he said, his upper-class accent barely masking his irritation. "I never wanted to spend the past few hours tracking you down."

"What in blazes are you going on about?"

The Musician kid ignored him, adjusting his spectacles. He coughed to clear his throat, then sang, "*Ffarro.*"

A muse shimmered before them a few moments later. The muse showed itself like an orange cloud of fireflies, spiraling around in a swarm until they spread out in a burst of orange light, shining against the black sky.

Jay stared up at the beacon of fireflies. He hated how impressed he felt.

As Jay looked up, there was another similar flash of light in the sky, coming from the direction of the hazel grove. The Musician nodded to himself, like he'd been expecting it, then turned to Jay again.

"All right, here are your options," he said. "Shut up and come with me quietly—or I'll drag you by force."

Jay stared at the other boy—who stood half a head shorter than him—and snorted. "Right. And here's *your* options: Beat it or get beaten."

The Musician kid frowned. "By force it is, then. *Rinnforzzanndo.*"

Jay flinched as another muse appeared on the Musician's wrist. It looked like a mix between a mouse and a monkey, with a long, curling tail and gripping toes. It blinked at Jay with owlish eyes.

Jay didn't react in time. The muse snapped its tail around his arm like a whip, squeezing tight—and before Jay could blink, the Musician was hauling him through the crowd like an ill-behaved toddler.

"Get off me!" said Jay, trying to twist free.

No use. With the muse's help, the Musician easily pulled Jay across the green, weaving toward the spot where the second flash of light had come from. Jay stumbled behind him, sputtering curses.

Once they broke free from the crowds, they came to a stop at the edge of the hazel grove, where the short, spindly trees gave way to a carpet of rusty leaves. Before Jay could wonder why the kid had stopped here, three other figures came forward from the trees.

"Took you long enough," said the scary Musician lady. The black fox muse was prowling at her feet.

"Nonsense," said the man who came up beside her. The bluebird muse was nestled comfortably on the crown of his head. "Adept Encore did well."

The other woman who followed slightly behind them said nothing, staring at the mechanical gizmo she was playing with.

The Musician kid sent Jay a long, sideways look. "*Libberro,*" he chanted.

The furry muse unwrapped its tail from Jay's arm. It scurried up the Musician's shoulder, then leapt into the air and shimmered out of sight.

Jay had been waiting. He sprang into a sprint.

"*Ferrmatta!*" the Musician kid sang, loud and commanding.

Jay yelped as a muse like a thatch of vines sprung up around his feet. The muse wrapped leafy tendrils around Jay's legs, snaring him. Startled, Jay tried to get away—

Only he couldn't. The vines held him in place. He was stuck.

"Sorry," said the Musician kid. "But no."

Jay cursed, pulling against the muse. *Bandersnatches.*

The man stepped forward, holding a black case at his side. "Easy," he said, raising his free hand like he was approaching a spooked animal. "There's no reason to be alarmed. We only want to have a few words with you."

Jay could think of a few very specific words he wanted to spit back at the man—but he held his tongue, yanking against the vines.

"It's pointless," said the Musician. "Stop struggling."

Even as he spoke, the vines grew thicker, sliding painfully along Jay's bare ankles and swallowing his legs. Frustrated, Jay yelled through his teeth—without thinking, he set his fingers and snapped.

The muse holding Jay recoiled, releasing him. Then the vines shrank back into the dirt, vanishing. Suddenly free, Jay stumbled, falling on his rear.

The Musician kid's eyes widened. "You dismissed my muse."

Jay scrambled to his feet, stammering. "I-I didn't mean—"

"Adept Encore was right," said the man, smiling. "You *are* a Musician."

Jay shot him a glare. "No, I'm not! I hate muses!"

The man's smile dimmed. The joyful sounds of Harvestide made the silence more awkward.

"I don't know what you skriffs want," Jay spat, checking his peripherals for the best way to run, "but whatever you're selling, I'm not buying."

"We're not street vendors," said the scary lady. "We're not selling anything. You can leave—*after* we finish our business with you."

Jay froze. Business? What business could they have with him?

The man stepped forward, reaching out a hand. "Let's try this again. I'm Dulcian. And this is Trillo, my patron muse," he said, pointing to the little bluebird muse now perched on his shoulder. "What's your name?"

Jay stuffed his hands deep in his vest pockets, saying nothing.

"Well, it's nice to meet you anyway," said Dulcian. He gestured to the others. "This is Callie Vielle, Mara Fipple, and Arkalin Encore. We have come to Hazeldenn on behalf of the Royal Conservatory."

Jay's eyes narrowed. He had no idea what a conservatory was—but it rhymed almost exactly with reformatory. Probably not a coincidence.

"And what d'you want with me?" he said, suspicious.

"Nothing difficult, I assure you," said Dulcian. "We need you to take a test for us."

Jay blinked. What?

"We need you to *fail* a test for us," Callie amended. "And you're not leaving until you do." She glanced to the fox muse at her side. "Fiero."

At her word, the fox muse bounded forward. It yipped and growled, wearing a vulpine scowl almost identical to the frown on Callie's face.

Jay cursed. He still had to find Lina. She could be anywhere by now.

"Fine!" he muttered. "So long as it means you leave me alone."

"Of course," said Dulcian. "After this, we won't bother you again."

With careful movements, he removed the black case from the chain around his wrist and unlocked the lid. Then he passed the case to the Musician kid—Ark-something, whatever his name was.

"All right, Adept Encore," said Dulcian. "You take it from here."

Ark took the case, exhaling.

"Right," he said. He stepped in front of Jay. "On behalf of the Royal Conservatory, and before these witnesses"—he gestured vaguely to the others—"I will now administer the evaluation. May Brio find you worthy."

He said the formal words as if he'd only learned them recently. He opened the lid of the case and held it up to Jay.

Jay arched an eyebrow. "Excuse me?"

Ark rolled his eyes. "Just pick this up and try to play it."

Jay peered inside. It was a fiddle, the kind he'd seen street buskers in the capital play for a few Whits in their caps. The fiddle was white except for the black string board along the neck.

Jay frowned at the instrument. "You're kidding."

Ark was still blank-faced. "I wish I were."

Jay shook his head. "I've never even touched a fiddle before."

"That shouldn't matter," Dulcian chimed in.

Jay eyed him. "How come? This a trick?"

"No trick," said Dulcian. "Just try. If nothing happens, that's that."

Jay's eyes shifted to the fiddle again. His gut instinct told him to walk away. But it wasn't like their test sounded hard. And they probably wouldn't let him leave 'til he did what they asked. The sooner he got away from these jerks, the sooner he could go look for Lina, say he was sorry, and try to forget this part of the night ever happened.

Jay stretched out a hand and plucked the fiddle from the case.

"All right," he said, bringing the fiddle close to his face as he squinted at its scratches and carvings. "There. Can't play it. Now can I—?"

Julian.

Jay almost dropped the fiddle in surprise. He looked up.

Ark was still holding the case. Callie had her lips pinched in a tight line. Dulcian waited with his hands behind his back. Mara was still staring down at the gizmo in her hands.

"Who said that?" hissed Jay.

Dulcian, Callie, and Ark glanced at each other. Mara looked up from her device.

"Said what?" said Ark.

"Somebody said 'Julian,'" Jay insisted. "One of you."

"Julian?" said Dulcian. "Is that your name?"

Callie looked straight at Jay. "None of us said anything."

Jay stared back at her, then down at the fiddle, not sure what to think. He wasn't crazy. He *knew* he'd heard—

Julian.

Jay gasped.

An unearthly melody rose around him, vibrating from the fiddle's core. It sang like delicate drops of spring rain whispering across the earth. It pulsed with the rich, resounding thrum of the ocean, rising and falling in majestic swells. The sound flowed over him as steady as a heartbeat— like it was alive.

Jay hardly dared believe it. It was the same thing he'd heard at the train station yesterday. *Perfect music.*

Julian, the perfect music sang out. *Come.*

Not at all sure what he was doing, Jay reached into the black case again, retrieving the fiddle's slender bow from the velvet lining. As the Musicians watched in disbelief, Jay lifted the fiddle and tucked it under his chin. Somehow, the fiddle's wooden surface felt warm to the touch.

Come. Come. Come.

Compelled by the call, Jay cradled the fiddle's neck in his hand and let his fingertips settle on the strings. With his other hand, he set the bow in place.

Then—as if he'd known all along he could do it, as if he'd done it a million times before—he set the music free.

CHRIS CROSS

The first clear, shivering tone took flight, ascending like a wild bird released from captivity, exulting in the open sky. The sound soared in all directions—sailing through the grove canopy, gliding across the town green. The laughter and babble of Harvestide fell quiet. Those nearest paused as the sound reached them, raising their heads to listen.

Jay didn't notice. He closed his eyes and kept his hands moving. The song pouring out of the fiddle felt familiar, though he wasn't sure why. It shook with tones so deep they trembled through his bones; it reached for pitches so high they made the hairs on his neck prickle. The fiddle sang with a voice that was hauntingly beautiful—and an inexpressible sense of relief overtook him, like a long-forgotten ache in the core of his being was suddenly gone.

Someone laughed, and Jay vaguely realized the laughter came from him. He was in tune with the fiddle, leaning into each push and pull of the bow, fingers flying. Notes flowed around him in a cascade of music as his hands flitted and danced over the strings, following a will of their own—

And then something inside the fiddle woke up.

Jay sensed it at once. He felt the slumbering presence within the fiddle rousing, like a beast opening its eyes.

Jay played on—and now he could feel the fiddle's power building under his fingertips. It strained against him, like it was trying to fling itself right out of his grasp—but Jay held on with all his might, channeling the fiddle's strength into phrases of melody. He put all he had into it, note by note—letting the music enter his very being, his very soul—

Then, too soon, the song was over.

Jay sucked in a startled breath, opening his eyes. The sudden silence was almost painful.

The town green was dead still. Everyone had stopped in the middle of their dances and games, as if caught in a trance. Some were smiling radiantly; others were weeping.

Startled, Jay faced the Musicians. Callie looked like she'd swallowed a hornet's nest. Ark was a stone. Mara's eyes protruded from their sockets. Dulcian's mouth opened and closed like a gibbering fish.

Jay pulled the fiddle away from his chin. His mouth dropped open.

The fiddle was radiant, suffused with a golden halo of light. The light shone over Jay, too, enveloping him in a glowing aura.

Jay gulped air, every part of his body thrumming. Then the light around him started to dim—and as it did, his energy dwindled. Jay's arms sank to his sides, out of strength.

"What happened?" he gasped, trembling.

Finally, Dulcian spoke, uttering two words Jay didn't comprehend: "You *passed.*"

Chapter Fourteen

THE UNRAVELING MAN

Jay was so lost in the echoes of the music that he couldn't think straight. "I . . . what?" he asked.

No one answered. It was so quiet that not even crickets were chirping.

Jay watched the motionless townsfolk, still transfixed by the music, and his earlier euphoria shifted to alarm. He tossed the fiddle to the ground, spooked.

"What the heck?" he cried. "What'd this thing do to me?"

Dulcian retrieved the fiddle, holding it at a distance like it was a sacred, dangerous thing. "The instrument didn't do anything," he said at length, as if he couldn't believe he was saying it. "*You* did."

Jay didn't like the way Dulcian was looking at him—like he was some kind of miracle.

The man turned to the other Musicians. "He *passed*," he said, beaming. "Do you understand what this means?"

The other Musicians weren't nearly so delighted. Mara was grim-faced. Ark looked like somebody had just played a cruel joke. Callie cursed aloud.

"Blast it all!" she hissed. "Give me that!"

Before Dulcian could stop her, Callie snatched the fiddle and the bow and shoved the instrument into Ark's hands.

"You! Play something!" she ordered.

"Callie!" Dulcian was aghast. "Brio has already chosen!"

"I don't believe it!" Callie snapped. She rounded on Ark again. "Play! That's an order from your juror!"

Looking like he was caught between two angry dredsnakes, Ark raised the fiddle, laying the bow across the strings with one smooth motion. He clearly wasn't a stranger to this type of instrument.

Even so, when Ark drew the bow across the strings, the fiddle didn't make a sound. The boy frowned; he tried again, his movements more insistent.

But the fiddle wouldn't obey him. It didn't even squeak.

"I—*can't*," Ark grunted through clenched teeth.

Callie's eyes widened. She took the fiddle, raising it to her own chin. Ignoring Dulcian's sputters of protest, she tried to play herself.

Nothing happened.

"Stop!" said Dulcian, snatching the fiddle from her. "None of us can play it. Only a Musician that Brio has accepted could ever make his instrument work. And that Musician is standing right in front of you!"

Jay found himself trapped under their stares. Part of him wanted to run in the opposite direction.

But he could still sense the presence within the fiddle, calling for him with a compelling, undeniable pull.

"Don't you get it?" said Dulcian. "He passed, unequivocally. The first person in centuries." He sent Callie a pointed look. "And *we* found him."

At once Callie's outrage deflated.

"*We* found him," she echoed, smiling in understanding.

"This wasn't such a worthless assignment after all," said Dulcian.

Jay glanced sideways at Ark, not sure what they were saying. But Ark was still looking at him with a mix of disbelief and disappointment. Jay scowled instead at Mara, who'd just stepped forward.

"We need to leave," she said in a breathy whisper. "Now!"

Dulcian and Callie broke off their discussion.

"Brio's Resonance carried for miles," said Mara, gesturing all around. "Who knows who else may have heard it?"

Dulcian started. "You mean—?"

Mara nodded grimly. "*Them.*"

Jay had no idea what Mara was talking about, but it was enough to spur the other Musicians into action. Dulcian quickly returned the fiddle to its case, and Callie grabbed Jay by the arm.

"*Move*," she ordered. She pulled Jay along beside her around the edge of the town green, the other Musicians flanking them.

"We need to get away from crowds," said Mara, casting wary looks at the townsfolk who were only just starting to come out of their daze.

"We'll head back to the stay-inn house," said Dulcian.

Mara shook her head. "I will gather our things. You can all make your way to the station and call our train to pick us up."

"Good idea," said Dulcian. He turned to Ark. "Arkalin, go with her."

But Mara shook her head again. "I can manage." She looked at Jay, her gaze as wide and heavy as the moon. "This boy needs to be protected. It would be better if you had Adept Encore's skills at hand. Just in case."

"Good point," said Dulcian. "Thank you, Mara."

Before Dulcian finished, Mara had already left them, vanishing into the crowd. Callie took off, holding Jay so tightly that her nails dug into his arm.

"Yow!" he cried, yanking against her. "Leggo!"

The scary lady held fast to Jay, stomping with each step as she led them straight into the hazel trees.

"Callie," called Dulcian, "where are you—?"

"I know where I'm going!" she snapped defensively. Dulcian and Ark shared a look and followed.

They walked further among the hazel trees, the light from Harvestide bonfires growing dimmer behind them. They passed through the grove's deepest shadows until another source of light glinted through the branches ahead. They broke through the trees into torchlight; all around, mounds of earth were speckled with the otherworldly glow of flickering candles.

"This is a graveyard," observed Dulcian.

"Blast!" barked Callie. "How do we get to the train station?"

Dulcian shook his head. "Callie, we can't go straight there."

"You heard what Mara said!" said Callie. "Hundreds, *thousands* of people may have heard Brio's Resonance for miles around—and not all of them will be happy about it. We're vulnerable. We need to bring him to the Maestrans Council right away." She smiled smugly. "Besides, I can't wait to see the look on all the Maestrans' faces when *we* return with a candidate who passed."

CHRIS CROSS

"We can't just up and leave with him," said Dulcian. "His family needs to know what's going on." He turned to Jay. "Julian, is it? Where are your parents? We need to talk to them."

Jay opened his mouth, but no words came. He wanted to ask if he could take the fiddle and play it again until the empty ache inside him was satisfied.

Before Jay could manage to speak, someone started clapping.

Jay flinched, startled. The other Musicians looked around. The sound was sharp and hollow, shattering the graveyard's sacred silence.

Clap. Clap. Clap.

"Who's there?" called Dulcian.

Peering past the quivering candlelight and torch smoke, Jay caught sight of something—something that shouldn't've been there.

A dim figure stood by itself at the edge of the graveyard. Jay squinted. The figure wore a hood over his head and a mask that covered his entire face. Most bizarre were the figure's clothes: They were pieced together from patches of frayed garments, of all colors and patterns imaginable. It looked like he'd unravel at every seam with the slightest snag.

At length, the Unraveling Man stopped clapping. Then he spoke.

"Well done," he said. Whoever was behind the mask had a smooth, languid voice, not deep but strangely imposing. "*Very* well done. We haven't felt a Resonance like that in many, many years."

The Unraveling Man approached. As he walked among the graves, the flickering candle flames winked out, one by one.

Jay shuddered, as if the icy breath of the Reaper had blown through the graveyard. Every instinct told him he should run, now, *now*—but he was mesmerized by the stranger. His feet were locked in place.

Callie and Dulcian swept forward. "Stop right there!" Callie spat, holding up a hand.

The Unraveling Man halted. "As you wish, Lady Vielle."

Callie narrowed her eyes.

"Of course we know you, loyal dog of Luthier," said the Unraveling Man. "But do you know us?"

Callie's glare was hard. "Sorry. I can't place your face."

The Unraveling Man laughed behind his mask.

"Identify yourself, sir," Dulcian ordered.

The Unraveling Man faced him. "Sir Mandore," he spat. "Always straight to business. But this business is not with you." He lifted his cloaked arm, pointing a linen-wrapped finger at Jay.

"We are here," he hissed, "for the Crafter's heir."

The words pounded in Jay's ears.

Crafter's heir.

Who, him? What did that mean?

"We heard it," said the Unraveling Man. "Brio's call. Ages have passed since that muse's Resonance has shaken us. We knew exactly what it meant." Contempt bled through his words. He lowered his hand. "*You* are the one who awoke Brio's instrument. You are the one we must speak with."

Jay somehow found his voice. "Who are you?"

The Unraveling Man bowed, then rose again.

"Our name," he said, pointing to his chest, "is Dubito, disciple of Din."

The statement had an immediate effect. Dulcian and Callie dropped into defensive stances. Fiero the fox muse snarled at Callie's feet, while Trillo the bluebird muse chirped with a piercing trill. Behind them, Ark stood petrified.

"Dischordian!" Dulcian spat. "How did you find us so quickly?"

Dubito held up his hands. "We are not here to challenge you. At least not today. We only wish to talk."

"There's only one thing to say," Callie growled. "You're under arrest."

Dubito *tsk*ed behind his mask. "Is it a crime to want to speak to the Crafter's heir?" He jerked his hood toward Jay. "He has a right to hear what we have to say."

Despite his instincts screaming *Danger!*, Jay felt a ruffle of curiosity. What did this creep want to tell him so badly?

Dulcian stepped forward. His smile was cold and sharp, like splintered ice. "*Dubito*, is it? What was your name before you became enslaved to a dischord? Do you even remember?"

The Unraveling Man laughed again.

"I have an idea," Dulcian went on. "Why don't you come with us? I hear the correction house in Fairdown Falls is lovely this time of year."

Dubito's laugh deflated as a sigh. "That doesn't sound appealing. Why don't we do something else?"

Before Dulcian or Callie could react, Dubito raised one hand high. He hissed a stream of harsh, unintelligible syllables, the sound grating against Jay's eardrums—then he made a quick clawing gesture, as if tearing the air with his fingernails. Then he turned his hand palm-side up.

Ark uttered a cry and covered his mouth. At first, Jay didn't understand what he was reacting to—until he saw something appear above Dubito's hand. And what he saw didn't make sense.

It was nothing. Nothing*ness*. A strange, dissonant blackness, void of light and life, seeped from Dubito's fingertips like an oily mist. Shrieking, shadowy tendrils lashed out in all directions like a rabid, hungry thing— searching for blood, for warmth, for anything to fill its infinite emptiness.

A shaft of ice shot down Jay's spine. Fear bled through his veins.

Dubito curled his hand into a tight fist—then he threw his hand wide open, fingers splayed. The discordant darkness screeched; in a blink, it was gone, flying away faster than Jay's eyes could follow.

Jay didn't understand what Dubito had done until he heard the screams.

He spun around. Flames, tainting the peaceful night sky an angry red, glowed from the direction of Hazeldenn. Fire danced from the town's distant rooftops. The air was punctuated by cries and shouts of confusion.

"*Batbeetle, batbeetle, fly away home*," recited Dubito in a horrible singsong. "*Your house is on fire and your children will burn*."

Jay went numb. Panic squeezed all thoughts from his mind except three:

Mr. Douse. Colton. Lina.

The Unraveling Man rolled his shoulders.

"We had hoped it wouldn't come to this," said Dubito. "If only you hadn't tried to keep the Crafter's heir all to yourself. So selfish."

As Jay watched, the fires devouring Hazeldenn grew stronger, tongues of flame licking the sky.

"It's your duty as Musicians to go put out that fire, isn't it?" said Dubito. He waved dismissively. "Go fulfill your vows. In the meantime, we will speak with the Crafter's heir. Or do you need more incentive?"

Dubito raised a clawed hand again.

"Five . . . four . . . three . . . two—"

"*SFORRZO!*" Callie interrupted, her voice a piercing yell.

In the next instant, Fiero shot off like a blast of black lightning, striking the Unraveling Man square in the chest. Dubito flew, his fraying garments whipping around him. Even before he hit the ground, Callie was running toward Hazeldenn.

"I'll find Mara! We'll handle the fires!" she shouted at Dulcian. She waved at Jay and Ark. "You take care of the rest!"

Dulcian was frozen, watching the flames. "But, Callie—!"

"*Go*, Dulcian!"

Dulcian snapped to it. He gathered Jay and Ark, pushing them in the direction of the hazel grove.

"Run!" he ordered, setting the fiddle's case on the ground and throwing off his long green coat. "I'll hold him off!"

Even while Dulcian spoke, the Unraveling Man regained his feet. He began to spew more unintelligible commands, stretching out his hands. The shrieking oily mist appeared again above his palms, ready to devour.

Ark shoved Jay forward, and they stumbled into a run. The last thing Jay saw over his shoulder was Dulcian, singing a melodic chant—Trillo answered with a piercing chirp, flying at Dubito as a blue blur.

"Hurry!" said Ark, pulling Jay into the refuge of the grove.

The cries and shouts from the burning town grew faint behind them, and soon all Jay could hear was the sound of their running feet thudding through the underbrush. They ducked around hazel trees and slid on hazelnut husks, their faces barely avoiding branches.

Jay panted for each breath, trying to ignore the weird sensation in his chest. It was like an invisible thread was tied around his heart, tugging at him. He wasn't sure how he knew—but Jay could tell the other end of the thread was back at the graveyard. The farther Jay ran, the stronger the tug in his chest became, making it harder and harder to keep going forward.

And then they broke free of the hazel trees. Ark reared up. Jay skidded to a stop and clutched at his chest, looking past him.

They'd hit a dead end. Hazel Lake was before them, the black waters stretching a hundred strides along either side. Ark cursed, out of breath.

"Which way?" he said, looking up and down the shore.

"It's too late for that," spoke a voice behind them.

Jay spun around in time to see a wave of black, oily mist rise from the ground before parting like a curtain before them. Dubito stepped out from the mist. His mask smiled wickedly at them in the moonlight.

"Dulcian!" Ark shouted.

"Sir Mandore won't be joining us," said Dubito. He shrugged. "We asked for something so simple. But you Musicians insisted on all this fuss." He gestured to the air, thick with smoke.

"You're a monster!" snarled Ark.

Dubito sounded amused. "Nothing gets past you, does it?"

Meanwhile, Jay was working out an escape route. He was just about to ditch Ark at the shoreline and make a break for the trees—but he was caught off guard when Ark stepped out in front, shielding him.

Dubito cast back his head in laughter. "Oh, yes, please!" He raised his arms, presenting a wide target. "Do your worst, child!"

Jay watched, seeing peripheral details in sudden focus. He saw sparks from out-of-control fires swirling above them. He saw the Unraveling Man's tattered garments rippling in the night air. Jay even noticed the dark, ugly scar on the back of Ark's left hand as the boy took a defensive stance, his arms up.

"*Deccipuulla vinncttuum!*" Ark chanted in a rush.

A muse answered his call almost immediately; it splashed out from the lake, looking like hundreds of little silver-green fish. The muse swam in midair around the Unraveling Man, creating a cage around him.

Dubito tilted his head like a snake studying its prey. "That form you used. It's ancient. Not something you would learn in Echostrait. Who in the world taught you that?"

Ark's face twisted in focus. "*Puurgo!*" he chanted, his voice cracking on the last syllable.

Each little fish turned inward, aiming at Dubito like hundreds of arrows. They began to sing as one, their song sharp and piercing.

Dubito threw his hands up and cried out, falling to one knee.

Ark turned to Jay, ashen with fear. "Go," he croaked. "Run!"

But before Jay could move, the Unraveling Man began to laugh. A great swarm of darkness appeared around him, striking out against the singing fish. The muse wailed, recoiling and retreating to the lake.

Dubito rose and dusted off his garments, looking Ark's way.

"You have some surprising skills, little boy, we'll give you that. But is that the best you can do?" He shook his head. "Such a disappointment."

Ark stared at the Dischordian with a haunted look, frozen in place.

Jay clenched his fists. There was no escape now. His eyes and nose stung from the smoke. His ears throbbed with the sound of the towns-folks' screams. He felt helpless, and he couldn't stand it.

The Unraveling Man stepped around Ark, still frozen where he stood, and faced Jay. "You *are* helpless," he said. "What could you possibly do?"

Jay gasped. Had this creep just read his mind?

"We don't understand why Brio's instrument played for you," Dubito went on. "You're no Crafter. You're not even a Musician. You're a mis-take."

Jay flinched. The words stung, more than Jay thought they could.

"Even so, those Musicians will drag you to Fairdown Falls," said Dubito, his voice going cold. "They will make you their puppet. They will use you, betray you, discard you. We've seen it before."

Jay didn't want to listen. But the Unraveling Man's voice slithered into his ears, the words worming into his brain, dropping seeds of doubt.

Dubito sidled up next to him.

"Here's what we came to tell you," he whispered. "There is a better option than what the Musicians can offer. We can show you a path to freedom. A fresh start. A life of your own. And it won't cost you a thing."

Jay felt a pang throb through him, squeezing his chest. His own life? A fresh start? That sounded too good to be true.

The Unraveling Man's hand fell on Jay's shoulder. This close, Jay could see through the sockets of the Unraveling Man's mask.

His eyes were completely black.

Jay tried to pull away. "Leggo," he heard himself squeak.

The Unraveling Man held his shoulder tighter. "This is a limited-time offer," Dubito hissed. "Won't you hear us out?"

Jay tried to cry out, but his voice was gone. A fresh wave of fear made his stomach roil.

Get away! Jay's brain screamed, but he still couldn't move. Dubito's mask smiled cruelly as he leaned in closer.

A blinding blue light flashed between them, forcing them apart.

The Unraveling Man recoiled. Jay staggered back and splashed into the lake. He stared up in awe at the blue light.

It was Trillo. The little bluebird muse flew high in a wide arc—then it swooped down, landing on Dulcian's shoulder. Dulcian was standing at the edge of the hazel grove, holding the fiddle's case. He had a nasty scrape on his forehead and his arm bore a deep gash, still bleeding.

"Julian clearly doesn't want to hear any more," Dulcian snarled.

The Unraveling Man recovered, hissing in exasperation. "Sir Mandore. As persistent and obnoxious as ever."

"Two of my finer qualities," agreed Dulcian with a fierce smile. He held his hands out toward Dubito. "*Coll pugnno!*" he chanted.

Trillo flew. The Unraveling Man was knocked off his feet as the muse struck him like a bright blue arrow, faster than Jay's eyes could follow.

While Trillo attacked, Dulcian ran up to Jay and Ark with a limp.

"Arkalin!" said Dulcian. The man's expression was intense, almost scary. "Get Julian to the Royal Conservatory. That is your mission! Do you understand?"

Ark sputtered. "Y-Yes!"

Dulcian threw the fiddle's case to him, then winced as he retracted his wounded arm. "Do not lose that!" he ordered. "Guard it with your life!"

Ark nodded—then his eyes went wide. "Dulcian!" he cried shrilly.

Jay and Dulcian both glanced behind them. The Unraveling Man was there, swathed in darkness, steadily approaching.

Dulcian grabbed Ark and Jay, shoving them shoulder to shoulder.

"Whatever happens, stay together!" he shouted. Then he sucked in a deep breath, bellowing in a resounding voice:

"*Locco mosso!*"

And before Jay could gasp, Dulcian gave them a mighty shove, straight into the lake.

In the split-second freefall, Jay saw Trillo shoot past them in a feathery blur, flying in rapid circles above the water. The lake started to glow and bubble on the surface, the muse's trilling cry piercing the night. Then, with a *sploosh!*, Jay and Ark fell into the lake, the water around them *stretching*, dragging them deeper and deeper—

And Dulcian, Dubito, and all of Hazeldenn rippled out of sight.

Chapter Fifteen

TRANSPOSED

Ark held his breath as he spun in oblivion, not sure where the water was taking him or how much time was passing. When the current stopped spinning, he let his body rise to the surface, toward light—and then he sat up. He was in a shallow pool of water.

Ark wiped water from his eyes and squinted. The sun was up. The world was a blurry smudge of color and confusion. He reached for his spectacles, dangling from one of his ears, and slid them on his nose.

The first thing Ark saw was the black case holding Brio's instrument bobbing in the water. Beside the case, a long shadow rippled on the water's surface. Ark followed the shadow to its source, glancing behind him.

A huge figure towered above him, glaring down.

Ark yelped, startled. He splashed through the water to get away—but then he realized the figure wasn't alive. It was a harmless bronze statue.

That's when his brain finally caught up to where he was: on his rear in the middle of a fountain pool, soaked from head to toe.

Dazed, Ark peered past water droplets on his spectacles and took a proper look around. There were tall buildings everywhere, built of pale stone. The paved streets were clean but empty. There was no sign of a hazel tree or any other living thing anywhere.

Nausea swelled in Ark's stomach. He wasn't in Hazeldenn.

What was this place?

Ark shivered, chilled. He pushed himself to his feet and peeled off his drenched talaris, wringing it out. He threw his talaris over his arm and waded over to retrieve the black case.

A few sloshing steps later, his foot caught on something floating in the fountain pool, almost tripping him. When he glanced down, he gasped.

It was Scarecrow. He lay face down in the pool, terribly still.

Frigits!

Ark crouched down, turning the limp boy over and shaking him by the shoulders. "Wake up!" he yelled. "Breathe!"

For an awful moment, Ark wondered if the boy wouldn't wake—but then his eyes snapped open. He lurched upright, gasping for air, thrashing like he was fighting not to drown.

"Hey!" said Ark, ducking away. "Knock it off!"

Scarecrow's eyes widened.

"Wha—?" He coughed and rose shakily. "What happened?"

Ark didn't know how to answer. "C'mon," he told him, stepping out of the fountain. Scarecrow fished his cap out of the water and staggered across the pool, sloshing out behind him.

"W-We're not in Hazeldenn," Scarecrow declared.

"No kidding," spat Ark. "Any other brilliant insights to share?"

That shut the boy up. Ark surveyed their surroundings, his eyes landing on the bronze statue. The figure was a middle-aged man with a smiling, rotund face. Water trickled from his outstretched hand, guiding Ark's eyes downward to the tarnished memorial plaque:

IN TRIBUTE TO THE LIFE AND WORK OF

SIR BENJAMIN GRIM

SCHOLAR AND HUMANITARIAN

Scarecrow cursed, chattering. "How in b-b-blazes did we get here?"

Ark frowned, trying to think.

Last night—had it only been one night ago?—Dulcian had shoved Ark and Scarecrow together into a lake to escape the Dischordian's attack. After the initial plunge, Ark had found himself enveloped in a strong current. It had felt like being sucked into a whirlpool much deeper than he knew the lake could reach. Then, when he'd floated to the surface, he was in a totally different place at a totally different time of day, with Sir Grim's statue spewing water on his head.

"Dulcian," Ark concluded. "He must have performed a Transposition."

Scarecrow stared at him, blank-faced.

"To Transpose something means to transfer it from one place to another," explained Ark. His voice sounded much calmer than it should have. "Dulcian and Trillo sent us from Hazeldenn to this place, with the water as a conduit."

"He *what?*" Scarecrow cried.

Ark could appreciate his amazement. Transpositions were extremely difficult. It required great expertise and absolute focus to relocate something over large distances, not to mention a powerful muse. Most Maestrans didn't have the chops to attempt them. Dulcian's Transposition had been ridiculously risky, but also magnificently skillful.

The problem was Ark had no clue where they'd ended up.

His chest gave a terrible squeeze. Ark pressed a hand to his heart, forcing himself to breathe.

Don't freak out.

Ark gripped the case's handle, forcing his brain to focus on a plan instead. Step One: Figure out where they were. Step Two: Find a way to get to Fairdown Falls. Step Three: Get Scarecrow to the Royal Conservatory and finish his mission.

Simple.

Ark glanced toward the boy. He was stamping his feet and cursing.

"What are you doing?" asked Ark.

Scarecrow didn't answer. Ark spoke louder.

"Hey. Julian."

"It's Jay," the boy spat back, rubbing his arms. "And it's blazing freezing out here!"

Ark was on the verge of chattering, too. "I can fix that." He cleared his throat. "*Asciugare,*" he chanted.

He waited, listening for a muse. Nothing happened.

"*Assciugarre,*" he chanted again, more insistently.

Nothing. He didn't even feel a muse stir.

Jay whistled. "Wow. That was real amazing."

Ark kept his mouth tightly shut. *Ignore him.*

"If we keep moving, we'll dry off," he said, putting on his best *I'm-in-charge* voice. He pointed down the lane. "Let's go this way—"

"Don't order me around," said Jay. He started going the opposite way, elbowing Ark as he passed and causing him to drop the black case.

Ark frowned at Jay's retreating back. Jerk.

He picked up the case, about to go down the lane anyway—until Dulcian's last command echoed in his mind:

Whatever happens, stay together!

Ark stopped midstride. Right. As impossible as it was to believe, he'd seen it with his own eyes: Jay had resonated with Brio's relic. He was Brio's chosen Musician. And it was Ark's duty to make sure the new Crafter's heir made it to the Royal Conservatory to assume his title.

By the time Ark caught up with him, Jay was pounding on the door of a nearby house, one of a dozen lined up together. No lights shone inside.

"'Scuse me!" Jay called out. "Anybody home?"

No answer.

Ark looked around, trying to gain his bearings. The streets were wide and straight, and the buildings were well made. It seemed like a respectable enough town, but the whole place felt eerily quiet. They hadn't yet run into a single person who lived here. And Ark still couldn't sense any muses.

"Is this town abandoned?" Ark murmured.

Jay sniffed the air. "I smell smoke. Maybe somebody's been cooking."

The mention of cooking made Ark's stomach twist and gurgle.

Jay started off again, heading into a commercial district. Ark followed, studying the shops lining the road. Various goods and sundries were on display in the windows, but each store was dark inside. Most shop doors had posters plastered to them, bearing sketches of people's faces.

"I bet this place *is* abandoned," said Ark. "Look at all the wanted posters."

Jay didn't look. He hunched his shoulders, hurrying past the posters.

"I've heard about towns getting taken over by outlaw gangs," Ark went on, matching Jay's pace. "The people who used to live here probably had enough of the outlaws and moved somewhere else."

"Sure—and they left without all their stuff," said Jay sarcastically, pointing to shop windows full of merchandise. He gestured above the rooftops, adding, "Besides, how d'you explain that?"

Ark squinted in the direction Jay was pointing:

Smoke.

"Somebody's here," said Jay. "Whoever it is can tell us where we are."

Ark was hesitant. Maybe they didn't want to find the source of the smoke.

But Ark's stomach grumbled louder than his cautious thoughts. Perhaps whoever was there would have food.

They walked for another ten minutes along the line of shops before they stumbled upon something new. The street they were on eventually spilled into a vacant town square, with a market plaza and taller buildings. A modest Designist sanctuary stood at the heart of the square, with a bell tower piercing the sky. Every building had its doors and windows boarded shut, including the sanctuary—and each entrance was marked by a red painted letter: *Q.*

Ark shuddered. Q. For quarantine.

A whole new chapter of the quiet town's story wrote itself across Ark's mind. This nameless place had been snared by sickness. The residents who were healthy enough to leave probably fled as fast as they could.

Ark was just about to mention the theory to Jay when Ark thought he saw something flicker in the edge of his vision.

Ark spun around. On the far side of the square, he thought he saw a shadow duck into an alley—but he wasn't sure.

A prickly sensation tickled the back of his neck. Ark tore his eyes away from the spot. "Maybe we should get off the street," he said aloud.

"Go wherever you want," said Jay, continuing forward. "I'm gonna find my own way out of here."

"Dulcian told us to stick together," said Ark.

Jay eyed Ark sideways. "I'd rather cover myself in honey and go jump in a bear pit."

Ark scowled. "The feeling is mutual, trust me," he spat. He stepped in front of Jay, making him stop. "Look—truce, okay? Just until we figure out what our next move is." He gave Jay a hard stare. "Unless you'd rather risk running into Dubito again? On your own?"

Jay's expression went grimmer than the statue of Sir Grim.

"Fine," he said, waving Ark away. "But stop stepping on my shadow."

Ark backed away a few paces, the black case thumping his leg with each step.

As they left the town square, Ark realized what else was bothering him about the town: there were no trees. No gardens, either.

Everywhere he looked, there were buildings, buildings, and more build-ings—but no natural spots of any kind. No wonder Ark couldn't sense muses anywhere.

They went down another residential road, eventually finding the source of the smoke. In the center of the street was a large rectangular vent. Smoke puffed through its iron grate.

Jay knelt next to it, covering his face. "What's down there?"

"A sewer," said Ark. "The smoke is probably just gases burning off."

Jay peered suspiciously down into the vent. "It's not a sewer."

"It doesn't matter what it is," said Ark. "Let's go."

To Ark's surprise, Jay followed without protesting.

Without a smoke signal to follow, Ark wasn't sure where to head next. He led them up wide lanes and down narrow alleys, trying to focus on the task at hand. Once they found their way from this place, they could hopefully secure transportation to Fairdown Falls. Paying fare would be tricky since he had no money, but as a Musician he could prob-ably barter for passage. Once they were in the capital, getting to the Royal Conservatory would be a piece of cake. And Ark would have successfully completed his jury mission.

Ark's imagination took over. He pictured Grand Maestran Luthier and all the other Maestrans of the Council standing in a row, waiting to greet him as he and Jay arrived. They'd want to give him a reward for safe-ly bringing the Crafter's heir, which Ark would graciously decline—so they'd insist on giving him a position in the Royal Conservatory in return for his efforts. . . .

"Watch out!"

Ark barely heard the warning through his daydreams. With his next step, his foot met empty space. Ark yelped as he tumbled down a stair-way—*Bonk! Bump! Thud!*—until he finally landed at the base of the stairs flat on his back. The black case chased him down, landing hard on his stomach. *Oof.*

Above him, he heard clapping. Ark peered up. Jay was descending the steps at a casual pace, applauding.

"Go jump off a bridge!" Ark spat at him.

"You first," said Jay. "I tried to warn you."

Ark grabbed the case and pushed himself to his feet, his pride more bruised than his body. He saw to his chagrin that the plume of smoke from before was in front of them.

"You've led us in a circle," said Jay, unhelpfully.

Ark glared at him. "Think you can do better? Be my guest."

"You're the Musician," said Jay, twirling a hand with sardonic flair. "Why don't you sing us some help?"

Ark closed his eyes and extended his senses. He didn't sense any muse around, but he cleared his throat anyway.

"*Aiuutto*," he chanted. "*Guiddammi*."

Like before, there was no response.

"What kind of rotten Musician are you, anyway?" said Jay. "You're pretty much as impressive as a wet sponge."

Ark clenched his jaw so hard his teeth squeaked. "I'm the Principal Adept of Echostrait," he said stiffly. "I'm the best student they have. But not even a Maestran can summon muses in a place where there aren't any!"

Jay rolled his eyes.

His flippancy made Ark's face burn with indignation. Before he spewed a biting retort, he remembered what he was carrying.

Ark stared down at the black case. Of course. There weren't any muses nearby who could answer his summons, but maybe . . .

Ark held the case out to Jay.

"This instrument is marked by Brio's power," explained Ark. "It doesn't matter that there aren't muses in this area. You could use the violin to tap into Brio's power and help us figure out how to get out of here."

For just a second, Ark thought he saw Jay's eyes light up—but then his expression soured. "Forget it. I hate muses."

"Its power responded to you once already—" Ark insisted.

"Are you deaf or just stupid?" Jay snapped. "I said *no*, bum-wipe."

The crude insult rolled off Ark. "Then what's your plan? Keep walking until we collapse from hunger?"

"I know exactly where we are," said Jay.

Ark scoffed. "Right. And where would that be?"

Jay pointed. "*Up-per Grims-borrow*," he said in a halting voice.

Ark followed Jay's outstretched finger. Across the way was a dingy public bulletin board: UPPER GRIMSBOROUGH LOCAL NEWS.

Ark frowned. Upper Grimsborough? He'd never heard of it.

Together Ark and Jay walked over to the bulletin board. Pinned across were more posters like the ones Ark had seen earlier. Ark took a closer look and discovered he'd been wrong.

"These aren't wanted posters," Ark said.

"They're missing persons notices," said Jay. "A whole lot of them."

A whole lot was an understatement. The board was littered with dozens upon dozens of relatively new notices. All of them were for missing kids.

Ark felt the uncomfortable prickly sensation crawl up his neck.

"What happened in this town?" he murmured.

Ark exchanged an apprehensive glance with Jay. Without a word, they pulled off the missing persons notices, searching underneath them. They found just what Ark had been hoping for: a map of the town.

Ark rested his finger on the red dot near the center of the map, which declared YOU ARE HERE. He traced a route along the crisscrossed roads to a box labeled TO FAIRDOWN FALLS printed in the top right corner of the map, with an arrow pointing past the map's borders.

"Here," said Ark, tapping the box with his fingertip. "If we can reach the Queen's Highway from here, we can follow it to the capital. Let's go."

Jay didn't budge.

"Nuh-uh," he said. He touched the box labeled TO THE COAST in the map's bottom left corner, with an arrow pointing the opposite direction from the capital. "I'm headed this way."

Ark stared at him. "You're going to the Royal Conservatory. Obviously."

Jay raised an eyebrow. "And why should I?"

Ark couldn't believe how dense he was. "Brio's instrument resonated with you. It's your responsibility to take the mantle of the Crafter. And it's *my* duty to take you to the capital."

"Guess you're gonna fail your duty, huh?" said Jay. He started walking, sending Ark a wave over his shoulder. "See ya."

Ark stormed in front of him, raising a hand to block Jay's path. "It isn't up to you!" he spat. "Brio *chose* you. You have to come with me!"

Jay smacked Ark's hand aside and sidestepped him. "Get over yourself. You can't make me do anything."

Ark wheeled around in front of him. "Let me ask you something.

Are you really this selfish, or are you just trying to tick me off?"

Jay smirked. "Lemme ask *you* something," he countered. "Do you have to practice being a totally stuffed-up jerk, or does it come naturally?"

It was the smirk that drove Ark over the edge. Seething, he stared Jay in the eye, tilting his chin to make up for their difference in height.

"You are *not* making me fail my mission!"

"Like I care about your stupid mission!" Jay snapped. "Get lost!"

Ark wasn't sure who pushed first. All he knew was that he and Jay were locked in a struggle a moment later—Ark trying to force Jay along, Jay trying to shove him off. Jay broke away and bolted, ducking down a nearby alley. Ark caught up to him on the other side, snatching Jay's vest.

"Lay off, bum-wipe!" Jay hollered.

"Stop being an idiot!" Ark shouted back.

Jay spun and slithered free from Ark's grip—and they were at it again. Ark grabbed his arm. Jay shoved him off. Ark spat insults. Jay spewed curses. Ark lunged. Jay ducked.

They were on the brink of hurling fists when Jay stumbled.

"What the—!" he yelled, barely catching his balance—and then he went dead still. Ark froze, finally seeing what was around them:

Bodies.

More than two dozen people were lying in the street. Some were slouched against buildings. Others were sprawled out in the middle of the road. One woman was slumped in the driver's seat of her cart while her horse, still hitched to it, was happily munching on the produce at the grocer's stalls. The grocer himself was curled up on a box of cauliflower.

"By the Design," Jay gasped. He covered his mouth like a mask, cursing through his hands. "Blast, blast, blast—we gotta get outta here!"

Ark was rooted to the spot. Something was wrong with this picture. He stepped up to the closest body on the ground.

"Are you nuts?" Jay cried shrilly. "It's a contagion! It'll kill you too!"

Ark scraped his nerves together and knelt beside the woman Jay had tripped over. He touched her wrist. Then he put his hand up to her mouth.

"She's alive," he confirmed. "She's breathing and her heart's beating."

With a new sense of urgency, Ark went over to the next person on the ground, then the next.

"Everyone's alive," he said after checking the grocer on his cauliflower bed. "They're just . . . asleep. And very weak."

"Who catches Z's in the middle of the street?" said Jay.

Ark didn't get it either. He studied the residents of Upper Grimsborough snoozing around them. He'd never heard of any disease that put people to sleep so fast they collapsed right where they stood.

Unless . . .

The prickly sensation tingled along his neck. What had Callie and Dulcian talked about back in Echostrait's transit station? Sickness, quarantines . . .

Nightcreepers.

Ark was so lost in thought that he didn't hear the strangers come upon them until it was too late.

"*Now!*"

The unfamiliar voice was so loud that Ark and Jay both jumped. Before they could react, a strong hand holding a cloth masked the lower half of Ark's face. Ark thrashed and reeled in panic, but the hands holding him were much stronger than he was. Ark's eyes watered as he tried not to breathe, until he thought his lungs would burst.

A sickly, cloying scent invaded his nose and mouth, carrying bizarre aftertaste of lavender and ash. The chemical vapors sent white dots flashing through Ark's vision. He staggered—the world spun, faster and faster.

The last thing Ark saw was strange, grotesque faces surrounding them, grinning ghoulishly. Then he fell down a long, dark tunnel that had no bottom, blacking out before he hit the ground.

Chapter Sixteen

NANNY MORA'S CIRCUS

Ark's ears regained consciousness before the rest of him did.

It started as a hissing psithurism at the edge of his awareness, which slowly transformed into muffled voices. The voices grew in clarity until syllables stumbled together into words Ark understood:

"... I *said* lemme go, you creeps!"

Ark recognized that voice. His eyes blinked open.

The world was sideways. The first thing he saw was a smoking torch flickering in a dark space. Ark searched for the voice that had roused him.

Jay, leaning against a rough stone wall, was yelling at a group of shadowy figures surrounding them. Ark's heart gave a jolt. There were ghoulish faces all around, their features distorted in the torchlight.

Ark tried to sit up, then immediately wished he hadn't. His head gave an almighty throb. He groaned as he staggered to his knees.

One of the ghouls noticed him. "Wakey, wakey!" he sang out.

Ark squinted against the light piercing his eyes, taking a proper look around. At once, he realized three things.

One: He and Jay had been abducted. Ark couldn't tell where they were. Everything was dark, and the air tasted stale and flat.

Two: Brio's instrument was gone. Ark's stomach dissolved in panic. Nothing else was missing, just the case.

And three: Their ghoulish attackers were just kids. The littlest had to be only seven years old, the oldest maybe seventeen. They looked perfectly ordinary—but their smiles were almost too serene.

The vacant hole of Ark's stomach gave a sickening pull. Among the flurry of questions that skated across Ark's mind—who these kids were, what this place was, where Brio's instrument had ended up—only one sat heavily in the center of his mind:

How the gavotte would they get out of this mess?

"Hullo there," one of the older kids said to Ark. He was maybe sixteen, with sunken cheeks and clothes a little too loose for his tall frame. He tipped his rounded derby hat in a friendly gesture. "You all right?"

Ark tried to swallow. A nasty taste lingered on his tongue, left over from the chemical he'd inhaled—as if he'd licked a dry, dead toad.

"What have you done to us?" he asked.

"They're crazy!" Jay snarled. He threw his arm out in a slow, clumsy punch. "Get away!"

"Take it easy," said Derby Hat, his smile still intact. "Enervapor fumes are still affecting you. You're gonna be sluggish for a while."

"Sluggy slugs!" a small girl with pigtails piped up, giggling.

Ark stared at Derby Hat. "Enervapor? You gassed us?"

The boy nodded. "For your own good. We couldn't let you stay on the surface and catch the sickness. Nanny gave us specific instructions to bring any kids we found to the safety of the circus."

"Yeah!" the pigtail girl squeaked. "Pescific instructions!"

Ark frowned. The response only generated more questions. What did he mean by "circus"? And "on the surface"? And "Nanny"?

"Where are we?" Ark wondered aloud.

Derby Hat laughed and raised his arms. "Welcome, new friends, to Lower Grimsborough—home of Nanny Mora's Circus!"

The other kids cheered.

Ark stared at the others, then looked up. Far above, he caught sight of a rectangle of light, covered by an iron grate.

Ah. *Lower* Grimsborough. Put that together with the musty air and their dark surroundings, and the rest fell into place so neatly Ark could almost hear the *click!*

"We're underground," he declared.

"Yep!" said Derby Hat. "These old caves run under the town. It's the only place the sickness won't get us. Nanny said so." He pointed to his chest. "Nanny calls me Sugar," he said. He gestured one by one to the other kids. "This is Honey, Peanut, Pepper, Cherry, Crisp, Cream, and Tart. You'll meet the others later. First, we'll bring you to Nanny."

Ark was trying to work out whether those could be their real names when Jay rose. His eyes were ice.

"You're not taking me anywhere," he snarled. "Now let me go."

The boy Sugar shook his head. "It's for your own good. You'll see."

Just then Pepper and Peanut grabbed Ark and hauled him along, while Crisp and Cream took control of Jay. Sugar held the torch, and soon the whole group of kids headed deeper into Lower Grimsborough.

"No!" Jay howled, trying to pull away.

Ark's body was still tingly from the enervapor fumes, so he knew it was pointless to try to shake the kids off. Instead, he stayed quiet, studying the kids escorting them through the caverns. They all looked inexplicably happy, if not a bit grubby. Like Sugar, their clothes hung loose, like they hadn't eaten in a while. But they went along in a euphoric daze, completely carefree.

The little pigtailed girl walked near Ark's side. He called to her.

"Um—Cherry?"

She turned to him, her gaze bright and vacant.

"Do you know where my case is?" Ark asked. "A black leather case, with a golden crest on the side? About this big?" He gestured with his hands.

"Oh, that?" said Cherry. "We left it behind in the tunnels."

"Where?" Ark pressed.

Cherry giggled. Then she peeled off, doing cartwheels as she went.

Ark stifled a sigh. So much for that approach.

Jay, who'd finally stopped trying to break free from the clutches of Crisp and Cream, turned to Ark, his voice a murmur. "Is it just me, or is something seriously wrong with these kids?"

Ark glanced around at the smiling kids. "It isn't just you."

Jay lowered his voice even further. "So, what's the plan? Jump 'em when they lower their guard and run for the exit?"

Ark sent him a dry look. "What exit?"

While Jay struggled to come up with a response, Sugar paused, raising a hand. "Here we are!"

Ark looked out, barely managing to keep his jaw from dropping.

Before them was an enormous underground cavern, so wide and open that Ark couldn't tell where the far side was. Stalactites hung from the ceiling like permanent icicles, and stalagmites lined the ground like stone sentries. Natural paths through the cavern were lit by countless torches, chasing away the subterranean gloom. Ark almost felt like he'd been brought to a giant, glittering ballroom.

"What the heck is that?" said Jay, pointing.

Ark followed Jay's gesture. In the middle of the cavern floor, flooded with light from dozens of torches, a huge empty ring was surrounded by a large crowd of young spectators. It looked just like—

"A circus," Ark and Jay said together. They glanced at each other, then looked on in amazement as Sugar's group led them closer.

There were easily a couple hundred kids watching performers in the ring. Ark saw some boys marveling at a giant man hoisting huge dumbbells over his head. A flock of girls applauded a group of lithe acrobats doing flips. One group was enthralled by a magician performing magic tricks, while others stared as a woman contorted her body into spine-wrenching poses. There were jugglers, clowns, and a lion tamer, too—and everywhere Ark turned, he saw the same smile of pure bliss on each kid's face.

Ark's eyes couldn't take it all in. A bona fide circus, underground. It didn't make sense. And yet here it was.

Sugar and his fellows hauled Ark and Jay right through the circus. None of the other kids spared them a passing glance. Their group cut between the jugglers and the acrobats toward a large canvas tent.

Sugar called out: "Nanny!"

A few moments later, a woman stepped out of the tent. She reminded Ark of the nurses at Echostrait. She wore a white frock that looked out of place in a cavern. She was small, with long hair that hung in a loose braid. She looked thin too, and weary—but even so, she was pretty. Ark tried not to gawp.

"What is it, Sugar?" she said. "New arrivals?"

She stepped over, reaching toward Jay. At once Jay recoiled, making Cream and Crisp stagger. "Back off, witch!"

The woman didn't react. "Let me look at you."

Jay edged further away. Ark stepped in.

"Pardon me, ma'am—who are you?" he asked.

The woman faced him. Her lips formed a half-smile, gentle and amused. "I'm Nockna Mora. But the children call me Nanny."

Ark's ears twitched. *Nockna Mora.* Why did that name sound familiar? Its significance floated in the vaults of his memory, but he couldn't retrieve it. He let it go for now. "And just what is this place?"

Nanny lifted her hands toward the cavern ceiling. "Sickness took Upper Grimsborough so quickly. Mothers and fathers collapsed where they stood. Someone had to look after the children. So I brought them here, to my circus."

"You put this together?" said Ark, gesturing toward the circus performers. "All of it? How?"

The half-smile crept onto her face again. "I can tell you all about it," she said, reaching toward him. "Let me examine you first."

It wasn't adding up—the sickness, the circus, none of it—but then Nanny touched his arm, and Ark felt his suspicions wash away. She was just a kind woman, trying to protect everyone. He could trust her, right?

Nanny's smile widened as Ark stepped closer. She placed her hands on either side of his head and inspected his eyes and ears. Ark stuck out his tongue when she asked, so she could check his throat.

"A fine specimen," she murmured.

Ark wasn't sure how to respond—but then Nanny placed her hands on either side of his head.

Ark stiffened. "What are you—?"

"It's all right," she said, "this will only take a moment."

Ark felt his muscles relax as a strange sound—high and ethereal, like a singing crystal goblet—whispered into his ears. It wasn't a loud sound, but somehow it drowned out the clamor of the circus.

"Mmm," hummed Nanny in an undertone. "The essence is salty, yet sweet. Complex. *Caramel.*"

Ark barely heard her, much less understood. A warm, gooey sensation dribbled through his mind, and his noisy thoughts were hushed, lost in the goo. He felt his body sink into the mysterious sound.

Jay smacked Nanny's hands away from Ark. Ark staggered.

"What're you trying to pull?" Jay snapped.

Nanny stared. "I am not hurting him," she reassured him, putting a hand on his shoulder. Her nose crinkled. "Ah. *Chocolate.* Delightful."

Jay threw off her hand, which seemed to surprise her.

161

"Trying to hypnotize us like you did them?" he spat, pointing at the kids. "You don't fool me, you witch!"

Nanny's face shone with a gentle smile. "This circus is for you." She gestured all around. "All children are happy here."

Ark's ears were still pulsing with echoes of the uncanny sound. He shook his head a few times, then rounded on Jay.

"Stop calling her a witch," he hissed. "What's wrong with you?"

Jay stared at him incredulously.

"What's wrong with *you?*" he spat back. He pointed. "Don't you see it?"

Ark followed Jay's finger toward the cavern floor—and then he finally understood what Jay was talking about. He gasped.

Based on the position of the nearest torch, Nanny's shadow should have been to her left. Instead, she had a dozen shadows, all stretching in various directions. Her shadows were connected to the strongman, the contortionist, the acrobats, and all the other circus performers.

Icy terror flooded Ark's veins, freezing his blood. His mind pleaded with his eyes, begging them to be wrong—but his eyes couldn't deny what they were seeing. Fear pulsed through his chest.

Please, no. Please, please, please.

Nanny glanced down at the impossible shadow at her feet, then back up at Jay. Her gentle eyes had gone sharp.

"You can see it?" she said in a hiss. "That is . . . unexpected."

Ark felt her glare, but he didn't dare meet her eyes now. Instead he kept his gaze fixed on her feet, following his old training.

Not like it was going to help him. They'd stumbled right into the heart of its lair. It wouldn't let them escape now.

"No matter," the pretend Nanny went on. "Soon you won't remember. Chocolate and Caramel—two more for my indulgence."

A dreadful laugh escaped Nanny's mouth, shrill and cruel—then, just as suddenly, she fell silent, staring at Ark's talaris.

"Musician," she said, eyes widening in realization. "You're a *Musician!*"

Her voice carried through the cavern.

The circus performers froze mid-act. The cheers and laughter of the kids stopped as if someone had clicked off a wireless. All fell silent.

Then, in a blink, the circus performers shrank to the ground. The shadows raced across the cavern floor like black snakes back to Nanny, where they merged and formed a dark pool beneath her.

At the same time, the children all straightened like puppets on strings. As one synchronized horde, they turned toward Ark and Jay. They were no longer smiling. Their faces were empty, blank.

"Take them away!" Nanny howled in a harrowing shriek. Her face was twisted like a beast's, revealing the monster within. Her voice became a terrible hiss: "*Take them away, take them away, take them away! Throw them into the pit! Let them rot in the dark!*"

The horde of kids moved as one. Jay tried to run in one direction, Ark in another—but there were too many of them. The kids circled until all Ark could see were glazed eyes.

Sugar was at the front of the horde, bearing a torch.

"Sugar!" Ark tried, shouting the boy's name. "Snap out of it!"

The boy slowly turned his head. His face was a hollow shell.

"*Take them away, Sugar,*" Nanny hissed.

Despite Jay's furious kicks and Ark's pleas, Sugar and the other children forced them along, one after the other. The ceiling dropped and the cavern shadows deepened, flickering in the torchlight. Lower Grimsborough was closing in around them.

Then, from ahead, Jay cried out, digging his heels into the ground. "No!"

Ark saw why he'd pushed back. Before them, the cavern floor fell away into a gaping hole. Ark stared down into the pit. There was no sign of a bottom, only empty blackness.

The kids pressed forward, shoving Jay closer to the edge.

"Stop!" Ark shouted—but no use. Ark watched as Jay lost his footing and fell backwards with a yelp, disappearing into the dark.

Ark stared into the pit, too shocked to move. His heart raced in terror. Jay was gone—and he was next.

The kids turned to face him. Ark fought to hold his ground, but his feet slid too easily on the loose rocks. They soon had him at the pit's edge.

"Sugar, please!" Ark shouted, barely keeping his balance. "Don't do this! You're mesmerized!"

For just a moment, Sugar and the other kids stopped pressing forward.

"Nockna Mora is controlling you!" Ark yelled, searching their faces for any sign that his words had reached them. "Fight back!"

The horde of children stared at him with empty gazes. A cold wave of dread rushed over Ark as Sugar stepped up, a serene smile on his face.

"It's for your own good," said Sugar—and he shoved Ark over the edge, down into the pit.

Chapter Seventeen

TROUBLE

*A*s lousy as the last few minutes had been, nothing was worse in Jay's mind than free-falling through pitch blackness.

At least it wasn't a long fall. He fell for maybe a second before he landed flat on his back.

Jay coughed, then rolled onto his side and sat up. It was a hard landing, but nothing felt broken or out of joint. Thank the Design for that.

He'd just about regained his feet when, from above, Ark started shouting. There was a scuffling sound of feet sliding on loose rock, and then—

Whomph!

Ark fell smack on top of him, knocking Jay back to the ground. Jay's head hit the stone, stars dancing across his vision.

"Get off!" Jay wheezed.

Ark scrambled over to the side of the pit, staring up to the edge. Jay could hear the mindless mob of kid puppets shuffling away, taking the only source of light with them.

"Come back!" Ark shouted. "*Come back!*"

No use. The torchlight faded and blackness filled the pit, wrapping them in pure, smothering darkness.

Jay closed his eyes, trying not to freak out. The only things that kept him from panicking were the reassuring touch of solid stone against his back and the sound of his own breathing: in, out, in, out.

"All right, stay calm, stay calm," came Ark's voice through the dark.

"There has to be a way out."

Jay winced as he pushed himself upright; his body felt like a sack of bruised apples. "Thanks for landing on me. Real swell of you."

"Well, now we're even," said Ark. "Shut up and let me think."

Jay scowled. "Should've known getting stuck with a bum-wipe like you would've ended with me in a rank whiz pit like this."

Ark didn't respond. Jay clumsily felt his way to the nearest wall, ticking off his mental checklist. Was he alive? Check. Was Ark a total jerk? Check. Were they in a huge heap of trouble?

Triple check.

Jay ran his hands along the rock wall, blindly investigating. The wall was carved smooth and went straight up. There were no crags he could find to serve as handholds or footholds. Climbing out? Not an option.

Jay clapped his hands once, listening. The echoes told his ears that the pit wasn't all that deep. Maybe, if they worked together, he and Ark could help each other scramble up and out of this hole. Then they could somehow get out of this cavern, with its creepy witch and her demented little puppets—

Jay's thoughts broke off as a growl, low and menacing, rumbled through the dark.

Jay's heartbeat stumbled a few paces. He'd been so focused on getting out that he hadn't considered something else could be down here with them. And by the sound of that growl, that *something else* was none too friendly.

Aw, bandersnatches.

"What was that?" Ark whispered, too loudly.

The creature growled again.

"*Shh!*" Jay hissed. He crouched and listened, groping for a loose rock in case he had to defend himself.

But before he found a likely weapon, a different voice spoke in the dark.

"Easy, girl. It's okay. No biting."

The low growls stopped.

"Who's there?" called Ark.

The voice didn't answer immediately. Jay heard a quiet shuffling from the far side of the pit. Then the stranger finally spoke up.

"Sorry. Didn't mean to spook you. I kept quiet 'cause I wasn't sure who else had been thrown down here with us."

The voice belonged to a boy. He had a quick, lilting accent.

"Us?" echoed Ark.

"Hotah and me," said the boy. "Hotah's my mate. Say hello, girl."

There was a loud bark followed by a steady *thump-thump-thump* on the ground. Hotah—a dog, Jay figured—was probably wagging her tail.

"Down here, I'm called Trouble," the boy added.

Jay almost snorted. "That's your name?"

"Nope," said Trouble. "But I can't remember my real name."

That shut Jay up.

"That Nanny woman . . . did something to me," said Trouble in the silence. "I don't know what. She put her hands on my head and said I was 'Trouble'—as in 'not worth the trouble.' And now I don't know my name or how I got down here in the first place. I can still remember Hotah's name, though."

Hotah barked again.

"Did she take your names, too?" said Trouble.

Jay shook his head before remembering that no one could see him. "Nuh-uh. She tried to, I think." He pointed to himself—another stupid gesture. "My name's Jay. The other voice over there is Ark."

"Arkalin," Ark corrected. "We're Musicians. That's why Nanny had us thrown down here."

"Musicians, nice," said Trouble. He sighed. "You're lucky. I've tried for ages to remember what my name is. Feels like I've walked into a night-mare."

Ark gasped like he'd been electrocuted.

"What?" said Jay, alarmed.

"Nightmare," said Ark. "*That's* what it means!"

Jay frowned in the direction of Ark's voice. "What means what, now?"

"*Nockna Mora*," said Ark. "I've just remembered. It means 'night-mare.'"

"Nanny Nightmare?" Trouble chuckled. "Could've told you that, mate."

Jay turned toward Trouble's voice. "Why did that witch throw *you* down here? Did you see her shadows too?"

"I don't know anything about shadows," said Trouble. "It's 'cause I caught her arguing with herself."

Jay blinked against the black. "That's it?"

"I thought it was two people at first, 'cause I heard two different voices speaking," Trouble went on. "One was like Nanny's own voice, but the other sounded harsh and rasping—like if a snake could talk."

Trouble paused. Jay and Ark waited for him to continue.

"Nanny was begging with the snake, saying she didn't want this anymore—but the snake said she had no choice," Trouble continued. He then spoke in an eerie voice: "*You're not in charge, Augusta. I am.*"

Jay shuddered.

"After that, she caught me listening, and that's when I found out there was no one else with her, and she was just arguing with herself," said Trouble. "Then she stole my name and threw me down here. I don't even know how much time has passed since. A couple days, maybe."

"You've been down here for *days?*" said Ark. "Alone? In the dark?"

"The dark doesn't bother me," said Trouble. "And I wasn't alone—I had Hotah. But I could go for some food, if you've got it."

The injustice of it all made Jay's ears burn. "She really is a witch!"

Trouble hummed. "Or she's insane."

"You're both wrong," said Ark. "She's possessed by a dischord."

He spoke quietly, but the word "dischord" echoed through the pit. The word immediately made Jay think of the Unraveling Man. The memory sent a nasty shiver down his spine.

"The signs line up," Ark went on. "Dischords can infiltrate a place if there aren't muses to guard it. Upper Grimsborough is a highly developed town. When they built it, they probably cleared out all the trees and natural spots without thinking to preserve some. Without dedicated spaces for muses or a Musician around to interact with them, the muses' connection to this place was greatly weakened. A dischord could have easily come here and overshadowed someone."

Jay heard Ark idly pacing, his footsteps echoing across the pit.

"And where dischords are, sickness follows," he continued. "Dischords feed on the vitality of living things. The people of this town felt the effects of the dischord's presence like a disease—that's why they set up the quarantine. Meanwhile, as the people grew weaker, the dischord grew stronger—until the entire population collapsed where they stood, too weak to move."

"And it's Nanny's fault?" said Jay, barely following. "Is she a . . ." He struggled with the word. "A Dischordian?"

"A Dischordian?" asked Trouble. "What's that?"

"Dischordians are the opposite of Musicians," said Ark, taking on an *allow-me-to-explain* tone of voice. "Musicians and Dischordians both summon spiritual beings—but that's where any similarity ends. Musicians and muses work together in a spirit of mutual giving. There's no ownership or control involved. Musicians study and perform music skills to communicate with muses because muses love harmony; muses in turn come at a Musician's call and lend their powers to carry out the Musician's requests. A Musician would never ask a muse to carry out a request that would go against its nature to create and protect, like killing or mindless destruction.

"But Dischordians are different," he went on. "Dischordians enter a ritual contract with dischords. Once the contract is sealed, a Dischordian can use the power of dischords however they choose: to extend their life, gain wealth, even murder. But there's a price. In exchange the Dischordian gives the dischords free reign over themselves—body, mind, will. Gradually the Dischordian loses their sense of individuality, and they come to hate anything to do with music. They especially can't stand Musicians and often attack them. Unless the dischord is exorcised, the Dischordian will eventually be totally consumed."

Jay swallowed. Hard to believe somebody would willingly choose such a lousy deal.

"But a dischord doesn't need a contract to overshadow someone who's vulnerable," Ark finished. "That's probably what happened to this woman, Augusta. She probably happened to cross Nockna Mora's path at the wrong time, in a moment of weakness, and it took her over. It'll control her until it gets what it wants."

"You sure know a lot," said Trouble. "What does the thing want?"

Ark hesitated.

"A long-term host," he said quietly. "Nockna Mora will consume the life from its current host all too quickly. Before then, the dischord will need to find someone else to possess, someone with plenty of energy to feed on." He paused. "Why else would a dischord lure so many children to its lair?"

The question sunk in. Chills washed over Jay. Trouble spat a curse.

"And once it takes its new host, Nockna Mora will consume the remaining kids," said Ark. "There will officially be nothing left of this town. Nockna Mora will then force its new host to wander until it finds another town to devour—and the pattern will start all over again."

As Ark finished, Jay found himself on his feet. The ever-present darkness was crushing him on all sides, and the mental images he'd created from Ark's words were impossible for him to shut out.

"That can't happen!" he declared. "We've got to do something!"

Jay heard Ark scoff.

"Like what?" said Ark. "It's us against a dischord, plus every kid it's mesmerized. That's three against a couple hundred."

"So we're just gonna let Nanny Nightmare win?" Jay spat. "Forget that!"

Ark's voice climbed in volume. "We are completely outmatched," he snapped. "If we try to challenge Nockna Mora, we won't save anyone. We'll lose everything. Because that's what happens when you cross a dischord—*people die!*"

He ended at a shout. The last two words ricocheted off the stone walls:

People die, people die, people die.

Jay didn't know what to say. He couldn't be sure, but it sounded like Ark was talking from experience. Maybe he'd dealt with dischords before.

"We can't fight Nockna Mora," Ark finished. "Not without muses to help. We need to report this to the Maestrans Council. Only a top-level Musician could banish a dischord as strong as this one."

"That's not good enough!" said Jay. "By that time, it'll be too late!"

"What other choice do we have?" Ark retorted.

"Well," said Trouble, intervening, "we won't have any choices until we get out of this pit, yeah? Luckily, with three of us, that should be easy."

His words ended Ark and Jay's argument in a blink. With careful, scuffle-shuffle steps, Trouble came to their side of the pit. His footsteps told Jay he'd walked right up to the rock wall.

"I'm about five 'n' a half steps tall," he said. "Which of you is taller?"

Jay could practically hear Ark scowl in the dark. "I am," said Jay.

"All right," said Trouble. "Then you and me will be here at the wall. You'll help me onto your shoulders, then we'll both help Ark climb out. Then Ark pulls me up and over, and we'll both reach down to get you. Sound good?"

"What about your dog?" said Ark.

"Hotah's a thoroughbred Southin lycalcyon," said Trouble. "She can get out on her own."

Hotah gave a confident bark, her tail *thump-thump*ing the floor.

"So," said Trouble, his tone changing. "I think I can trust you two. But I'm relying on you guys not to ditch me 'n' Hotah. Yeah?"

Jay didn't know whether to feel surprised or offended. "Are you kidding? Why would you even worry about that?"

"Because I can't see," said Trouble.

"None of us can see," said Jay. "It's pitch black."

Trouble laughed softly. "That isn't—"

"We're wasting time," Ark interrupted, exasperated.

Jay shot a pointless glare in Ark's direction, then made his way over. He bumped into another person.

"Hey, there you are," said Trouble. "Give me a boost."

Jay set his feet and braced himself against the wall. After a couple awkward bumps, Trouble stepped on Jay's folded hands, and Jay hoisted him up. There was an awful moment when Trouble wobbled and almost fell backward, but he recovered his balance on Jay's shoulders.

"Blast, this is hard," said Jay. If he could just see what he was doing!

"I can feel the top!" said Trouble. "Ark, you ready?"

Ark managed to kick Jay in the shins and smack him in the face—*by accident*, he claimed—before he made the slow, painful climb. By the time Ark was halfway up, Jay could feel his legs turning to jelly.

"Take your time, bum-wipe," he grumbled.

"In case you didn't realize, this is almost impossible!" Ark snapped back.

Every muscle in Jay's body was burning by the time Ark pulled himself over the edge of the pit. "Hurry up!" he grunted.

Ark pulled Trouble out, and Jay's legs buckled in relief. While he rested, he heard Hotah give a happy *woof!*—and then she dashed across the pit.

With eager snuffling and wildly scratching claws, the dog jumped her way to the top.

"Ready, Jay?" called Trouble. "We're reaching down."

Jay pushed himself up and stretched his arms as far as he could. He tried jumping. It took a dozen tries before Ark and Trouble snatched Jay's wrists at the same time. They pulled while Jay used his legs to scramble up along the rock wall, until Jay at last tumbled over the edge.

"We made it!" cheered Trouble. Hotah gave a bark.

"And it's still pitch black," said Ark cynically. "Hooray."

Jay waved a hand in front of his face. He hated being blind down here.

"What now?" asked Ark. "We can't risk wandering around and falling into another pit. Jay and I were knocked out before we were taken here. And Trouble, you said you don't remember how you got down here. So how are we supposed to get to the surface?"

Jay felt around his pockets. "I've got spark stones. If we had something to burn, we could make a torch. Ark, gimme your jacket."

"You're not burning my talaris," said Ark.

"No need," said Trouble. "*I* may not remember how I got down here—but Hotah does. She's smart. You two, grab hold."

Jay wasn't sold on the idea of following a dog, no matter how smart she was, but he sure as heck didn't have any other ideas.

Jay took Trouble's shoulder. Ark grabbed Jay's elbow. Trouble whistled in a pattern; Hotah responded with a *woof* and sniffed around, padding forward. Soon they all started off, shuffling in a line.

After some minutes of shuffle-walking, Ark spoke up.

"Is that light?"

It was. Gradually Jay's eyes could make out the outlines of stalagmites and stalactites, which grew more distinct the closer they got to the light. Soon they stumbled into a shaft of pure sunlight, shining in through a rectangular vent high above. It was too far up to be an escape route—*blast*—but at least they were no longer in the dark.

"Found your bearings, yeah?" asked Trouble.

In the light, Jay studied the boy. Trouble was around Jay's height, with a deep russet brown complexion like his own and shaggy black hair woven into a short braid behind his head. He wore lightweight clothes that Jay recognized as Southin-made, including a wide belt along his waist, with colorful glass beads sewn on it. Next to Trouble was a creature with a blend of orange and silver-gray fur. Hotah looked like a mix between a wolf and a fox, with a soft bushy tail, long pointed ears, slender yellow eyes, and a fang-filled canine grin.

Jay was about to ask Trouble how Hotah knew what path to follow—but then he did a double-take. Trouble's eyelids were fused closed.

"Wait," Jay sputtered. "Trouble, you—are you *blind?*"

Trouble flashed a grin. "Took you awhile to pick up on that."

Ark snorted. "Idiot."

Heat fanned through Jay's cheeks. He was about to tell Ark to go jump back into the pit when Hotah gave a low *woof!*—and then, whimpering, she nuzzled Trouble's hand, her ears flat. The grin fell from Trouble's face.

"She's agitated," he said. "Someone might be nearby."

"Let's move," said Ark.

Trouble whistled softly. Hotah sniffed the ground—and then she was off, Trouble keeping pace. Ark followed behind.

Jay steeled himself. With one last look at the shaft of sunlight, he set his jaw and followed, back into the dark.

Chapter Eighteen

BRIGHT IDEAS

Jay didn't know whether the second trip into the dark was better or worse than the first. The blackness felt heavier than before, like a suffocating blanket. Occasionally, though, they passed clusters of glowing crystals nestled along the rock wall, shining yellow, green, blue, and violet. Ark called it *fosfer essence*. Jay had never heard of a fosfer before, but it sure was pretty.

They made their way in near silence, following the sound of Hotah's paws and Trouble's quiet directions: "Step up here . . . this way . . . hang left . . ."

Jay took up the rear, antsy to find the exit, wherever it was—but he had no idea what he was supposed to do once they got there. He still had his original plan: make it to the coast, get on a boat, and ditch his debt with the Capo for good.

But he didn't think he could leave this town knowing that hundreds of kids were about to become Nanny Nightmare's dinner.

He had to do something.

Jay was still trying to work out what that something was when a soft noise made him freeze in his tracks. It was coming from behind.

"Guys," he whispered, "did you hear—?"

Then his voice died.

Come.

The perfect music breathed over him like a gentle gust of wind. It swirled through his brain, the rush making him feel lightheaded.

But that wasn't all. Jay rubbed his eyes, thinking he was seeing things—but when he opened them again, it was still there: a ribbon of golden light, hovering in midair. It unfurled behind him, rippling and pulsing like a beacon.

"Ark, are you seeing this?" said Jay, glancing back.

Wuh-oh. He'd stopped too long. Jay turned in time to see Ark and Trouble disappear around a bend ahead.

Jay glanced between the slender ribbon of light and the dark path Ark and Trouble had just gone down. Great. What was he supposed to do now?

Before he could decide for himself, the perfect music washed over him again, louder this time. He felt a strange pull in his chest—the same sensation he'd felt when he'd run through Hazeldenn's groves to escape the Unraveling Man. The music tugged at him—insistent, relentless.

Julian. Come.

Jay spun on his heel and followed the pull, chasing the ribbon of light.

The ribbon danced and flickered ahead of him, always just beyond his reach, guiding him along. Jay backtracked until he reached a narrow path in the stone, so tight that he had to squeeze through sideways. On the other side, he found himself in a manmade tunnel carved from the rock. The dusty floor was marked by dozens of footprints.

Jay knelt, studying the tracks. This must've been the way he and Ark had been brought down here. If he followed the tracks, he'd find the exit!

But the tug in his chest wasn't pulling him straight down the tunnel; he felt it tugging him toward the left. The golden ribbon curled along the ceiling before it seemed to disappear straight into the wall.

Jay rose and followed it. He found a crevice in the stone wall, camouflaged by the shadows. The ribbon of light flickered brightly as soon as Jay reached his hand inside. His fingertips landed on leather.

Come.

Jay was compelled to obey, pulling out the black case. The case itself wasn't glowing, but there was golden light shining inside it, seeping out through the crack of the lid. Jay never would've found the case here on his own, not in a million years. The fiddle didn't want to be lost.

Jay spread his hand over the case. Inside, the golden light pulsed, and the perfect music responded to his presence; he felt it soften and lean into his touch, like a purring cat asking for its ears to be scratched.

Jay flinched, pulling his hand away. Nuh-uh. Whatever mystical, musical power this was, Jay didn't trust it. He didn't trust muses, period.

The perfect music turned petulant, apparently miffed that Jay had withdrawn his hand. Then, just like a spooked cat, the perfect music broke off, fleeing. The golden light dimmed to almost nothing.

In the sudden dark and quiet, Jay went still, his own breathing loud against the shivery silence.

Then, closer than Jay would've guessed, he heard the uproar.

Jay froze. He backed into the crevice, melting into the shadows, and listened. There were voices—lots of them—laughing, yelling, screeching. But above the ruckus, he heard a loud, frightened howl.

Jay gasped. *Hotah*.

Oh, no.

Jay pulled away from the shadows, peering out. He saw firelight from torches a bit farther down the tunnel, casting slithery shadows from around a corner. If the brainwashed kids were here, the witch couldn't be far.

Jay swallowed the sour taste in his mouth—then, clutching the black case to his chest, he crept down the tunnel, keeping to the shadows as best he could. The closer he got, the louder the voices became, until—

"Hush, morsels."

The voices fell silent at once. Jay ducked low and peeked around the corner. He almost cursed aloud.

Ark and Trouble were there, with Hotah between them. Sugar, Cherry, and the whole mob of brainwashed kids had trapped them on all sides. Nanny Nightmare stood among the throng, shaking her head.

"What naughty brats," said Nanny. "I must find a deeper pit."

"Go ahead," said Trouble. "And then throw yourself in it."

Nanny barely spared him a glance. "Sightless one," she sneered. "Mortals breed offspring with such repulsive defects and yet allow them to live. I cannot fathom it. I will do your kind a favor by consuming you."

Trouble's fierce expression cracked.

"Augusta," said Ark in a shaky voice, "are you there?"

Nanny snapped her head toward Ark. She laughed in a high, nasty way.

"*Augusta is gone*," she jeered—but it wasn't Nanny's voice. The foul voice was just as Trouble had described it: like a snake, primed to strike.

"Augusta!" Ark called, louder. "Answer me!"

"*It's no use,*" hissed the snake voice. "*Augusta will never—*"

But then the snake broke off. Jay followed Nanny's glare and saw her hand flapping uncontrollably at her side. The snake snarled, and Nanny grabbed her own hand and forced it to stop.

"*We have no time for this,*" hissed the snake. "*Where is Chocolate?*"

Trouble's face was blank. Ark blinked at her.

"*The other child! The one with eyes that see too much!*" she spat. She paced in front of them, impatient. "*I never let free food escape. Tell me where he is, and I will make your end a merciful one.*"

Jay's pulse churned. If any of her minions stepped too far in his direction, he'd be caught. And then he'd become dessert.

Which meant he had to leave now and escape to the surface while Nanny's attention was elsewhere.

Your chance, his sensible side whispered. *This is it! Run!*

Jay snuck another glance around the corner at Ark and Trouble, feeling a twinge of conscience. If he ran, they'd pay the price, wouldn't they?

He cursed under his breath. What choice did he have? It wouldn't do them any good if he got caught too. If he made it out, he could find help and rescue them. Miracles happened.

Jay bet Ark would do the same thing in his place. Ark would leave him behind for the chance to find help. It wasn't an easy thing, but in this case, maybe it was the right thing.

But if it was right, why did it feel so wrong?

Jay squeezed the case. Bandersnatches! What was he supposed to do?

Caught under the twisty dilemma, Jay almost didn't hear Ark's reply: "Sorry, Nockna Mora. Jay already escaped."

All the whirring thoughts in Jay's brain screeched to a halt.

Huh?

Nanny clutched Ark's chin, jerking his face upward. "You're lying."

Ark forced a laugh—and then his eyes flashed in Jay's direction. He held Jay's gaze for just a heartbeat; then he turned to Nanny, his face defiant.

"Even if he were still here, I wouldn't sell him out," he declared. "But Jay did find a way out. Looks like he's off the menu."

Nanny's face blistered with fury. She screeched in outrage.

Jay ducked around the corner, exhaling a shuddery breath. Ark's look had only lasted for a second, but his message had been clear:

Go. Now.

Jay felt a weight in his chest. Ark had made Jay's decision for him: Leave them behind.

Still fixed in place, Jay leaned around the corner for one last look. Nanny had stepped right up to Ark, raking clawed hands through his hair.

"Well. At least I have you, Musician. We'll have so much fun."

Jay gulped. Nanny made "fun" sound like a death sentence.

"Do your worst," said Ark—but his bravado was ruined by the tremor in his voice. Ark's pale face had gone ashen.

Nanny flashed a disturbing smile. "You will make a fine vessel."

Ark's eyes widened in terror.

"No!" Trouble yelled.

Nanny stroked Ark's face. Ark flinched.

"*Annstoss!*" he chanted desperately.

Nanny laughed. "No muse can save you. Stop fighting."

She clasped a hand behind Ark's head, forcing him closer, and lay her other hand over his face and smiled, dark eyes glinting.

Jay didn't think about what he was doing. He didn't even realize he'd decided to move until he'd burst out from around the corner. He charged straight through the kids, yelling and swinging the case like a battering ram. Nanny snapped her head in Jay's direction just as he careened into her.

"Back off!" Jay hollered.

Nanny clumsily regained her feet, whirling around.

"Filthy child!" she screeched. "They said you escaped!"

"Like I'd ever ditch them!" Jay spat. He was sorry he'd been tempted.

"How noble," she sneered. "Now you can all be eaten together. But first, I will claim my new vessel."

The brainwashed kids cut off the exits.

Jay swallowed hard. Come to think of it, he didn't actually have a plan to get out of this. He'd only been trying to stop Nanny from possessing Ark. And she was at it again, zeroing in on him.

Julian.

The moment Jay registered the perfect music calling to him, a thought dropped so abruptly into his brain that he felt a shiver race from the hairs on his neck to his toes. He glanced at the case in his arms.

"I'd like to see you try!" Jay blurted before he could stop himself. He held the case up. "Don't make me use this! You'll be sorry!"

Ark gaped at him, dumbfounded. Nanny didn't even twitch.

Cursing himself for following such a stupid impulse, Jay opened the case and took out the fiddle.

"Ha!" Nanny cackled. "What a fearsome instrument!"

She didn't look the slightest bit intimidated. Not surprising, really. In the torchlight, the scuffed white fiddle looked even more pathetic than Jay remembered—like any knock would shatter it to splinters.

"What will you do, attack me with a jig?" sneered Nanny. "No muse will answer you here."

Her scathing words reminded Jay of what the Unraveling Man had told him, stirring up doubts: *You're no Crafter. You're not even a Musician. You're a mistake.*

Jay shook his head, forcing out the echoes. None of that mattered. He'd gotten what he wanted: Nanny's attention. He'd be duffered if he wasted this chance.

Jay shot Ark a sharp look, meeting his gaze. He tilted his head toward Trouble, then jerked his chin upward. He hoped Ark got the message.

You two. Go.

Then Jay picked up the bow and clutched the fiddle's neck in a death grip, his fingers fumbling on the strings.

"This should be good," Nanny hissed with a nasty laugh.

Jay's heart galloped like a terrified stallion, his blood pounding. He didn't know what to do next. Nanny was leaning toward him, her eyes gleaming with hunger. At once Jay forgot how to move, to think, to breathe.

"Do it, Jay!" Ark shouted. "Play!"

Startled, Jay pulled the bow across the strings without thinking.

The fiddle sang out a majestic note, clarion clear through the cavern. The single note rang through Jay's being, clearing his head. He remembered the last time he'd played the fiddle: letting his instincts take over, following the perfect music's lead. He remembered the fiddle's dance under his touch, the warmth of its voice, the strength of its Resonance.

Nanny's smile vanished. She stared at Jay as he played on, like she couldn't look away.

Somehow, as Jay played on, he felt calm. The perfect music pervaded the cavern with a sound no earthly instrument could've made. Each note folded neatly into the next, the whole of it sharp and smooth together like an icy mountain runoff cascading into a deep, sun-warmed lake.

Nanny snarled in pain. She clawed at her chest.

"*Stop*," she hissed, face contorted in agony. "Stop it! Stop him!"

The brainwashed kids snapped their heads up as one, coming for him with vacant faces. Hotah leapt, knocking a few back with a snarl. Trouble took a position beside the lycalcyon, ready to knock some heads. Ark flanked Jay from the other side, a stray rock in his hands.

"Finish it!" said Ark, struggling to block Sugar's tackle.

Jay gave everything over to the fiddle, letting its power sing through him. The fiddle thrummed with energy, so warm that Jay's hands were starting to feel the sting.

Then a golden light burst out of the fiddle's center, shining as brightly as a shooting star through the cavern. The light soared high, then tapered to a point, drawing back like an arrow toward Nanny.

Nanny recoiled, her face twisted.

"*Brio?*" the snake inside her gasped in horror. "*No!*"

Jay cringed against her screeches, struggling to play on. Drops of sweat ran down his face. He felt the perfect music taking aim.

Then, with a burst of power and harmony, the golden light shot forward. Nanny wailed, shielding herself. Jay struck the final note.

The golden light pierced Nanny's chest. She arced backward, eyes wide. The light filled her, making her glow from within.

FWOOM!

There was a thrum of deep pressure. Something else was pushed out of Nanny, thrashing and convulsing. The dark thing dissolved in the light with tormented shrieks.

And then, it was gone.

The percussive blast nearly knocked Jay off his feet. He felt the pressure wave overtake him, then pull him in like a riptide, overcoming his senses.

Augusta sat at someone's bedside, her face creased with concern—she mopped the sick person's forehead—

Jay blinked against the vision, disoriented. What was this?

Before he understood what was happening, the vision shifted:

Augusta stood before a council, arguing with stern-faced men—"There is no cure! The children should be protected! They must be sent away!"

Jay barely grasped what he was seeing when the scene changed again:

Augusta knelt before a grave, weeping in frustration—someone from the shadows called to her—"Why do you cry?"—Augusta clenched her teeth—"I must take the children!"—the stranger agreed—"Yes, we will take the children!"—Augusta couldn't even scream as a black shadow overtook her . . .

Jay gasped, snapping out of the vision.

"*Jay!*" Ark was shouting, shaking his shoulder. "Can you hear me?"

Jay shook himself from his daze. He was still in Lower Grimsborough. The kids were looking around in confusion, like they'd been lost in a dream.

Beside them, Trouble gave a loud *whoop!* of joy.

"Andi!" he cheered, pumping his fists in the air.

Jay blinked. "What?"

"I've remembered my real name!" said Trouble. He held a fist to his chest. "I'm Andi!" He grinned. "What did you *do?*"

Jay didn't know how to answer. Other kids were coming to their senses, repeating their names like they were scared of forgetting them again.

The sight filled Jay with bewilderment. He stared at the fiddle, then turned to Ark. "Did you . . . *see* anything just now?"

Ark stared like Jay had hit his head. "Like what?"

Jay hesitated, not sure whether to explain—and then he saw Nanny. She looked the same, yet totally different. Her face no longer looked evil. She was slumped on her knees, tears flooding her eyes.

"I'm free," she whispered, her face shining in relief. "I'm *free.*"

Jay didn't know how, but when that dischord was pushed out of her, he'd glimpsed her memories of what led to her being possessed.

Jay turned away. Maybe he should ask Ark about it. He was smart.

But how was he supposed to do that? *So, when I played the fiddle, I read this lady's mind. Saw her memories. That's not crazy, right?*

Before Jay could decide, Ark took Brio's instrument from him, returning it to its case. "Let's get out of here. I don't want to wait around for something else to happen." He turned to Sugar. "Where's the exit?"

The boy shrugged. "Dunno. Before Nockna Mora lured me here, I'd never come to Lower Grimsborough before. It's like a bad dream."

Ark scanned the group of kids. "Do any of you know how to get out?"

Heads shook in all directions.

"No worries, mate!" said Andi. "Leave it to us. C'mon, girl."

He rested his hand on Hotah and whistled. Hotah gave a happy bark and took off, sniffing a trail. One by one, Jay, Ark, and the rest of the kids followed, with Augusta taking the rear, leaving the caverns of Lower Grimsborough behind.

Chapter Nineteen

TRAIN RIDE

Ark was just waiting for something else to go wrong. Would Andi lead them the wrong way? Would they get lost in the dark? He was almost expecting the dischord to come back.

But Hotah led them straight to a set of stairs leading up and out of Lower Grimsborough. Perhaps Ark had earned a respite from his rotten luck.

Ark left the stairs and stumbled into the open, squinting against the brightness. He'd never been so happy to see sunlight or taste fresh air. Judging by the sun's position in the sky, it was well past noon. How much time had they lost to Lower Grimsborough? Hours? Days?

He looked around. They'd emerged pretty much at the last place Ark remembered seeing before they were knocked out—only there were no more bodies lying in the street. Instead, dozens of stupefied adults were waking up. Some held their heads like they were recovering from a headache, while others stretched stiff hands and necks.

"Father!" cried Sugar and Cherry, running up to a bearded man in the middle of the street. There were similar reunions happening all around, kids dashing up to their parents. The street was soon filled with cries of joy and relief.

Ark was amazed. It was remarkable how different Upper Grimsborough felt with the dischord gone. The effects of its presence had vanished; instead of an unquiet stillness along empty streets, there was the natural energy of people. Everyone looked happy, albeit a little hungry.

Ark caught sight of the grocer who'd been asleep on a crate of cauliflower, hungrily munching on his own tomatoes.

"Excuse me," someone called.

Ark turned. Augusta stood before them.

"Forgive me," she said, her face filled with regret. "What I did to you was reprehensible. It wasn't truly me, but that's no excuse."

Ark wanted to reassure her, but Jay beat him to the punch.

"You were being controlled by a dischord," he said with an easy shrug, though he seemed to be avoiding her gaze. "I'd say you're clear."

Augusta's face was haunted by guilt.

"I lost my son to a disease, not long ago," she said softly. "I didn't want another mother to go through that." Her voice grew quieter. "My desire to protect the town's children from the contagion became my obsession. That's how the dischord manipulated me."

Ark struggled to find appropriate words. At last, he spoke.

"Nothing you've done is unatonable," he said. "There's no point in blaming yourself or dwelling on what's in the past. Focus on moving forward. The memories may haunt you for a time, but they will fade. It's over now."

A gentle smile spread across Augusta's face. "It is over," she echoed.

"You should hire a Musician for this town," Ark added. "With muses here to protect you, you shouldn't have to worry about dischords again."

"I will," she said. She laid a palm on her chest. "I am Augusta Grim. If not for you, everything my great-grandfather built would have been lost."

Ark's mind flashed to the bronze statue of Sir Grim they'd seen when they'd first been Transposed here. Her great-grandfather, most likely.

"I am deeply in your debt," Augusta went on. "How can I repay you?"

The spark of an idea flashed in Ark's mind.

"We need to get to Fairdown Falls," he answered. "Fast."

Augusta nodded. "There is a waystation not far from town. Several routes stop there on their way to the capital. Consider yourselves on board the next train. I will take care of it."

Jay looked like he was about to spit out some churlish protest—but then Augusta swept up to him. She leaned in, wrapping him in an unexpected hug.

Jay went dead still, arms rigid at his sides.

"Thank you," Augusta whispered, her eyes glistening. She stepped back, holding him by the shoulders. "You saved me. I will never forget it."

She released him. Jay bent his head, trying to hide his self-conscious face under his cap before he shuffled away.

Ark watched him, frowning. He had no idea what was going on in that idiot's head.

Ark broke his stare when Trouble—Andi, rather—sidled up next to him.

"Fairdown Falls, huh?" said Andi. He flashed a hopeful smile, resting a hand on Hotah's head. "Can we come with?"

∞

Their seats on the train were modest and not terribly comfortable, just hard benches with little leg room—but to Ark, it was an enjoyable ride. Their misadventure in both Upper and Lower Grimsborough had been quite a detour, but now they were back on track. *Finally.*

After Augusta told everyone how he, Jay, and Andi had rescued their town from a parasitic dischord, the people of Upper Grimsborough were exceedingly generous. They not only paid for train fare all the way to the capital, but they also insisted on packing food for them, more than Ark could eat in a week. Ark had to politely turn down other gifts for fear of being buried under their offerings of gratitude.

Augusta then escorted them to the waystation, ensuring they got on safely. If she hadn't been there, Ark wasn't sure whether Jay would have climbed aboard. Even now, as the train rumbled along, he sat across from Ark as close to the car window as possible, like he was waiting for a chance to jump out.

Andi was enjoying himself even more than Ark was. He sat next to Jay with Hotah stretched out at his feet, happily digging into the food.

"I was sure you'd gotten lost, Jay," Andi was saying, chomping into his fourth sandwich while he rehashed their escape. "I thought you'd gotten turned around in the dark, and I blamed myself for leaving you behind. Then we get captured—and you come in out of nowhere—and *pow!* You use your music powers to thrash that dischord!"

Jay said nothing. Ark eyed him, feeling a twinge of irritation.

"My brother's a Musician," Andi went on. "He can see muses, I mean—he doesn't practice music. I've been traveling around trying to find him."

"Is that why you were in Upper Grimsborough?" said Ark.

Andi polished off his sandwich. "Yeah. My brother left our village weeks ago without saying goodbye, right before his coming-of-age ceremony. That's not like him. So I hopped on a boat and followed him." He wiped his hands on his trousers, adding, "Some folks at the port said they'd met a guy who sounded like him and that he'd gone toward Upper Grimsborough. I followed their directions—and now, here I am."

"You're from Southin?" Ark guessed aloud.

Andi chuckled. "The accent kind of gives it away, yeah?" he grinned. "My full name is Andimakanani. My brother is called Hoku, but his name is really Kahokuokalani. Doesn't get more Southiner than that."

"You traveled all the way to Merideyin by yourself?" said Ark, unable to hide his surprise. "Must have been hard."

Andi tilted his head. "Not so hard. It's just been a lot of walking. Hotah's kept me company."

He reached down and scratched her ears. Hotah snuffled his hand, licking crumbs from his fingers.

"Fairdown Falls is most likely where Hoku's gone," said Andi. "Growing up in Southin, it's the only city in Merideyin we ever heard of. Whatever he's up to, I think I'll be able to find him there." He shifted his head in Ark's direction. "What are you two heading there for?"

Ark glanced down at the black case, resting in the empty seat next to him.

"We're on our way to the Royal Conservatory," said Ark, choosing to be honest but vague. "Jay and I need to get there as soon as possible."

Jay cut in with a grumpy snort. "After all the crazy things you've put me through, you still think I'm going anywhere with you?"

Ark shot him a pointed look. "You *know* why you have to go there."

Jay held up two fingers. "I know two things. One: You're a bum-wipe. Two: You won't drag me anywhere near that city."

Ark clenched his hands, fighting against his desire to kick Jay in the shins. Andi was listening to their exchange with blatant curiosity. Ark wasn't sure how much they could go on without giving away privileged information. Andi was a nice guy, but Ark hardly knew whether to trust him with the knowledge of who Jay was or what Ark's mission entailed.

"Jay—a word?" said Ark. He grabbed the black case—he refused to let it out of his sight again—then snatched Jay by the vest and, ignoring the boy's sputters, pulled him from his seat toward the car door. He pushed Jay through, joining him on the outside landing.

"I'll only say this once," said Ark, speaking just loud enough to be heard over the *clack-a-clack* of the train wheels. "We're going to the Royal Conservatory. *Together.* You can complain and curse all you'd like— but if you don't come with me, others might come looking for you. Like Dubito." He let that name hang in the air.

Jay stared at Ark from beneath the brim of his cap. "So?"

Ark wanted to shake him. "*So?* You're the Crafter's heir!"

Jay went rigid.

"Your best option is to come with me," said Ark. "If nothing else, we have a responsibility to get *this* back safely." He held up the case.

Jay's frown darkened.

"I'm gonna say this slowly, so you understand," he said. He jabbed Ark's chest with his finger. "*I'm. Not. Going.* Do I need to repeat that, or did the message finally make it through your thick skull?"

Ark felt his temper spiking. "Why?" he yelled. "*Why* are you being so stupid about this?"

"Because," Jay yelled over him, "I *can't* go there!"

Ark stared, taken aback. "Why not?"

"None of your business!" said Jay. He swept his cap off and pushed his hair out of his face. There was a shadow of desperation in his eyes. "I can't be seen there, all right? If certain people find me, I'm worse than dead."

Ark shook his head, not understanding. "What are you saying—?"

"Nuh-uh," said Jay, cutting him off. "You listen to me now. You think I'm supposed to be this Crafter's heir? News flash, pal: I'll never, ever be a Musician. I hate muses—always will." He gestured to himself, head to toe. "Besides, d'you really think the Royal Conservatory would accept *me* as the Crafter?"

Ark stared at Jay. The vitriol behind Jay's words drowned out any reasonable response Ark could have had.

"Didn't think so," said Jay, answering his own question. "I'm the last person they'd want for the job *and* the last person who'd take it. You can tell them that yourself. And you can bring that fiddle home on your own."

As he said it, Jay shot a glance at the case—and then he jammed his hat back on his head and returned inside the train car.

Ark followed slowly, not looking in Jay's direction as he returned to his seat. Jay had resumed his previous position, pressed up against the window. Andi seemed to have sensed that they'd argued; he kept quiet, rubbing his bare feet along Hotah's furry back.

They rode in stuffy silence for the rest of the day. Eventually the sun dipped beyond the horizon, and night bathed the passing scenery in darkness. Jay fell asleep slouched in his seat; Andi propped his feet up on Hotah and dozed.

Ark couldn't sleep so easily. He took out his notebook and a stub of a pencil, doodling on a blank page. As he sketched, his thoughts returned to his earlier conversation with Jay:

I hate muses. Always will.

I'll never, ever be a Musician.

The echoes of Jay's words played on a loop between Ark's ears. He couldn't reconcile Jay's aversion to music against his obvious affinity for it. Back in Lower Grimsborough, Jay had summoned enough harmonic power to not only exorcize a dischord but *eradicate* it. Only Musicians with the most outstanding ability could do that.

Jay had saved their lives.

Now Ark knew his duty. Once word of the Crafter's return broke out, people would come for Jay. Enthusiasts. Enemies. Opportunists looking for an advantage. Escorting Jay to the Royal Conservatory was more for his safety than anything else.

And yet, no matter how much Ark hated to admit it, Jay had a point.

D'you really think the Royal Conservatory would accept me as the Crafter?

Given Jay's aversion toward muses, did it even make sense for Jay to be the new Crafter? It'd been two hundred years since the last one, and yet Crafters were still revered today. Even if he'd wanted the Crafter's title, Jay was nowhere close to being the kind of person the world expected as a Crafter.

Besides, Jay had his own reasons for avoiding the capital. *Certain people*, he'd said. Ark frowned. Despite knowing Jay was the Crafter's heir, there wasn't much he knew about the guy.

Ark tucked his notebook away, absently tracing his fingertips over the scar on his left hand. His eyes traveled to Jay and Andi. For a moment, he wished he wasn't on his jury mission—that he was instead on a trip with friends, without some unquestionable duty deciding his every move. That would have been nice.

He leaned his head against the car window, shutting his eyes.

KWEEEEEEEE!

Ark jolted in his seat, the train whistle piercing through his sleep. It felt like he'd only shut his eyes for a couple of seconds—but outside, the sun was up and the scenery had completely changed. Gone were the wide-open fields and occasional trees; now he saw an uneven landscape with a flat-topped mountain peak growing ever closer.

Even as Ark took in the sights, the train car abruptly lurched. He scrambled to catch the black case before it fell off the bench.

Jay and Andi startled awake. "Hwa—wha's goin' on?" said Andi.

"I think we're stopping," said Ark, feeling the train lose momentum as it passed under a wide brick gate. There was a plaque alongside the gate: CINDERTOWN.

"They must need to trade out draft beasts and refuel," said Ark. "We'll probably leave again in a few minutes."

Jay was already searching out the window for the likeliest place to hop off. He needn't have bothered. The train hadn't even come to a full stop when the coach attendant entered their car and addressed the passengers.

"Ladies and gentlemen, I apologize for the inconvenience, but I must ask you all to disembark," he said in an exceedingly polite voice. He held up a stack of paper slips. "You will all receive a ticket voucher as you exit. Please make your way down to the platform."

Ark stared in confusion as the other passengers got up and gathered their luggage.

"Excuse me," he called to the attendant. "Aren't we headed to Fairdown Falls? Why are we getting off?"

The attendant looked down at him. "Cindertown's lava flows are too high right now to lead a team of draft beasts through safely. All train travel to and from the city is suspended until the flow returns to lower levels."

He handed Ark ticket vouchers. "You three can use these in place of fare to the capital when travel resumes in a week or so." He shuffled off.

It was a clear explanation, but Ark got hung up on one word:

Lava?

Jay wore an irritating grin as they all stepped off. Ark gave Andi his elbow to use for balance as he hopped onto the platform, while Hotah leaped nimbly down and began sniffing around.

"Ugh!" said Andi, holding a hand to his nose. "What's burning?"

Ark stepped out from the shelter of the platform, getting his first glimpse of the city. What he saw made him whistle aloud.

Before him, countless buildings climbed up the mountain slope, along with slender trees, bubbling natural springs, and flourishing gardens. Many buildings Ark saw were either mechanic workshops, alchemy supply stores, or hot springs bath houses. Huge chunks of dark igneous glass had been carved into shimmering black statues and placed on street corners. Way up toward the summit, a brilliant orange cascade poured out of the mountain, oozing along a deserted black plain on a distant side of the slope.

The panorama of the fiery city was one thing—but Ark marveled when he saw the local muses. Bird-shaped muses with long beaks and fiery wings flocked near smoking chimneys. Monkey-like muses with green mossy fur lounged in the trees. A muse that looked like a huge tortoise crawled along the street, its shell as black and sleek as the volcanic glass statues on the street corners. Everywhere else, muses swam through spring water, scurried around gardens, and made themselves at home among the citizens.

"So?" said Andi. "Is someone going to tell me what's up?"

Ark fumbled for a response. "We're in Cindertown."

"That means nothing to me," said Andi. "Does it look like a safe place?"

Ark almost laughed. They were literally standing on a volcano.

"I'm sure it's perfectly safe," he said.

Behind him, someone snorted. Ark turned. Jay stood there, arms crossed.

"No such thing as perfectly safe," he said.

Ark glanced back toward the train station, a sour taste in his mouth. All he wanted was to get to Fairdown Falls and get his jury mission done.

Why did his rotten luck always interfere? He felt more like the Jinx than ever.

"We need to get our bearings," said Ark. "We don't know how long it'll be until the trains start running again. We should find some way to contact the Royal Conservatory, let them know we're here."

"You have fun with that," said Jay. "Count me out."

He started walking off.

Ark watched him, torn. Two sides of him argued in his head, alternating between Dulcian's and Jay's voices:

Whatever happens, stay together!

I'll never, ever become a Musician.

Get Julian to the Royal Conservatory. That is your mission!

You won't drag me anywhere near that city.

Ark chased the voices out, focusing on his own reasoning. He made his decision.

Jay paused and glanced at Ark over his shoulder. "You're not gonna try to stop me?"

Ark shook his head. "How could I stop you? I fell asleep on the train, and when I woke up, you were gone. You must have slipped out the window. You're probably headed back home to Hazeldenn."

Jay blinked.

"That's what I'll tell Dulcian and Callie, anyway," Ark added.

Jay eyed him, suspicious. "What's your game?"

"No game," said Ark. "Go before my moment of lapsed judgment ends."

Jay slowly relaxed his guard. "You're serious. How come? What about your mission?"

Ark stepped up to him. "I thought about what you said. I know what it's like to have someone force you on a path you weren't cut out for. No one should make you go to the Royal Conservatory." He lowered his voice so Andi couldn't hear. "Besides, Musicians who've been so eager to see the next Crafter return don't deserve to have someone like *you*, so obviously reluctant, fill the role. It'd be better to wait another hundred years for a Crafter's heir who'll accept the responsibility instead of run away from it."

The words struck home. Jay stared at him, abashed, maybe even ashamed.

"Andi and I will take Brio's instrument back," Ark finished, patting the case. "You don't have anything else to worry about."

Jay held Ark's gaze for a long moment. "'Kay, then," he said, uncertain. "Have a nice life."

He began shuffling down the street, hands in pockets, disappearing into the flow of people.

"Wait, Jay's not coming?" said Andi. "What gives?"

Ark watched Jay go, not sure what to feel. Disgust? Disappointment? Neither, really. Maybe regret?

Ark frowned. He had a bigger issue to deal with. He wasn't looking forward to seeing Callie's and Dulcian's faces when he showed up with Brio's instrument, but not Jay. He'd officially failed his jury mission.

No—his mission had been doomed from the start. When Ark was sent back to Echostrait, maybe he could convince Maestran Pandoura to give him another one, with different jurors.

"We should get moving," he told Andi.

But then, in the corner of his eye, he saw Jay come to an abrupt stop, like he'd run straight into a brick wall. Ark watched from a distance. Jay wagged his head, like he was trying to chase away a bug that'd flown into his ears. Then he pressed a hand to his chest, his head bowed like he was in pain.

Then, inexplicably, Jay did an about-face and came storming back up to them. His glaring eyes were locked on the black case. Ark studied him, hesitant.

"Changed your mind?" he asked, genuinely curious.

"Shut up," said Jay, still glowering at the black case.

"Jay!" said Andi. "Coming with us after all?"

Jay didn't answer. Ark tucked away his own questions and returned to the matter at hand. "All right, then. Same plan. We should find some way to contact the Royal Conservatory, and then we'll—"

Andi cut him off. "Do you guys hear that?"

After some moments, Ark heard what sounded like a rowdy crowd some streets away. A hot blast of fire burst over the rooftops, followed by surprised shouts.

Images of Hazeldenn on fire burned through Ark's mind.

"We're checking it out," he said, determined. "Let's go."

He stepped off, Andi and Hotah at his heels. Jay followed, grumbling curses under his breath all the way.

Chapter Twenty

THE KING STREET SALAMANDERS

Ark was certain Jay would change his mind again. He expected Jay to find some opportunity to slip sideways through the passersby and leave. But every time Ark glanced over his shoulder to make sure Andi was keeping up, he saw Jay there too, following them even though it looked like it was the last thing he wanted to be doing.

"Is that . . . clapping?" asked Andi.

Ark looked up and listened. He wasn't sure. They reached the street where the fire burst had come from. Ark braced himself, rounding the corner.

There were about ten people, boys and girls alike, all wearing costumes in fiery colors: orange tunics and trousers with yellow belts. Many of them had dancing staves, hoops, and torch sticks. Others carried drums and flutes. They looked like they were warming up. One of the performers, a lanky guy with spiky blonde hair and a pair of grease-smeared spectacles, walked along the perimeter of the crowd.

"Ladies and gentlemen!" the spiky-haired guy called out, catching everyone's attention. "Today, you're the luckiest people in Cindertown! You're here in time to see some of the best fire-breathing anywhere in the world!" He swept his hand along the crowd. "What you are about to witness are the most beautiful and dangerous stunts ever attempted with fire—so cheer and clap if you like what you see!" He raised both hands high. "And now I present: *The King Street Salamanders!*"

The spectators cheered as Spiky Hair stepped aside and another performer came forward. The girl wore a different costume than the others: a yellow Eastirn-style dress with orange leggings stretching down to her yellow shoes. Golden paint had been applied to her forearms in curving strokes, highlighting her naturally tan skin. Her raven hair was knotted behind her head and pinned up with a hair ornament in a fiery design. She gazed at the crowd with fierce amber eyes.

One of the performers struck a hand-held gong, and the drums and flutes struck up a rhythmic tune. On cue, the girl in the yellow dress began to dance while the Salamanders all lit their props, turning torch sticks into fans of fire and hoops into circles of flame.

The spectators *ooh*ed and *ahh*ed. The fire breathers performed stunts one after the other in perfect coordination: juggling lit torches, tossing burning rings into the air, and extinguishing fires in their mouths. Spiky Hair took a flask from his belt, sucked in a mouthful from it, and then spewed it out in a roar of flame over the crowd's head. Ark was fascinated.

"Ugh—smells like burning," muttered Andi. "Can we go now?"

Ark didn't want to leave, but he knew Andi was right. He was just about to say they were moving on when the raven-haired girl came forward again. She clapped her hands to the beat of the drums, getting the spectators to clap with her. Then the girl held out her left hand, palm up. Finally, keeping her focus on her left hand, she raised her right hand, twirled it around, and snapped her fingers.

With a flash and a flicker, a large, multicolored flame flared to life in the middle of her left hand, changing from red to blue to green to yellow in a matter of seconds. Somehow, the girl wasn't burned. She rolled the flame around her palm—the fire grew higher, higher, higher—and then she threw the flame up high into the air. It exploded in a sparkling burst, showering glittering confetti over the crowd.

Everyone went wild, whooping and whistling. Ark clapped along.

"Thank you!" called Spiky Hair. "I am Ignazio, captain of the King Street Salamanders—and if you liked what you saw here today, come vote for us at the twenty-third annual Fire Festival! Until then, we bid you—"

"Cheater!" someone shouted over the applause.

Ignazio broke off. Ark, along with the other spectators, turned as a boy with a shaved head and a burn scar near his mouth shoved his way through. He was followed by a pair of watchmen wearing silver badges on their coats.

Ignazio stared at the rude boy in recognition.

"Aiden," he said, narrowing his eyes. "What's this about?"

Aiden scowled, then pointed to the raven-haired girl. "That trick wasn't done with fire-breathing!" he spewed. "That yellow-eyed fennik cheated! Your team should be disqualified from the Fire Festival!"

The raven-haired girl flushed at the slur. Her team erupted in outrage.

"Don't you *dare* call her that," said Ignazio, gesturing to the girl. "Hana is the most talented person on our team. Just because *your* team doesn't want to face her in the competition doesn't mean you get to spout accusations against her. The Salamanders don't need to cheat to beat you!"

The Salamanders all cheered in agreement and surrounded Hana in a protective arc.

"As captain of the Firebirds, I'm only protecting my team!" Aiden puffed. "We won't compete against frauds!"

The remarks spurred more shouts and yelling.

"Sounds like trouble," murmured Andi. "Can we please get out of here?"

Ark was inclined to agree. He nodded at Jay, then started to make his way through the spectators pressed in around them.

"I *know* she cheated!" Aiden yelled above the rest. "She used muses!"

The stunned crowd went silent. Hana and Ignazio stared at Aiden in shock. Aiden smiled back like a smug shark that'd found its dinner.

Ark frowned. He hadn't seen muses anywhere near this street. The girl hadn't performed any musical forms, either. Should he speak up?

While he dithered, Jay snorted next to him.

"Yeah, right," he said, too loudly.

Aiden snapped his head in Jay's direction. "You got something to say?"

Soon the whole crowd was looking at Jay. Jay was unruffled.

"That wasn't a muse," he said. "It was just a great trick."

Aiden glared at him. "You calling me a liar?"

Jay shook his head. "Nah. I'm calling you an idiot."

Before they could carry on, one of the watchmen—a squat, imposing man with a mostly bald head, a chubby red face, and a thick mustache that curled up on either side of his mouth—stepped in. "Listen, son," he said, pointing to Jay, "if you can't contribute anything helpful to this inquiry, I'm going to ask you to butt out. How do you know there wasn't a muse involved here?"

Jay didn't answer. He shot a cold look at the watchman and clammed up.

Ark sighed. He supposed he should play mediator.

"He's right," said Ark, stepping forward. "That trick wasn't done with musical arts." He turned to the girl. "Alchemy, right?"

She looked at him in chagrin.

"A fire-breather shouldn't reveal her secrets," said Hana, sounding reluctant. She lifted her hands, which had a sparkly sheen that matched the golden paint on her arms. "My skin is covered with a fire-retardant base," she explained. Then she held up a small transparent cylinder. "I keep a capsule in my right hand, filled with extracts of quickfliss and brightbane. When I toss it into my left hand, the extracts react, the capsule combusts, and the result is a multicolored fire in my hands. It's alchemy combined with stage magic, that's all."

"See? There you are," said Ignazio, triumphant.

"Liar!" Aiden barked. "Quickfliss and brightbane are too unstable to mix without immediately combusting!"

"Not if you combine them with æthermist," Hana retorted. "A quarter measure of æthermist stirred in keeps the extracts from reacting until it evaporates. We time it precisely for our performance—"

"That's garbage!" Aiden yelled. "It was muses, I tell you!"

Ark sighed. "Perhaps a test would settle things?"

He glanced around, surveying the buildings to see whether any muses were nearby. He saw a collection of muses in the form of firebirds, roosting on the rooftop of a small jewelry shop.

"What do you see up on the roof there?" he asked the girl.

Hana, and the whole crowd with her, turned to look.

"What am I supposed to be looking at?" she asked, blinking.

Ark raised his hand. "There are at least half a dozen muses up there. Even the most novice Musician would be able to see them."

The crowd murmured. The two watchmen exchanged uncertain glances.

"Says you!" said Aiden, glaring at Ark. "Why should we believe you?"

Ark set his jaw. Fine then. Proof.

"*Accesso*," he chanted in a low, soft voice.

One of the muses on the roof swooped down, its lustrous body and fiery tailfeathers bright against the daylight. Following Ark's direction, the muse flapped its brilliant wings and flew in a dizzying upward spiral, trailing fire from its tail and creating a whirlwind of sparkling, colorful flame. Then, from high above, the muse flashed its wings once more and sent down a burst of shimmering golden sparks before flying off.

The crowd gasped. Someone even screamed.

Ark turned to Aiden, crossing his arms. "Now *that* was a muse."

Aiden's mouth was hanging wide open. Hana and Ignazio gaped at him too. Most of the spectators stepped away.

Then the mustached watchman came up to Ark.

"Quite a display," he said—though it didn't sound like a compliment. "Right in front of us, too. Bold, aren't you?"

Ark glanced over to Andi and shared an uncertain look with Jay before answering the watchman. "Is something wrong, sir?"

The mustached watchman put a heavy hand on Ark's shoulder. The other watchman who'd stood by the whole time—a dark, wolfish man with furry black hair, a long duster coat, and unsettling silver eyes—came forward too, flanking Ark from the other side.

"It's against the law to summon muses within Cindertown's city limits," said the mustached watchman. "You're under arrest!"

Chapter Twenty-One

WANTED

All the way to Cindertown's watch house, Jay glared at the back of Ark's dumb head, mumbling curses. Ever since they'd crossed paths in Hazeldenn, Ark had dragged him into one mess after another. First it was the Unraveling Man, then Nanny Nightmare—and now they were being led away by rotten lawmen. Jay swore the guy was jinxed.

But since Ark still had the stupid fiddle, Jay had no choice but to follow him, no matter what mess he stepped into.

It wasn't fair. As the watchmen escorted Ark across Cindertown, Jay tried again to walk his own way—but he couldn't. It was like the fiddle somehow *knew* Jay was trying to leave it behind, and now he couldn't get five strides away without the perfect music tugging at his chest with a sharp pull, stopping him in his tracks. He was a dog on a leash, yanked invisibly along by its master.

The fiddle was smug about it, too. Jay could sense it even now, humming faintly in its case, happy to have Jay nearby. Jay swore again under his breath.

"Any idea where we're going?" asked Andi, keeping pace with Jay.

Jay tuned out the fiddle's self-satisfied hum. "The watch house, most like," he muttered. He scowled again at the back of Ark's head.

"They won't lock Ark up, will they?" Andi whispered.

Jay didn't answer. Ark was apologizing to the two watchmen—as if saying sorry could help. He'd probably never crossed paths with lawmen in his life and was now overwhelmed by their authority.

Jay wasn't. Back when he was the Quickstep Kid, he'd met enough watchmen in Fairdown Falls to know most were no better than the criminals they locked up. He'd once seen a trio of watchmen beat up an old man just 'cause he was homeless. He'd seen a rich lady who'd run over a poor vendor's cart with her carriage get off scot-free after passing fat wads of cash to the watchmen on the scene. He knew half a dozen watchmen were under the Capo's thumb, too, trading her favors in exchange for coin.

Jay grunted. Watchmen. Jerks and crooks, all of 'em.

If he hadn't been forced to follow Ark and these watchmen against his will, Jay might've enjoyed walking around the city. It was so much different than Fairdown Falls, which was all water, and Hazeldenn, which was all dust and hazel trees. Jay spied alchemy shops selling rare minerals, all organized in tidy glass bottles. In machine shops, mechanics were all hard at work, fiddling with tinkerbit tools and metal parts. On the sidewalk, a hawker in a bowler hat was peddling what he claimed was the "Elixir of Life" (which looked like plain water)—along with a young woman who sold mechanized animal figurines that hopped and wriggled at the turn of a key.

Jay dawdled too long watching the wind-up figurines. The fiddle pulled him with an insistent tug in his chest, compelling him to follow. Jay winced, pressing a hand to his heart. *Bandersnatches.*

They'd walked a dozen blocks before they came to the watch house, a dull brick building with bars on the windows. "Wipe your feet," the furry-faced watchman said as he led Ark inside. The other watchman— the guy with the sharp gray eyes—held the door open for Jay and Andi. Hotah padded in behind them with a low *woof.*

The watch house was one large, bland room. Men and women sat at desks, going over reports and sorting files, not sparing them a glance.

Jay looked around, trying to squash his uneasiness. The last time he'd been in a watch house, he'd been handcuffed to a desk just like the ones here, while the watchmen celebrated his arrest. Jay had turned himself in, horrified about what'd happened at Windfalle—but in his arrest report, the watchmen said they'd caught him and brought him in themselves. Liars.

The mustached watchman led Ark to a large, disorganized desk, bearing an embossed brass name plate: CAP. WALLACE RUSS. The sharp-eyed watchman peeled off and went to a puny but tidy desk beside it, with its own cheap wooden nameplate: DEP. INS. JAMES ARGENTINE.

The captain took his place behind the large desk. "Sit!" he barked at Ark.

Ark sat on the sole stool with the black case resting across his lap. Jay and Andi stood to the side while the captain settled in, folding his hands and giving Ark a stern look over the mess on his desk.

"I'm Captain Russ, head of Cindertown's musical enforcement unit," he declared. "I have two jobs: to protect the citizens from muse-related mishaps, and to make sure troublemaking Musicians are properly catechized."

In his seat, Ark blinked. Jay raised an eyebrow. Catechized?

"*Chastised*, sir," whispered the deputy inspector from his desk.

"Whatever!" snapped the captain. He narrowed his gaze on Ark. "Did you know that ignoring the restrictions on music around here can land you in jail?"

Ark's eyes went wide. "Please, sir—"

"Don't interrupt!" the captain barked. Ark's mouth shut with a *clop*.

"You should be happy we were there to stop you," the captain went on. "Better to be punished now than get carried away with muses later, causing major damages and suffering greater competences."

The deputy inspector coughed. "*Consequences*, sir."

"Whatever!" the captain hissed at him.

"I apologize for interjecting," said Ark in a rush before the captain could cut him off again, "but, sir, the reason I summoned a muse was to prevent that fire-breather from being falsely accused of cheating. She was innocent, and the only way to prove it was to perform a *real* music form."

The captain considered Ark's words, his furry mustache twitching. "However noble your motives, it doesn't change the fact that they were unlawful. In this city, improper summoning of music spirits is on the same level as arson!" He eyed Ark, then added, "An arsonist is someone who malevolently incriminates someone else's property."

"*Incinerates*, sir."

"Whatever!"

"I *know* what arson is," said Ark. "I didn't set anything on fire. In fact, I was only trying to put a fire out, figuratively speaking—"

"Don't try talking your way out of this!" said the captain, cutting him off. "What kind of fool do you think I am?"

"The annoying kind?" Jay muttered before he could stop himself.

Ark shot him an irritated look. Andi snorted, unable to stop a laugh. Even Hotah looked amused.

The captain sent Jay a cool glare, then turned to Andi, who was still trying to stifle his chuckles.

"Think that's funny, do you?" the captain grumbled. "You kids—you have no idea how many situations I deal with every year." He reached into the rumpled papers on his desk, grabbing a document with scribbled columns. He brandished it in front of Andi's face. "Take a look at this!"

Andi tilted his head. "It's . . . a piece of paper, right?"

"Don't be smart!" said the captain. "Our infraction rate is awful! Are you blind?"

Andi smirked. "What gave it away?"

The captain tossed the document aside and leaned against his desk. The heap of papers behind him shifted, sending other files spilling to the floor.

"I've met dozens like you," said the captain, while the deputy inspector collected the fallen documents. "Teenaged Musicians who think they're above the law, using music willy-nilly. They all end up here at my desk eventually—for destroying property or disturbing the lives of honest citizens with their instructive shenanigans—"

"*Destructive*, sir," murmured the deputy inspector.

"*Thank* you, Argentine, you may resume your own duties!" the captain snapped. The deputy inspector obediently returned to his desk.

"All that said," said the captain, turning to Ark, "I consider it my duty to put wayward Musicians in their place. And *you* should consider it *your* duty to keep your musical mischief to yourself—oh, for the love of lava, what is it now?" the captain barked as a clerk came up to him.

"Apologies for the interruption, sir, but the chief's called for you."

The captain perked up. "What's the situation?"

"A theft at the mayor's house. A painting has disappeared from his gallery. It's possible a Musician may have done it."

The captain harrumphed. "I suppose I should check it out." He turned to the deputy inspector, waving vaguely in Ark's direction. "Argentine, you finish this up. I'm off to comprehend a thief."

The captain departed like a blast of hot air. The deputy inspector sighed.

"*Apprehend*, sir," he muttered. He turned to Ark, Jay, and Andi, motioning for them to come over to his desk.

"Don't mind the Walrus too much," he said as the three of them took a seat. "He's not the best with words, but he's a good man."

Ark and Andi chuckled. Jay blinked, confused.

"Captain Wallace Russ," said the deputy inspector, spying Jay's puzzled look. "Our friendly nickname for him around here."

Jay mouthed the man's name to himself. Wallace Russ . . . Walrus. Heh.

"I'm Inspector James Argentine," the deputy inspector went on. "I'm also with Cindertown's musical enforcement unit."

"Please, Inspector," said Ark, diving right in, "had I known there was a ban on musical arts in your city, I never would have—"

"Calm down," said Argentine. "You couldn't have known. I already gathered that none of you are from Cindertown." He turned to Andi, looking closely at the bead pattern on his belt. "You're a member of the Hawkingale tribe of Southin. Is your island Aramoa or Te'emaru?"

Andi straightened, surprised. "Te'emaru."

Argentine nodded. "And you're a student from Echostrait," he continued, pointing his pen at Ark. "A bit young to be an Adept, aren't you?"

Ark stared at the man. "How . . . ?"

Argentine gestured to Ark's white coat. "I haven't seen a talaris like that in some time." He turned last to Jay. "And you . . ."

Argentine's sharp silver eyes narrowed as he searched Jay's face. Jay tucked in his chin, hiding under his cap. What was this guy's problem?

"Let's start from the top," said Argentine, breaking his gaze. He retrieved a pen and a paper pad from his desk. "What brings you to the city?"

Ark began to explain, but Jay didn't pay attention. He'd noticed the flyers lining the wall behind Argentine's desk, featuring sketches of outlaws and details of their crimes. One flyer in the middle caught his eye. Instead of a sketch, that flyer had only a silhouette, as if the artist didn't know the outlaw's face, though the silhouette clearly belonged to a woman.

Jay read the name on the flyer—then gasped:

CHRIS CROSS

WANTED
THE CAPO

LORELEI THAYNE

DESCRIPTION:
CURRENT HEAD OF THE STACCATO GANG. FEMALE, LATE THIRTIES,
BUTTERFLY-SHAPED BIRTHMARK ON RIGHT SHOULDER
CHARGES:
THEFT, BURGLARY, LARCENY, FRAUD, ASSAULT, TRAFFICKING, DE-
STRUCTION OF PROPERTY, AND DISTURBING THE PEACE

WARNING! THAYNE IS CLASSIFIED AS **HIGHLY DANGEROUS**
CITIZENS ARE EXHORTED TO AID THE
CABINET OF JUSTICE IN HER ARREST

Jay bit his cheek to stop himself from scowling. In his mind, he pictured the letter the Capo had sent, remembering what she'd written:

Pay back the rest of your debt by midnight on Wintertide Eve . . . If you don't pay, someone else will . . . I'll be waiting for you.

Jay tried to drive the letter from his thoughts—and then his heart skipped a few beats. There was another criminal flyer on the wall behind Argentine's desk:

The Quickstep Kid.

Jay couldn't look away. There was his own face, pinned up next to a dozen others like a suspect lineup.

The poster sent a flood of memories rushing through him:

Lounging in the Capo's office, practicing his lock-picking on an old safe while the Capo and the rest of the gang planned the next job—hunching in the shadows outside some fancy mansion, his heart thudding the way it always did before a heist—slipping through dark corridors on silent feet, clutching treasures crafted from gems and gold—racing back to the Staccatos' hideout, the whistles of watchmen in the air.

Jay let the memories drift away, gazing at his wanted poster. The

Quickstep Kid's expression was so angry, his glare hard and hollow. Is that what he'd looked like to other people?

Jay looked at Argentine. He caught the deputy inspector staring at him before quickly shifting his gaze back to Ark. Jay's gut twisted like a wrung dishcloth. Did Argentine know who he was?

Jay kept his head down while Ark finished speaking.

"... and that's how we stumbled across the fire-breather performance," said Ark, wrapping up his explanation.

Argentine nodded, scribbling notes on his notepad.

"If I may ask, sir," said Ark, "why are musical arts illegal here?"

Argentine, still writing, shook his head. "They're not *illegal*. Despite what the Walrus said earlier, Musicians can summon muses within city limits—though only if they follow regulations. The risk is otherwise too great."

Argentine gestured out a nearby window, pointing to the city's peak.

"As you may have gathered, Cindertown stands on volatile ground," he explained. "Mount Vakra is an active volcano. While her lava flows are naturally effusive and follow a predictable cycle, there's a chance that any irregular forces could lead to a more explosive eruption. The muses dwelling in this region are capricious and strong. If a Musician were to summon one carelessly, Vakra could stir—and the results would be catastrophic."

Jay didn't follow all the words the man used, but he got the basic idea. Summon a muse, go kaboom.

"That's why the Walrus reacted the way he did when you performed a music skill right in front of him," Argentine went on. "He came down hard on you, but that's his job. And he's the best man for it."

Ark balled his fists in his lap, like he was bracing himself. "Inspector, I'm willing to accept whatever the punishment is for summoning that muse."

Argentine set down his pen and pad. "I won't be formally charging you. The music skill you performed was relatively minor, and since you only summoned a muse to prevent an innocent person from being accused of the same offense, I consider your actions justified. Though I'll keep your information. If I hear any report of you using music again, I will have to arrest you." He gestured to the exit. "You're free to go."

Ark sat in his seat for some moments, like he didn't dare trust his luck. "Thank you, sir," he gushed with a grateful smile. At once he rose to his feet—but then he paused, hesitating.

Argentine looked up. "Yes?"

Ark glanced around the watch house. "May I please use your wireless? I need to contact the Royal Conservatory. It's important."

Argentine shook his head. "I would let you, but wireless doesn't work in this city. Volcanic activity underground interferes with transmission lines and signals. The best you could do is post a letter by express courier. Since the lava is high now, the fastest it would get to the capital is three or four days."

Ark did a slow blink of disbelief. "Three or four *days?*"

"It depends on the shipping rate," said Argentine. "If you want it there in less time, you'll need to pay an airship-handling fee."

Ark lowered his head, patting his empty pockets.

"Is it an emergency?" asked Argentine.

The anxious look on Ark's face was enough of an answer. Argentine hummed, then tore a sheet from his notepad, handing it to Ark with his pen.

"Write out what you need to say. I can't afford air shipment, but I'll post it for you by the next-fastest rate. That's the best I can do."

At length, Ark inched forward, hastily scribbling a few lines on the paper.

"Leave it to me," said Argentine, folding up the note. "Good day."

Ark stood, looking both grateful and uncomfortable. "Thank you," he finally managed. He shuffled toward the exit, with Andi and Hotah following. Jay lurched to his feet and started after them.

"Hold up," said Argentine, catching Jay's shoulder.

Jay slithered out of the man's grasp. "What?"

Argentine sent Jay a steady look, saying nothing. Jay could already sense the fiddle starting to pull at him, urging him to follow. He tried to shake the first nagging murmurs of the perfect music from his head.

"What d'you want?"

Argentine held his silence. Then he turned to the wall of criminal flyers behind his desk.

"Have you ever heard of the Capo, Lorelei Thayne?" he asked.

Jay froze.

Argentine crossed his arms. "I recently read an interesting report from the Cabinet of Justice's Department of Organized Crime. According to informants, Thayne is apparently after someone."

Jay could feel his emotionless mask slipping. "That so?"

Argentine nodded. "She's put a bounty on an old member of the Staccatos—someone who'd deserted her gang a couple of years ago and has been keeping a low profile ever since," he said. He looked Jay square in the face. "The Quickstep Kid."

Jay turned to stone. No doubt, now: Argentine knew exactly who he was.

"I hope the Kid's not planning on trying to leave Merideyin," Argentine went on. "Word from the street is that Thayne's sent some bottom-feeders from her gang to keep an eye on all port cities, in case the Kid shows up. She's also got sniffers searching some of the larger waystations. Seems she's real keen to get her hands on him."

Those words sank into Jay's ears, drowning out the whispers of perfect music. The Capo had guessed his every move. She'd put the word out about him in the underground and had sent her muscle out to the ports and waystations, all so she could put a barrier around Merideyin to hold him in. Soon she'd run him down like a fox hunting a fenced-in hare.

Jay couldn't swallow. What was he supposed to do now?

"Why are you telling me this?" he asked in a husky voice.

Argentine's silvery eyes made him look like a wise gray wolf.

"If the Quickstep Kid wants to go straight, he should be allowed to," said Argentine at length. "He doesn't have to go back to the gang life. If he needs help, he can always come see me. I'd keep Thayne off his back." Argentine's sharp eyes softened. "Think you could tell him that for me?"

Jay stared at the deputy inspector, not sure what to say. He'd expected Argentine to tell him off and order him not to get into trouble. He'd never figured the lawman would offer to protect him.

Jay coughed at the sudden tightness in his throat. "Yeah, sure," he said gruffly, trying to sound tougher than he felt.

The corner of Argentine's mouth quirked in what might have been a smile. He nodded, sitting behind his desk once more.

"Take care of yourself, Kid," he murmured.

Jay didn't hear him. He was already halfway across the watch house. He couldn't get away from the place fast enough.

Chapter Twenty-Two

THE CARTWRIGHT SCHOOL FOR YOUNG LADIES

"What was that about?" asked Ark when Jay rejoined him and Andi. They had waited by the exit while Argentine had spoken to him, and Ark looked more than a little curious.

Jay answered with a shrug. Now that Thayne had put out a bounty on him and had eyes on the ports, Jay's plan to take a boat and sail far beyond Thayne's reach sunk like a capsized ship before his eyes. He had no idea what he was supposed to do now.

"All right," said Andi in the awkward silence. "I vote we find food. And maybe somewhere we can sleep and get a bath."

Hotah gave a throaty bark.

"Hotah votes for those things, too," said Andi, rubbing her snout.

Jay surveyed the street. That was a good sum-up of his own priorities. The autumn night would be a cold one, and he wasn't keen on sleeping outside. And the food they'd had on the train had been ages ago.

"Until the trains are running again, it looks like we're stuck in this city for a few days," said Ark. "Unless we try walking to Fairdown Falls?"

"*No*," said Jay.

"Forget that, mate," said Andi.

"Then we'll need to find someplace to stay while we're here," said Ark, trying to sound in charge again. He stepped out into the road.

Before Jay could follow him, Hotah gave a sharp bark. At once, Andi threw his arm out in front of Jay, stopping him from stepping off the sidewalk. Alarm flashed across Andi's face.

"Watch out!"

Ark glanced back. Seconds later, a roaring machine on four wheels came flying toward him down the street. Other pedestrians jumped out of the way, but Ark was right in the motorcar's path. The driver didn't slow down.

"Ark!" Jay hollered. "*Move*, bum-wipe!"

Ark was frozen—until a girl in a yellow costume dove into the street. She shoved Ark from behind, sending him spilling out of the car's path.

The speeding motorcar swerved, just barely missing Ark and the girl who'd saved him. The driver fled, tires screeching.

Jay left Andi on the sidewalk and ran into the street. Ark was fine—he'd landed on top of the black case with a couple scrapes—but the girl was on her side, clutching her ankle.

Jay recognized her at once. It was the girl they'd seen in the fire-breather performance—the one who'd been accused of cheating.

"You okay?" said Jay, kneeling next to her.

The girl hissed through her teeth. "Define 'okay.'"

Ark, who'd collected himself, snatched up the black case and joined Jay at the girl's side. He blinked, surprised. "You!"

The girl sat up with a wince. Her knot of black hair came undone in the process, spilling over her shoulders. "Hello again."

"C'mon," said Jay. "Let's move her."

Jay and Ark each took one of the girl's arms over their shoulders, hoisting her up. Witnesses to the near collision hovered around the scene. Andi stood at the front of the crowd, his face anxious.

"What happened?" he called out nervously. "Ark?"

"I'm fine," said Ark while he and Jay helped the girl up. "But she's been hurt."

"She who?" said Andi.

Jay and Ark settled the girl down on the curb. Her face was tight with pain.

"My ankle. It's sprained," she said, exasperated. "The Fire Festival is next week! I can't have a bad ankle!"

"Be glad you don't have worse," said Jay. "That driver almost plowed right over you." He glanced in Andi's direction. "Andi, how'd you know that thing was coming?"

Andi shrugged. "Hotah warned me." He rubbed her head. "Good girl."

Hotah gave a howl.

Meanwhile the girl pulled up her orange leggings, inspecting her ankle. It was swelling and turning the color of a ripe plum.

"Do we need to get you a brace?" Ark asked her.

"No," said Jay, "we need to wrap it up so it doesn't get worse."

"That's what a brace *is*, genius," Ark muttered.

"I should elevate my foot and put my ankle on ice first," the girl said. She glanced between Jay, Ark, and Andi, looking sheepish. "Um . . ."

Jay read her expression. He sighed. "Yeah, we'll help you home."

The girl blushed as Jay and Ark once again took up places on either side of her, serving as crutches. They started down the sidewalk, the girl hobbling between them while Andi and Hotah followed behind.

"I'm Arkalin Encore, by the way," said Ark, all proper-like. "This is Andimakanani and Julian."

"Hana," the girl answered. "Forgive me if I don't curtsy."

Jay chuckled while Ark asked, "What were you doing outside the watch house?"

"To come bail you out, actually," explained Hana. "I couldn't let you get in trouble for helping me. I never got a chance to thank you for clearing my name, either."

Ark caught her eye. "It was nothing," he said, sounding oh-so-superior. "Thanks, too, for saving me from getting run over. That was a crazy stunt."

"Yep, we get it—you're both very thankful," Jay cut in, huffing for breath already. "How far away do you live, exactly?"

Seventeen blocks. That's how far they shuffled along, by Jay's best guess. It was a downhill walk, at least—but it was slow-going with Hana's ankle. Not only that, but all along the way, Jay felt dozens of muses watching him. They were all over the place, drifting in serene harmony wherever they pleased. The sight of so many music spirits put him on edge.

At last, Hana said, "We're here."

Jay looked up. Beyond an iron fence and several trees stood a building that looked like somebody had pieced a bunch of different houses together. The original building had been a simple brick structure, but somebody had gone back to it and built on more wings, another floor, and a large mechanic's garage on the far side of the yard.

"What is this place?" asked Ark.

Jay glanced at the gate: CARTWRIGHT SCHOOL FOR YOUNG LADIES. Jay blinked between the sign and the odd building. This place was a school? He'd never been to a school before.

They brought Hana through the gate to the front door. Before turning the knob, she sent them an uncertain look.

"Just so you know," she said, almost defensive, "the teachers here, the Cartwright sisters, are geniuses. They've both studied hard and built things other inventors couldn't dream up. Keep that in mind, okay?"

Jay didn't know what Hana was trying to say until she led them inside. Beyond the door were some of the weirdest sights and sounds he'd ever seen. All along the walls were metal shafts, steaming cylinders, whirring fans, and turning gears of all sizes. Mechanical fixtures and implements stretched from floor to ceiling, filling the space with *tick-tick-tick* and *click-clack-whir* noises. Jay felt like he'd just walked inside a clock.

"What is this stuff?" he asked.

"Don't touch," said Hana. "It's all part of a geothermal power system the sisters designed. Water reservoirs in the ground below us are constantly being heated by Mount Vakra's magma, and that super-hot water usually boils over and escapes to the surface as geysers. The sisters figured out how to use that hot water and pressure to power dozens of things, including the turbines in the cellar, which generate our electricity."

Jay wasn't sure she'd answered his question—he had no clue what she was saying—but to demonstrate, Hana reached over to the wall and flipped a shiny brass switch. There was a squeak and a puff of steam—and then the lamps along the ceiling came to life, filling the hallway with light.

Ark whistled. Jay gaped.

"This way," said Hana, guiding them further inside.

They had to be careful to avoid touching any mechanics as they helped Hana limp along. Eventually they came to what must've been a kitchen—though it wasn't like any other kitchen Jay had seen. By the sink, drying dishes had been placed next to polished tinkerbit apparatuses. On the counter, a basket of knitting sat beside a basket of wires and cables. An open drawer was filled with silverware and wrenches mixed together. Opposite the sink were jars and bottles labeled with words like SUCROSE, SODIUM CHLORIDE, SODIUM BICARBONATE, and other chemicals that didn't sound like they belonged in a place where people cooked food.

Jay had just peeled his eyes away from two identical jars on the shelves (one was labeled COOKING OIL and the other COG OIL—NOT FOR COOKING!) when he realized somebody else was in the kitchen. The girl was bent over the kitchen table in concentration. She had a rich ochre complexion and bright hazel eyes that were focused on the gizmo she was building. A pair of hand-painted goggles rested on top of her head, holding back long, twisted braids of black hair, woven with multicolored ribbons. She wore a mechanic's jumpsuit up to the hips, its sleeves tied around her waist. She also had on an oil-stained shirt with the sleeves torn off, which revealed her extraordinary arms.

Jay couldn't stop staring. The upper parts of the girl's arms were normal—but at her elbow, both arms transitioned from skin to machinery. The girl's forearms and hands were built of the most intricate tinkerbit apparatuses Jay had ever seen: copper wires, brass gears, and dozens of steel pulleys worked together to create functioning mechanical hands.

"Hi, Hana!" greeted the girl without looking up. "Welcome home. How was practice?"

Hana rocked on her feet, wincing. "It was—"

"You're back just in time, actually," the girl went on without letting Hana answer. She held out one of her tinkerbit hands. "Could you pass me the runcible screwdriver? I need to loosen this—"

"Not now, Rye," said Hana.

The other girl finally looked up to see Hana limping between Jay and Ark. She gasped. "Oh!"

"It's just a sprain," said Hana, settling into a chair and carefully stretching her leg out on the seat next to her. "I need bandages, a washcloth, and ice."

"Sure thing!" said Rye, leaping from her chair. Jay tried not to stare in wonder as Rye went around the kitchen, opening cabinets, pulling drawers, and balancing all the items Hana had asked for in her prosthetic arms. Rye even helped Hana remove her shoe and wrap her ankle in bandages, setting the bundle of ice on top.

"Maybe jacabean tea for the swelling," Hana murmured.

With that prompt, Rye retrieved a tin from the cupboard, carefully measured out a scoop of dark green powder into a cup, and added hot water.

"You all can sit," she said, waving Ark, Andi, and Jay toward seats at the table. Rye handed Hana the cup. "All right—what's the story?"

Hana sipped her tea while she told Rye everything, from the moment Aiden accused her of cheating to the mishap with the motorcar.

"Wow," said Rye. She smiled at Ark. "Thanks for sticking your neck out for Hana like that. I've never met a Musician!"

Ark replied with a humble shrug. Jay didn't know why he suddenly felt the need to punch him in the face.

"My name's Rye," she went on, waggling her tinkerbit fingers in a wave. "Ryanna, actually, but everybody calls me Rye. Don't call me Anna, please and thank you." She glanced down to Hotah. "Oh, wow—that's a gorgeous dog you've got. What's her name? Is she your seeing-eye companion?"

"Yup—this is Hotah," said Andi, scratching Hotah's ears.

"May I pet her?" Rye asked. "Pretty please?"

Andi nodded. Rye squealed in delight as she went over to see the lycalcyon. On the way, she knocked into Jay, bumping him with her metal elbow.

"Whoops!" said Rye as Jay winced. "Sorry."

Jay bit back a scowl, rubbing the bump on his head. "Forget it," he said, feeling more and more irritated for some reason. He rose from his chair. "We should get going."

"Aw, please stay!" said Rye, waving him back into his seat. "There's hardly anybody around right now. Most of the other girls are off with their families for autumn holidays, and they won't be back for the rest of term until the Fire Festival is over—so it's just me, Hana, and the sisters here." She traced the fingerpads of her hands through Hotah's fur; Hotah leaned into her touch. "You guys in town for the competition?"

"Not exactly," said Ark. Jay tapped the table impatiently while Ark explained how they'd gotten kicked off the train.

"Oooh," said Rye, making a face. "Bad timing."

"She's right," said Hana, sipping her tea. "The lava flow will be high for a few more days, at least."

"And you'll never find a place to stay overnight in the city," added

Rye. "People have been coming in from all over for the Fire Festival. The hotels have been booked for weeks."

Ark blanched. He glanced at the black case in his lap. "We'll figure something out."

A bright smile blossomed across Rye's face. "I have a great idea!" she said, bouncing up. "Be right back!"

Without explaining, she flitted out of the kitchen.

"So," asked Ark, filling the silence, "who are the Cartwright sisters?"

Hana set aside her empty cup.

"As I said before, they're geniuses," she said. "Susanna's designs have influenced half of current tinkerbit engineering. And Rosetta's experiments have made it into dozens of alchemy journals. They know a ton about the other subjects they teach us, too—literature, foreign languages, history."

"They sound like quite the pair," said Ark.

Hana beamed.

"Wanna meet them?" said Rye, who'd reappeared just as suddenly as she'd left. She stepped aside and held out her arms like she was presenting a prize. "Ta-da!"

Behind her came two elderly women with leathery brown skin and bristly white hair. Both women had the exact same face; they peered at Jay and the others through a web of identical wrinkles. Still, though they were obviously twins, the women were very different. The lady on the left was muscular for her age, with a spot of grease on her cheek and tools sticking out of the pockets of her baggy trousers. The lady on the right was lithe and willowy, and she wore a stained lab apron over her lacy dress along with a pair of long rubber gloves.

"Guests, how lovely!" said the woman with the lab apron, wearing a warm smile. She removed her gloves with a graceful tug, offering her hand to shake. "How do you do? My name is Rosetta Cartwright. I'm an alchemist."

The woman on the left remained rooted where she stood, offering them a wave instead. "Susanna Cartwright, engineer," she greeted them curtly, biting down on a toothpick and squinting. "Rye says you wanna stay at our school."

Ark waved his hands. "Oh, no, we didn't ask for that—"

"Ryanna just told us how you helped Hanabi during her practice," said Rosetta, cutting him off. "And that the lava flows have interrupted your travel plans."

Ark nodded.

"Then putting you up for a few days feels like the least we could do," Rosetta concluded, smoothing her lab apron. "You're most welcome to stay here."

Ark shook his head. "We don't want to impose—"

"Nonsense!" said Susanna with a hearty chuckle, giving Ark a pat on the back that nearly sent him toppling off his chair. "We've got spare beds. Pitch in around here, and you can stay."

"Of course!" said Andi, chiming in. "Hotah 'n' me are happy to help."

Hotah *woof*ed in agreement. Rosetta and Susanna beamed twin smiles.

"Then it's settled," said Rosetta, gesturing for them to follow. "Come along. Before dinner, let's get you cleaned up."

∞

That night Jay lay awake in an unfamiliar bed, staring at an unfamiliar ceiling. He wished he could be snoring right now, like Andi and Ark were on the other side of the dorm room. But Jay's brain was somersaulting over too many thoughts to let him sleep, and it was impossible to keep his eyes closed for even a few minutes.

After the Cartwright sisters had decided to let them stay, they'd had Jay, Ark, and Andi all take baths before having them help prepare dinner. It was one of the best meals Jay had eaten in ages. Now, just a couple hours later, he was lying in a cozy bed, squeaky clean and with a full belly.

Still, Jay couldn't relax. He felt helpless knowing the Capo had blocked off his escape routes and was slowly drawing in her net. Maybe her people were in Cindertown already, closing in on him.

Jay tossed under the covers. So much for sleeping.

He glanced outside the dorm window, thinking back to his conversation with Argentine. The deputy inspector had said he'd help keep the Capo off his back. Maybe now was the time for Jay to put his mistrust of watchmen aside and ask one for help. He needed help.

But then Jay shook the idea from his head. Nuh-uh. Even if he went to Argentine for protection, there was no way the man could give it. Jay knew the Capo. There was a reason why the current head of the Staccato Gang had never been arrested, why hardly anyone knew what she even looked like—and why she always got what she wanted. She was smart, and coldblooded, and didn't let little things like laws and watchmen stand in her way. She'd knock Argentine down like a stuffed dummy, without a second thought. And then she'd be sure to make Jay pay.

Jay had just shoved that not-so-happy thought from his head when he heard Ark moan in his sleep. Ark's eyes snapped open and he sat up, squinting like he didn't recognize where he was.

"Hey, bum-wipe," Jay whispered. "You wet the bed or something?"

Ark was too sleepy to even glare. He grumbled something about a bad dream, then rolled over and returned to snoring.

Jay folded his arms behind his head. It felt like forever since he'd slept in his own bed in Mr. Douse's shop loft. How was the old man doing? And Lina and Colton—were they all right? Jay still had Lina's bracelet, deep in his pocket. He'd never apologized. Did she miss him? Did she hate him?

Jay closed his eyes and saw flames scorching the rooftops of Hazeldenn. The fire swirled and roared . . . and then the flames were burning Windfalle, too, destroying everything he'd come to love.

Jay opened his eyes again, haunted by the memories. He didn't need to fall asleep to have nightmares tonight.

Julian.

The perfect music sang out to him from inside the black case next to Ark's bed. Jay listened. The perfect music whispered a gentle, soothing melody, one Jay swore he'd heard before but couldn't place. It made Jay think of warm starlight, cool evening breezes, and the peaceful, sacred hush of night.

Jay felt his body relax. His eyes grew heavy.

"Leave me alone," he whispered. Then he fell asleep.

Chapter Twenty-Three

BREAKING NEWS

As usual, Ark's nightmare ended with him dying.

He was in a cold, twilit forest, running for his life. He flew through the brumal brush and bracken at top speed, trees whipping past him, his feet slipping on snow as he ran.

The Beast gained on him, dogging his every step, bellowing like a demon of Din's design. The Beast was hungry, and it was hunting.

There was only one path Ark could take. Despite knowing what lay at the end, he was compelled to follow the same route through his nightmare every time. He ran straight through snow and shadows until the ground inevitably fell away beneath him. Ark stumbled and tumbled into a hollow in the forest floor, trapped at the bottom with steep, icy embankments on all sides.

Ark cried out, but no sound came from his mouth. He could not move. He could only wait until the Beast found him, as it always did.

The Beast came. It was all fangs and claws and spines and red eyes, the very image of the Reaper coming to collect his soul. It approached him slowly, squeezing all hope from Ark's terrified heart.

You are a disappointment, his father's voice whispered from all around.

The Beast leapt. Its fangs flashed. He was gonna die.

Ark screamed, throwing out his hand to save himself—

Pain splintered through Ark's knuckles, yanking him from his fitful dreams. He hissed aloud, awake at once. It took him a moment to realize what had happened: He'd punched the wall next to his bed in his sleep.

Ark shook out his hand and put his spectacles on, replacing night-mare visions with his real surroundings. The dormitory room he'd been sharing with Jay and Andi for the past few days was bright with midday sunlight. The other beds were empty.

Ark got ready in a groggy daze, pulling on his talaris and taking Brio's instrument along in its case as he headed downstairs.

Eight days had passed since they had come to Cindertown, and Ark had worried his last nerve to the frayed end. He'd stopped by the train station and the watch house each day, hoping for news—but he had nothing. No word from the Royal Conservatory in response to his message. No sign that Mount Vakra's lava flows were ebbing. No clue what his next move should be.

Ark passed through the corridors of the Cartwrights' school, already accustomed to the rumbling mechanics winding along the walls like brass vines. As he made his way toward the kitchen, he glanced into the nearby classrooms. Some were workshops with tools hanging on the walls. Others were laboratories filled with glass alembics and blackboards covered in formulas Ark couldn't read. There were other classrooms that had art supplies, anatomical science dummies, and books on every subject: poetry to politics, theater to theology, languages to logic.

Ark wished he could grab a stack of books and take refuge in their pages—but he had to be ready to leave at a moment's notice. As generous as the Cartwright sisters had been, and as much as he was enjoying spending time with Andi, Rye, and Hana—even Jay, to a slightly more tolerable degree—Ark still had to reach Fairdown Falls.

He tightened his grip on the black case, heading into the kitchen.

Jay, Andi, Hana, Rye, and the Cartwright sisters were all there. Hana washed plates while Andi helped her dry them. Rye chatted with Susanna over mugs of tea. Jay, meanwhile, sat rigidly in a chair while Rosetta stood behind him, wielding a pair of clipping shears.

"Don't fidget," she gently chided Jay, brushing his unkempt hair. "You're long overdue for a proper haircut." She caught sight of Ark in the doorway. "Hello, Arkalin. It's late. Did you sleep well?"

"Yes, thank you," Ark lied. Since he'd encountered the dischord in Lower Grimsborough, he'd had exhausting nightmares almost every night.

Rosetta smiled and turned her attention back on Jay. Jay froze as she began to clip away, sending clumps of hair to the floor.

Susanna nodded to a plate of hash on the table. "Hana made lunch. Dig in."

Though he didn't have much of an appetite, Ark started on the hash while Rye and Susanna chatted next to him. Rye rested one of her arms on the table while Susanna prodded at it with a miniature screwdriver, giving Rye's hand a tune-up.

"Why can't you just use hydrovapor instead of fluviengas to get the Morning Star to fly?" Rye was saying while Susanna tweaked and tinkered. "Hydrovapor is more efficient for achieving lift, right?"

"When you do the math, yes," said Rosetta, going after Jay's fringe with the scissors. "Hydrovapor gets you about fifty percent more buoyancy for the same weight of fuel. But it isn't cheap."

"Besides, the problem isn't lift," said Susanna, tightening a screw at Rye's thumb. "The Morning Star only has room for about five passengers, maybe six. When those people get off, something's gotta balance their weight—or else the ship'll fly too high when it takes off again. You don't wanna have to vent the gas, either, or else you won't have enough left to return to the air when more passengers come aboard. We could use water as a ballast, but then we'd have to land at a water source every time—and we want the Morning Star to be free to fly and land anywhere. We need to figure out some other way to maintain the ship's weight ratio."

Ark didn't pay much attention to their aeronautics discussion. He'd heard Rye talk with the sisters about the Morning Star for days on end. The Cartwright sisters' small airship prototype was currently sitting in the school's mechanic garage, awaiting final adjustments before the sisters pumped up her balloon and put her on display at the Fire Festival later that evening.

Rye frowned in thought, flexing the fingers and testing the grip of her newly serviced hand. "You'll still be doing low-altitude demo rides at tonight's Inventor's Expo, though, right?"

Susanna nodded. "And before you ask, yes—you can help pilot."

Rye pumped her fist, mouthing a *yes*.

"But until we solve the weight problem, we'll postpone the Morning Star's official maiden voyage," said Rosetta. She sent Ark a knowing smile.

"Perhaps a muse will drop in on us and offer a solution. We could use the inspiration."

Ark nodded politely in response, saying nothing. Over the past few days, he'd noticed numerous muses visit the Cartwrights' school. When he'd mentioned as much to Susanna and Rosetta, they'd been delighted. They'd asked him all sorts of questions, curious to know what forms the muses took and whether they were attracted to any particular areas of the school.

Ark had kept his answers vague, mostly for Jay's sake. He hadn't said aloud what he'd observed: that the muses who stopped by almost always went to Jay, like they were drawn to him. A couple days ago, when Jay and Ark had gone outside to weed the garden beds, a muse in the form of a moon lily had sprouted between Jay's hands, opening and closing its petals to get his attention. Jay had pretended not to see it.

Not long after, while Jay, Ark, and Andi were helping to sweep and mop the floors, another muse in the shape of a pearly white bat had flown in and circled Jay's head, its wings flapping with the sound of wind chimes until Jay had shooed it away with an irritated hiss.

The most bizarre incident had been when Ark and Jay had first stumbled upon the school's library. Ark had found a pristine copy of *Darcy Harper and the Sorcerer of Nozz* and happily plucked it up, diving into the first chapter; Jay had poked around the shelves and stared at the covers like he wasn't sure he was allowed to touch them. Then an eagle-like muse with ochre feathers and ruby eyes had swooped in, perching on the marble bust next to Jay. Jay had given it the cold shoulder until the muse, with a resonant *caw*, had lowered its gleaming feathery head in a bow. Jay had stormed out of the library without looking back.

Ark had witnessed each instance with bewilderment. Sure, muses would interact with Musicians, even when they weren't summoned by a cantus or tonus. But Ark had never heard of muses intentionally seeking out a Musician—especially one who obviously didn't care for their attention. It didn't make sense why the muses would take such an interest in some random person.

Ark checked himself, staring at his half-eaten plate of hash. It *wasn't* just some random person they were drawn to, though, was it? Jay had resonated with Brio's instrument. He was the Crafter's heir. Perhaps the muses could sense that, somehow.

"There, all done," said Rosetta, pulling Ark from his thoughts. She dusted hair clippings from Jay's shoulders. "That feels much better, doesn't it?"

Jay swept a hand self-consciously through his cropped hair and mumbled, "Thanks."

Rosetta patted his arm. "Think nothing of it, dear," she said. She turned to Ark, holding up the shears. "How about you, Arkalin? Want a trim?"

Before Ark could answer, Rosetta spied his half-eaten plate. "You've hardly eaten, honey." She placed a calloused hand on his forehead with a motherly touch. "Feeling out of sorts?"

Ark shook his head. "I'm well. Just a little anxious."

"Fresh air—that's what you need," said Susanna. "Boys shouldn't be cooped up indoors too long. Why don't you all head out to the news stand together? You can get the latest lava flow updates."

"Great idea," said Rosetta. "Hanabi and Ryanna can take you."

Hana shook her head. "I'm meeting up with the Salamanders to rehearse before the competition. All of Iggy's spiky hair will fall out if I'm late."

"And I want to help you with the Morning Star before the Expo!" said Rye, sending Susanna an imploring look.

"Go on to the news stand," said Susanna. "Just there and back again. And then you can help with the Morning Star while Hana goes to practice."

Rosetta nodded in agreement, then gestured to the door. "Hurry along, girls."

After that, Ark found himself following Rye and Hana along the sidewalk with Jay and Andi on either side. Ark was glad for his talaris when he felt the end-of-autumn breeze, promising a chilly day. He gripped Brio's instrument case tight in his hand.

"Sounds like a lot of people are out here," said Andi.

He was right. Despite the frosty air of the colder morning, the streets were packed. Pedestrians roamed around, taking in the sights or scoping out souvenirs, which savvy street vendors proudly put out for passersby to pick over. In anticipation of the fire-breathing competition that evening, plenty of people were wearing the colors of the various local fire-breather teams. Some fans wearing the orange and yellow colors of the King Street

Salamanders recognized Hana, telling her "Good luck!" and "Crush those Firebirds!" in passing. She thanked each of them.

"What's all happening tonight?" asked Andi. "There's more to the Fire Festival than the fire-breathing competition, yeah?"

"The competition is the biggest event," said Rye, falling into step beside him and Hotah. "There's also the Inventor's Expo, where Susanna and Rosetta will be presenting the Morning Star prototype. Other than that, there'll be food stalls, vendor stands, all that stuff." She casually added, "Maybe we could all go to the festival tonight. It's always a lot of fun each year."

Andi grinned like he thought that was a grand idea. Hana glanced Ark's way and smiled. Even Jay, who'd been sullen and preoccupied the past few days, managed a nod. Ark opened his mouth before he could stop himself.

"Not if the trains are running again," he said. "If they are, we'll need to leave for the Royal Conservatory as soon as we can."

Rye's and Hana's faces fell a little, but they nodded in understanding. Andi's grin dimmed in disappointment. Jay rolled his eyes.

"Nice one," he muttered. "You deserve 'Wet Blanket of the Year.'"

Ark frowned. "We have bigger things to worry about—"

"Stuff it, bum-wipe," Jay interrupted. "All you ever talk about is getting to the Royal Conservatory—and finishing your 'mission,'" he added in air quotes. He shook his head. "You know, if you weren't busy acting like such a stiff-neck all the time, you might remember you're just a kid. And you *might* even be okay to hang around with—that is, if you didn't get your dandies in a twist over every little thing."

The rest of them walked ahead, leaving Ark stunned on the sidewalk. After a moment he hurried to catch up, his face burning.

Ark was glad when they finally arrived at their destination. They stopped in a wide-open plaza surrounded by specialty shops. In the center of the plaza stood a large circular stage with four sets of stairs leading up to it. Standing around the stage near the stairs were men and women in brightly colored clothes—vibrant blues, shocking oranges, lurid greens. Around the stage's circumference were weather-stained signs, all bearing the same warning: PERSONS THROWING STONES AT NEWS CRIERS WILL BE PROSECUTED.

"Looks like we beat the start of the broadcast," Hana remarked.

Ark scanned the stage, confused. "I thought we were going to a news stand. Where are the bulletins?"

Rye explained. "We don't print news bulletins in Cindertown," she said, guiding them toward the group of bystanders. "Bulletins are a waste of paper, not to mention flammable—and not everyone can read, anyway. So the city hires news criers to share current events instead."

Rye gestured to the people in vibrant clothes. "The news criers are just about ready to go up, I think."

As she said it, a bald man in a pristine white suit climbed up the stairs and took center stage, getting the crowd's attention.

"On behalf of the Curtiss and Felixson Dispatch Company, welcome to today's afternoon broadcast," he said in a baritone voice, hushing the crowd. "Today's reports are sponsored by Cindertown's fire-breathing champions, the East End Firebirds. Aiden Flaire, captain of the Firebirds, invites you to come cheer on your number-one team at tonight's Fire Festival."

As the man made the announcement, a familiar figure ascended the stage: Aiden, the same guy who'd accused Hana of cheating. He was dressed in an all-black costume with a golden sash around his waist. The bystanders cheered as he flashed a winning smile at the crowd.

Hana glared at Aiden. "Number-one team?" she echoed.

Rye scoffed, waving dismissively at the stage. "*Pff*, please. Not after tonight, buddy. The Salamanders are gonna put your flames to shame."

She held up a hand, and Hana high-fived it.

Meanwhile, the bystanders hushed as Aiden raised his arms, taking a dramatic pose. He held out his right hand, palm up—and then, with a familiar gesture, he snapped his fingers. At once a quivering flame appeared in his bare hand for a few seconds before burning out with a sizzle. The bystanders clapped and cheered.

Hana's mouth fell open.

"Say," said Rye, glancing Hana's way. "Wasn't that quickfliss and brightbane?"

"That thief!" Hana growled. "He stole my move!"

There was nothing she could do about it; Aiden had already left the stage, and the criers in colorful outfits ascended, taking positions around the stage's circumference. The man in white spoke again.

"And now, the daily broadcast!"

On cue, two dozen criers all held up their reports and began talking at once, shouting to the bystanders below. Ark winced at the chaotic babble:

"—still no leads regarding the break-in at the mayor's gallery—"

"—Wystian leadership declines meeting with Southin chieftains—"

"—quarantine in Upper Grimsborough lifted—"

Andi tilted his ear more intentionally toward the stage, a confused look on his face. "Say, mates—is it weird that some of them are shouting different things about the same story? How are you supposed to know who's right?"

Ark tried to listen. Andi certainly had better hearing than him; it was hard enough for Ark to pick out individual stories in the noise.

Rye tapped Ark on the shoulder, then pointed to a crier standing on the far side of the stage: a man with a beige suit and thick spectacles.

"That man reports on Mount Vakra," she said. "C'mon."

Ark and the others followed her around the stage, finding a spot where they could hear the beige-dressed crier. Ark strained his ears:

"—monitors at Vakra's summit reported a decrease in gaseous emissions and a drop in effusive flow as of three o'clock this morning," the man was saying, his voice droning like a tired gramophone. "Travel restrictions through the lava field will be lifted at three o'clock this afternoon. Trains may resume operations starting at four p.m.—"

"There you are," spoke Rye over the rest of the report. "Sounds like you'll be able to leave tonight." She shrugged. "Too bad you'll miss the Fire Festival. But at least you'll finally get to Fairdown Falls." She forced a bright tone in her voice. "Next time you're in Cindertown, we'll hang out again!"

Ark thought through how to respond: thank them for their hospitality, offer a noncommittal agreement to visit Cindertown at some point in the future. But he couldn't form the words. Ark stared at Rye, then glanced to Andi, Hana, and finally Jay. He recalled what Jay had just told him:

If you weren't busy acting like such a stiff-neck all the time, you might remember you're just a kid. And you might even be okay to hang around with.

Ark clenched the black case even tighter.

"Nah," he said, shaking his head. "We shouldn't leave tonight. The trains could be packed with others trying to leave. We'll wait until morning."

Jay and the others stared at him in surprise.

"Besides, we don't know when we'll be able to visit Cindertown again," he added, trying to keep his tone casual. "We should make a night of it." He glanced at Andi. "But only if that's okay with you, Andi. I know you want to reach the capital to find your brother."

Andi's face turned thoughtful. "I've been chasing Hoku for weeks now. If he really is in Fairdown Falls, it won't make much difference if I take one more day to get there."

Rye glanced between them. "So . . . Fire Festival?"

Ark nodded. Rye and Hana cheered, loud enough to earn annoyed glances from bystanders still listening to the broadcast. Jay regarded Ark with a sideways glance. For once he didn't call Ark a bum-wipe.

Hana, Rye, and Andi started off from the news stand. Ark and Jay were just about to follow when a woman in a vivid red dress clambered up onto the stage.

"Extra! Extra!" she shouted, silencing the other criers. "Breaking news!"

That got Hana, Rye, and Andi's attention, too. They walked back to where Ark and Jay still stood. All the bystanders drew a little closer to the stage, murmuring in curiosity.

"This just in!" the woman in red cried out. "*A Crafter's heir has been found!*"

The crowd gasped. Ark's mouth fell open.

"Sources from the Royal Conservatory confirmed a team had been sent to the town of Hazeldenn for a Crafter evaluation," the woman in red shouted.

"Hazeldenn," Andi echoed. "Say, Jay—isn't that where you're from?"

"Shh," hissed Hana and Rye together, listening. The crier cried on:

"According to local testimony, in the evening during local Harvestide celebrations, a large-scale musical event occurred. Inhabitants saw a golden pillar of light and felt a profound Resonance. Witnesses claim to have seen a teenaged boy playing a glowing violin. The Royal Conservatory has since identified the phenomenon as the positive response to a true Crafter's heir."

As she spoke, Ark drew the case to his chest. How the gavotte had the news spread so quickly?

It took Ark a moment to realize Hana had glanced his way, her eyes focused on the case in his arms, her face unreadable.

The woman in red continued to shout:

"The Crafter's heir is believed to be en route to the Royal Conservatory, whereupon he will undergo the necessary final rites to assume the full Crafter title," she bellowed. "Grand Maestran Johann Luthier was unavailable for comment, but notice was sent to members of the International Maestrans Congress, presumably in preparation for the Crafter's appointment."

The end of her report was drowned out by the crowd, now jabbering in excitement.

"Well, *that's* something you don't hear every day!" said Andi with a bright grin. "The Crafter's returned? Are they serious?"

"Hmm," said Hana absently. Her stare was still fixed on Ark.

"Jay?" asked Rye, studying him. "You all right?"

Jay didn't respond. He looked shaken, staring at the crier.

"We should leave," said Ark. He didn't like the way Hana was studying them—like she had just seen through a complex alchemical formula. He cuffed Jay on the shoulder, breaking his daze. "C'mon."

But none of the others budged.

"Ark?" said Andi, suspicious. "You sound weird. What's going on?"

"Nothing's going on!" said Ark, exasperated.

Rye pressed her lips into a tight line. "No, something's wrong."

Ark saw the gears turning in her head. Then the light of understanding blinked on.

"Oh. My. Gosh," she squeaked. "Is *that* why you're going to the capital?"

"I don't know what you're talking about," said Ark. Frigits, they were perceptive. Dangerously perceptive.

Ark looked over to see Hana staring hard at him. His temper spiked. "What?" he snapped.

Hana's clear, amber-eyed stare was unflinching. At length, she spoke.

"One question—and be honest," she asked, her voice low. She pointed. "What's in the case?"

At her question, the black case in Ark's arms felt twice as heavy. A little voice in his head told him to deny it. The fewer people who knew the truth, the safer they were.

But he couldn't get his mouth to form a likely lie. He stared at Hana, Rye, and Andi. He couldn't hide the truth from his face.

"Thought so," said Hana triumphantly.

Rye squealed, practically jumping up and down. She pointed at Ark. "It's *you!* It's you, isn't it, Ark? *You're* the Crafter's heir!"

"What?" said Andi, too loud. "The Crafter's heir?"

"Shh!" Ark hissed, hushing them. He shook his head.

"Not me," he murmured. He pointed to Jay. "*Him.*"

They all turned their heads. Jay was standing in the same spot, arms crossed, head down. He was hiding his face under the brim of his cap— something Ark had noticed Jay always did when he didn't want to be noticed.

"Julian?" Hana whispered, stunned. Rye and Andi were mute with shock. Ark saw Jay clench his hands, sweating under their stares.

"Am I interrupting something?" someone asked.

Ark jumped, startled. All of them spun around.

Inspector James Argentine was hovering behind them. Ark wondered how long the man had been standing there.

"Inspector Argentine!" said Ark, his voice cracking in surprise. He cleared his throat, adding smoothly, "Can we help you?"

Argentine's face was a mask. If he'd overheard something, he didn't show it. "I'm here to help you, actually. Would you mind coming with me?"

He gestured for them to follow, setting off at a brisk pace. Ark obeyed. Jay and the others trailed behind.

"I tried to find you earlier at the Cartwrights' school," said Argentine over his shoulder. "Miss Rosetta said I'd likely run into you at the news stand."

"What's this about?" asked Ark as they left the news stand behind.

"Your message," Argentine replied, guiding them through the throngs in the streets. "I'd sent it to the Royal Conservatory, as you'd asked."

Ark started. "Did you get a response?"

Argentine pursed his lips. "You could say that."

After that puzzling response, the man kept a frustrating silence— though thankfully he didn't take them much farther. When they stopped, Ark stared up at the tall building they'd come to. It was a nice-looking place, with lots of windows and rows of torches leading to the entrance. An ostentatious crimson sign said THE GOLDEN EMBER HOTEL.

Argentine walked straight through the hotel entrance, with Ark, Jay, Andi, Rye, and Hana following on his heels. Ark was about to ask again why they were here when a familiar voice called out:

"Arkalin! Julian!"

Ark blinked, watching a figure approach from the far side of the hotel lobby. Before Ark was ready for it, Sir Dulcian Mandore swept him and Jay into a brief, firm hug.

"You're here!" said Dulcian, laughing. "Thank the Design!"

Chapter Twenty-Four

THE CRAFTER'S HEIR

Ark rubbed his eyes and cleaned his spectacles on his talaris, positive he was seeing things. But when he slid his spectacles back on, Dulcian was still there, shaking hands with Argentine.

"Thank you for all you've done, Inspector," said Dulcian.

"Not at all," replied Argentine. His eyes flickered between Ark and Jay once more. "If you need further assistance, you can find me in the city square, just south of here. I'll be patrolling the Fire Festival tonight."

With that, the deputy inspector exited the hotel.

Dulcian grasped Ark and Jay by the shoulders. "Are you all right?"

Ark and Jay assured him they were fine, and Dulcian exhaled a sigh of relief. Ark studied him. The man's hair was ruffled, and dark circles under his tired eyes spoke of sleepless nights. Trillo, perched on his shoulder, looked as lively as ever, fluffing its blue feathers and twittering happily.

"You have no idea how glad I am to see you," said Dulcian, managing a smile. His eyes soon found the case in Ark's arms. "And I must say, I'm *extremely* glad to see you didn't lose *that*. I'll take it back now, if you please."

Ark passed the case to Dulcian, who held it in his arms for a reverent moment. "I don't think there are sufficient words for me to express how relieved I am right now."

"Excuse me," said Hana, politely interrupting. Ark had almost forgotten that she, Andi, and Rye were still there. "You know Julian and Arkalin?"

Dulcian looked at her kindly. "Indeed. And who are you?"

Andi answered first. "I'm Andi."

"Himawari Hanabi," said Hana.

"I'm Ryanna Inyanga!" said Rye.

"Oh, we're using full names?" said Andi. "Then I'm Andimakanani ne Te'emaru. And this is Hotah."

The lycalcyon sniffed the hem of Dulcian's talaris.

"Hanabi, Ryanna, and Andimakanani—it's a pleasure to meet you," said Dulcian. "How are you all acquainted?"

Ark's mind fast-forwarded through memories of the past couple weeks.

"It's a long story," Ark admitted. He was about to elaborate, but Jay cut in.

"What happened to Hazeldenn?"

Dulcian's gaze lingered on Jay's face a second too long.

"After I'd Transposed you to safety, Dubito disappeared," he explained. "We gave up looking for him and spent the rest of that night extinguishing fires. There was some damage, but no townsfolk were harmed."

Jay closed his eyes as if offering up a thankful prayer.

"After that, we tried tracking you," Dulcian went on. "My Transposition was supposed to send you both directly to the Royal Conservatory—but Dubito interfered, sending you off course. We didn't have any clue where you'd ended up until the Royal Conservatory contacted us, saying they'd received word that you were here. We had a difficult time pinpointing your location, what with the city-wide restrictions on music—but Inspector Argentine was tremendously helpful in finding you."

"Where is Callie? And Mara?" asked Ark.

Just then, another voice from the back of the lobby—shrill, imperious, and quite familiar—called out, barking orders.

"—stand aside—let me pass—oh, for the love of—*move!*"

The other hotel guests moved aside as if an angry boar had been set loose. Lady Calliope Vielle stormed through, as domineering as ever. Fiero padded beside her, wearing the same stern expression on its foxy face. Behind her came Mara Fipple, trailing Callie like an extra shadow.

"You two have *no idea* how much you've put us through!" Callie shouted by way of greeting. She closed her eyes and swallowed, apparently trying to choke down her bile. "I suppose it's enough that you're all right, at least." She shot Dulcian a fierce glare. "No thanks to *you*."

Dulcian balked. "How many times must I apologize?"

"A few more," Callie snapped. She gestured to Ark and Jay. "After your failed Transposition, we're lucky they didn't both end up in the ocean!"

"Do you know how difficult it is to perform an improvised Transposition under duress?" Dulcian countered. "Let's just be grateful they're safe!"

Dulcian and Callie kept squabbling. Looking like she felt out of place, Mara retrieved her calculations device from her pocket and began idly punching buttons. The device spewed out a line of numbers in sequence:

$$0\ 1\ 1\ 2\ 3\ 5\ 8\ 13\ 21\ 34$$

Ark didn't realize he was staring until Mara caught him at it. She held up the strip for him to get a better look.

"See the pattern?" she said, tracing a finger along each number.

Ark frowned and studied the number series, curious by what pattern there could be—but he never got the chance to work it out.

"Enough," Callie snapped, cutting Dulcian off with a sharp flick of her hand. That's when she finally noticed Andi, Rye, and Hana.

"What are commoner kids doing here?" she said.

"Apparently, it's a long story," replied Dulcian. "One I'm most curious to hear. Anyway, we should probably report back in."

He gestured toward the lobby stairs.

The next thing Ark knew, he, Jay, and their commoner friends were making their way up to the hotel's third floor. They arrived at a set of double doors at the end of a corridor. Dulcian opened the doors, ushering them through.

Ark did not expect to see so much green. The space beyond was a large, well-tended sunroom. The outer walls were made of tempered glass, and a door opened onto a balcony that offered a perfect view of the city square below. The room was filled with plants of all kinds: spiny plants in individual terrariums, miniature trees in pots, sleek ivy plants with vines unfurling to the floor. The air had a humid, floral taste that filled Ark's lungs.

"Smells like home," Andi remarked.

"It's the only room the hotel would offer," said Dulcian. "Apparently we came at the wrong time of year. Something about a local festival."

Hotah *woof*ed and padded into the sunroom. Andi followed her, along with Rye, Hana, and Jay. Ark paused at the threshold.

The plants weren't the only green things in the room. At least a dozen other people were gathered, all wearing green talarises bearing the Royal Conservatory emblem on the back. It looked like they had transformed the sunroom into a base of operations.

Dulcian shut the door behind them, nudging Ark forward.

"Say hello to our colleagues from the Royal Conservatory," he said. "They were sent by Grand Maestran Luthier as an additional escort—"

"Introductions can wait," Callie cut in. She pulled a few wicker chairs together, then snapped at Ark and Jay: "Sit!"

Ark and Jay obeyed. Callie sat as well, and Dulcian took the only vacant chair left, leaving Mara to stand behind them. Andi, Hana, and Rye hovered awkwardly, like they weren't sure they belonged there.

"Now then, Arkalin," said Callie, ignoring everyone else, "report."

Ark took a deep breath, then recounted everything from the moment they'd emerged from the fountain pool in Upper Grimsborough to their stay at the Cartwrights' school. Callie remained silent during the whole story—though Dulcian gasped when Ark mentioned the dischord Nockna Mora and how Jay had used Brio's instrument to defeat it. Ark felt like hours had passed by the time he'd finally finished explaining.

"You were right," said Dulcian at length. "That was a long story."

"Indeed," said Callie. She turned her gaze toward Andi, Rye, and Hana.

"On behalf of the Royal Conservatory, I want to thank the three of you for helping Arkalin and Julian," she told them. "You did us a service."

Andi, Rye, and Hana barely had a chance to look pleased with themselves before Callie added curtly, "That said, we no longer need your assistance." She motioned to a few of her green-clad comrades, who stepped forward. "These agents will see you out. Good day."

Ark and Jay sputtered objections as Rye, Andi, and Hana were swiftly ushered out of the room, so fast they didn't even get to say goodbye.

"Why'd you dismiss them like that?" Ark demanded. "They're our friends! They don't deserve—!"

Callie didn't let him finish. Her eyes blazed.

"You forget your place, Adept Encore!" she snapped. At once the storm of her fury was upon him.

"Your foolish decisions these past weeks have only been outshone by your reckless actions!" she spat. "You panicked in Hazeldenn when you were supposed to be vital support against Dubito and the threat he posed to the townspeople. Since then, you've gallivanted around with a centuries-old relic like it was nothing but a toy, and by your own admission you nearly lost it. You've put your life and the lives of others at unnecessary risk several times over—and not only that, but you jeopardized the future of the Crafter's heir before his inauguration!"

Just when Ark thought Callie was finished, she added, "You should request to be excused from the rest of your jury mission. You'll spare yourself the embarrassment of a dishonorable failing mark and a permanent stain on your record."

Each rebuke stabbed Ark in the chest, and it was all he could do to keep his emotionless mask intact. Inside, he felt like everything around him was rising, building into a terrible wave that was about to crash down and sweep him away. *Request to be excused?* But his jury mission was his chance to prove himself. Had he failed so spectacularly that they were sending him back to Echostrait?

Ark was painfully aware of Dulcian and Mara, who were avoiding his gaze, along with the other Royal Conservatory Musicians, who'd paused just long enough in their tasks to catch his reaction. The awful wave rose even higher around him, filling his ears with a horrible roar.

Then, unexpectedly, Jay spoke up.

"Jeez," he said, not bothering to keep his voice down. "No wonder Ark's turned out to be such a stiff-neck. He's got ugly skriffs like you ragging on him all the time. Now it makes sense."

Callie's head snapped in his direction. "What did you call me?"

"An ugly skriff," Jay repeated, unaffected by her venomous look. "And if you believe even half the stuff you've just said about Ark, you're also a total duff-for-brains."

Ark stared, stunned. Dulcian and Mara gaped in shock. The other Musicians were openly watching, forgetting their tasks completely.

Callie's tone turned waspish. "What the gavotte would you know?"

Jay sent her a level look.

"I know what I've *seen*," he said. "In Hazeldenn, I saw Ark put himself between me 'n' Dubito to protect me when you guys were nowhere to be found. In Grimsborough, I saw him all set to offer himself up to a dischord so I could escape. He goes on and on about protecting that fiddle and fulfilling his duty—and the only wrong thing he's done this whole time is put up with your stupid criticism." His words gained a biting edge. "You don't fool me. You're just chewing him out to make yourself feel better for all the stuff *you've* screwed up. What a jerk move."

The sunroom went dead silent. Mara and Dulcian exchanged a nervous look. The other Musicians changed tack, pretending they were absorbed in their tasks and hadn't overheard anything—presumably to avoid the eruption of Callie's inevitable wrath.

But Callie remained frozen in her seat. She looked like she was struggling to keep her own mask on her face, but the red tint in her cheeks gave away her shame.

Ark, meanwhile, couldn't believe his ears. Jay had defended him?

He glanced sideways, noting the way he and Jay were squared off in their chairs, facing Callie and the other Royal Conservatory Musicians. For a moment, it was like the two of them were on the same side. Friends, even.

"I know Ark's a screw-up, too, and he's annoying as heck," Jay added, breaking the silence. "But it's not like being a bum-wipe is a crime."

Ark sighed. And the moment was over.

"Now that the lecture's done, can we leave?" said Jay, standing from his chair.

"Stay, please," said Dulcian. Jay flopped down on the chair with a *hmph.*

"Let's put this discussion behind us," said Dulcian, playing moderator. He nodded to Jay. "What matters now is our Crafter's heir."

Jay sat rigidly as the other Musicians, as if on cue, stopped what they were doing and came over, standing behind Jay like a row of trees.

"Before we return to the Royal Conservatory, we've been instructed to prepare you a bit for what comes next," Dulcian began. "Tell me, Julian—how much do you know about the Crafter?"

Jay tilted his head to duck behind his cap brim, saying nothing.

"Then we'll start at the beginning," continued Dulcian, folding his hands. "Throughout history, the Crafter has always stood as the leader of all Musicians in Sedrinel. Do you know why that is?"

"'Cause Brio chose 'em," Jay muttered.

"That's half-correct," said Dulcian. "They were indeed chosen by Brio and so were deemed worthy to assume the Crafter title. But ultimately the reason the Crafter has always been appointed the leader over all Musicians is because of the gifts Brio bestows on the Crafter."

Jay peeked out from under his cap. "Gifts?"

Dulcian smiled. "It's much like a muse patronage ceremony," he explained. "During a patronage ceremony, a Musician and muse choose one another. They forge a special bond and are connected in spirit for life." He stroked Trillo's beak as he said this. "In some instances, the muse even bestows unique gifts on their Musician—gifts beyond natural understanding. Some Musicians have received the ability to tell when someone is lying, for example, or an enhanced aptitude for teaching, healing, and so on."

Jay sat up a little more. Ark sat up too, curious.

"Brio is the most ancient and powerful muse in existence—and each Crafter who has bonded with Brio has received multiple gifts in return," Dulcian continued. "These gifts are what set the Crafter so far apart from other Musicians—even Maestrans."

"What gifts will Jay receive?" asked Ark, unable to stop himself from asking.

"We looked into the biographies of Crafters who came before, but I'm afraid they are woefully vague on those details," said Dulcian. "But we learned that these gifts will manifest throughout Julian's time as Crafter, as his bond with Brio deepens and his musical skills improve. Whatever they are, these skills are what give the Crafter the ability to fight discord and preserve harmony in Sedrinel."

Ark glanced Jay's way. Jay was staring blankly at his hands, like he wasn't sure what to think.

"Until you perform the bonding ritual with Brio at the Royal Conservatory, though, you're technically still just the Crafter's heir," Dulcian told Jay. "Brio has chosen you, accepted you—and through the ritual, you'll accept him back and formally receive the Crafter title. It's our duty now to make sure you get to the Royal Conservatory in one piece."

Dulcian gestured to the other green-clad agents.

"We have secured a private train that will depart for Fairdown Falls at ten o'clock this evening," Dulcian went on. "Factoring in necessary stops, we're scheduled to arrive at the capital by noon tomorrow. It seems details about the Crafter's heir have already been leaked, so we may need to contact the Grand Maestran ahead of time to prepare a stronger security detail—"

"Hold on," said Jay, trying to speak up.

"—and there's a chance we'll encounter another Dischordian, perhaps even Dubito," Dulcian continued over him, addressing the Musicians standing behind Jay. "We must take every precaution. Teams of three at all times, and the Crafter's heir doesn't go anywhere without an escort. Understood?"

"Yes, Sir Mandore," the Musicians answered in unison.

"Now wait just a minute!" Jay blurted.

"We should also employ a stunt double to throw off any unsavory company, if the need arises," said Dulcian, speaking over Jay. "Two enemies we have to fear just as much as Dischordians are politicians and the press. We may need a decoy to keep them from devouring the Crafter's heir when he arrives at the capital." Dulcian smiled at Ark. "Perhaps we can appoint you to the task?"

"I—yes," said Ark, who hadn't known until that moment whether he was even still involved. "I can be a decoy."

"I don't need a—!" Jay protested.

"Now, then," said Dulcian, interrupting Jay yet again, "we'll only have a short time to give Julian a crash course in etiquette. Once we arrive in Fairdown Falls, he'll meet with Grand Maestran Luthier before being presented to the rest of the Maestrans Council. Following the final ritual with Brio's instrument, we'll hold a public audience where he'll be officially recognized as the Crafter." Dulcian held his chin pensively. "We should start thinking about who should serve as your liaison. The Maestrans are still working out how the Crafter will fit into the international council structure. Luthier has said he's willing to abdicate his position, but other Grand Maestrans may not be ready to relinquish their authority—"

"*Stop it!*" Jay exploded, bursting from his chair.

Dulcian's mouth snapped shut.

"Will you just lay off?" Jay yelled. "You think I wanna hear any of this?"

Dulcian sent him an apologetic look. "I realize it's rather a lot to take in at once. Unfortunately, time is not on our side—"

"That's not it!" Jay spat. "Stop acting like you've made all these choices for me. What makes you think I'm gonna go along with anything you've said?"

Dulcian tried on a placating smile. "Because you are our Crafter's heir. You have to."

Jay's glare turned as cold and sharp as a blade of ice. "I don't have to do *anything* for you skriffs. You can't force me to be the Crafter!"

He thrust his hands toward Ark.

"Why can't you just let *him* be your Crafter?" said Jay. "We all know Ark would be way better at the job. He's Mr. Perfect at everything. Oh, yeah—and he actually knows music!"

"It doesn't work like that," said Dulcian, ever-patient. His eyes met Ark's for a moment before he kept speaking. "None of us would question Arkalin's skill—he's a genuine virtuoso. But we don't bring out Brio's relic for just anybody. I don't know many specific details, but before an official Crafter evaluation ever takes place, there's a thorough selection process first—very private, very discreet—and it can take years to complete." He tilted his head toward Ark. "I can't say whether Arkalin was ever vetted as a Crafter candidate before—but you were observed *and* positively selected, Julian. That's why Luthier sent us to Hazeldenn."

"What d'you mean, observed?" Jay cut in. He peered suspiciously at Dulcian. "Are you saying—was somebody *spying* on me? Who? For how long?"

Dulcian simply ignored the questions. "Besides, as you may recall, Arkalin wasn't able to play Brio's instrument, even when he tried," he pointed out. "But you did."

"Shut up!" Jay snapped. "Just stop talking—!"

"We're not forcing you to become anything more than you already are!" Dulcian spoke over him, getting louder himself. "Brio chose *you!*"

"He chose *wrong!*" Jay hollered, losing it completely. "How many times do I have to tell you people? I'll never be the Crafter! I'm not a Musician! I *hate* muses! I hate *all* of you!"

The only thing worse than Jay's outburst was the terrible silence that followed. Ark felt like he was the sole audience member of a play that'd gone catastrophically wrong, falling apart before his eyes. Dulcian looked stricken. Callie, Mara, and the other Musicians averted their gazes.

Even the muses seemed cowed; Trillo and Fiero shrank away, like they could feel Jay's rage.

Only then did Jay's angry expression crumble. He hid his face under his cap.

"I didn't—" he began, then faltered. He clenched his trembling hands into fists. "I never asked for this," he said instead, his voice now barely a hiss. "You all came barging into my life without giving me a say-so. You don't even know me—what I've done—!"

He choked on his words, like he'd said something he hadn't intended. The atmosphere in the sunroom tensed, like even the plants were waiting to see what happened next.

At length, Dulcian stood, reaching for Jay's arm. Jay jerked out of reach.

"I can't," Jay spat, backing up. "You don't get it—you don't!"

"Julian!" said Dulcian, but too late. Jay bolted from the sunroom. Ark heard his rapid steps grow faint as he ran down the corridor.

"I'll get him," said Dulcian, dashing after him.

Callie's sigh was intentionally loud and exasperated. "Wonderful. This assignment really was a waste of time."

She stormed off across the room, staring out the wide windows to the plaza below. The other Musicians spoke in hushed voices. Ark sat alone, feeling tremendously awkward. It was almost a relief when Mara came over—at least until he saw the expression she was wearing.

"Miss Fipple?" he asked. He didn't understand why, but Mara looked anxious, frightened even, just before she spoke.

"Arkalin!" said Mara in a breathy hiss, leaning in close so none of the others could hear. "There's something you have to know!"

Ark stared at her. "What is it?"

Mara gaped at him, her face pale. "Can't say—!" she gasped. She looked terrified, but she was desperately trying to tell him something.

As she trembled before him, Ark studied her, his mind whirring.

Then it clicked. Ark dove into his talaris pocket, pulling out his notebook and his nub of a pencil. He offered them to her.

"You don't have to *say* anything," he told her meaningfully.

Mara's watery eyes widened. She snatched both from his hands, flipping his notebook open to a random page and scrawling along the edge. At one point, she viciously scratched out what she'd written and kept on scribbling.

"Mara!" barked Callie.

Mara flinched, the pencil and notebook jumping in her hands.

"Coming!" she said. She handed Ark his notebook.

"*See the pattern*," she hissed. Then she hurried over to Callie.

Turning his back to the door, Ark furtively flipped his notebook open. She'd written a code inside along the margin:

$$34 - 33 = A$$

$$30 \quad 19 \quad 20 \quad 19 \quad 14 \quad 14 \quad 16 \quad 13 \quad 15 \quad 14 \quad 21 \quad \blacksquare \quad 12$$

First number: 34. He'd seen the number 34 in the sequence Mara had been typing out on her calculations device, not long after they'd first arrived at the hotel: 0, 1, 1, 2, 3, 5, 8, 13, 21, 34. It must have been fresh in her mind.

Ark studied her code. Here, "A" equaled 34 minus 33—which was just another way of saying "A" equaled one. After staring at the row of numbers Mara had scribbled out, Ark finally understood: He had to subtract from 34, *then* convert the result into a letter.

Ark pulled out his notebook, making calculations on the same page:

$$34 - 30 = 4 = D$$
$$34 - 19 = 15 = O$$
$$34 - 20 = 14 = N$$

As the message formed, Ark's stomach retracted to the size of a marble:

D-O-N-O-T-T-R-U-S-T

Uneasily, Ark studied the last two numbers of the code: 12 and 21. He worked out the letters from the code one at a time:

$$34 - 21 = 13 = M$$
$$34 - 12 = 22 = V$$

Ark breathed a silent gasp.
M. V.
Mandore and Vielle.
Dulcian. Callie.
Do not trust.

Chapter Twenty-Five

THE TRUTH

*J*ay had barely made it to the second floor when the fiddle's sharp pull stopped him in his tracks.

"Let me *go!*" Jay snarled, clawing at his chest.

At first, Jay thought the fiddle had actually listened. The pull in his chest eased—but then he heard footsteps chasing after him.

"Julian, wait!" called Dulcian. He had the fiddle in its case with him.

"Leave me alone!" Jay snapped. He started jumping down the steps two at a time, trying to gain as much distance as he could against the fiddle's tug, now almost painful.

Dulcian still followed him. Jay darted across the lobby and ducked into a random room, looking for a way out of the hotel. Wrong turn: It was an empty parlor, filled with stuffy furniture and amusements.

Jay tried to backtrack to find another escape—but Dulcian had already arrived in the doorway, blocking Jay's path.

"Please," said Dulcian, out of breath. "I'm in no shape to chase you."

Jay edged back into the parlor. "Stay away from me!"

Dulcian held up his free hand in truce. "All I want is to talk."

From Dulcian's shoulder, Trillo trilled in an anxious chirp and flapped its wings, as if the bluebird muse were also urging Jay to stop running.

"I got nothing more to say," spat Jay, looking for a way around Dulcian. "So unless you wanna stare at each other 'til we're both cross-eyed—"

"Why do you hate muses?"

Jay staggered at the question, missing his chance to dash. "What?"

"Muses," Dulcian repeated. "Do you really hate them so much?"

Jay tensed up again. "I don't—!" He flinched. "I don't have to tell you!"

A faint smile spread over Dulcian's face. He closed the door behind him.

"*Chiusso*," he chanted. Trillo tweeted in response, flying in a path around the door. Jay felt a thrum of pressure; the door sealed with a *click*.

"There. Some privacy," said Dulcian. He went up to a table in the parlor with a checkerboard on it. "Do you play?"

Jay glanced at the board. "Who doesn't play checkers?"

Dulcian took a seat and blew the dust off the board, setting the green and red pieces on the squares. "Perhaps a game can help us break the ice."

Jay crossed his arms. That guy could go break ice all by himself.

He tried the door. It wouldn't budge.

Bandersnatches.

"Come sit," said Dulcian.

There was no point in refusing. Jay sat, scowling.

Dulcian sat with the black case across his legs. "You have the first move."

Jay slumped in his chair, moving a red piece. Dulcian moved a green piece, waiting for Jay to go next. Jay grudgingly made another move. Their pieces slid across the board as they played in silence. Every so often, Trillo would chirp in Dulcian's ear, as if advising him.

At length, Dulcian sighed in dismay.

"A trap!" he said, staring at the board. "Clever. You're quite formidable."

It was a compliment, but Jay didn't thank him. Dulcian sighed again and jumped over one of Jay's pieces. Jay then jumped Dulcian's last piece.

"That was quick," said Dulcian. "I never stood a chance."

Jay frowned. Why wasn't he getting on with it?

Dulcian must have sensed Jay's thoughts. "I've met a bit of anti-Musician sentiment in my life," he said, changing the subject. "Some people don't like us because they don't understand our gifts. But you're the first *Musician* I've met who claims to hate muses."

Jay's hands clenched the chair's armrests.

"Don't call me that," he snarled. "I'm not a Musician."

"Of course you are," said Dulcian. "Why deny it?"

"Shut up! I'll deny it all I want!"

Dulcian glanced up. His tone changed. "But why?"

The question sank into Jay's ears. He stumbled over a response.

"'Cause I don't—I'm not—I'm not like you!" he blurted.

Dulcian straightened up, curiosity flickering in his eyes.

"Now why would you say that?"

Jay thrust out his arm and sent the checkerboard to the floor, red and green pieces flying.

"Stop messing with me!" Jay yelled. "I just hate muses, okay? I hate seeing them wherever I go! I hate having them follow me! I wish they'd all go away!"

Jay wanted Dulcian to be shocked, or angry, or something—but the guy just hummed thoughtfully, like he'd been expecting the outburst.

"And there's the lie you keep hiding behind," he murmured. Before Jay could figure out how to respond, Dulcian glanced at Trillo.

"*Primmo locco*," he chanted.

At once, the muse flew between the floor and the checkerboard, retrieving all the pieces in a flurry of bright blue feathers. Dulcian reset the board.

"It's okay, Julian. No one's here but us." His gaze settled over Jay like a cloak. "You can tell me the truth."

The truth. An ugly lump of shame swelled in Jay's chest.

"I can't," he hissed.

Dulcian's stare sharpened. "Can't, or won't?"

Jay bit his lip. He couldn't meet the man's eyes. The silence around them went tight.

Then realization flashed over Dulcian's face. "Something happened to you. Something that involved muses." His voice softened. "Did someone get hurt?"

Jay clenched the armrests. *No. I don't want to remember.*

"Please," said Dulcian. "Tell me."

The truth fluttered inside of Jay like an anxious bird trying to escape its cage. Against his will, Jay's mind drifted three years into the past.

∞

CHRIS CROSS

The Quickstep Kid, the youngest and quickest member of the Stacca-to Gang, had had a lousy run of luck. All week he'd gone back to the Capo's place at night with nothing to show for his thieving, nothing of value to count toward his parents' debt. After he'd come back with empty hands for the fifth day in a row, the Capo had kicked him out, saying he shouldn't come back until he'd brought in something more than pocket lint.

Homeless and unwelcome with the gang, Jay had wandered to the slummy west side of the city, where all the streets smelled like fish. Hungry and desperate, Jay had ended up shuffling into a small Designist sanctuary, a dinky little chapel called Windfalle. Near the chapel door was a poor box where people dropped spare change to help feed the orphans in the church's care. All it took for Jay to get past the lock was a simple snick-'n'-twist with his lockpick wires.

Jay's gnawing hunger must've dulled his senses, though, because he never heard the monk approach. Jay still remembered the panic he'd felt when a heavy hand fell on his shoulder, catching him in the act. But the monk who'd caught him hadn't called for the watchmen. Instead, he'd only made Jay return all the coins he'd pilfered from the box—"That's for the orphans," he'd said—and then the monk had reached into his simple robes and pulled out a solid gold Medallion.

"Take this, but promise to come back tomorrow," the monk had said. Then he'd given Jay a blessing and let him go.

Jay had no obligation to keep that promise—but the next day he'd gone back to Windfalle anyway. The monk, Brother Elfenbein, had been delighted to see Jay when he shuffled into the chapel. He'd told Jay that, if he wanted, he could earn money instead of stealing it: The monk had promised to pay Jay every day if he helped around the place. Jay hadn't been sure what the old monk was up to, offering a twelve-year-old outlaw a job—but when Brother Elfenbein offered to feed Jay every day too, Jay had accepted on the spot.

And that's how the Quickstep Kid came to Windfalle. Every morning, instead of heading off to pickpocket in the market, Jay would head to the sanctuary, where Brother Elfenbein would give him something to do: clean the chapel, sweep the grounds, help cook. If there was something Jay didn't know how to do, Brother Elfenbein would teach him.

After Jay had finished for the day, Brother Elfenbein would thank Jay for his hard work, pay him, and say "See you tomorrow."

Windfalle was unlike any other place Jay had known. The little sanctuary doubled as an orphanage. At mealtimes, the orphan kids treated Jay as one of their own, sharing food and laughs. After dinner, Jay would usually linger to hear Brother Elfenbein tell stories, hanging on every word. As time passed, Jay even started to drop in on Brother Elfenbein's sunrise service. Jay was fascinated by everything: the colors of the altar candles, the rose scent of the incense, the rumble of the monk's voice as he sang blessings over the people. Jay had asked Brother Elfenbein what all the prayers meant. Jay remembered the look in the monk's eyes whenever he talked about his faith, staring off at something both near and far away—like a night watchman at midnight, looking toward the horizon for the dawn.

After a few weeks of working at Windfalle, Jay had begun to realize how much he was enjoying his time there. With Brother Elfenbein, he was simply Jay, not the Quickstep Kid. The monk had never demanded anything from Jay, but he did expect a lot from him—more than Jay thought he was capable of.

Jay had visited Windfalle every day for a couple months when he'd finally worked up the courage to tell Brother Elfenbein his darkest secret.

"I see things," Jay had said. The two of them had been sitting on the sanctuary steps; Jay remembered how his hands shook, how scared he'd been to tell the monk the truth. "Critters nobody else does."

Brother Elfenbein hadn't called Jay crazy. He'd asked what the critters looked like, when and how often they appeared. Jay had pointed to the tree that grew beside Windfalle, where a glowing creature that looked like a great big slithery eel was swimming in midair through the tree branches. The eel opened and closed its mouth like it was singing to itself, its slippery body flashing different shades of blue.

"It's right there!" Jay had insisted. "Do you believe me?"

Brother Elfenbein had smiled. "Of course I believe you," the monk had said. "You're a Musician!"

Jay had listened in amazement while Brother Elfenbein explained that the creatures Jay could see were muses, spirits closely tied to nature and life.

"Musicians are special people," he'd explained. "They can see muses when others can't. With some practice, I'm sure you can do many incredible things with your gift. You'll be like other Musicians and call upon muses at will—just like that!" he'd added, snapping his fingers.

After hearing Brother Elfenbein's explanation, Jay had felt like his whole life had started over. He'd always pretended the weird, uncanny beings nobody else could see weren't real. But after that moment on the sanctuary steps, Jay had stopped ignoring muses. Instead, he would go up to different muses that passed by Windfalle. Then he'd do what Brother Elfenbein had said other Musicians did: He'd snap his fingers, trying to call muses with his will. The muses would react in different ways, though most often they went along with what Jay had asked them to do in his thoughts.

Brother Elfenbein had called him a natural. One day, after watching Jay snap his fingers to summon a bushy-tailed muse to help sweep the sanctuary steps, the monk had admitted that Jay was quite talented.

"You should go to school to study music," the monk had said. "I bet you could become a full-fledged Musician for the Royal Conservatory."

It had been one of Jay's happiest moments. For the first time, Jay had felt there was a life he could have beyond the streets of Fairdown Falls. And he'd wanted it. He'd wanted to learn everything about music. He'd wanted to become a real Musician, to play with muses and help people, like Brother Elfenbein had helped him.

But then he'd remembered his parents' debt.

"The Capo," Jay had said, his hopes sinking again. "I owe her too much money. She'll never let me go until I pay her back."

After he'd said it, Jay remembered the strange look Brother Elfenbein had given him. There was a determined glint in the monk's eye.

"We'll see about that," Brother Elfenbein had said. He didn't say anything more about it; he'd thanked Jay as usual and sent him home.

Jay hadn't figured out what the monk had meant until a few days later. When Jay had arrived back at the Capo's place that evening, a few other members of the gang—Longshot, Backstabber Blake, and Small Fry—had cornered him, demanding to know what he'd been up to, hanging around a church all the time. Startled, Jay asked how they'd found out.

"Some high-'n'-mighty holy man came here, saying he'd followed you," Longshot had said. "He demanded to see the boss, then told her to cancel your debt—elsewise he'd take you away 'n' turn the rest of us in. Boss didn't take it none too well."

Jay remembered the horror he'd felt, hearing Longshot explain what'd happened. Before any of the other Staccatos could stop him, Jay slithered out of their grasp and ran from the place, back to Windfalle.

The Quickstep Kid had never run so quickly in his life.

∞

"Julian?"

Dulcian's voice broke through Jay's memories. Jay blinked, looking up. He'd been sitting silently in his chair, staring blankly at the checkerboard.

Dulcian's face was full of sympathy. "I'm here to listen."

Shame pounded through Jay's bones. Fighting to keep his voice even, Jay finally spoke.

"You're from Fairdown Falls, right?" he asked Dulcian, struggling to meet the man's eyes. "You know about Windfalle?"

Dulcian stiffened in his chair.

"Yes," he said, his voice quiet. "I know it. An old Designist sanctuary. The Capo of the Staccato Gang burned it down."

Jay hid under his cap, too ashamed to speak. Dulcian's eyes went wide.

"Great gavotte," he said. "Were you there?"

Jay nodded. His guilt grew claws, ripping his insides raw—but Jay kept talking, afraid the truth would slip away if he didn't speak.

"The Capo didn't do it," he said.

Dulcian blinked, nonplussed. Jay took a deep breath.

"Brother Elfenbein—the monk from Windfalle—he was my friend," Jay began. Already he could feel the wave of shame swelling within him. "I'd gone to see him that night."

As he spoke, images flashed before his eyes, as sharp and vivid as they'd been three years ago:

Jay flew back to Windfalle faster than fast, hurrying to warn Brother Elfenbein that the Capo was coming for him—he burst through the chapel doors, shouting for the monk—but the monk wasn't alone—

"The Capo was there, with Brother Elfenbein. Threatening him."

Lorelei Thayne was screaming at the monk, saying he should never have come to the Staccato Gang, should never have interfered—she said if he tried to take Jay away, she'd make him pay—

"I told her to get away from him."

Jay yelled at her to stop—Thayne looked his way, angrier than he'd ever seen her—she called Jay ungrateful, said that he'd forgotten who he was, what he owed her—Jay tried to talk her down—he said he'd go back with her, do anything she'd ask, if she wouldn't hurt Brother Elfenbein—but Thayne said it was too late—Brother Elfenbein tried to defend him—

"Brother Elfenbein told me to run. The Capo knocked him out."

The monk fell to the floor in a crumpled heap—Thayne stared down at his unconscious body, a deadly decision in her eyes —

"Then the Capo grabbed a candle from the altar. I saw what she was about to do. I couldn't let her hurt Brother Elfenbein, so—so I—"

The candle flickered as Thayne brought it close to the altar, about to set it aflame—Jay's heart stopped—

"—I snapped."

Jay screamed and snapped his fingers—his only thought was to save Brother Elfenbein, to make Thayne stop—

"A muse answered me."

An enormous golden spirit with flaming wings came to him, its voice beautiful and terrible—the muse flew through the chapel, making the whole building groan and shudder and quake—

"Next thing I knew, everything was on fire—"

There was a storm of heat and confusion—flames erupted in every direction, consuming the pews, the altar, the whole chapel—

"—and I couldn't stop it. Everything burned. Everything."

Jay froze in horror—it wasn't supposed to happen this way—Thayne bolted from the sanctuary, dragging Jay behind her—

"I got out. But Brother Elfenbein, h-he was trapped."

Raging flames scorched the sky—Thayne stood before the inferno, firelight burning in her cold eyes—Jay screamed for the muse to come save Brother Elfenbein—

"I begged the muse to stop the flames. But it didn't listen. It just disappeared."

The flames kept rising—the heat blistered Jay's skin, stung his eyes, scorched his soul—

"It all happened so fast. I couldn't stop it. I couldn't—!"

"Julian," Dulcian cut in, as gently as possible. "Breathe."

Jay sucked in a sharp gasp. Sweat clung to his forehead, and his limbs felt shaky. It was a long moment before he found his next words.

"That muse let Windfalle burn to the ground with Brother Elfenbein still inside," he spoke, his words husky with disgust. "*That's* why I hate muses." His lips quivered. "But I hate myself even more."

Dulcian shifted in his seat, his gaze sharpening.

"If it weren't for me, that muse never would've come," Jay whispered, his voice hoarse. "Brother Elfenbein was always so kind to me—and because of me, he . . . he's . . ."

But Jay couldn't bear to finish. Shame bled through him. The night Windfalle burned, Jay had turned himself in to the watch. In the reformatory, he swore an oath that he'd never call for a muse again. He couldn't let himself hurt more people like he'd hurt Brother Elfenbein.

The two of them sat in silence. At last, Dulcian spoke.

"He's alive," he said. "In case you didn't know."

Jay's head snapped up. "He—who?"

"The monk, Brother Elfenbein," said Dulcian. "The Capo escaped, though."

Jay stared at Dulcian, stunned. "How d'you . . . ?"

The man picked up one of the checker pieces from the board. "You have been honest with me—excruciatingly honest—so I shall be the same." He rubbed his thumb over the checkers piece.

"I was there that night, too," Dulcian finally said. "At Windfalle." He sent Jay a soft, sad smile. "Small world, isn't it?"

Jay blinked. His mouth opened, but he had no words.

"The Cabinet of Justice had received a tip about the Capo, Lorelei Thayne," said Dulcian. "A citizen said he'd discovered where the Capo was, that he knew how to lure her out of hiding. It was the best lead the Cabinet of Justice had had on her in years."

Jay's head spun. "Brother Elfenbein . . . he tipped off the watch?"

Dulcian set his checkers piece down with a *clack*. "He'd agreed to get the Capo to come to his sanctuary at Windfalle, and that's where the watch could arrest her."

Jay was stunned. There was a reason the Capo had never been arrested. Everybody in Fairdown Falls knew turning her in would be a death sentence. Nobody would dare cross her.

Nobody except Brother Elfenbein, it seemed.

"Callie and I had helped the Minister of Justice catch and detain dozens of criminals over the years," Dulcian explained. "It was no surprise when he asked us to assist in apprehending Lorelei Thayne." A shadow fell over the man's eyes. "When we got there, Windfalle was already in flames. We'd assumed the Capo was the one who'd started the conflagration. We knew our duty was to identify Lorelei Thayne and seize her—but then we heard that a monk was still inside the sanctuary. Callie and I had to choose: follow orders, or save the monk." His voice went quiet. "We chose the monk."

Jay gripped his armrests, anxious for Dulcian to continue.

"The sanctuary was still burning, but we went inside as fast as we could, expecting the worst," Dulcian went on. "The monk had been spared. A stray muse, a great golden spirit, had shielded him from the worst of the flames—but right as we got there, the muse used up the last of its power and vanished. We'd assumed the muse just happened to be nearby and had acted on its own to protect the monk." He gave Jay a direct look. "But it seems the muse had been summoned, after all."

Jay's heart pounded in his throat. A confusion of emotions—joy, guilt, relief, and half a dozen others—churned inside him, making him nauseous.

"You mean . . . that muse I'd called . . . it *saved* him?" he whispered.

Dulcian nodded.

With that, Jay felt a twist in his chest, and his last chain of resistance finally snapped. He tried to cover his face before Dulcian saw—but Jay couldn't stop the tears. After a long stretch he wiped his face and looked up again, meeting Dulcian's gaze.

"All this time," he hissed, his voice breaking. "I thought he was dead. I thought it was my fault." He swallowed, a lump choking him.

Dulcian's gaze was unreadable.

"I wish I could say it ended happily for me and Callie," he said, finishing his story. "But we'd disobeyed orders, letting the Capo escape. Brother Elfenbein had suffered terrible injuries, and he was forced to go into protective custody in case the Capo went after him again. And the Maestrans Council suspended me and Callie from all missions until we'd worked our way back into their good graces." He shook his head. "I know we made the right decision, letting Thayne go to save a life—but there was still a cost." Dulcian glanced at Jay. "Your choice to summon a muse that night had a cost, too. And you've punished yourself ever since."

Jay bent his head to hide under his cap.

Dulcian set his hand on Jay's shoulder. "Why do you think Brio chose you?"

Jay shrugged.

"I can't say for sure," said Dulcian, "but now that you've told me what happened at Windfalle, I have a fair guess." He reached up and stroked Trillo's beak. "You didn't call for a muse to take advantage of someone, or flaunt your power, or punish your enemies. Otherwise, the muse never would have answered you. But it came to you because, in that moment, it resonated with a deep, selfless desire within you: the desire to protect others, without a thought for yourself." Dulcian's gaze shone diamond clear. "Brio never would have chosen you if that desire weren't still in your heart. That speaks volumes about the person you are—and about the Crafter you'll become."

Those words snagged Jay's attention.

"You have a choice here—a chance to start again, take a new path," said Dulcian. "You're not just gifted. You are a gift, Julian. That's why Brio chose you. You were made for something greater than you can imagine."

Jay stared at Dulcian, the man's words rebounding through his brain.

"It's time you stop denying who you are," said Dulcian. "You are the Crafter's heir, called to step out and save people who need you, people who believe in you. It's written inside of you."

Jay swallowed hard. He spoke without thinking.

"But—what if I can't do it? What if I mess up again?"

Dulcian laid a firm hand on Jay's shoulder.

"Trust yourself a little more and your fears a little less," he said. "You're going to be an amazing Musician and a brilliant Crafter one day. Believe that Brio, the one who has called you to it, will be faithful to you. And know that, no matter what challenges you face, you won't be alone." He clasped a fist to his heart. "*Fortes soli, fortiores una.*"

Jay had no idea what those funny words meant. But somewhere inside him, a great weight he hadn't realized he'd been carrying was suddenly gone.

Before he realized what Dulcian was doing, Jay accepted the black case from him.

"Here," said Dulcian. "This is technically yours now."

Jay could sense the fiddle's presence, humming serenely. For once, Jay didn't mind.

Chapter Twenty-Six

A BARGAIN

When Jay and Dulcian made it back to the sunroom, the others hardly noticed they'd returned. Callie was barking orders at Ark, Mara, and the other Musicians, who for some reason were all in a frenzy.

"What's going on?" said Dulcian, speaking over the chaos.

Callie turned to him, startled. Before she could answer, Ark spoke.

"We just heard from Argentine," he said. He looked pale. "The watch received a threatening letter. Someone's planning to attack the Fire Festival."

"What?" said Jay. His mind immediately flashed to Andi, Hana, and Rye.

"Who?" said Dulcian.

"That's why the Inspector contacted us," said Callie. "The letter was from an anonymous, self-proclaimed Dischordian."

Jay tensed. Everybody went quiet, turning their eyes to different corners of the room. Still, Jay got the uneasy feeling that they were all watching him without actually looking his way.

"It's just a coincidence, right?" said Jay, asking aloud what he hoped the rest of them were thinking. "I mean, it's not because of *me*."

No one answered. Dulcian's mouth became a tight line. Callie and Ark reflected the same expression. Mara looked even more anxious than the rest.

"It could be a coincidence," said Dulcian, his tone totally unconvincing.

Jay shot him a look. Gee, that made him feel better.

Ark spoke up. "How could it be related to Jay, though? No one could possibly know the Crafter's heir is in Cindertown." He paused, then added, "Except those of us in this room, that is."

Jay didn't get why Ark was staring between Dulcian and Callie with such a strange frown on his face.

"It may be coincidence or a conspiracy—either way, the captain of the city's musical enforcement unit has requested our assistance," said Callie, bringing them to focus. "Music is restricted here to maintain a precarious natural balance. I'd hate to imagine what an unscrupulous Dischordian could do if they were to attack tonight."

Dulcian nodded. He turned to Mara and the other Musicians.

"Callie and I will take half the agents to go help the city watchmen," he said. "Mara and Arkalin will stay here with the rest. From this point, this room is on lockdown. Eyes on all points of entry. No one gets in, and no one leaves—not until we give the all-clear." His eyes flashed to Jay. "Understood?"

Jay nodded. The other Musicians saluted. Mara looked like she wanted to protest, but the moment passed.

"Arkalin should keep Julian company in the room," Mara suggested. "The rest of us can guard it from the outside." She turned to Ark and Jay. "Don't unlock the door for anyone unless you hear this knock."

Mara did a *knock-tap-knock-tappy-tap* rhythm on the door.

"Excellent idea," said Dulcian. He turned to Ark. "Stay with Julian."

"Yes, sir," said Ark, sounding more relieved than anything.

"Let's go," said Callie. She, Dulcian, and half of the guys in green hurried off. Mara sent Ark and Jay one last glance, then followed the other group of green-coats, shutting the door behind her.

Ark locked the door as their footsteps retreated down the hall.

"Frigits," he said, cursing softly. "A Dischordian. Here."

"Lucky us," Jay muttered. He set down the fiddle's case and sat sideways in one of the sunroom's chairs, his legs dangling over the armrest. The fiddle's quiet, serene voice hummed in his ears.

Ark settled down into the chair next to Jay's. His gaze flickered between the exit and the balcony door, as if making sure nobody was trying to break in—and then he stared at Jay, his expression unreadable.

"What?" said Jay, more sharply than he'd meant.

"Nothing," said Ark. His face formed a half-smile. "You know, when you called Callie an ugly skriff earlier, I thought she was going to maim you." He sent Jay an even look. "You stood up for me."

There was an unstated question behind Ark's words: *Why?*

Jay shrugged. "She was out of line."

Ark didn't try to make more conversation, instead taking out his pocket notebook. Jay fiddled with one of the nearby plants; when he poked it with his fingertip, its leaves closed at his touch, like praying hands.

The praying plant got old, fast. Jay sighed. Bandersnatches, this was dull.

Bored, Jay stepped over to the balcony windows, staring out over the city square below. The Fire Festival looked like the worst party in the world to miss. People roamed the vendor stalls that had been set up for the occasion, finding treats and souvenirs. Fire breathers in shiny costumes were warming up for their competition, while on the far side of the square people were setting up bizarre mechanisms for the Inventor's Expo. Every so often, a firework cracked to life, filling the sky with color and light.

Jay searched the faces below, looking for Andi, Rye, and Hana. No luck. It was no fun watching a party he couldn't go to, so Jay went back to his chair and flopped down once more.

"This stinks," he grumbled.

"Hmm," said Ark, not listening.

Jay glanced his way. Ark sat bent over his little pocket notebook with a frown. What was he doing?

A few days ago, while they were at the Cartwrights' place, Jay had asked if he could see Ark's notebook. Ark had refused—so Jay had picked it from Ark's pocket without him noticing. The notebook wasn't as interesting as Jay had hoped: scribbles that made no sense, along with a sketch of a woman. Jay had slipped it back into Ark's coat before he'd found it missing.

Now, though, Ark had the notebook open to a page with fresh notes Jay hadn't seen: lots of numbers in a row, kind of smudged.

Jay leaned closer. "What's that?"

Ark quickly flipped the notebook closed—but before he did, Jay saw the words DO NOT TRUST scribbled across the bottom.

"It's private," he said, stashing his notebook away.

Jay harrumphed. "Right. Whatever."

Ark shifted, sitting up. "Why were you and Dulcian gone so long?"

Jay shrugged. "We were just talking about stuff."

"What stuff?"

"It's private."

Ark sighed, like he'd expected that response. "Right."

Silence again. Jay stared out the windows at the darkening sky, his thoughts drifting back over his conversation with Dulcian.

You're not just gifted. You are a gift, Julian. That's why Brio chose you.

Jay didn't know whether to believe that—but as Dulcian's words echoed in his mind, Jay felt a gentle warmth spread through him from the inside out.

Nobody had ever told him that before.

A low, deep *boom!* from outside shook Jay from his daze. Startled, Jay and Ark both glanced out the windows. A shower of red sparks filled the sky.

"Think they've caught the Dischordian yet?" Jay wondered aloud.

Ark frowned. "I don't know. I wish we knew what was going on."

More *booms!* thundered through the air and rumbled through the floor, with red sparks blazing like firebirds over the city rooftops. A fireworks show, maybe? Jay turned to ask Ark—

But then Jay heard a different noise, coming from the hallway outside:

Thump. Thump.

Jay stood from his chair, spooked. "What was that?"

Ark held out his hand. "Wait."

Jay and Ark held their breath. Then the knock came, exactly as Mara had done it earlier: *knock-tap-knock-tappy-tap.* Ark exhaled in relief.

Jay watched Ark go to the door. It was probably Dulcian coming to give them the all-clear. But then Jay felt the fiddle pull at him. The perfect music whispered through his mind:

Don't.

It took him a second to understand what the fiddle was trying to tell him. Jay jumped up.

"Ark, don't—!"

Too late. Ark opened the door, then froze. Jay gasped.

"*There* you are!" said Dubito, delighted. "We thought you'd never answer."

The Unraveling Man looked just as he had that night in Hazeldenn's graveyard. He was hooded and masked, and his entire body was disguised by robes pieced together by scraps of frayed, unraveling garments. In the hallway beyond, two of the green-coats who'd been stationed outside the door were sprawled on the floor, unconscious.

Jay swallowed a yelp. So *that's* what those thumps had been.

"Mara!" Ark hollered, his face going white.

"Don't bother," said Dubito, shaking his head. "Miss Fipple is occupied elsewhere. Won't you invite us in?"

The Unraveling Man swept past him into the sunroom. The lamplight in the room went dim as shadows climbed the walls. Jay shivered, feeling cold.

Ark jumped between Jay and the Dischordian, holding out his hands in a defensive pose. Just as Ark took a breath to shout a cantus, Dubito waggled a finger at him.

"*Ah, ah, ah,*" he said, like he was scolding a toddler. "No music. Or did you forget the volcano?"

Ark froze, hesitating.

"Fool," Dubito snickered. He threw out his hand. A black, oily shadow burst from his palm, screeching and howling, striking Ark square in the face.

"No!" Jay cried.

No use. The blow knocked Ark to the floor. When he finally sat up, his eyes were blank, like he could no longer see the room. Ark scrambled to the corner and crouched, shaking in fear, his face full of terror.

"*No,*" he moaned, ". . . help . . . Father. . ."

Jay stared, horrified. "What did you do to him?"

The Unraveling Man calmly adjusted his mask.

"Don't worry about him," said Dubito. "He's just reliving his worst nightmare, that's all."

"Stop it!" Jay demanded. "Let him go!"

The Unraveling Man held up his hands, shaking his head.

"Not until we speak our piece." Dubito waved toward the chairs. "Shall we sit?"

It was like Dubito was asking Jay to join him for lunch. A bizarre image of the Unraveling Man offering him tea and sandwiches flashed through Jay's mind as he sank into the chair across from the Unraveling Man, every muscle tense. He didn't want to take his eyes off the Dischordian for one second—but he kept track of Ark from the corner of his eye.

"Why're you here?" said Jay.

Dubito folded his hands, sitting perfectly still. Jay fidgeted as the silence stretched as thin as a wire. At length, Dubito spoke.

"As a thief, how would you break into a guarded vault?"

Jay started. The way Dubito had asked the question . . . it was almost like he was asking Jay personally, like he knew Jay had experience with that sort of thing. But that wasn't possible—this guy couldn't've known—

"You would light a fire," Dubito went on, answering his own hypothetical question. "The fire causes the guards to leave the vault to investigate. With the vault abandoned, the treasure is ripe for the taking." He waved toward the balcony and the city beyond. "We did the same. We dropped off a letter for the watch, lighting a small fire in their minds about a threat to Cindertown. While Sir Mandore and Lady Vielle ran off to investigate, they left their precious treasure behind with little protection." He gestured grandly at Jay.

Jay glared at him. "You didn't answer my question."

Dubito cackled behind his mask. "Oh-ho! You're smarter than you look." His volume dropped. "But you are pretty *quick*, aren't you?"

Jay didn't like the Unraveling Man's wily tone. What did he know?

In the corner, Ark was moaning:

"Father, *please*, I don't want to die . . ."

Jay clenched his jaw. He had to get this creep gone so he could help Ark.

"You gonna tell me why you're here?" Jay snapped.

Dubito let the silence stretch on, broken only by Ark's soft moans. After an eternity, the Unraveling Man spoke.

"We are here because we know who you are. Who you *really* are." He leaned in closer. "*Quickstep*."

A thunderbolt of shock shook Jay to his core. He leapt from his chair.

"H-How—*how* do you—?" he stammered.

Dubito shrugged. "Unlike those fool Musicians, we did some digging. We barely had to scrape the surface to get all the dirt on you."

Jay's heart thumped painfully in his chest.

"So, Brio chose the infamous Quickstep Kid to be the Crafter's heir," said Dubito. He hummed in dark amusement. "How *pathetic*. That doddering muse doesn't know how to pick 'em like he used to." He clicked his tongue. "And you haven't even told the Musicians the truth—that you're just a worthless outlaw. Goodness, what would Sir Mandore think if he knew?"

The words sank into Jay's ears, stirring up old feelings of shame. Jay tried to shrug them off, to remember the things Dulcian had told him earlier—but the Unraveling Man's voice was louder, filling him with doubt. It took all Jay's willpower to respond.

"That's not who I am anymore." The words came out in a quiet murmur, not nearly as convincing as he'd hoped.

Dubito stood from his chair, circling Jay like a cat around a wounded bird.

"Then what are you?" he hissed. "You're no Musician. You're *nobody*. A menace. A *mistake*. Why else would Brio have sung for you?"

Jay opened his mouth to protest, but no words came. A weight settled onto his shoulders. He could hardly hear Ark's moans.

"What do you want from me?"

Dubito returned to his chair, picking at loose threads on his sleeve.

"We know the Capo of the Staccato Gang is after you," he said. "Lorelei Thayne is tracking you down because you owe her a debt. How much?"

Jay's mouth answered without asking his brain's permission.

"Four hundred and four thousand, two hundred forty-seven Medallions, plus interest," he said. The number tasted flat and heavy in his mouth.

Dubito whistled. "*Whoo*. What a sum. It'll take a lifetime to pay it."

Jay scowled, hating that the creep was right.

"You can't clear that debt," said Dubito. He pointed to himself. "But we can."

Jay's head snapped up. "What?"

"Four hundred and four thousand, two hundred forty-seven Medallions. Plus interest," said Dubito, repeating the number back perfectly. "We can give you the full amount you need to pay the Capo back."

Jay blinked at the Unraveling Man, too surprised to speak.

"But favors aren't free," Dubito went on. "We want something from you."

Uh-huh. 'Course he did. Jay scowled. "What?"

Jay could feel Dubito grinning. He raised a cloaked arm and pointed. "*That.*"

Jay looked down:

The black case. Brio's instrument.

Jay scanned the Unraveling Man's mask, trying to understand. "You want the fiddle? How come?"

"No, no, no," said Dubito, waving his hands. "This isn't about what *we* want, or why. What matters is what *you* want."

He put a hand on Jay's shoulder, but Jay couldn't feel his touch.

"We told you before—we can show you a path to freedom," said Dubito. "We know Brio chose wrong. No one will accept you as the Crafter. They'll cast you out—or worse, they'll make you a plaything, a puppet to do their bidding until they get bored and throw you away."

The Unraveling Man's tone changed.

"But if you accept our offer, you'll be free," said Dubito, opening his arms wide. "You haven't been formally named as the Crafter yet. There's still time to choose. You can be free from the Capo. Free from the Crafter's burden. Free to go where you wish, do as you wish, chart your own course!"

The words bled through Jay's brain. In his arms, he thought he felt the fiddle humming in its case, trying to get his attention.

"This is a generous offer," hissed Dubito, taking Jay's focus again. "But such generosity won't last forever. What's your answer?"

Jay picked up the case. He narrowed his gaze at the Unraveling Man.

"I'm supposed to just hand the fiddle over and hope you've got thousands of Medallions on you right now?"

Dubito scoffed. "Of course not. We don't have the money here. But we can give it to you in Fairdown Falls."

Jay chewed his lip, not sure what to say. The conversation he'd had with Dulcian felt like ages ago, and he could barely remember what the Musician had told him then. But what Dubito was telling him now sounded like a good move: pay off the Capo, break his ties with the Staccatos, ditch the daunting destiny of the Crafter being thrust on him. Choose his *own* life.

Jay heard a moan. Startled, he glanced at the corner. Ark was clutching the scar on his left hand, his face contorted in agony.

Jay felt a throb of guilt. He'd forgotten Ark was still there.

"You need a few days to think this over," said Dubito. "Meet us in Fairdown Falls. If you accept our bargain, bring Brio's relic to Butcher's Block before midnight on Wintertide Eve, and we'll give you the cash."

The Unraveling Man stood, sweeping his arms wide. "It's your choice, Quickstep. Your life. Be a puppet—or be free."

He gestured toward Ark.

"He's all yours now," said Dubito. "By the way. Before coming here, we sent your Musician friends at the festival a little . . . *gift*. You should get going."

Dark oily mist poured from between the Unraveling Man's hands. Jay cringed and covered his ears as the mist shrieked and swirled, swallowing the Dischordian in a cloud of nothingness. Then he was gone.

Jay only took a couple seconds to recover. He hurried over to Ark. He was as pale as death, covered in sweat, still clutching his scar.

"*Save me*," he pleaded, "*save me, Father!*"

"Ark!" Jay yelled. He shook Ark's shoulders. "Snap out of it, bumwipe!"

Ark couldn't hear him. His eyes were still clouded by horrors.

Jay drew his hand back—

WHAP!

The smack across the face did the trick. Ark came to, disoriented. He slowly formed words. "I was . . . how . . . ?" He sat bolt upright. "Dubito!"

"He's gone," said Jay. He helped Ark find his feet. "He put you under some kind of spell."

Ark glanced down at the scar on his hand, then up at Jay, like he'd been exposed. "What did I—?"

He didn't get to finish. A low, terrible *BOOM!* shook through the hotel. Jay and Ark ducked as the ground quaked. Windows creaked and cracked. Plants tumbled, their clay pots shattering on the floor.

Then the tremors subsided. Jay still felt his bones rattling as he and Ark stood. They scanned the ruins of the sunroom, then looked at each other.

"We have to go," they said at the same time. Jay snatched up the fiddle's case and ran alongside Ark, Dubito's words chasing him all the way.

∞

The Musicians who'd been lying unconscious in the hallway were no longer there. Jay barely had time to wonder where they'd gone as he and Ark booked it down the stairs, racing for the front doors. The lobby was abandoned, with chairs toppled over and a fancy chandelier in pieces on the floor. Jay and Ark stepped around the wreckage and bolted for the exit.

Outside, a mass of people surged like a river. Women carried kids while men helped the elderly. Watchmen urged everybody along: "... to the designated safety area ... no running ..."

Another rumble shook through the ground. People in the crowd screamed while the watchmen shouted for everybody to stay calm.

"What happened?" Ark called out.

"Nightcreepers!" a man passing by cried aloud. "At the Fire Festival!"

"I saw them too!" a woman said. "They've woken Vakra!"

Jay gaped at the flat-topped mountain. A plume of thick smoke churned from its peak. Lava spewed like a cauldron about to bubble over.

Jay cursed with every swear word he knew. This was the Unraveling Man's "gift." Dubito was trying to wake a volcano.

"We've got to find the others!" Ark shouted over the evacuating crowd.

"How?" Jay shouted back.

He felt a hand on his arm. Jay twitched when he saw who it was.

"Mara!" said Ark. "Are you okay? Did Dubito—?"

"No time!" she said hoarsely. Mara's fingers dug deep into Jay's skin as she hauled him toward the city square.

"Why're we going *toward* the volcano?" Jay yelped.

She didn't answer. Mara led him and Ark against the rush of people. They'd only gone a short distance before Jay heard someone call out:

"Jay! Ark!"

Jay felt a thrill of happy relief when he saw Andi, Hana, and Rye running toward them.

"You're okay!" said Rye, giving them both a hug.

"Where are Susanna and Rosetta?" asked Ark, worried.

"They're helping with the evacuation," said Andi. His face was drawn. "Everyone's talking about Nightcreepers."

"And they say Mount Vakra could erupt," said Hana. She was wearing her yellow and orange Salamander costume. "What's going on?"

Jay was about to answer, but then Mara yanked his arm so hard he felt his shoulder pop. He yelped as she pulled him onward. Ark and the others chased them as they edged past another building and ducked through an alley—until at last they spilled into the abandoned city square.

Jay stared. The remains of the Fire Festival were all over the place. Wrecked vendor stalls were scattered like splintered matchsticks. Small fires burned everywhere. Only a handful of people remained amid the rubble. Jay saw Captain Russ and Inspector Argentine arguing with Callie and Dulcian. Trillo and Fiero were on their own, dashing around the square and putting out the more dangerous flames.

"It's unthinkable!" the Walrus was shouting, his mustache twitching.

"It's your only option!" Callie shouted back. "That or a full eruption!"

"You can't use muses *now!*" the Walrus blustered. "If something goes wrong, we could all be deliberated!"

"*Obliterated*, sir!" shouted Argentine.

"Captain Russ," said Dulcian, "we could stop the reaction and save your city with the help of local muses. Dischords are behind this. We don't know the Dischordian who summoned them, but—"

"It was Dubito!" Ark cried out.

Dulcian, Callie, Argentine, and the Walrus snapped their heads in his direction.

"Julian! Arkalin!" cried Dulcian. "Thank goodness—"

"Dubito was here!" Jay interrupted. "He was in the hotel!"

Callie snapped her eyes at Ark. "What happened?"

Ark lowered his head, clenching his fists like he was bracing himself. He opened his mouth to speak.

Jay beat him to it.

"Dubito told us he'd sent a 'gift' for tonight," Jay blurted, skipping the part about Ark being incapacitated. "Must've been the dischords."

Jay could feel Ark staring at him in disbelief.

Dulcian's eyes narrowed. "What else did Dubito say?"

"Nothing," said Jay, too quickly. Dulcian's gaze sharpened.

"There's no time!" Mara broke in, breathless. She turned to Jay. "*You* stop the eruption! Use the instrument!"

"I won't allow—!" the Walrus barked.

Callie cut him off with a sharp gesture. In the firelight, her eyes shone with a strange glow. "Can you do it?" she asked Jay.

The ground rumbled with another tremor. No time to waste.

Jay's body shivered with nerves as he held the fiddle to his chin, his fingers trembling on the strings, listening for the perfect music to guide him.

But this time, a different voice whispered between his ears:

You're nobody. A menace. A mistake.

Jay tried to shake the words from his head. He shifted his position, straining his ears to hear the perfect music—but Dubito's voice only grew louder.

Nobody. Menace. Mistake.

After an agonizing minute, Jay lowered the fiddle in defeat. "I can't."

The ground shuddered beneath them. Jay burned under their gazes like a bug under a magnifying glass.

"It's okay, Julian," said Dulcian, trying to be kind. "You did your best."

That only made Jay feel worse. He returned the fiddle to its case, unable to look at any of them.

Argentine pointed to the sky. Jay saw stuff like black snow falling.

"The ash fall," said Argentine. He pulled a kerchief from his coat and wrapped it around his nose and mouth. "We need to seek shelter."

Callie shook her head. "We have to catch any dischords on the loose."

"And we *must* get Julian out of here," added Dulcian.

"No one's going anywhere," Argentine insisted. "We'd risk too much traveling through the ash. The only way we could go anywhere now is if we grew wings and flew."

At that, Rye's head snapped up.

"The Morning Star!" she cried out.

Everybody looked to where she was pointing. In a trashed corner of the city square that had previously been the Inventor's Expo, a smallish airship sat mostly undisturbed. The Morning Star was attached to a display frame by ropes, floating safely above the other rubble—though the balloon was in danger of being punctured by the surrounding wreckage.

"What is that supposed to be?" said Callie.

"An airship!" said Rye. "Come on!"

Jay and the others followed her over to the Morning Star, stepping over the broken mechanics of a dozen other inventions that'd been destroyed in the first quake. Rye reached the ship first, yanking away sharp shards, scorching hot pieces of burned wood, and other dangerous debris with her metal hands like it was nothing. Then she vaulted over the side of the ship and hurried to the navigation dash, flipping switches and turning knobs.

"We can fly out of here!" said Rye, beaming—though her smile faded as she scanned their faces. "But not everyone. Maybe four or five of us."

Jay caught Dulcian and Callie sharing a tight-lipped look.

"Forget it," said Callie. "That doesn't look sky-worthy at all. I'd rather risk a Transposition."

"Besides," added Dulcian, "if that ship can't fly with all of us, it's not a good option. Callie and I won't let Julian out of our sight again."

Ark spoke up at once. "I think we should take it."

Dulcian's and Callie's eyes snapped toward him.

"Just me, Jay, Andi, Hana, and Rye," Ark added. "We can fly out of here together and get to safety." He sent Dulcian and Callie a strange look. "Unless you want to risk Jay getting burned by lava or attacked by a dischord horde?"

Dulcian frowned at him. "Of course not."

"Then it's settled," said Ark. "The five of us will take the Morning Star."

"Nothing is settled—!" Callie protested.

Ark ignored her, turning to Rye. "Could this ship make it all the way to Fairdown Falls right now?"

Rye studied the gauges on the navigation dash, whispering calculations to herself. "There's *probably* enough fuel," she said at length. "But only for a one-way flight."

Callie and Dulcian exchanged another glance, looking ready to object.

"I agree with Arkalin," said Mara, speaking up in his defense. "A proper Transposition may take too much time, and dischords may find us any moment. Sir Mandore, Lady Vielle—you both have been trained to combat dischords and natural disasters, too. These children have not." Her eyes seemed to flicker toward Jay when she added, "They can't help, so it's best if they stay out of the way."

Jay wished he could disappear on the spot.

The ground shook again. Mount Vakra gave a terrifying grumble. Splots of lava shot from the peak like crimson stars.

"If you Musicians are planning to do anything, you'd better be quick!" said the Walrus, covering his mustache with his own kerchief.

"Right," said Dulcian reluctantly. He waved at Jay and the others. "Get on."

Ark immediately helped Hana and Andi climb aboard the airship. Jay was the last to follow. He hugged the fiddle's case to his chest, his heart racing.

Rye adjusted a dozen settings on the control panel. The propellers at the back of the ship whirred and spun to life.

"Everybody, hold on!" cried Rye, setting her goggles over her eyes. She pushed the throttle.

Before Jay could gasp, the Morning Star rose into the air, higher and higher, trading the streets of Cindertown for the cold, black sky.

Chapter Twenty-Seven

INTERLUDE IN THE SKY

*A*rk wasn't sure how much longer he could take the silence.

Standing along the port side of the Morning Star, Ark crossed his arms and leaned on the bulwark, the freezing wind stinging his face. If he wasn't so cold right now, he would've sworn he was dreaming. After his humiliating encounter with Dubito and the threat of Mount Vakra erupting, flying through the sky like a bird was too surreal.

Cindertown was far behind them now. As they'd climbed into the air, Mount Vakra had become nothing more than a crimson blot on the horizon, growing fainter until it had finally blinked out. Ark hoped that meant Dulcian, Callie, and the other Musicians had calmed the volcano, and not that Cindertown was now buried in ash.

After they'd reached sailing altitude, Hana, Andi, and Rye had begged for Ark and Jay to tell them everything. Jay had made no motion to speak up, so Ark stepped in. His breath had turned to mist in the cold air as he told them about Dubito, how he'd attacked them in Hazeldenn, and how he'd tracked them down again in Cindertown. The others were stunned.

"A *Dischordian?*" Andi echoed.

"And he's after Julian?" said Hana.

Ark nodded. They all turned to Jay, who was avoiding their gazes.

"Well, Dubito can't catch us in the sky," said Rye, pushing the throttle forward. Ark felt the ship gain speed, the night wind slicing through him.

After that, silence had settled over them like fog, heavy and dismal. Andi and Hotah sat between coils of rope, exhausted. Hana carefully removed vials from her pockets—pyrotechnic powders and extracts meant for her performance with the Salamanders—and stashed them in the cargo hold. Rye was focused on the controls, her attention shifting between a navigation chart and the fuel gauge. Jay crouched with the black case across his knees. For the next hour, the Morning Star sailed on with only the wind whispering into their ears.

Ark breathed in deeply, imagining the freezing air blowing around inside him, clearing the thoughts clotting his mind. But even his frosty breath and the sky's sacred stillness couldn't rid him of the guilt he felt, leaving Mara behind with Dulcian and Callie—or his anger at the dischords who woke Mount Vakra and put so many innocent people in danger—or his shame, letting Dubito get past his defenses so easily.

"How-w-wling spirits!" said Andi through chattering teeth, breaking the silence at last. "I'm s-so cold I think my nose is gonna f-fall off!"

"It's not *that* bad," said Rye. She operated the helm expertly, looking comfortable despite the freezing air. "Feels like home to me."

Andi shivered, surly. "*My* home is a t-tropic island! I don't do cold!"

Ark was on Andi's side. He couldn't feel his fingers or toes anymore, and his ears ached. Ark concentrated, listening, then cleared his throat.

"*Callorre*," he chanted.

It took some moments for a muse to respond—but at last, one with the long, twisting body of a horned lizard shimmered on the air beside them, its body radiating with a warm orange glow. A wave of warmth flooded the airship's deck, and everyone sighed in relief.

"Thanks, Ark," said Andi. Rye and Hana echoed him.

Ark was resigned to enter another stretch of silence when Jay rose from his crouched position and stepped up beside him, setting the case at his feet.

"Well done, bum-wipe."

Ark couldn't tell if the remark was sarcastic or sincere. He ignored it.

Jay hummed to himself, then pulled something from his pocket: a girl's bead bracelet, brand new. Jay rolled the smooth beads between his rough fingers.

"You all right?" asked Ark.

Jay wore a blank look, so Ark elaborated. "What happened back there—when you tried playing Brio's instrument but couldn't—you don't have to beat yourself up about it. It's common for Musicians to blank when they perform in front of other people. It's happened to me before."

Jay snorted, hunching his shoulders. "Yeah. Sure."

Ark frowned. He'd intended to reassure him, but Jay clearly didn't want to hear it.

"What happened after Dubito attacked me at the hotel?" Ark asked straight out. "How did you get rid of him? Did you use Brio's instrument then?"

Jay shook his head. "Didn't need to. Dubito said some things, then left."

Ark stared, puzzled. "What things?"

Jay shrugged, fiddling with the bracelet's colorful beads. Ark frowned. Jay was hiding something. Ark was about to press him further, but then Jay spoke up, glancing his way.

"When Dubito attacked you, he said he'd made you relive your worst nightmare," he said. "Was yours . . . about your dad?"

The suddenness of the question stopped Ark short.

"You called for him," said Jay quietly. "Begged him to save you."

Ark sealed his lips. Jay's face broke into a lopsided smirk.

"I get it," he said. He turned to rest his back against the bulwark, leaning on his elbows. "Dads are a sore subject for me, too. Mine ditched me right after I was born. Left me behind with a—" Jay stopped himself, then shook his head. "Let's just say he ran off and I've been paying for it ever since."

Ark blinked. Jay went quiet, twirling the bracelet between his fingers.

Ark let the silence grow, not sure whether to speak. A moonlit lake surrounded by a dense, dark forest passed by below. At length, Ark's hands moved on their own. He retrieved his notebook, delicately pulling out the sketch tucked inside the cover.

Jay peered at it, curious. "Who's she?"

Ark held the sketch close so it wouldn't get snatched away by the wind. He managed a soft smile.

"My mother. Father drew this portrait of her holding me."

Jay's eyes skimmed the sketch. "She's a pretty lady."

Ark stared at the picture of himself sitting on his mother's lap. He retreated to a cold, still place inside.

"She was killed by a dischord."

Jay's easy smile faded away.

"I was there the day it happened—but I was only a baby, so I don't remember," said Ark. The words came easier than he'd expected. "Mother had gone down into the cellar to summon a dischord. Father said afterward that she'd tried to make a contract with it."

Jay's eyes widened. "You mean . . . she was . . . ?"

"A Dischordian," Ark finished for him. "Who knows, really." He felt numb, and not just from the wind's chill. "The ritual failed somehow, and the dischord devoured her."

Jay went tight-lipped, his face grim.

"Father never got over it," Ark went on. "He was a talented Musician. He could have been a Maestran—but after Mother died, he traveled, exorcizing dischords wherever he went. I think it was his way to atone for not saving her."

Jay was quiet, listening.

"When I turned four, he taught me to fight dischords," said Ark. "My father's family, the de Canis, have exorcized dischords for generations. Father made me learn ancient arts—exorcism rites passed down along the de Cani line for centuries. I trained day and night." He shook his head. "But I wasn't cut out for it."

Nightmare images from Ark's memories flashed through his mind:

Fleeing through a dark winter forest—a ravenous Beast hunting him, trapping him in an icy pit—Father nowhere to be found—

"One night, I—I messed up a dischord exorcism," said Ark. A tremor made his voice shake; he coughed to cover it up. "A wolf had been possessed by a dischord and was terrorizing a local village. Father made me try to exorcise the wolf by myself, as a test."

Ark held out his left hand. In the firelight glowing from the airship burners, the scars there looked even more ghastly.

The Beast cornered him—Ark screamed for Father to rescue him—the Beast lunged, its fangs sinking into his hand . . .

"I almost died."

At that, a bizarre little laugh escaped him. Ark wasn't sure why. Maybe, by saying it out loud for the first time, he'd finally realized how absurd and awful it was. Tristen de Cani had sent his *son*—a skinny eight-year-old—against a wild, dischord-possessed beast. Ark had cried at the memories so many times that the only thing left to do now was laugh.

"I still have nightmares about it," Ark admitted, lowering his scarred hand. "All dischords terrify me now."

Jay blinked at him. "And you still wanna be a Musician?"

Ark searched for the words. "After that botched exorcism, Father said I was a disappointment," he answered, his voice cracking on the word. "He disowned me—said I wasn't worthy of being called a de Cani anymore."

"Wait," Jay cut in. "De Cani? I thought your name was Encore."

Ark shook his head. "That's my mother's family name. I was allowed to use that."

Jay whistled. "That's cold."

Ark knew it. He felt a spike of frustration—how could his father have been so callous?—but old shame smothered his anger.

"Not long after, Father dropped me off at Echostrait. He told me to learn as much as I could and become stronger. When I proved myself, he said that I could come home. And then I could be Arkalin de Cani once more."

Ark put the sketch and his notebook away.

"This was supposed to be it. My jury mission was my chance to prove I wasn't a disappointment anymore." Ark made himself say the rest of the fears in his head. "But if I fail this, I'll lose everything. My home, my name—for good."

Ark didn't understand it, but when he was done speaking, he felt . . . not better, exactly. He was mortified, and anxious, and sad—but admitting his fears felt like a tiny step forward from where he'd been before.

"Your dad's a jerk."

Jay's response caught Ark off guard. Jay stood with his head tilted back, his eyes watching the reptile muse soaring alongside them.

"But at least he cares," Jay went on. "Sending you off to school, having you study up, being all strict—I bet it was his way of saving you. Like the best way to protect you was to have you learn how to protect yourself, but far from real danger. It doesn't make what he said or did to you okay, but at least he was trying to look after you." He snorted. "Better than what my dad ever did for me, anyway."

Ark had no response. In his mind, he'd only ever been a source of shame for his father. Ark supposed it was possible his father had left him at Echostrait out of concern. Maybe even love.

Jay turned, knocking Ark's shoulder with his knuckles.

"Lemme cheer you up," he said. "You're a bum-wipe. And a stiff-neck most of the time. And you always act like a know-it-all. And your snooty accent gets on everybody's nerves—"

"Do you know how 'cheering up' works?" said Ark, arching his brow.

"—but even *I* can tell you're a real decent Musician. Maybe even a good one," said Jay. He tilted his head toward Andi, Hana, and Rye. "They know it. Dulcian and Callie know it, too. Heck, back in Hazeldenn my friend Lina couldn't stop talking about how incredible she thought you were."

Ark's face went pink in surprise. Jay stared at the bead bracelet he was holding, then stashed it back in his pocket.

"And you're not a good Musician 'cause of how good you are at music," Jay went on. "It's 'cause you always use music for other people." He gave his head a little shake. "I can't speak for your dad. He's a jerk anyway. But based on what I've seen, you're not a disappointment."

Ark was speechless. He didn't know whether to feel uncomfortable by Jay's blunt candor or to be suspicious of his words. Ark's personal motto had always been *Leave other people alone*—mainly because he found other people too hard to get along with.

But he supposed he never stuck to his motto when it came to people in trouble.

Ark glanced sideways at Jay. Not for the first time, Ark wondered whether they could have been friends in some other life. Ark cleared his throat.

"Thanks."

Jay gave an unassuming shrug.

"I should probably tell you, too," Ark went on. "You are an idiot most of the time. And stubborn. And irritating. And you could probably stand to bathe more often—"

"Are you trying to be nice right now?" said Jay, frowning.

"—but based on what I've seen, you're going to make a real decent Crafter." Ark smirked. "Maybe even a good one."

He thought his remarks would have made Jay smile, or at least scoff—but instead, a shadow fell over his face. He looked away, folding his arms like he felt cold again. His reply was so quiet that Ark wasn't sure he was meant to hear it:

"I doubt it."

Ark didn't get the chance to ask Jay about that, though.

"What are you guys talking about?" asked Andi, calling to them.

At once Jay spun around, wearing a slapped-on grin.

"Daddy issues," he answered. "Mine and Ark's. Who else?"

Andi rocked his head to the side. "I get along fine with my dad. Though he'll probably kill me when I get home."

"Why's that?" asked Jay.

Andi laughed weakly. "When I left home to find my brother, I didn't exactly tell my parents first. But I knew my folks would never have let me go. They've always been afraid of me getting hurt." His voice softened. "My dad was really upset when Hoku left. They used to do everything together—sailing, hunting, sports. Dad's never done much with me since I'm . . . well." He quickly brushed a hand along his closed eyes. "But if I bring Hoku home, I'm sure Dad will be happy."

Andi sounded so hopeful. Ark wondered whether he was trying to find his brother partly so he could please his father.

"I haven't seen my papa in a while," said Rye, chiming in. "He built me my first pair of arms. He gave me my very own tinkerbit toolkit." She pursed her lips, then reached up to her elbow. With a few switch-flicks and a twist, she removed her arm.

"A few years ago, a regiment of Wystian soldiers occupied our town," Rye went on, massaging her stump with the other hand. "The soldiers planned to ship all the kids to Wystian education camps, including me. We'd heard rumors that kids who go to those camps forget their Nurthican roots and never come home. So my mom and dad smuggled me out of the country instead. My home is still occupied territory, so it's not safe for me to go back yet." Rye popped her arm back into place and shrugged. "Hana's got it tough, too."

Ark and Jay glanced her way. Hana stiffened.

"How come, Hana?" asked Andi. "C'mon, we're all mates here."

Hana hesitated, clearly not wanting to speak—so Rye answered for her.

"Hana's parents were doctors for the emperor," she said.

Ark's mouth fell open. "Emperor Odayaka? The Lord of Eastir?"

"Your family rubs elbows with royalty?" said Andi, grinning.

Hana shook her head. "Not really. My parents weren't part of the emperor's court. They technically aren't physicians, either—they're both alchemical herbalists. But when the emperor's daughter, Princess Arashi, got sick, he called for everyone in the imperial capital with some knowledge of medicine to help cure her. My parents were the ones who found a remedy for her illness."

She tried to make it sound like no big deal, but Ark was still amazed.

"So what happened?" said Andi, prompting her.

Hana huffed. "Some jealous doctors in the court told the emperor that my parents were only able to cure the princess because they poisoned her in the first place," she said bitterly. "They were both imprisoned. The government seized our home, taking everything. No one wanted anything to do with me, the daughter of the disgraced Himawari family— but Princess Arashi had pity on me and helped me get to Merideyin."

Ark didn't know what to say.

"Hana and I met in the same immigrant compound," said Rye, trying to recover the conversation. "We stuck together while we were there. Eventually the Cartwright sisters agreed to sponsor both of us in Merideyin." A newborn smile dimpled her cheeks. "I'd call that lucky—right, Hana?"

Ark glanced between the two of them, grasping for words. "You've both gone through a lot."

Rye pulled a tiny screwdriver from her pocket. "I enjoy tinkerbit mechanics—and not just because I'm part machine," she said, grinning with a playful wink. She twirled the screwdriver through her metal fingers. "There are so many forces in the world that want to destroy, to tear things apart. I guess I always thought that, if I choose to fix things instead of break them, I can help make things better. Someday I want to invent machines to help people, even in some small way."

"I feel the same way about alchemy," said Hana. "I won't change the world by solving formulas or performing experiments—but maybe what I discover will someday help someone else invent new medicines or other compounds to make lives easier. I hope that will make a difference."

Hearing that, Ark's desire to prove himself to his father felt trivial. He struggled to respond.

"That's amazing," he said—and as soon as he did, Ark wanted to eat his own foot. Great gavotte, he sounded like a total duff-for-brains. He wanted to say what he really believed: that they were brave, and strong, and incredible—and he was glad to know them. But his good-for-nothing mouth couldn't manage to say what he truly meant.

Ark felt the silence squirm around them until he couldn't stand it. The deck creaked beneath him as he wandered over to stand at the bow of the airship. Here, the view of the night sky was clear and vast; the stars were like clusters of fireflies.

The thought reminded him of the lullaby his father sang to him when he was small. Ark hummed the melody; the tune was slow and somber, delicate and dark. He closed his eyes and began to sing the words, tasting the sorrow of the lyrics on his tongue:

Adieu, adieu, ma luciole
La nuit est presque terminée
Les étoiles se fondent dans le soleil

Adieu, adieu, ma luciole
Il est écrit dans l'aurore
Bientôt, bientôt tu seras une ombre

Hélas, hélas, ma luciole
Serait-ce votre dernière danse?
Tout va disparaître dans le silence

Courage, courage, ma luciole
Cet adieu est temporaire
Un jour, tu reviendras à moi encore,
À moi encore . . .

The last note flew into the sky and melted into the darkness, letting the silence advance once more, washing over the airship in a peaceful wave. When Ark glanced back, he saw Andi and Hotah curled up next to Hana, their eyes closed in sleep. Rye was yawning, her eyes half-lidded.

"Just gonna close my eyes for a few minutes," she said. "If anything starts beeping, wake me." Then she flipped a couple switches on the navigation dash and locked the helm before sliding down beside Hana.

Jay joined Ark at the tip of the bow.

"You speak Wystian," Jay snorted. "Show-off."

By the way Jay was grinning, Ark could tell he was joking. Ark smirked.

"'Wystian' isn't a language," he said. "What you're thinking of is *languax d'ouii*, a Wystian dialect spoken in the—"

"Sure, yeah, *real* interesting," Jay interrupted, faking a yawn. He started to walk toward the stern.

Ark called him back. "Wait. There's something I should show you."

Jay paused. He looked surprised when Ark pulled out his notebook.

"Back at the hotel, after you and Dulcian left the room, Mara gave me something," he explained. "A coded message."

Ark opened his notebook to the page with Mara's handwritten formula:

$$34 - 33 = A$$

$$30 \quad 19 \quad 20 \quad 19 \quad 14 \quad 14 \quad 6 \quad 13 \quad 15 \quad 14 \quad 21 \quad \cancel{} \quad 12$$

Jay read the notes, frowning. "It's all smudged," he said. He pointed to the scribbled-out number. "What's that?"

"A mistake," said Ark. "Mara was writing very fast."

"*Do not trust* . . . M? V?" said Jay, pointing to the message Ark had written out below. "What's that supposed to mean?"

"I believe they're initials," explained Ark.

Jay's eyes went wide. "*M!* Mara!"

Ark tried not to roll his eyes. "Mara gave me this message, remember? It's not her. I think Mara was trying to warn us about Dulcian and Callie."

Jay blinked with a blank stare.

"Sir *Mandore*, Lady *Vielle*," said Ark, tapping the two letters that finished the code. "Those are the only names M and V together could stand for."

Jay's brow bent in confusion. "Why warn us about them? They fought Dubito."

Ark looked at him. "Maybe they weren't really fighting. Maybe it was an act."

Jay frowned. "What d'you mean?"

"How did Dubito find us in Hazeldenn so quickly after you Resonated with Brio's instrument?" said Ark. "How did Dubito even know to look for us in Cindertown? How could he have possibly known the secret knock to get into the hotel's sunroom?" He stared into the night. "Maybe someone has been secretly working with him. Or *two* someones."

"What?" said Jay. "Dulcian? Callie? No way."

"We can't ignore the possibility," said Ark. "Before my jury mission began, Mara warned me not to go with them. She said I'd regret it. Perhaps she's known all along that Dulcian and Callie were up to something . . . maybe that they were working with a Dischordian."

Saying it aloud was more frightening than Ark expected. He thought of Dulcian's kind smile and Callie's fierce resolve. Could they really be in league with a Dischordian? It was hard to believe. But factoring in all the coincidences and Mara's coded warning, what other explanation was there?

Jay shook his head. "I don't know much about Callie, but Dulcian's really nice." He grabbed the notebook from Ark's hands and stared at the message. "It doesn't make sense. Why wouldn't Mara turn them in if she knew they were up to no good?"

"She might not have enough evidence to accuse them—or maybe she's just afraid of them," said Ark. He frowned. "Mara is an Aphonian. She can see muses, but she can't use music to defend herself. If Dulcian and Callie *are* working with Dubito, and if they discovered Mara was on to them, she wouldn't stand a chance."

Jay matched his frown. "Hard to know what to believe."

Ark considered the possibilities. "Maybe Dulcian and Callie hired Dubito to fake a fight with them. That would make them look good in front of the Maestrans Council. Or maybe they're Dischordian sympathizers. Or maybe . . . ," Ark winced, pinching the bridge of his nose as a needle of pain stabbed between his eyebrows. "I'm not sure what to believe, either. Mara's message has gotten me so turned around that I can't see straight."

Jay stared at the message a long moment. Then he closed the notebook.

"Look, we can't worry about it now," he said, passing the notebook back to Ark. "We'll be in Fairdown Falls soon enough. In two days, it'll be Wintertide Eve. At that point, none of this will matter."

Ark blinked, puzzled. What did Wintertide have to do with anything?

"I'll stay awake," said Jay. He shoved Ark away. "Rest up. You look like something Hotah spat out."

Ark could feel the exhaustion pulling at his limbs. He nodded, then laid down on the deck. "Good night, then."

Jay didn't answer. He was staring into the night sky, looking lost and small against the immense sea of stars. As Ark closed his eyes, he heard Jay begin to sing to himself, his voice so quiet it was almost stolen by the wind:

> *Courage, courage, ma luciole*
> *Cet adieu est temporaire*
> *Un jour, tu reviendras à moi encore . . .*

Ark was too tired to be surprised. So, Jay knew the song too. Huh.

Ark drifted, the notes of the lullaby carrying him off to sleep.

Chapter Twenty-Eight

THE ROYAL CONSERVATORY

Ark was still sound asleep on the deck, enjoying an incredible dream. He was flying on his own through the air, gliding with outstretched arms above glittering white clouds. Ark flapped his arms and soared, completely free . . .

Then an almighty lurch threw him from his dreams. Ark staggered as the airship dove at a stomach-flipping angle.

"Ratchets, ratchets, *ratchets!*" Rye was cursing.

Ark found his feet, trying to understand what was going on. Jay, Andi, and Hana were all clinging to the rigging ropes. Hotah was whining. Rye was pulling against the helm, glaring through her goggles.

"What's happening?" Ark shouted, grasping at the rigging ropes.

Before anyone could answer, the airship fell into another stomach-turning dive—and then the Morning Star climbed up on a fresh gale. The wing sails groaned with the strain; Rye's hands flew over the navigation dash, madly trying to adjust the controls against the drastic wind shear.

"Storm!" she shouted back. "It's mucked up the airstream."

Rye pointed off the port side. Ark stared, his heart galloping. A glowering mass of ugly clouds were grumbling off the horizon to the north.

"The headwind off that storm blew us off course a few spans before I could correct it!" she shouted over the shrieking wind. "Then the headwind became a tailwind and made the air all choppy. If we don't get out of these currents soon, we might get blown right past our destination!"

She nodded toward starboard. Ark turned—and his mouth fell open. Fairdown Falls.

He hadn't expected to be flying over it already. The enormous Fairdown River was below them, shining like liquid silver as it flowed over the land. It was the biggest river Ark had ever seen—so wide that, had he been down on the riverbank, he wasn't sure he'd be able to see the other side. On its way to the sea, the river cascaded over sheer cliffs, creating a magnificent waterfall.

The sight was breathtaking—but Ark gasped when he caught his first glimpse of the capital city.

Ark had never seen so many tall buildings before, all in one place. They seemed to rise right out of the river, but really they were all squished together on a group of bumpy islands in the heart of the river's current. Long wharfs sticking out from the islands were crowded with boats. Dozens of bridges connected the islands to one another, weaving together a crisscross network of streets and canals on each island. People were everywhere, swarming marketplaces, public plazas, and parks. Everywhere Ark looked, the capital was bustling with life.

"Great gavotte," he breathed, awestruck.

Then the airship lurched, buffeted by a sharp breeze. Ark felt his stomach somersault up into his throat as the deck slanted again.

"Blast it!" Jay cursed. "At this rate, we're gonna crash!"

"We're crashing?!" Andi cried out.

"No, we aren't!" Hana yelled back, shooting Jay a hard look. "Rye has studied everything about aeronautics. She's helped with all the Morning Star's hover tests. She knows what she's doing!"

Ark didn't think reading theory and practicing hovering were the same as real flight—but he had to admit that Rye was handling the helm like an expert, making precise adjustments to the controls to counter the shifting winds.

"Where should we land?" said Hana between blasts of wind.

"Good question!" shouted Rye. She looked straight at Ark.

Ark wobbled as he crossed the deck, gripping onto the navigation dash as he stood next to Rye. He squinted at the city below.

Finally, he spotted it. Positioned at the highest point on the smallest, bumpiest island, titanic statues of two people stood in proud splendor. The statues were surrounded by scaffolding and renovation equipment, but Ark could still tell that one statue was a fierce, beautiful woman dressed in armor—the First Crafter—while the other was a winged figure with an ageless face, dressed in robes—Brio. The statues gazed benevolently down upon Fairdown Falls, holding an enormous stone lantern between them.

"Look!" said Ark, pointing to the statues. "That's Harmony Monument. The Royal Conservatory is supposed to be just below it."

"All I see are trees!" said Rye.

Ark scanned the land below the statues. The rest of the island did look like it was covered by one big forest, but then he noticed a few rooftops peeking out from the foliage. As they got closer, Ark finally saw the Royal Conservatory. It was easily twice as large as Echostrait's campus, and its many gardens, groves, and buildings stood in harmony with the ancient trees.

"There!" shouted Ark, drawing Rye's attention to a large circular lawn. "Can we land there?"

Rye altered the Morning Star's heading, pulling against the controls. Another screeching alarm made her curse again.

"Not enough distance!" she said. "We're caught in an upper current. It's negating the engines and countering decreased thrust—"

"Use words we can all understand!" shouted Jay.

"We're too high up and going too fast!" Rye shouted back. "I've cut back on the throttle, but the tailwind is pushing us so hard from behind that we won't be able to descend fast enough. We'll miss the landing site!"

Ark tried not to envision the Morning Star landing miles off course in the middle of nowhere.

"But we have to land now!" shouted Jay. He was squeezing the black case in his arms like a lifeline. "What can we do?"

Rye glanced above, and her eyes lit up.

"I'll vent the balloon," she said. "With less fluviengas keeping us airborne, our weight should help us descend. Everybody, hold on!"

They all scrambled for a handhold. Ark's heart punched his ribs as Rye turned a large knob on the navigation dash. Seconds later, Ark smelled a strange, spicy odor as fluviengas hissed out of the balloon.

Almost immediately the airship began to lose altitude—slowly at first, but then rapidly like a cart that had just rolled past the peak of a hill. Ark held the navigation dash in a death grip while Rye steered them toward the flat stretch of lawn in the heart of the Royal Conservatory grounds.

"It's gonna be close!" said Rye. "Let's hope we miss those trees!"

Ark swallowed, his mouth dry as dust. He could see immediately that they weren't going to miss the trees. As the airship careened toward the treetop, everyone yelled in alarm. Ark chanted on instinct:

"Sppingicci versso l'allto!"

At the last second, something rolled beneath the ship, pushing them up just enough to make it over the trees. A muse in the form of a luminous whale appeared from beneath the Morning Star. The whale swam in midair, flicking its tail to say *You're welcome* before it vanished.

The ship glided a few more strides before it finally struck ground. The Morning Star shuddered as the hull tore into the trimmed grass, sending dirt flying everywhere. Ark and the others cried out as they were thrown across the deck, and the whole ship shook like mad.

And then, at last, the ship gave an awful groan and stopped at an angle. Ark and the others lay still, breathing heavily, not daring to move.

"So," said Andi, clutching Hotah, "I take it the flight's over?"

That was enough to break everyone from their shock. Ark helped Hana slide off the ship while Jay helped Andi and Hotah jump down. Rye tumbled onto the grass and tore off her goggles, circling the ship to inspect the damage.

"I'm dead!" she wailed. "Susanna and Rosetta won't speak to me again!"

Ark felt for Rye. As he watched, the propellers sputtered and died. The broken foremast gave a *crack!* and fell off. The balloon sank with a *whomph* as it deflated, while the stern engines belched black clouds. Hana lay an arm over Rye's shoulder, trying to reassure her. Rye looked like she wanted to throw up.

Ark straightened, looking around.

The Royal Conservatory. He'd finally arrived, and it was better than he'd imagined. Ark had grown up navigating the cramped, twisty-turney grounds of Echostrait, where everything was squished close together. But here, the majestic, centuries-old buildings were spread out, nestled harmoniously within the island's foliage. Ark spied well-worn paths weaving through the trees, connecting each building in a natural network. Aside from buildings, more property was dedicated to vast, winter-bare gardens,

286

sparkling ponds, quiet grottos, and cool brooks. The whole place was more like one huge nature reserve than the center of all Musician affairs in Merideyin.

"You there! Halt!"

Ark looked around. Three Musicians in gray talaris coats were marching across the lawn. The one in the middle—a chiseled statue of a man with silver bars on his collar and a muse in the form of a wasp on his shoulder—looked particularly formidable, his gaze fixed on Ark.

"Adept Arkalin Encore?" he said, taking in Ark's white talaris.

Ark nodded.

The captain's expression remained stern. "We were informed you would be arriving by airship," he said. He turned to the still-smoking heap of the Morning Star. "If that's what you call this absurd machine."

"What did you say?" blurted Rye, storming forward. Hana grabbed her before Rye could tackle the man. The captain's wasp muse flicked its antennae and buzzed angrily, its bulbous eyes on Rye.

"Stand down, Kreuz," the captain told his muse. Once the wasp's buzzing stopped, the captain asked, "Which of you is the Crafter's heir?"

His eyes traveled expectantly over Hana, Rye, and Andi before finally settling on Jay. Jay sent the man a sour glare, then held up the black case.

Incredulity flew over the captain's face. The other gray-clad Musicians shared doubtful looks.

"That's quite enough, Sharpe!" a new voice called out. "I'll take it from here."

The captain and the other gray-clad Musicians stepped aside. A heavy-set man with terra cotta skin and a close-shaven head approached them. He wore a red talaris that reminded Ark of Maestran Pandoura. At his side was a muse in the form of a handsome white rabbit.

"Maestran Ruan Bao," said the man, introducing himself. He gestured to the white rabbit muse. "And my patron, Luta. Greetings, Adept Encore and companions. We are relieved you arrived safely."

He clasped each of their hands for a handshake. When he came to Jay, he instead offered a deep bow.

"It is the highest honor to meet a Crafter's heir in my lifetime," he said, his voice full of emotion. "Welcome to our Conservatory, Your Eminence."

Jay blinked at the man, looking stunned.

"The Maestrans Council is waiting," Maestran Ruan added. He whistled softly to the white rabbit, who twitched its nose in response. Then he turned to the gray-clad Musicians. "Lead the way, Captain."

The captain saluted the Maestran and bowed deferentially to Jay, though the disbelief on his face stayed put. Then he and his coterie stepped off, with the Maestran, Ark, Jay, and the others following.

"Don't mind Captain Sharpe. He scowls at everyone," said Maestran Ruan. "He leads the Gray Wolves, our security unit. He specializes in defensive forms and being suspicious of everything."

They crossed the length of the lawn toward one of the wider paths leading into the trees. Ark kept pace easily with the others, eager to reach the Maestrans Council—but the moment they passed into the wooded grounds, he stopped dead in his tracks. Jay froze too.

"Uh, hello?" said Andi, who was right behind them. "What's the holdup?"

"Are you all right?" asked Hana. Rye glanced back.

Ark and Jay shared a wordless glance. Ark knew they were commoners and so couldn't detect muses—but even so, he could hardly believe they didn't notice. A tingly sensation raced up his spine.

Muses. *Everywhere.*

Ark felt countless gazes lock onto him at once, immediately aware of his presence. After a few moments, he began to spot them: above in the trees, below along the ground, hovering in the air. Muses of every size and shape surrounded them—birds, beasts, and more bizarre forms—watching him curiously. He'd never seen so many muses in one place.

"Great gavotte," Ark breathed, eyes wide. "There's hundreds of them!"

"Hundreds of what?" asked Rye.

Ark wished he could show her what he saw. "Muses. This place, this whole island . . . it's singing with their presence."

Ark glanced toward Jay. Jay's face shone with unguarded awe.

Maestran Ruan afforded them another moment to take it all in, then coughed. It was enough of a signal to get Ark's feet moving again—though as they continued walking, he couldn't keep his eyes from wandering. To his right, a serene muse with moss-green hair and horns covered in bark, its neck as tall as the trees; to his left, a playful muse like a squirrel bounding from tree to tree, chittering merrily and flicking its golden tail; up above, a muse like an albatross with feathers of pure silver, gliding through the air. Ark was so distracted that he didn't even notice they'd left the trees behind until Maestran Ruan spoke.

"Welcome to our Maestrans Hall," said the man, raising a hand.

Ark gaped at the opulent structure before them. An enormous building made of gilded alabaster stood right up against one of the bumpy island's sheer rock walls, tucked beneath blankets of ivy. The building looked like a cross between a temple and a castle, at once welcoming and imposing.

"Allow me to guide you all through several points of protocol," said Maestran Ruan, leading them on toward the front entrance. "When entering the assembly room, you will wait at the back to be announced before you approach the Grand Maestran. When you are asked to step forward, you will first bow to the Grand Maestran and the Council Chair. Do not speak unless the Grand Maestran speaks to you first."

While he spoke, Captain Sharpe and the other Gray Wolves stepped around to open the doors for all of them. Maestran Ruan slid aside to let Jay walk in first. Jay shuffled forward, with Ark right behind him.

The atrium inside wasn't what he'd expected. A long strip of the floor was polished stone—but on either side, the stone floor gave way to tiered gardens overflowing with flowers. Elsewhere, windows fitted with prismatic stained glass cast mosaics of color on the floor. The most eye-catching part of the space was a splashing fountain in the middle. The fountain featured a statue of an armor-wearing woman and a winged man standing back-to-back in a victorious pose, with a wretched monster writhing beneath their feet.

Ark studied the fountain. This was probably the fountain he and Jay were supposed to have emerged from when Dulcian performed his Transposition back in Hazeldenn. If only Dulcian had gotten it right—that certainly would have saved them loads of time.

Then again, if Dulcian had been successful, they never would have met Andi, Hana, or Rye.

The Maestran coughed again. Jay shuffled forward along the stone path, reaching another set of doors on the opposite side of the atrium.

"Remember," said Maestran Ruan in a low voice, "don't approach until you're introduced. Do not speak unless spoken to. And don't forget to bow."

With that, he pushed the doors open.

Ark squinted against the bright light. It felt almost as if they'd stepped outside again. Beyond the doors was an enormous circular chamber. Wide windows reached from floor to ceiling, letting in sunlight and a brilliant view of the forested grounds. Between the windows, wooden columns were carved to look just like trees growing along the perimeter of the room, holding up the domed ceiling with strong, polished branches. Portraits of men and women in purple coats lined the walls, gazing eternally from their paintings with the same expression—like they were forever wondering, *Is it lunchtime yet?*

"Who are all these people?" Rye whispered.

At first Ark thought she was talking about the portraits—but then he shifted his gaze down to the main part of the room. Men and women were dressed in different colored talarises: most in bright red, but some in orange, ochre, and emerald. Most had patron muses at their side. They sat at slender tables set in rows, all facing a raised platform at the far end.

"This is Merideyin's Maestrans Council," replied Ark under his breath. "They're the most powerful Musicians in the country."

"What about those guys?" asked Rye.

Rye was pointing at the two people sitting on the raised platform. One was a man with tan, leathery skin, a white beard, and a wise, earnest gaze. He was the only person wearing a purple talaris. Behind him perched a muse in the form of an owl with bronze feathers. Next to the man was a woman in a maroon talaris, with deep olive skin and wooly black hair. An elaborate sapphire hair ornament sat on top of her head.

"That's Grand Maestran Johann Luthier," said Ark, starstruck. "And next to him is the Council Chair, his subordinate."

Ark reflexively smoothed his hair and tweaked his collar as Maestran Ruan left them by the doors, heading down a side aisle toward the front of the chamber. He stepped up to the side of the platform, waiting for the woman in maroon to notice him. She didn't.

Suddenly Hana gasped.

"What's wrong?" asked Andi, alarmed. He drew close to Hotah.

"It's nothing," Hana whispered. She turned to Ark. "But how in the world did *they* make it here before us?"

Ark turned. Standing before the Grand Maestran's bench were two people in green talarises. Their backs were to the entrance, but Ark recognized Trillo and Fiero right away.

"Dulcian and Callie?" he said, stunned. "I—I have no idea."

It was only after he'd spotted them that he realized a man in an orange talaris was standing at the front of the room too, addressing the Grand Maestran like a lawyer to a magistrate.

"—the facts remain," the orange-clad man was saying. "Sir Mandore's and Lady Vielle's decisions concerning the Crafter's heir have been highly questionable. For nearly *two weeks* following the incident in Hazeldenn, the Crafter's heir could not be accounted for. And after he was finally recovered in Cindertown, instead of bringing him along through the same Transposition they used to return here this morning, Sir Mandore and Lady Vielle made the dubious decision to send him off in an unregistered airship prototype with virtual strangers. And where is he now?"

The Maestrans murmured and their muses rustled. Ark's eyes stayed on Callie and Dulcian. Was this some kind of disciplinary hearing?

Meanwhile Maestran Ruan was still waiting by the Grand Maestran's bench, trying to get her attention. The woman in maroon was unaware.

"—and the conclusion is clear," the prosecutor in orange went on through the murmurs. "In light of their injudicious actions concerning the security of the Crafter's heir, the panel believes they are not yet fit to return to service and recommends their suspension be extended."

Ark could see Callie tighten her fists. Dulcian's shoulders sank. Fiero and Trillo grew agitated. Grand Maestran Luthier turned his steady gaze on them.

"How do you respond?" he asked in a soft, deep voice.

Callie stepped forward. "With respect, Your Excellency, a Transposition is what caused us to lose track of the Crafter's heir in the first place. And as we *just explained* in our report, the situation in Cindertown left us little time to discuss options. The best way to remove the Crafter's heir safely from the city and keep him out of Dubito's reach was the airship. Adept Encore was the one to recommend it."

"In other words, you followed the lead of an inexperienced teenager instead of using your own judgment," the prosecutor said scathingly. Callie pressed her lips into a tight line, saying nothing.

The Grand Maestran looked grim as the prosecutor stepped away to speak with a group of other orange-clad people near the front.

"Does the panel intend to amend its verdict?" the Grand Maestran asked.

The prosecutor returned. "Excuses don't change facts. The panel stands by its decision. Lady Vielle and Sir Mandore's suspension will be extended indefinitely." With a superior expression, he added, "If Julian were here right now, I am sure he would recommend the same thing."

"What the heck do *you* know?"

Ark jumped, startled by Jay's outburst. He turned to where Jay had been standing—but Jay was already stomping swiftly down the center aisle. Every Maestran turned to stare as Jay reached the front of the chamber.

Ark swallowed back a million curses. *Moron!*

"What is this?" demanded the prosecutor, outraged. "This is a closed meeting! Guards!"

Captain Sharpe hurried to the front of the assembly room.

"Please escort this reprobate to the security hall," said the prosecutor.

Captain Sharpe didn't move, his gaze flickering between the prosecutor and Jay. Maestran Ruan, who had kept to the side, finally stepped forward. "If I may interject—"

"What is the problem?" the prosecutor interrupted impatiently.

Ark stared hard at the back of Jay's head, willing him to keep his mouth shut for once. But it was no use.

"The *problem* is you figure you can stuff words in my mouth when I'm right here!" said Jay, glaring at the prosecutor. "I don't know what you're all going on about—but I speak for myself, got it?"

Ark hid his face in his hand with a groan. Leave it to Jay to break every single point of protocol in one go. Now all of them would be kicked out.

But that didn't happen. It took everyone a moment to process what Jay had said—then, one by one, they seemed to notice the black case Jay was carrying. The room exploded with gasps and shouts. Faces shone with amazement. Even the prosecutor's mouth fell open.

The only person who kept his composure was the Grand Maestran. He raised his hand. All the jabbering voices hushed.

"Forgive us, Your Eminence—we had not realized you'd arrived," said Grand Maestran Luthier, without the slightest hint of sarcasm. "How relieved we are to find you safe and unharmed. You are most welcome here!"

Jay shifted uncomfortably, clutching the case in a tight grip.

"I'd prefer it if you spoke for yourself in this matter," added the Grand Maestran, speaking to Jay like an equal. He leaned forward. "Based on your experience, what would you say Sir Mandore and Lady Vielle deserve?"

Ark crossed his fingers, hoping Jay wouldn't say anything stupid before the entire Maestrans Council.

"Well," said Jay at length, "they dragged me off in the middle of the town festival, forced me to play a fiddle, threw me into a lake, made me play checkers, and let me go onto a dinky airship that almost crashed."

Ark could practically feel the wave of incredulity ripple across the Maestrans. Callie and Dulcian were soon sweating under dozens of hard stares.

Apparently, though, Jay wasn't finished speaking.

"But I guess they were just doing their job," he went on. "And their job was even harder thanks to that Dubito creep." He shrugged. "I figure you should let them off the hook."

"I see," said the Grand Maestran. "Well, one thing is certain: the Crafter's heir does not mince words, does he?" He smiled at Jay. "Please take it easy on us old Maestrans, Your Eminence. Such pure-hearted honesty may be too much for the crotchety politicians in the room."

The Council Chair chuckled. A few other Maestrans shared grins, though most seemed to be trying to hide their disapproval at the Grand Maestran's sideways jab. Jay frowned, like he didn't get the joke.

"So be it," the Grand Maestran continued. He turned to the panel in orange. "As it is His Eminence's decision, let it be known that Sir Mandore and Lady Vielle's suspension is now ended. I recommend they report for duty at the end of Wintertide, following the Crafter's inauguration. What say you?"

A chorus of *ayes* responded throughout the chamber.

"Then this hearing is concluded, and our assembly is adjourned," said the Grand Maestran, rising from his seat. Every other Maestran followed suit. They all began to bow to Grand Maestran Luthier.

But the Grand Maestran held up his hand, shaking his head. Then the man turned toward Jay and, with one smooth, deliberate motion, bowed to him.

Gradually, everyone else in the room—including Dulcian and Callie—mimicked him, bowing instead in Jay's direction. Rye whispered something to Andi, and the two of them also bent forward, along with Hana.

Ark was the only one who didn't lower his head, so he was the only one to see Jay's flabbergasted expression. Jay glanced over and caught Ark's eye, raising his hands like he had no clue what to do. Ark shrugged back.

Thankfully, the bowing ended. The Maestrans shuffled out of the chamber, though not without sideways glances at Jay. Ark caught the words "Brio," "Crafter's heir," and "*Him?*" in their conversations.

Soon the only ones left in the assembly room were Jay, Dulcian, Callie, Maestran Ruan, Captain Sharpe, the Grand Maestran, and the Council Chair—along with one person Ark hadn't noticed at all. Mara had apparently been there all along, practically invisible behind the other Maestrans.

"C'mon," hissed Ark to Rye, Andi, and Hana. The four of them hurried up the center aisle just as the Grand Maestran and the Council Chair descended from the bench.

"Your Eminence, we are well met," said the Grand Maestran, walking up to Jay with a warm smile. "Please call me Luthier. Tallon is my patron."

At that, the owl muse that had been perched behind the Grand Maestran flew down to the man's shoulder. Tallon gave Jay a wide, owlish stare.

Then the Grand Maestran gestured to the woman in maroon. "Allow me to introduce Council Chair Ilona Tadellos and her patron, Morceau."

Maestran Tadellos acknowledged Jay with a bow. As she bent forward, Ark realized the sapphire hair ornament on the top of her head wasn't an ornament at all. It was a muse in the form of a large blue spider, clutching her bun of dark hair with long, spindly legs. Jay looked even more uncomfortable than before—though Ark wasn't sure what bothered him more, her bowing or Morceau the spider muse.

"I know you have only just made it here, Your Eminence—may I call you Julian?" the Grand Maestran asked, interrupting himself. Jay nodded stiffly, and the man continued. "You and your companions all deserve a rest, Julian, but I'm afraid we mustn't delay. We must carry out your inauguration as soon as possible. Otherwise, the risk is too great."

"What do you mean?" asked Ark, realizing too late that he'd forgotten to add "Your Excellency." Thankfully, Maestran Ruan covered Ark's gaffe.

"His Excellency has been in contact with the Grand Maestrans of the other nations," he explained. "While Grand Maestran Luthier is in favor of letting the Crafter assume his rightful place right away, the others aren't of the same mind."

"They've been grumbling," Grand Maestran Luthier interjected. "*I* may be willing to step aside to let the Crafter lead, but the other Grand Maestrans aren't willing to hand over their authority so easily. If it were up to them, the Crafter would remain a figurehead, or at least under *their* control. They want to summon Julian to the next International Maestrans Congress meeting and evaluate him themselves—no doubt to delay his formal investiture or somehow tether his influence to their own positions. That's why we must hold his inauguration immediately, before the Grand Maestrans can carry out their intentions."

"How soon is 'immediately'?" asked Jay, tapping the case.

"Wintertide Day," said Maestran Tadellos. "The day after tomorrow. But no need to fret, Your Eminence—we'll guide you through every step."

"My fellow Grand Maestrans will no doubt be furious with me," said Grand Maestran Luthier. "But by then Julian will be the Crafter, and they'll no longer have any power to object."

"You can rest assured the likes of Dubito won't interrupt, either," said Captain Sharpe. "The Gray Wolves will be covering every inch of the Royal Conservatory grounds. No foul Dischordian will dare show their face here."

"Thank you, Captain," said the Grand Maestran. He faced Dulcian and Callie. "I am pleased our two best agents will be returning to active service. This is a happy occasion for you both." He glanced at Mara, as if just remembering her. "And Miss Fipple! You deserve our thanks, too." While Mara meekly bowed, the Grand Maestran told all three, "It seems only fitting you should all be in attendance at Julian's inauguration."

Callie, Dulcian, and Mara all stammered their thanks.

"Good, good," said the Grand Maestran. He then faced Andi, Hana, and Rye. "You must be Hanabi, Ryanna, and Andimakanani. Lady Vielle and Sir Mandore informed the Council of your commendable actions in helping the Crafter's heir. Please allow me to extend to you the full hospitality of the Royal Conservatory. You are free to decline, but I hope you will at least join us for the Crafter's inauguration. We will have seats reserved for you."

At that, Hana, Andi, and Rye looked delighted. Hotah gave a happy bark.

Ark fought to keep his disappointment in check. He should be *happy*. He *was* happy that Andi, Rye, and Hana got the credit they deserved; they'd helped Jay out of pure kindness, without any thought of reward. And it made sense that Dulcian, Callie, and Mara were praised for their efforts as the Royal Conservatory's representatives. The Crafter's heir had arrived safely at the Royal Conservatory; that's what mattered.

Besides, it was foolish—arrogant even—for Ark to have secretly hoped that the Grand Maestran would acknowledge him, too.

Ark tilted his head to let his fringe fall in front of his spectacles, wishing he were anywhere else. A second later, it dawned on him that he'd copied Jay's move of ducking under his cap.

Ark only realized Grand Maestran Luthier had started speaking again when he heard his name.

"—our steadfast Adept Encore."

Ark glanced up. Everyone was looking at him.

"Remind me, Adept Encore," said the Grand Maestran, regarding him with a serious expression. "How old are you?"

Ark swallowed. "Fifteen, Your Excellency."

"Fifteen," repeated the Grand Maestran, marveling. He turned to Jay, Andi, Hana, and Rye, explaining for their benefit. "Most students who go out on their jury missions are eighteen or older, and they merely assist their jurors with rather simple assignments—allowing them to field-test their musical skills with professional support. Not all pass on the first try."

He faced Ark again, a smile at the corners of his mouth. "I know of no other young Musician who would have performed as admirably as you. Despite the unprecedented situations thrown your way, you handled yourself better than many veteran Musicians. I already assumed you were a unique talent, based on what Maestran Pandoura had written me about you—but you've proven yourself even more exceptional than advertised."

The stone fist around Ark's chest dissolved. He felt himself blushing.

"Sir Mandore, Lady Vielle," said the Grand Maestran, turning to them, "as the Adept's jurors, what is your final decision about his performance?"

Ark glanced between them. He didn't know whether he should still be wary of them, after Mara's warning—or if he should feel guilty for being so suspicious without any real evidence. He quashed the worries in his head, holding his breath.

"Isn't it obvious?" said Callie at length. "He's passed."

"With flying colors," added Dulcian, grinning.

Fiero barked and Trillo chirped, as if echoing their verdict.

Ark's heart pounded hard. The Grand Maestran spread his arms wide.

"Excellent," he said, extending a hand. "Congratulations, Sir Encore. You are a full-fledged Musician. Well done. I will inform Maestran Pandoura that you have passed with distinction. In the meantime, you will receive your credentials and your new talaris before the inauguration."

Ark was too dumbfounded to speak. The Grand Maestran of Merideyin had shaken his hand and told him well done. If only his father could have seen that.

But who cared? Ark's face stretched in a broad grin. He'd done it. He was a Musician in his own right, and for the first time in ages, he no longer felt the yearning ache to prove himself.

For a moment, Ark thought about speaking up and correcting the Grand Maestran—he was going to be Sir de Cani, not Encore. But he held himself back.

Sir Encore. Ark smiled. Had a nice ring to it.

"Come, everyone!" said the Grand Maestran, sweeping his arms so high that Tallon had to flutter to keep his perch on his shoulder. "We have many preparations to make, but right now I believe lunch is in order. Will you all please join me?" He waved his arm toward Jay. "Your Eminence?"

Ark had been so caught up in a euphoric wave that he only just noticed Jay standing on his own, hugging the black case. Ark couldn't say why, but for some reason Jay looked grim.

"Your Eminence," the Grand Maestran repeated gently.

Jay snapped from his daze. He started off, walking beside the Grand Maestran while the rest followed. Ark couldn't hide his grin as Andi, Hana, and Rye congratulated him. As they left Maestrans Hall, Ark promised himself he'd catch up with Jay later.

But first, lunch.

Chapter Twenty-Nine

A TRADE

As tasty as the food smelled, Jay didn't feel like eating it.

Which was a lousy shame, considering. Jay stared at the plate, wishing his mouth would start watering. Most of the food was just the kind of stuff he liked best, including apple dumplings, cracked pepper cheese, and a honey-nut crumble that made him miss Hazeldenn in an awful way. But instead of scarfing all that hearty, spicy, honey-sweet goodness, he let it grow cold.

Since they'd arrived at the Royal Conservatory the day before, every meal set in front of Jay had looked just as lip-smackingly delicious—but he'd barely tasted anything. When he was the Quickstep Kid, he'd always lost his appetite before a big job with the Staccato Gang. It was the same now.

Jay heard a delicate chime. He glanced over to the clock on the wall.

Six hours until the Capo's deadline.

Bandersnatches. He still didn't know what to do. Jay hunched in his stiff shirt as he paced, his new shoes scuffing the plush carpet.

The past day and a half had been a total blur. Since going to lunch with Grand Maestran Luthier yesterday, Jay felt like he'd been thrown into a game of hot potato—except *he* was the spud. After lunch, the Grand Maestran had tossed Jay to Maestran Tadellos, who brought him to see Harmony Monument, the gigantic statues of Brio and the First Crafter at the very top of the island. Maestran Tadellos went on and on about the history of the ritual Jay was supposed to perform there, but Jay had been too distracted by the creepy spider muse sitting on her head to pay attention. Then—hot potato!—Spider Lady had tossed Jay over to Maestran Ruan, who'd swept him off to dinner with lots of people in red coats. They all talked a lot, but not to him. Jay had never felt so out of place.

This morning had been no better. After a twitchy night of no sleep, Jay was tossed out of bed by a bunch of strange people who'd come to measure every inch of him. They'd made him stand real still while they forced him into dozens of stiff, itchy outfits with high collars and weird buttons and not nearly enough pockets. While they'd poked him like a pincushion, Spider Lady had made him read over the inauguration schedule so many times that Jay went cross-eyed. The only part he remembered was that he was supposed to wear his new black talaris to Harmony Monument, where he'd perform the official Crafter ritual by lighting the big stone lantern that the two statues were holding. Then he'd recite the ancient vow of the Crafters, promising to serve and protect, forever and ever, *yadda yadda yadda*.

And that was it. Lighting the lantern and saying the vow would make him a Crafter.

Of course, nobody bothered to explain *how* he was supposed to light that stupid lantern. Nobody asked whether he even *wanted* to make the vow. Nobody understood anything. They probably just assumed he was loving every minute—like Ark, Andi, Hana, and Rye seemed to be. Ark and the others got to pal around together and explore the island while Jay was dragged this way and that, getting all prepped up for an inauguration ceremony he wasn't even sure he'd be attending.

Jay wanted to tell somebody—about his old life, the Capo's deadline, Dubito's bargain—about the target on his back and the ticking clock over his head. But he couldn't find the words, much less somebody to talk to. The only thing left was to make a choice on his own: stay or go.

Fed up with pacing, Jay went over to the balcony doors and stepped outside. From here, he could see all of Fairdown Falls. As he gazed out, the city winked back at him.

"I missed you too," Jay whispered to the city, his breath fogging on the cold air. He scanned the knot of islands, remembering places he'd haunted as the Quickstep Kid: over there, a good street for pickpocketing; over there, a market where he'd score free meals; way over there, a secret entrance to the sewers, in case he'd needed to hide from watchmen.

Jay gazed at the cityscape for what felt like ages. Eventually, his eyes drifted over to the west side, where Windfalle used to be. He quickly turned away and went back inside, checking the clock again.

Five and a half hours until deadline.

Jay cursed. Blast it! He couldn't take much more of this—

Tap tap!

The knock on the door made Jay jump. The door opened, and Mara poked her head inside. "Your Eminence?"

Jay felt a sour twist of disappointment. It took him a second to realize he'd been hoping to see Ark and the others at the door instead. But they hadn't dropped by all day. Not once.

"What d'you want?" said Jay. He hadn't meant to sound so grumpy.

Mara smiled meekly, stepping inside. "I heard you'd requested to have dinner alone in your room tonight. I wanted to make sure you were okay."

That was the last thing he'd expected her to say. "I'm good," he said, somewhat touched. "Thanks."

Mara raised her shoulder in a half-shrug. "You're going through a lot," she said. She spied his untouched plate. "Big day tomorrow, yes?"

Jay grunted. Mara crossed the room and retrieved Jay's uneaten dinner.

"I'll take care of this for you," she murmured, heading to the exit. She opened the door and started to leave—but right before the door closed behind her, she caught it, turning back around to face him.

"There is one thing I wanted to tell you," she said.

She spoke in a halting, hushed voice. Jay perked up. "Yeah?"

Mara glanced out the door, looking down the hallway both directions—then she slipped back in, shutting the door and setting the plate down. She bit her lip, then spoke in her wispy, whispery voice.

"It isn't true."

Jay blinked. "What isn't true?"

Her eyes finally met his. "You *aren't* the first person in two hundred years who was able to play Brio's instrument. There were other Crafter's heirs."

Jay's brow crinkled in confusion. What was she saying?

"It's something only very few others know about," Mara went on. She clutched her skirts and sat on his bed. "I found out when I was put in charge of Crafter evaluations. Grand Maestran Luthier also knows the truth."

The significance of what Mara was saying finally sank into Jay's brain.

"That's—but—I—" he stammered, too many thoughts trying to escape at once. Finally, he managed, "How many?"

Mara glanced at the ceiling. "Nine, I think. The Royal Conservatory has kept it hushed for ages."

Jay absently reached a hand up to his chest, clutching at his shirt. It felt too tight. The air in his room turned thick, suddenly hard to breathe.

"What happened to them?" he asked huskily.

Mara shook her head. "Nothing *happened* to them. They just chose not to become the Crafter. I think many of them went on to be great leaders and famous thinkers in their time." She shrugged. "They may have made good Crafters, too, who knows—but they chose their path for themselves."

She stood up from the bed, turning her wide, watery eyes on him. Then she took up the plate of cold food and headed to the door.

"Why'd you tell me this?" he called after her.

Mara paused in the doorway. She turned around for a moment, sending him a sympathetic look. Then at length she said, "Good luck tomorrow."

Like a ghost, she was gone.

Jay felt blood pounding in his ears. His whole body pulsed in shock. Dizzy, he staggered to his bed, flopping down before the weight of Mara's words knocked him to the floor.

It isn't true.

A sharp pain squeezed Jay's skull. He bent forward, holding his head in his hands—and saw the black case with Brio's fiddle just a few paces away.

There were other Crafter's heirs.

Groaning, he flopped backwards, sinking into the bed. He stared at the ceiling, trying to digest what he'd just heard.

They got to choose?

At once he felt the spark of something fierce and angry in the pit of his stomach. There had been others like him, other candidates who'd played the fiddle. And they still chose other things. Meanwhile, everybody Jay had met was acting like he was *the* Crafter's heir, the first in centuries, and he had no choice but to become the Crafter.

They acted like he was something special.

And he wasn't.

The anger in his gut burned hotter. Jay felt trembly all over. What was he supposed to do now?

Words spoken by Dulcian and Dubito began swirling through his mind in a storm:

You're not just gifted. You are a gift, Julian. That's why Brio chose you.

They will make you their puppet. They will use you, betray you, discard you.

You are the Crafter's heir, called to step out and save people who need you, people who believe in you.

You can be free from the Capo. Free from the Crafter's burden. Free to go where you wish, do as you wish, chart your own course!

Soon more voices joined the storm in his mind, adding to the confusion:

Pay back the rest of your debt by midnight on Wintertide Eve, plus interest.

It's your choice, Quickstep. Your life. Be a puppet—or be free.

If you don't pay, someone else will.

Good luck tomorrow.

Jay lay on the bed for what felt like a lifetime, the echoing voices whirling his thoughts into a muddle. Eventually, one voice won out above the others.

His choice made, Jay lay still, waiting.

∞

Ding!

The clock above him chimed the eleventh hour. Jay sat up.

Time to go.

His new clothes weren't suited for a midnight escapade, so Jay quickly changed into his old threads, donning his vest and cap for good measure. Then he yanked one of the silky sheets off his bed and ripped it, making a simple sack to carry the fiddle's case. He slung the sack over his shoulder, the case resting against his back. He was ready.

Jay took one final look around the room. His eyes landed on the black talaris coat made just for him, laid out on a chair. The Crafter was the only one who ever wore black, the Spider Lady had said. Jay could've sworn the black talaris was staring back at him in disapproval—almost like it knew Jay was never going to wear it.

Jay slinked across the room, slipped out to the balcony, and flung himself over the side.

Climbing down from the balcony was cake. The rough stone walls gave him plenty of handholds; in no time, he was close enough to jump down to the ground, landing softly on the winter-bare bushes below. Jay paused, checking that the coast was clear—and then he took off.

Night wrapped around Jay like a cloak, and Jay's old instincts kicked in. He snuck across the Royal Conservatory grounds as silent as moonlight, his movements fluid as he ducked swiftly through the trees.

Only a few muses drifting in the trees saw him, watching him curiously as he passed; Jay hurried faster so the music spirits wouldn't catch up. Soon enough his feet crunched on the gravely shore. A handful of public rental rowboats sat in a line at the water's edge, each anchored and chained to a coin-drop meter.

Jay paused to catch his breath, his heart hammering on his ribs—

Don't.

The sudden voice made Jay jump. He glanced over his shoulder to the sack, where the fiddle was tucked snuggly away.

Don't, the perfect music whispered again, pleading.

Jay ignored it. In a blink, he chose one of the shabby rental boats, snicking off the chain with a twist-pull trick everybody from the city knew how to do. Then he hopped in and pushed off, heading for the main islands.

He flowed with the river current, but even so Jay's muscles had forgotten how much effort it took to row. By the time he reached the far shore, his arms quivered like mad and his lungs burned from gasping in the icy, damp air. Jay ditched the boat underneath an abandoned pier to avoid suspicious eyes—then for the first time in three years, he stepped into Fairdown Falls.

He was home.

Jay's feet crossed from gravel to pavement as he entered the city proper. Tall buildings were squished within each block, their shuttered windows turning a blind eye to the streets below. Lamps lit the way for the passersby still out: rich young revelers out on the town, lonely homeless folks trying to stay invisible, stern watchmen on the beat.

As Jay walked forward, he saw the main avenues all bore Wintertide decorations: sparkly frostsilk garlands dangling over doors, spruce boughs strung between lampposts. Festive braziers were spaced along the sidewalk, burning merrily with the scent of sweet hickamore berries.

Jay paused by a brazier to warm himself. In another life, he might've enjoyed the holiday like everybody else. Any other kid like him would be in bed right now, dreaming of Wintertide feasts and fun to be had the next day. Part of Jay wanted to be back in bed, instead of shivering in the cold.

Don't, the fiddle whispered again, more insistent.

Jay smacked his ears, drowning out the whisper. He clutched the strap of his makeshift sack and headed toward the meeting spot, weaving through the streets like a dancer who'd memorized the steps and rhythm of the city. The promise of snow was hanging from the heavy clouds above, so Jay hurried. At long last, he arrived at Butcher's Block.

Jay had never stepped foot in Butcher's Block, and for good reason. It used to be an alley row of butcher shops back in the day—but even after the meat businesses moved out, Butcher's Block kept a bloody reputation. Most folks on the streets knew it as a spot for shady business and cutthroat dealings—emphasis on throat-cutting. Anybody with any sense stayed away from the grunts and goons who chose to make a deal there.

The moment Jay set foot into the alley row, his senses flipped on high alert. Butcher's Block was shrouded in river mist and shadows. He stepped cautiously forward, staring in morbid fascination at the rusty meat hooks still hanging above empty shops. The place was dead silent—but even so, Jay swore he felt eyes watching him.

"Hullo?" he called, clutching the strap of his sack tighter.

No response. The night was cold, but sweat made Jay's neck prickle. The thought hit his brain too late: What if this was a trick? What if—?

"Happy Wintertide," a voice spoke from everywhere and nowhere.

Jay stiffened like a spooked cat. He spun around.

Nobody was there. The mist curled at his feet.

"We knew you'd show up," the voice spoke again, closer this time.

Jay felt a shiver that had nothing to do with the frosty air. He blinked—and there was the Unraveling Man, standing in a place that a second ago had been only shadows and mist. Jay jumped, cursing aloud.

"Such language," said Dubito, sounding amused behind his mask. "Do you have Brio's relic?"

Jay pulled the sack off his shoulder, taking out the case and opening it.

"You have the coin?" said Jay gruffly.

Dubito reached into the folds of his frayed garments, retrieving a bundle.

"Four hundred and four thousand, two hundred forty-seven—plus interest," said Dubito, tossing it at Jay's feet. "Your debt in full."

Jay opened it and gasped. Inside were stacks and stacks of printed notes, all worth a thousand Medallions apiece. *Blessed Seraphs.*

From the corner of his eye, Jay saw the Unraveling Man reach back into his patchwork sleeve.

"Here's a final gift from us," said Dubito.

Jay dropped the bundle of cash, throwing up his hands. "Back off!" he snapped, winding his fist up for a swing.

Dubito laughed. "Easy, there." He pulled his hand out again, tossing a small pouch in Jay's direction. It clinked when Jay caught it.

Jay stared. It was filled with gold Medallion coins. "What's this?"

"Call it a bonus," answered Dubito. "You can't build a new life of your own from nothing."

Jay blinked up at him. "What's the catch?"

"No catch," Dubito went on. "We like you. You think for yourself— not easy to do in the company of Musicians. We thought you could use a little help." He waved at the case. "Hand over the instrument."

Still holding the pouch of Medallions in one hand, Jay reached for the fiddle's case. Seemed Dubito was gonna stick to his word after all.

Wrong.

Jay flinched. The perfect music's voice was fierce, piercing his brain: *Wrong. Stop. Don't.*

Jay felt the air tremble with the fiddle's vibrations. The mist pulsed as the perfect music's words grew even sharper:

Stop! Wrong! Stop!

Jay winced in pain, trying to shake the echoes from inside his skull.

This is my choice! he shouted back at the fiddle through his thoughts. *I'm not the Crafter! Let me go!*

The perfect music sang mercilessly around him, reverberating like a head-splitting gong. Jay cringed.

Stop! Don't! Wrong! Stop!

"Shut up!" Jay hollered. "*Let me go!*"

He threw the fiddle's case. It skidded across the alley, stirring the mist.

At once, Jay felt a *crack!* splinter from his very center. The sensation raced through him, snapping, shattering like glass—then, nothing.

Jay swallowed hard. He felt . . . off. His hand went toward his chest. He hadn't even noticed until now—but since he'd played the fiddle the first time in Hazeldenn, a strange warmth had been inside him, unlike anything he'd ever experienced. That peaceful feeling had been with him the whole time since, like the reassuring hand of a friend on his shoulder.

But no more. Panting for breath, Jay's eyes found the fiddle's case.

Silence. Not even the tiniest vibration.

The perfect music was gone.

The Unraveling Man gleefully snatched up the case. Jay heard his slow, humming laugh as he stroked the case's imprinted crest. Then, still laughing, he turned his mask toward Jay.

All at once, Jay felt an awful coldness rush over him, worse than the freezing waters of the river. He gasped, the air sucked from his lungs.

"A pleasure doing business with you," said Dubito. "You should get going. Don't you have a debt to pay?"

With that, the Unraveling Man took a step backward and melted away into the shadows, leaving nothing but mist in his wake.

Chapter Thirty

A DEBT AND A PRAYER

Snow began to fall as Jay fled from Butcher's Block. It collected on his cap, clung to his eyelashes, made every slippery step on the sidewalk a risk—but he hardly noticed. He barely paid attention to where he was going, letting his feet lead him over bridges, across canals, and down narrow alleys. His mind was lost on other things: the heavy weight of the money thumping his back with each step, Dubito's low, slow laugh . . . the hollow ache in his chest that wouldn't go away.

By the time he stopped moving, Jay's hands, nose, and toes were blocks of ice. He stared at the place he'd ended up, dread flickering through him.

The Staccatos' place wasn't an obvious choice for an outlaw gang to hide. It used to be a courthouse, where the Cabinet of Justice held trials and charged criminals. Then a new courthouse had been built some blocks away, and the abandoned building had been bought up and renovated as a restaurant. Now the Old Courthouse was a local landmark, pride of the neighborhood—

Though only the Staccato Gang knew the Old Courthouse's real owner.

Taking a deep breath, Jay set his cap over his eyes and stepped forward, passing the old marble columns and slipping through the restaurant entrance.

Late as it was, the Old Courthouse was full. Patrons slouched at round tables and nursed warm mugs of festive spiced wine. A woman was hunched over an upright tinkerbit piano, plinking out subdued tunes.

There was no one at the host station to greet him, so Jay waited, blowing on his hands to warm them. Thoughts drifted through his head like falling snow. Would Ark and the others ever figure out what he'd done? Jay frowned. Maybe he should've left a note to explain, to apologize—but it was probably better if he just disappeared.

Finally, a girl with bouncy blonde curls and a cheeky smile stepped up to the host station. "Welcome! Table for one?"

The words came automatically to Jay. "I've got a reservation on the second floor."

There was no second floor, not to the average customer—but Jay figured the code hadn't changed since he'd been gone. The girl nodded knowingly.

"What name?" she said, still smiling.

Jay tilted his head back to meet the girl's eye. "Quickstep."

The girl's eyes widened. She nodded again and stood aside to let him in. "This way, please."

The girl escorted him around the tables. Jay cast his gaze around every corner, noting the muscle-bound goons hovering near the back doors, watching him pass. Soon the girl led him to a flight of stairs with a rope across it that declared STAFF ONLY. The girl lowered the rope for him.

"She's expecting you," she squeaked, then scurried away.

Jay took the stairs two at a time, trying to ignore his nerves as he circled the upper level. He made his way to the Capo's den, a secret office positioned just above the old judge's bench. Jay heard the piano plinking away below as he knocked his old pattern on the office door.

"About time," an all-too-familiar voice called from inside.

Jay took a deep breath, bracing himself—then he walked in.

"Got a question for you," he said, speaking straight off. "If I bring myself in, does that mean I can collect the bounty you put on my head?"

Jay's abrupt entrance took everybody by surprise, giving him a chance to take in his surroundings. Half a dozen gang members were in the Capo's office. Small Fry stood just beyond the door, his tall body and huge frame taking up an entire corner of the room. Longshot, Zoë Maclaine, Backstabber Blake, and Hunchback Willie were all gaping at him in amazement. Sweetie, sitting on a chair with her feet swinging far above the floor, stared open-mouthed. Jay sent a sharp grin to each of them.

"Look at that," the familiar voice spoke again. "The wayward jay-bird's come back to the nest. On his own, too."

Jay felt his body seize up as he spied the woman behind a desk. Three long years, and the Capo of the Staccato Gang hadn't changed a bit. Lorelei Thayne was tall, and proud, and stunning. Her face, with its broad nose and high cheekbones, belonged in a painting, not on a wanted poster. Her cinnamon hair was short—it made it easier for her to wear the wigs she used to throw off the watchmen—and her sleeveless corseted tunic showed off her warm brown skin and the scarlet, butter-fly-shaped birthmark on her arm. Her umber eyes were trained on him like a hunting falcon.

"For somebody so quick, Quickstep, you took ages to get here," Thayne went on.

Jay shrugged, trying to act casual. "I beat your deadline."

"By two minutes," said Thayne. She glanced at an antique clock sitting on the shelves next to her desk, one of many stolen prizes stored there. "I thought for sure you'd pull some fool stunt like trying to leave the country. Looks like I didn't give you fair credit."

Jay glued his teeth together.

"I figure you wouldn't be here if you weren't ready to deal," Thayne went on. Her smile took on a crooked slant. "Can you pay?"

She folded her hands expectantly, her eyes watching Jay. Her smile said it all: Thayne was waiting for him to say he didn't have her money. She figured she'd calculated his every move, leaving him no choice but to come back to work for her as the Quickstep Kid.

Jay smiled widely. Then he threw the sack of cash on her desk.

"Every last Whit."

Thayne's crooked smile dropped off. The other Staccato members rushed over, gathering behind Thayne as she opened the sack, assessing the sum.

"*Whoo-ee*," said Longshot, whistling. "That's a pretty slice of cheese."

"What the heck he done?" whispered Backstabber. "Rob the Queen?"

Thayne counted the stacks of printed notes three times over. When she was finished, she looked at Jay, her face disappointed.

"You must've pulled one heck of a heist," she finally said. She bent one of the stacks in her hand, letting the notes slide out along her thumb.

"I'll bet you crossed more than a few folks to get your grubby hands on this."

Jay's mind flashed to Ark, Dulcian, Andi, Hana, and Rye. *They* were the ones he'd crossed. Somehow thinking about them—about how he'd turned his back on them—made him feel even more empty inside than when he'd handed the fiddle over to Dubito.

"Sure you don't want my protection?" Thayne asked, locking gazes with him. "Come back. Work for me. No matter who you've crossed, no one will lay a finger on you. Not if you're one of mine."

Jay's frown deepened. Thayne watched him with keen eyes, trying to read him. Was she really trying to get him to come back on his own?

He snorted, shaking his head. "Forget it. I've paid back what my folks owed. You got nothing on me anymore. We're *done*."

He turned his back to her, making for the door. Before he could squeeze through the exit, Small Fry stepped in his way.

"What now?" Jay snapped with a scowl, spinning around.

Thayne stepped around the desk, approaching him until Jay could smell her peppery perfume.

"What happened that night, at the chapel?" she asked in a murmur. Her gaze went razor sharp. "We both know *I* didn't set that fire."

Jay felt his stomach flip inside out, remembering Windfalle. He turned his stone-hard glare on her. "Don't know what you're talking about."

Thayne flashed a slanted smile. "You're still a lousy liar," she whispered. "You can't outrun the truth, no matter how quick you are."

She returned to her desk, putting the stacks of cash away.

"Your parents' debt is cleared," she declared. "But don't think this is the end of our . . . relationship. You have unique skills, Quickstep—more unique than I realized. Together we can put them to good use."

Jay scoffed. "I'll never do any more favors for you."

Her eyes cut into him, peeling him apart with her gaze.

"I'm certain you will," she murmured, smiling. "See you around."

∞

Jay slipped out the exit as fast as he could, his heart thumping as he ran into the night. It was only a quarter past midnight when Jay finally stopped to rest, but he felt like he'd been running for hours. Every muscle quivered. Sweat chilled his forehead. He gasped frozen air into his raw lungs, coughing as the last bit of energy he had left puffed from his mouth in clouded breaths.

When his breath finally caught up with him again, Jay's face was stinging from the frigid air and his limbs were aching with the cold. He stomped his feet and slapped his hands, trying to get feeling back into them—then he looked around, wondering where he'd ended up.

He'd followed his feet to the Cathedral Plaza, a wide expanse of smooth pavement hemmed in by humble businesses. The cathedral itself—a wooden church that dominated everything else with its tall bell towers and massive windows—stood at the head of the plaza, with wide stairs leading to its entrance. The windows glowed from within, beckoning him inside.

Jay followed the Wintertide braziers lining the plaza and climbed the steps, aching for warmth and for something else he couldn't put his finger on.

Inside, the cathedral was dimly lit by sconces on the walls. Only a few people were here: a monk sitting by the entrance, dozing; a drunk snoring in the aisle; a woman weeping on the far side, crying over a small child's toy. Jay shuffled in and removed his cap, unobserved by the other visitors. The air inside was heavy with the echoes of uncountable prayers, all still hanging in the rafters like wisps of drifting incense.

Jay slid into a pew, bone-weary, too tired to sleep. He let the still, sacred air chase away the numb tingles in his toes and fingers . . . but something heavy and cold in his pocket kept stealing his warmth. Jay reached into his vest and pulled out the pouch of gold Medallions that Dubito had thrown at him.

Jay stared at the coins. This much money could take him to any country he wanted, send him on any adventure he chose. Jay closed his eyes, trying to think of a next step, a starting point where his new life could begin.

But he kept coming up with blanks. Instead of possibilities, he only saw dead ends.

The holy silence of the cathedral rang in his ears. The hollow ache in his chest throbbed. Jay pressed a fist to his heart, gritting his teeth. It wasn't supposed to be like this! He was supposed to be free now—free from the Capo, free from the Crafter's duties. But shouldn't his freedom have felt more . . . freeing? If being free to go anyplace in the world with more money than he knew how to spend wasn't enough, what had he been looking for?

Unexpectedly, memories from the past few days popped into his head. Andi and Hotah, wearing matching grins. Rye, her arms wide and welcoming. Hana, watching with gentle eyes. Ark, a shy smile behind his deadpan gaze.

Jay stared blankly as more memories took over:

Dulcian, talking to him over a checkers board.

The Cartwright Sisters, caring for him like he was family.

Inspector Argentine, offering him a helping hand.

Augusta Grim, hugging him, whispering in his ear: *Thank you.*

Mr. Douse. Colton. Lina.

Brother Elfenbein.

The fiddle, singing just for him, its celestial sound breaking through his ordinary noise like blue sky peeking through black clouds.

The memories warmed Jay more than a bonfire ever could . . . but then the emptiness in his chest bared its teeth again. He could sense the truth approach him from behind, waiting for him to glance over his shoulder and face it.

But Jay didn't want to turn around. He didn't want to admit he'd been wrong. He couldn't face the idea that the thing he'd wanted all along was the very thing he'd already had . . . and tonight, he'd just walked away from it in exchange for a pouch of icy coins and a void he couldn't fill.

Jay gritted his teeth so hard they squeaked. The truth was tapping him on the shoulder now, insisting that he pay attention. He clutched the pouch of coins in a shaky grasp. His mouth spoke on its own.

"I messed up, didn't I?"

The truth was finally standing in front of him—along with the total, horrible realization of what he'd done.

He'd betrayed his friends, lied to them, thrown them out like trash.

He'd tangled himself worse with the Capo, making himself and his abilities even more valuable to her.

And worst of all, he'd been duped into giving Brio's fiddle away. And without the fiddle, Brio could never choose another Crafter to replace him.

"What've I done?" Jay cast his eyes up to the cathedral ceiling. "Why in blazes didn't you stop me?" he hissed. "How could you let me make such a stupid move?" His frustration turned bitter. "How come I'm such a screw-up, huh? Why am I even here? I'm just a stupid nobody! A lousy no-good ex-outlaw who only causes trouble!"

Jay forced himself to bite his tongue. He took a deep breath and started over.

"Listen," he hissed, praying that whatever holy being was in charge would hear him with a friendly ear. "I don't know what to do. I've made a mistake—a huge mistake—and I don't know how to fix it. It's all one big mess that I can't clean up, and . . . and I'm . . ."

The words caught on their way out of his mouth.

". . . I'm scared."

All at once, Jay's fear became a sticky glob in his throat. A double surge of dread and resolve kneaded into each other in his gut. Jay swallowed the fear, slid down onto his knees, and closed his eyes.

"I let everybody down," he whispered, his stomach twisting in knots. "I know I don't deserve another chance. But I wanna fix this. I have to. If there's something I can do . . . if I can set things right . . . *please*."

Jay sat still, heart pounding, not sure whether to wait for an answer. The emptiness in his chest wasn't gone, but it didn't feel so painful anymore.

The silence of the cathedral had surrounded him again when, out of nowhere, words that Dulcian had spoken just a few days before rippled to the front of his mind:

You were made for something greater than you can imagine.

The echo faded—but it seemed to take the weight on Jay's shoulders with it. Suddenly, inexplicably, Jay knew what to do. What he had to do.

Not like it was gonna be easy, going back to the Royal Conservatory. Once he admitted everything he'd done, they'd probably call ahead to the watchmen so they could reserve a prison cell for him for the rest of his life. But at least they'd finally know the truth.

And then Jay would be free. *Really* free.

Jay pushed up from his knees, making the Designist sign of blessing over himself. Afraid he'd try to talk himself out of it if he hung around any longer, Jay headed for the exit.

But before he stepped out, Jay spied something that made him pause. A humble poor box sat by the doors, opposite the dozing monk. Based on the number of spider webs on the box, there hadn't been many donations lately.

Jay held up the pouch of Medallions, looking at the fortune in his hand. Then, without thinking twice, he stuffed the whole pouch in the poor box. With that, Jay threw his cap on and shuffled out into the night.

The moment his feet hit the pavement, Jay felt it.

Something was wrong.

Very wrong.

The sensation came from the ground, as if the bones of the earth were screaming. Jay felt it crawl over him, shivers of terror racing up his spine. A steady, high-pitched shriek stabbed his ears; it was faint, as if it came from a distance—or maybe it was all in his head.

Even so, Jay found himself stumbling down the cathedral steps and shuffling away from the plaza. He followed the awful sound through festive streets and down empty lanes, dread dogging his every step. At length he left the tall buildings of the city behind, reaching the shore. Finally, Jay could scan Fairdown River for the shriek's source—

Jay gasped. He blinked, rubbed his eyes, and looked again—but he wasn't seeing things.

The Royal Conservatory's entire island was surrounded by pitch-black river mist—except the mist was alive. Tendrils of oily, dissonant darkness writhed up from the river's surface like the tentacles of some giant sea monster, preparing to grab the island and swallow it whole. Glowing dots of orange flame speckled the island, burning bright.

Unable to look away, Jay staggered in a daze toward the docks.

Then he began to run.

Chapter Thirty-One

THE CHALLENGE

As the alarm bells rang, Ark and Andi ran together down the hall to Hana and Rye's room, with Hotah chasing their heels.

"Wake up!" Andi called while Ark pounded on their door. Hotah barked. Seconds later, Hana and Rye emerged, blankets wrapped over their shoulders.

"By the stars, you're both loud," said Hana, rubbing her eyes. "What time is it?"

"And why're you dressed?" said Rye around a yawn—then she straightened. "What's that clanging?"

"There's trouble," said Ark. As groggy as he'd been five minutes ago, now he was wide awake. "It's an emergency alarm. Something's wrong."

"We heard people running and shouting orders outside our room," Andi added, reaching for Hotah's head in search of a comforting touch. "Sounds like someone could be attacking the island."

At that, Rye and Hana snapped to attention.

"Dubito?" said Hana, pulling her blanket around herself.

"Is Jay okay?" asked Rye.

"Not sure," said Ark. "But I plan to find out. Let's go."

"You're not going anywhere," said a voice from behind.

Ark and the others spun around. A pair of Gray Wolves, a woman and a man who both towered above them, came down the hall at a near-run, their gray talarises whipping behind them.

"Captain Sharpe's orders," said the woman, giving them each a stern look.

"You are to stay put in your rooms. Do not leave until we return with the all-clear." She turned her eyes on Ark. "Do you understand?"

Ark matched her gaze. "I understand."

Satisfied, the Gray Wolves ran off. When they'd left, Andi groaned.

"Are we really just going to wait here?" he said, frowning.

"Of course not," said Ark. "I told her I *understood*. I never said I intended to obey."

Andi chuckled. Rye and Hana shared a grin. "Give us two minutes," said Hana.

The girls disappeared back into their room. While he and Andi waited, Ark tugged at the stiff collar of his new green talaris, hoping the Gray Wolves wouldn't walk past again and spot them loitering.

"What now?" asked Hana when she and Rye returned.

Ark cleared his throat. "*Adiuvva*," he chanted softly.

He felt a thrum in the air; seconds later, a muse that looked like a hound padded through the wall of a nearby room, its fur mottled with browns and greens like the forest floor.

"Oooh—did a muse come?" Rye squeaked in excitement. Ark shushed her, then turned back to the muse, clearing his mind of everything but the Gray Wolves.

"*Innseggui con vellocce!*" he chanted.

The forest hound muse bellowed with a throaty, brassy howl—and then it was off, galloping down the hall. Ark chased after it, hissing at the others.

"Hurry!"

The hound muse followed its quarry, the two Gray Wolves, through the corridors of the guest housing and right out the front door. Ark and the others followed it outside into the falling snow. The alarm wasn't so loud anymore—but now Ark could hear a different noise: an awful, skull-splitting shriek that seemed to come from all directions. He winced, gritting his teeth.

"You guys hear that?" he asked.

"Not sure what you're hearing," said Hana, looking pale. "But something isn't right out here. The air is foul. And the ground feels unstable."

"I feel it too," said Rye, going green. "I don't feel so good."

"I felt something like this in Lower Grimsborough—but it's a million times worse," said Andi. He leaned toward Ark. "It's a dischord, isn't it?"

Ark felt a tremor of fear run through him. He was a full-fledged Musician now, but he wasn't magically cured of his dischord phobia.

The hound muse barked at them, wagging its tail impatiently. Ark and the others ran to catch up, and the hound muse took off, leading them down well-worn paths through the trees. Ark had to stay right on top of the muse so he wouldn't lose him in the forest camouflage.

As they ran, Ark realized he could hardly sense any muses across the Royal Conservatory grounds. The few that he spotted seemed agitated, their harmonic voices blending in warning against the unsettling shrieking. Dread washed through Ark's stomach. He ran faster.

Suddenly the hound muse stopped, gave another brassy howl, and vanished. Ark soon realized where the hound had brought them. He skidded to a stop at the edge of the trees before he and the others could spill out into the open. Maestrans Hall was before them, all its windows blazing. Maestrans in red were leading groups of green-clad agents, dashing off across the Royal Conservatory. In the center of the lawn, Grand Maestran Luthier stood with Tallon on his shoulder, fresh snow sticking to his purple talaris. Captain Sharpe and his fellow Gray Wolves were relaying a report.

". . . Sir Encore and our commoner visitors have been secured," the captain was saying.

"Good," said Grand Maestran Luthier. "And what about His Eminence?"

"No report yet, Your Excellency."

Ark saw the Grand Maestran frown.

"Is that Mara over there?" Rye whispered behind him. She pointed to a lone figure standing a few strides away from the others.

Ark nodded, glad to see a familiar face. Though Mara seemed distracted. She stared toward the sky with glassy, vacant eyes.

Ark stared up too—and immediately saw that Mara wasn't staring at the falling snow. He covered his mouth to keep from crying out. No wonder the air tasted so foul.

Above the Royal Conservatory, the sky was filled with the swaying, shrieking shadows of dischords, even blacker than the midnight sky. They twitched and stretched over the Royal Conservatory like the fingers of some horrible monster: the whole island was sitting on the monster's palm, and its fingers were slowly curling in, ready to crush it in its grasp.

Ark's knees trembled. "We shouldn't be out here."

"What is it?" hissed Andi. Hana and Rye studied him too.

But Ark didn't get to explain. Dulcian and Callie were running out of the trees, out of breath. Ark and the others listened.

"Lady Vielle, Sir Mandore—at last," called the Grand Maestran. "What of His Eminence? Have you moved Julian to a safer area?"

Callie gasped for breath. Fiero yipped, snuggling against her ankles.

"We couldn't find him, Your Excellency," said Callie at length.

Ark froze. *What?*

The Grand Maestran straightened. Tallon rustled on the man's shoulder with a nervous *hoo-hoot*.

"Couldn't *find* him?" he echoed.

Dulcian looked distraught. Trillo circled his head with panicked cheeps.

"Julian wasn't in his room," said Dulcian.

All the nearby Maestrans jabbered in panic. Ark's feet moved on their own; he left the trees, moving closer. The other three followed.

None of the adults took notice of them.

"I don't understand—weren't you two guarding his room?" the Grand Maestran asked. "How could he be gone?"

"We found the balcony windows open," said Callie. "But it was the top floor, so we'd assumed that entrance was secure—"

"You *assumed?*" barked Captain Sharpe in outrage, while his wasp muse Kreuz flew angrily above his head. "When you volunteered to help guard His Eminence's room, you were to cover all entrances!"

Dulcian and Callie began to speak in their defense, but Captain Sharpe kept interrupting. The other Maestrans joined in. Soon everyone there was squabbling except Grand Maestran Luthier and Mara.

Ark wanted to scream. Why the gavotte were the adults bickering at a time like this? They had to go find Jay!

He very nearly snapped, about to tell them all to shut up and search— but a loud, booming voice bellowed at them instead, thundering overhead:

"WE KNOW WHERE HE IS!"

Everyone was so startled that they cowered in surprise—except Mara, who was still staring glassy-eyed toward the sky.

Ark recovered with a start. He knew that voice.

"*FOLLOW THE LIGHTS!*" the voice roared in a teasing singsong. Before Ark could wonder what lights the monstrous voice was referring to, the terrible shrieks grew in volume. Ark gasped and plugged his ears.

A bright flash dropped from the sky and exploded before his eyes, followed by another, and another. Bonfires soon blazed throughout the frosted trees, lighting a path of fiery destruction.

The Grand Maestran quickly stepped off along the fiery path, and the other Maestrans, agents, and Gray Wolves followed. Even Mara went with them. Ark led Andi, Hana, and Rye along at the rear. He hoped Jay would be at the other end of the path.

They'd only been running along the scorching trail a few minutes when they once again came out into the open. A recognizable circular lawn was lit by a ring of dancing flames. Ark and the others skidded to a halt inside the fire barrier.

The wreckage of the Morning Star sat in the firelight like the haunted remains of a ghost ship, cordoned off by ropes. Sitting on the bulwark amidships was an all-too-familiar figure in tattered clothes and a mask.

"If it isn't Grand Maestran Luthier!" said Dubito, spreading his arms wide on either side. "Even the old dog left his bed for us."

The Grand Maestran fixed his gaze on the Dischordian. Meanwhile, Dulcian, Callie, and the other agents took positions behind him, poised to attack. The other Maestrans and Gray Wolves fanned out along the fire barrier, surrounding Dubito. Mara held back behind the Grand Maestran.

"Take aim," said the Grand Maestran quietly. He lifted his arm; Tallon pumped its wings and swooped high, its steely eyes glinting. Grand Maestran Luthier began to utter a cantus, his voice deep and resonant; Dulcian, Callie, and the others joined him, chorusing an attack.

"Ah, ah!" warbled Dubito, wagging a finger. "Not so fast, Your Excellency. If you attack us, you might damage *this*."

He pulled something from the folds of his garments.

Ark gasped. The Maestrans and agents exclaimed in shock.

Even Grand Maestran Luthier's dispassionate expression fractured.

"What is it?" hissed Andi.

Rye clutched his hand, her face grim. "It's Julian's violin."

Ark's brain told his eyes to look again—but his eyes insisted they were right. The white, scuffed-up violin looked even more fragile in Dubito's merciless grip. The Dischordian choked the violin's neck in one hand, throttling it like a broken-winged bird that'd lost its will to escape.

Horror and fury churned together in Ark's gut. How had Dubito gotten hold of Brio's instrument? Just what had he done to Jay?

"Where is the Crafter's heir?" demanded Grand Maestran Luthier.

Dubito cast his head back in a cackling laugh.

"Somebody's betrayed you!" he crooned. He kicked his heels against the bulwark. "They've been close to you the whole time. You shouldn't have trusted them. They aren't who you think they are."

"Nice try," Callie snapped. "You won't trick us into pointing fingers."

Ark glanced back to the Grand Maestran—but instead he caught Mara's gaze. She made no signal—no nod, no hand gesture—but based on how intently she was staring at him, he knew what he was supposed to say.

Ark stepped forward. "Hold on!"

All heads turned his direction. The Grand Maestran and his muse blinked at him with wide-eyed surprise. Callie and Dulcian looked startled.

"Arkalin, what are you—?"

"You two," Ark interrupted, waving between Dulcian and Callie. "They said you *volunteered* to guard Jay's room tonight?"

Dulcian and Callie exchanged glances. "We heard the Gray Wolves were stretched thin with security preparations," said Dulcian, defensive. "We offered to guard Jay's room so they could monitor the rest of the island—"

"And every other time Dubito managed to track Jay down, you two just happened to be nearby?" Ark cut in again.

They caught on quickly enough to what he was implying.

"How *dare* you!" hissed Callie, her glare sharpening to daggers.

"Arkalin," said Dulcian, "are you saying you think *we*—with *him*—?"

"You two led Jay away from the crowds in Hazeldenn, and Dubito showed up," said Ark. "You two went off in Cindertown, leaving me and

Jay alone in the hotel, and Dubito found us there. And tonight, *you two* were put in charge of guarding Jay's room—and now Dubito has him!"

As Ark spoke, Dulcian's and Callie's faces transformed. He'd never seen such a cold look from Dulcian. Callie's took on the same shade as Mount Vakra's red-hot lava, ready to blow.

"Why you little—!" she snarled, storming toward him—but before she could get to him, the Gray Wolves had Dulcian and Callie surrounded.

"It's not true!" Dulcian protested.

"Mara tried to warn me from the very beginning," Ark spoke over them. "She told me not to go with you on my jury mission."

That startled them to silence. "Mara?" murmured Dulcian.

Grand Maestran Luthier looked confused, but resolute. "Captain," he finally spoke, "please escort these two away for questioning."

Captain Sharpe saluted. Callie cursed and Dulcian sputtered more protests of innocence as the Gray Wolves led them away.

Dubito, meanwhile, chuckled in amusement. "Well done, little Encore," he said, rocking on the bulwark.

Grand Maestran Luthier stepped forward. "What do you want, Dubito?"

Dubito rolled his head sideways, like a marionette whose neck string had snapped. "What do we want? Something you have, obviously."

The Grand Maestran gestured to Brio's instrument. "You already have our Crafter's relic and the Crafter's heir. What else are you after?"

Dulcian carelessly waved Brio's violin. "What, this? We have no use for this. But *you* want it back, yes?"

"Please," said the Grand Maestran genially, as if this were a pleasant business exchange. "Return the relic—and Julian, if you'd be so kind."

Dubito clicked his tongue behind his mask, shaking his head. The genial tone in the Grand Maestran's voice evaporated.

"Enough with the games, Dischordian," he growled.

Dubito perked up. "I *like* games. Let's have a game!"

He jumped to his feet, standing on the bulwark. He swept his arm out like a master performer, his hand passing over the remaining Maestrans and Musicians positioned around the Morning Star.

"We challenge you by the ancient rites," he said, as if intoning a ritualistic verse. "One against one, and only one prevails. Defeat us, and we will return to you what you want."

Then Dubito rested his hand on his chest, turning his mask to face the Grand Maestran squarely.

"But if *we* win, you'll tell us where your Magnum Opus page is," he hissed, his tone menacing. "We know you have a page hidden somewhere—in the place only *you* know about."

Ark was so focused on Dubito that he almost didn't see it. When Dubito said the words "Magnum Opus," the Grand Maestran stiffened in shock.

Ark frowned. Magnum Opus? What was that?

The wave of shock that had washed over the Grand Maestran subsided, and he swiftly resumed his calm, expressionless stance.

"The Magnum Opus is a fairy tale, nothing more," he said, shaking his head. "I can't offer something that doesn't exist."

Dubito snarled, clutching Brio's instrument in his hands.

"*Don't lie!*" he hollered, thrashing like a beast. "We know you have it! And you'll tell us where it is!" He squeezed the violin between his hands like he was prepared to crush it. "If you don't, we'll pulverize this to dust!"

Grand Maestran Luthier blanched. The other Maestrans yelled and cursed at him. Sensing he'd won, Dubito held Brio's instrument close.

"We're trying to play nice here," he insisted, straightening the tatters of his garments. "Who will accept our challenge?"

Ark clenched his jaw. Anger that had only been frost minutes ago now burned in an icy rampage. He spoke without thinking.

"I will!" he yelled, raising his hand. "I'll challenge you!"

"Yes!" Dubito blurted, practically yelling over him. "It's done!"

"Sir Encore!" snapped the Grand Maestran. "Stand down!"

"Too late!" cackled Dubito. "No withdrawing. No substitutes or seconds. So say the ancient rites!"

He tossed Brio's violin in the air, letting it spin high above his head before catching it—making every Musician in the area cry out in alarm.

"Get ready to hand the Magnum Opus page over," Dubito jeered.

Ark wasn't intimidated. He didn't even register the fact that he'd gone and willingly accepted a one-on-one confrontation with a Dischordian—which probably would have made him faint not long ago.

His only thought was Jay. He tried not to let his imagination get the best of him.

"Don't think I'll make this easy on you, creep," Ark snarled, rolling up his talaris sleeves. "I'll make you pay for whatever you've done to Jay!"

Dubito snorted. He covered the lower half of his mask like he was trying to stifle a giggle—but then he let loose with a full-on roar of laughter, hugging his sides like they hurt, wiping a fake tear from his mask's eye.

"What's so funny?" Ark snapped.

"You!" said Dubito, pointing straight at Ark's face. "You still haven't worked it out yet, have you? None of you have! You're such fools!"

"Worked what out?" said Ark.

Dubito shook his head. "We never kidnapped your little friend!" he cried. He held out Brio's violin. "Did you think we stole this?"

The announcement was so unexpected that Ark couldn't even blink.

"We never said Sir Mandore and Lady Vielle were the ones who betrayed you," said Dubito, goading them. "No, no: *Julian* betrayed you!"

"That—that's not—" Ark sputtered, his mind struggling to comprehend what the Dischordian was saying. "Jay isn't—"

"We struck a deal," Dubito went on, gleeful. "He had quite a heart-to-heart with us when we were alone in Cindertown. He chose to give us Brio's relic in exchange for cash. He's long gone by now!"

The ice in Ark's veins melted, leaving a puddle of uncertainty behind. "You're lying. You have to be."

"Are we?" said Dubito, a sneer behind the words. "Tell me, does the name 'Quickstep Kid' mean anything to you?"

Ark blinked, thinking. The Quickstep Kid? Wasn't he an outlaw?

"Don't change the subject," Ark spat.

Dubito snickered. "He *is* the subject."

Ark's brain froze mid-thought.

Jay . . . the Quickstep Kid.

Was Dubito saying—?

"Your little friend has quite the colorful past," said Dubito, answering aloud the question Ark was too afraid to ask. "Julian never mentioned he was an infamous outlaw, huh? Imagine that. And still you trusted him without question, just because he could play a few notes on *this*." He stroked Brio's violin with his fingertips.

Ark's head pounded out of sync with his racing heart. His mind flew through memories of Jay from these past few weeks—the way he spoke, the way he dressed, the way he moved—trying to piece together a complete picture of the truth. It wasn't possible. It *couldn't* be.

Could it?

"There is no point giving Julian another thought," said Dubito, beckoning him forward with a flap of his hand. "Come, little Encore. You want Brio's relic back? Come and get it."

Chapter Thirty-Two

DUBITO UNMASKED

One of Ark's favorite games as a kid was hide-and-go-seek. But Dubito's version—hide-and-go-kill—was not at all what Ark would call "fun."

Ark was still reeling from the news that Jay had betrayed them. He was hardly prepared when Dubito appeared in front of him—teleporting between blinks, moving faster than was humanly possible.

"Encore!" the Grand Maestran shouted.

Ark slipped, his feet sliding on the slick, snowy grass, right as the blur of Dubito's fist swung past, brushing the hair at the top of his head. Ark froze on the ground like a terrified rabbit, trying not to think about how bashed his face would've looked if Dubito hadn't missed.

"Want to forfeit?" asked Dubito. "Give up, and we'll kill you quickly!"

The claws of fear scraped down Ark's back.

Focus, he told himself. Ark stood and shook off his nerves with the snow. Ignore distractions—this was no time for phobias—

"Arkalin!" he heard Hana cry out.

Her warning was just enough for Ark to dodge another of Dubito's attacks, which would have hit him like a hammer to the skull. Dubito pressed his advantage, never giving Ark a chance to find sure footing. Ark wobbled away, staggering backwards, his mind racing.

"We should thank you!" said Dubito, speaking like they were having a casual chat. "Sir Mandore or Lady Vielle would have been *much* more challenging opponents. Had they been here, we probably would be fighting one of them. But they're off trying to prove their innocence on the far end of the island—all because *you* jumped to conclusions. Jump, little frog, jump!"

Dubito thrust out his hand, hissing garbled speech. A burst of screeching darkness shot from his palm toward Ark's feet. Ark leapt out of the way, but he compromised his footing and lost his balance, crashing to a knee.

"Goodbye!" cheered Dubito, pulling his arm back for a final strike. His hand was a knife, ready to stab through Ark's heart.

Ark stuck his fingers in his mouth and whistled a desperate tonus. With the dischord shadows choking the island and the toxic presence of dissonance in the air, Ark wasn't sure a muse would even come.

But just before Dubito knife-handed him, a muse in the form of a pale blue river turtle swam up from beneath the ground, placing itself between Ark and Dubito just in time. Dubito's fingers crunched against the turtle's shell. He howled, staggering back.

Ark didn't think. In half a heartbeat he was already bolting across the lawn, every muscle on fire. Once he was on the other side of the Morning Star, he slid feet-first several strides through the snow, ducking behind a broken wing-sail that sheltered him like a tent, hiding him from view.

"So, you'd rather be hunted before you're killed?" Dubito called out, cackling. "Ollie, ollie, oxen free! Ready or not, here I come!"

Ark held his breath, trying not to make a sound. His heart raced like a tinkerbit motor about to explode. All at once he was eight years old again, hiding in a frozen place while a Beast chased him down, ready to devour.

Ark shook the memory from his mind. *Think.* Dubito was a Dischordian, someone willingly possessed by a dischord—but the dischord could still be purged from him. And thanks to his father, Ark knew the techniques.

"Oh, little Encooore," called Dubito in an awful singsong, interrupting Ark's thoughts. "Come out, come out, wherever you are! If you won't come out, we'll have to find some *new* playmates!"

Ark blanched. Andi. Hana. Rye. They were still out there, along with the Grand Maestran, Mara, and the handful of other Musicians who were watching from the edge of the lawn. He couldn't afford to keep hiding.

He retreated to his mind, recalling the training his father had drilled into him for fighting dischords. He could hear Tristen de Cani's voice in his head:

Get ahold of yourself. Ark slowed his breathing, trying to calm his galloping heart. He needed a clear head and steady hands for what came next.

Always fight discord with harmony. Opposites counteracted. Whatever attack Dubito tried on him, Ark needed a counterattack.

Strike first. Dischords were beings of pure malevolence. They deserved neither mercy nor hesitation. Ark would have to be ready to do his worst.

A plan wove together in Ark's head. He braced himself, waiting.

Not even a minute later, he saw Dubito walk around the far side of the Morning Star, coming into view. Dubito's head was twitching in all directions like a wolf trying to catch his scent.

"Where are you?" he snarled, sounding annoyed.

Ark waited. Dubito passed right by the wing-sail, his silhouette crossing the canvas like an evil ghost. He was almost exactly where Ark wanted him . . . one more step . . .

Ark leapt out from his hiding spot, sliding on the snow behind Dubito. "*Fullgueo—caecco!*" he chanted at a shout, every syllable crisp.

A keening cry responded to his canti. Ark and Dubito looked up to see a shining muse like a silver albatross circling overhead. The albatross keened again—then its feathers shone like a beacon, brighter than midday.

Dubito screeched, ducking down to cover his eyes from the blinding light. Ark didn't waste a second.

"*Neccto!*" he chanted. This time, a muse in the form of a cluster of golden spiders appeared, dangling on gossamer threads. The spiders moved swiftly, weaving their silk around Dubito at dazzling speed.

"Are you kidding—?" Dubito blurted, just before the webs covered his mask. Soon Dubito was completely wrapped in the muse's glittering strands.

Ark vaguely heard a cry rise from the border of the lawn. The other Musicians were cheering him on. For the first time, Ark felt a glimmer of hope. His fellow Musicians were at his back, and the muses were on his side.

They answered his every call, coming to put discord in its place.

Ark held out his hands, concentrating. He thought through the steps his father had taught him a thousand times: Envision the dischord inside the possessed host as a monstrous fist, clutching onto the host's heart. Guide the muse's power through his imagination, picturing the muse smashing each finger of the dischord's fist. As its grip weakened, the dischord would have no choice but to flee its host—and that's when Ark could take the no-longer-possessed Dischordian down.

Ark was ready. "*Puurrgo!*" he bellowed.

The ancient cantus thundered across the snowy lawn, resonating through the air. The webs around Dubito began to glow white-hot. Dubito screamed.

Ark didn't blink. He kept his eyes on the Dischordian, looking past the exterior to envision the grip of dischord clinging to him. Ark was almost bowled over by the disturbing presence of dissonance coming from Dubito—a hungry, harrowing void that wanted to suck him in and drain him down to nothing—but Ark held firm, sweating from exertion. He guided the muse's power through his thoughts as Dubito began to scream and thrash—

But then his screams broke off. Dubito laughed darkly.

"Just kidding," he sneered.

A second later, the webs surrounding Dubito were blown to bits. A shrieking, oily darkness slashed through the glowing spider silk. In an instant, the Dischordian was free.

"You know many dangerous ancient songs, little Encore," said Dubito, readjusting his mask. "But you're no match for us."

Ark stood there dumbly, shivering from his wasted effort. He didn't understand. His technique was flawless. He'd watched his father perform this same exorcism a thousand times.

What was he doing wrong?

Nothing, a voice in his head told him. He'd done everything exactly right. Dubito should have at least been marked by the muse's harmony, like an afterimage echoing around his body—but even that wasn't there.

Why wasn't it working? What trick was Dubito using?

Ark was missing something. Something right in front of him.

Meanwhile Dubito circled around Ark, spiraling like a falcon about to swoop in and snatch its prey.

"Too bad you were on the losing side," he hissed, speaking low so only Ark could hear. "You're a fair Musician—but you would have made a better Dischordian. If we didn't have to kill you, maybe we could have trained you."

Ark tuned Dubito out, furiously trying to come up with what he was missing. He studied the Dischordian's ridiculous patchwork clothes, but he didn't see anything strange about them. His eyes locked onto Dubito's mask, drawn once again to the eye holes, trying to see within. Ark tore his eyes away from the mask and looked down, studying his hands, his feet—

There.

The truth exploded in his head like a bombshell, making his ears ring. Ark glanced between Dubito and the spectators along the edge of the lawn.

So *that's* how Dubito was doing it!

Ark almost laughed aloud. He'd been dead wrong about everything this whole time. How the gavotte had he missed something so obvious?

"It's time to end this," Dubito said, raising a clawed hand. "No hard feelings."

The shrieking darkness of dischord gathered in Dubito's palm— Hana, Rye, Andi, and all those watching from the edge cried out in alarm.

"Time out!" Ark shouted, holding his arms in front of him in an X.

The outburst caught Dubito off guard. He froze mid-attack.

"We're abiding by the ancient rites," said Dubito, lowering his hand. He shook his head. "There are no time-outs in a duel."

"You're cheating," snapped Ark. "There's no cheating in a duel, either."

Dubito went dead still. The Musicians watching from the edge of the lawn broke into surprised murmurs.

"Oh, dear—this is embarrassing," said Dubito, his tone mocking. He raised his arms in a derisive shrug. "And how are we cheating?"

"As you said, ancient rites forbid the use of seconds," said Ark matter-of-factly. "And the real Dubito isn't even on the field."

The murmurs grew in volume. Dubito laughed.

"You're delusional," he said—though there was an edge in his voice that wasn't there before. Ark's smile grew sharp.

"And you're a coward," Ark replied. He spun around, arm outstretched, pointing along the spectators until his finger landed on the right one:

Mara.

"Hello, Dubito," said Ark.

Every head turned toward Mara, who stood so still that she was hardly noticeable. Her stringy, snow-damp hair covered half her face. She looked at Ark like a spooked mouse, sputtering protests.

"Me?" she squeaked. "I'm an Aphonian! I'm not a—"

"You conveniently weren't there when Dubito showed up the first time in Hazeldenn's graveyard," said Ark, speaking over her. "And you weren't at your post outside the hotel room when Dubito attacked, either—but it's no wonder how he knew *your* knock to get us to let him inside." He felt a bubble of anger grow in his stomach. "Your codes made me suspect Dulcian and Callie. You tried to make me doubt them from the very beginning!"

"It isn't true!" said Mara, her cheeks pink. She lifted the sleeve of her brown talaris, showing off the Royal Conservatory emblem sewn there. "I have served loyally for years! I have conducted countless evaluations to help bring our true Crafter back!" Her tone turned angry. "You can't keep accusing everyone of being Dischordian conspirators!"

Ark set his mouth in a straight line, thinking again of Dulcian and Callie. He shrugged off his guilt. Priorities.

"I don't know your reasons," said Ark. "But I haven't even gotten to the best evidence." He pointed downward. "There."

Everyone looked down, including Mara. There was nothing remarkable about the ground at their feet. Even the Grand Maestran looked doubtful.

"*Più a più luminnoso*," Ark chanted, looking up at the albatross muse still soaring overhead. "*Rivvellato*."

The albatross clicked its beak, stretching its wings and flying closer to the ground, bringing its light with it.

"See it?" said Ark, pointing again.

This time, it was more visible. Based on where the albatross muse was soaring, all their shadows should have been small, hidden beneath their feet with the light overhead. But Dubito's shadow stretched far longer than it should have, going in the wrong direction. Ark pointed again, tracing Dubito's unnatural shadow to its source:

Mara's feet.

"Miss Fipple . . . ," said Grand Maestran Luthier, aghast.

By now, Mara had stopped crying. She wore a sour look, glaring at Ark.

"Not bad," she said—and her voice was changed, no longer weak and breathy. "A bit late, though, don't you think?"

In a blink, the masked Dubito that Ark had been fighting melted to the ground, taking Brio's instrument with it. It retreated toward Mara like a fishing line being reeled in. The shadow puppet vanished and left the violin at Mara's feet. She retrieved it, then straightened up—she was taller than Ark had realized—and swept her hair out of her face.

"Do you mind if we take our mask off?" she asked, smirking.

Ark stared in horror as the skin around her face began to crack and peel. Then parts of her face began to flake away, revealing reptilian scales beneath. Mara blinked, and her eyes transformed to colubrine slits. She grinned to bare her fangs, letting the tip of a forked tongue lick her lips.

"That's better," she sighed. Her voice sounded eerily like her masked puppet. She held Brio's violin by the neck and set it on her shoulder like a bat, smiling at all the faces gaping at her in mute shock.

"Shall we get on with it, then?" she sneered—then, with a low hiss that sounded all too much like a snake, she uttered a dissonant command. Her skin began to smoke with darkness, black mist steaming around her. She raised her free hand, then swept it across the air in a clawed motion.

"*Diffenndi!*" Ark barely managed to chant, ducking to the ground.

Blackness burst from Mara's hand and expanded outward in a percussive blast, cutting across the lawn with a howling shriek. Ark had dodged it in time; the blue turtle muse he'd summoned once more had swum in front of Andi, Hana, Rye, and the Grand Maestran as he'd intended, creating a shield to protect them. But all other Musicians on the lawn were hit by Mara's surprise attack. They collapsed to the snow, unconscious, their eyes blank with horror. The albatross muse was also hit; with a cry of pain, it flew off, vanishing in a flicker.

Ark staggered to his feet. He could barely grasp how many Maestrans Mara had taken out with that single attack. *Great gavotte.*

"Thirty-two down, two to go," said Mara, waving between Ark and the Grand Maestran. Her smile showed off her fangs and forked tongue. "And then the Magnum Opus page will be *ours*."

Ark never saw her move. He only felt her blow hit his face with devastating force, knocking him clean off his feet.

Ark landed in the snow with a bone-shaking *whumph!*, stars dancing before his eyes. A warm, sticky wetness ran down his cheek. He tasted metal.

"Stop this!" said Grand Maestran Luthier. "It's over, Miss Fipple. You forfeited this duel the moment you admitted to cheating—so say the ancient rites." He stepped away from the protective shield the blue turtle muse was still holding around Hana, Rye, and Andi. He shook his head in pity. "You will never find what you're looking for. It's impossible—"

"Shut up!" howled Mara. She whipped around and flung out her hand, snarling garbled speech. Dischord rage flew from her palm and struck the Grand Maestran through the chest.

Ark sat up, mouth open. The Grand Maestran lay terribly still against the trunk of a tree, his head lolling to the side. Tallon fluttered anxiously over him, pecking at his talaris, trying to wake him.

"We will destroy every muse and Musician on this island!" Mara screamed, her serpent eyes glowing as she clutched Brio's violin in a choking grip. "We will burn everything until we find the Magnum Opus page!"

Her voice echoed across the terribly still lawn, over unconscious bodies. Only four people were left standing: Ark, Andi, Rye, and Hana.

Mara cleared her throat, regaining her composure. She turned to Ark.

"First things first."

It was like every nightmare Ark had ever had. His boots kept slipping on snow. His talaris was tangled under him, keeping him from crab-crawling away from her. He scrambled for a cantus, a tonus, any skill he had in his arsenal—but he blanked.

In half a second, Mara was on top of him, pinning him to the ground with her knee. She grabbed his face with her free hand and forced him to look up.

"We are no average Dischordian," she said. "We are one of the Wretched. We have feasted in this world since the time of Din. You never stood a chance."

Mara stroked his hair. Ark tried to wriggle out from beneath her, but then she grabbed his hair in her fist, yanking hard. Ark yelped.

Mara's face was empty of any human feeling. She raised her free hand high, clawing her fingers. Oily darkness swirled in her palm, ready to devour.

"At last," said Mara, relishing the moment. "The Crafter will finally be no more. The Magnum Opus will be gathered and rewritten! The age of the dischord will dawn! Goodbye, little Enc—*oof!*"

In the middle of Mara's victory speech, someone Ark was not at all expecting came blitzing toward them, lightning quick. He rammed right into Mara, bowling her over. Mara squawked and landed head-first in a snowdrift.

Ark blinked in disbelief.

Jay skidded in the snow, out of breath, a wild gleam in his eye. He glanced at Ark with a zany grin.

"Miss me, bum-wipe?"

Chapter Thirty-Three

SACRIFICE

Ark scrambled to his feet, gaping at Jay like a wide-eyed fish that'd just been saved from a fisherman's net.

"Thanks," he finally said.

Jay shrugged, trying to be casual. "Don't mention—"

Ark's eyes went wide. "Duck!"

Ark dragged Jay down to the ground right before something fast and horrible shrieked past their heads.

"What the blazes—?" Jay blurted, glancing up.

A hideous snake-woman stood a few paces away, with scaly skin and glowing eyes. Jay yelped, jumping to his feet.

"*Whattheheckisthatthing?*"

"The real Dubito!" said Ark. "Run!"

"Is that—*Mara?*"

"I said *run*, moron!" Ark snapped. He whipped around.

"*Acciaccato*—!"

"Nuh-uh!" Mara interrupted. She held up a familiar white fiddle.

Jay stared at the fiddle, a sickening twist in his gut. He couldn't sense the perfect music. It was as silent and dull as an ordinary fiddle.

Ark swallowed the rest of his cantus. Mara spoke weird, harsh words as a ball of swirling darkness formed in her hand. She smiled nastily, ready to strike.

Then two figures barreled into Mara from behind, making her cry in surprise. Rye and Hana both shoved Mara face-first into the snow.

"Take *that*, you witch!" shouted Rye, flashing her a triumphant hand gesture.

"C'mon!" said Hana, grabbing Jay's elbow. Rye took hold of Ark—and before Jay knew what was happening, the girls were pulling them away, Andi and Hotah following right behind.

"Andi! Rye! Hana!" Jay cheered. "You're okay!"

"Just move it!" Andi growled.

Mara was already regaining her feet. Thinking fast, Rye and Hana dragged the boys onto the slanted deck of the Morning Star. They kept their heads low, ducking behind the bulwark.

"Where were you?" demanded Hana in a whisper.

Jay squirmed under their stares. "It's a long story—"

"Make it a short one," interrupted Andi. "Where've you been, mate?"

Jay didn't know how to answer. He peeked over the edge of the bulwark. Mara was on her feet again, fuming in more ways than one. Her face was dark with rage; her skin was smoking.

"There isn't time—" Jay hissed.

"Make time!" said Rye, sending him a hard look.

Jay looked at each of them, his eyes reaching Ark last.

"Is it true?" Ark murmured. "Are you the Quickstep Kid?"

Jay felt another sickening twist inside. So *that's* why they were all staring at him like he was a stranger. All at once Jay felt naked, exposed. No use denying it.

"I *was* the Quickstep Kid, years ago," he said. "But not anymore."

He left most details out, but in the span of a minute, he managed to explain how he'd left the Staccato Gang, how the Capo had called in his parents' debt, and how Dubito had offered to pay it in exchange for the fiddle.

"That's the truth," Jay finished. He glanced over the bulwark again; Mara was on the move, circling the Morning Star like a predator out for the kill.

He turned away from Mara, catching Ark's gaze. Ark wore a grim, tight-lipped expression. Jay figured he knew the thoughts going through Ark's head: *Why didn't you say something? How could you have been such a moron?* But when Ark spoke, he said something different.

"I need to know," he murmured. "Why did you come back?"

The answers played in Jay's brain—*I couldn't run anymore, I couldn't leave you behind*—but they sounded lame. Instead, Jay smirked.

"What, you thought I was gonna leave a creep like Dubito to a bum-wipe like you?" he replied. "Couldn't let you have all the fun by yourself."

At that, Ark smiled a little.

"Ark isn't by himself, you know," said Hana, gesturing to herself, Rye, and Andi. "We're stopping Mara together."

"One thing I don't get," said Rye. "Why aren't muses attacking Mara on their own right now? Aren't there hundreds of them nearby?"

Ark sighed. "Mara is a Dischordian, but she's still human. Muses can't attack the dischord inside Mara without possibly harming her. The only way to beat her is to expel the dischord from her first."

"Is that the plan, then?" asked Hana.

Jay and Ark shared a look.

"First, we get the fiddle," said Jay.

"*Then* we purge the dischord," finished Ark.

"Right," said Andi. "And how are we going to do that, exactly?"

Jay frowned in thought. "A distraction. What've we got?"

They thought for an eternal few seconds—then Hana started with a gasp. She slid across the deck and pulled open the hatch leading into the cargo hold. Then she pulled out a few familiar glass vials filled with colorful liquids and powders.

Rye smiled. "Are those what I think they are?"

"A few shattered in our crash landing, but there's more than enough still intact," answered Hana. "We've got the distraction covered."

Jay grinned. "Okay," he whispered, leaning in. "Here's what we do . . ."

When the plan clicked together, they all kept low, going to their positions. Jay took one last deep breath—then, as Mara stepped in just the right spot, he jumped off the Morning Star.

"Can I ask you something, Mara?" he called out.

Mara spun around. Her snakelike face made Jay want to run fast in the other direction.

"Us first," Mara answered. Her fang-filled mouth stretched in a nasty sneer. "Why did you come back?"

Jay didn't answer. Mara's sneer darkened in amusement.

"Oh, we get it," she hissed. "You think you're some kind of hero. *You!*" She cackled. "You're a filthy outlaw. You're not worth spitting on!"

"I'm an *ex*-outlaw," said Jay, shifting his ground to keep her right where she was. "And I know I'm no hero. Never figured I was."

Mara narrowed her eyes.

"Tell me," he went on. "When you told me about the other Crafter's heirs—the ones found before me—were you lying?"

It seemed that was the last question Mara expected him to ask. She paused, thinking—just what Jay wanted her to do.

"Yes," she finally said. "We lied about one thing." She put on a sly smirk. "There were more than nine."

"What really happened to them?" he asked, trying to delay a little longer.

Mara said nothing.

"You duped them too, didn't you?" Jay went on, answering his own question. "You probably pulled the same routine on them as you did on me." He held her gaze, shaking his head. "After they played Brio's fiddle, you moved in. You cornered them and filled them with all kinds of doubts. Told them they'd only be puppets if they took the Crafter's title. Told them they'd be happier if they chose for themselves. And, sadly, it worked. You scared them all off, and there hasn't been a Crafter since. 'Cause of *you*."

"*Yes!* Because of *us!*" Mara snapped, squeezing the fiddle's neck. She gestured to herself. "Ever since this vessel first hosted Dubito, we have had but one task: to prevent the Crafter's return. We have succeeded for centuries."

"Centuries?" Jay blurted. "How old are you?"

"Enough," said Mara, rolling her eyes. "You're stalling."

Jay froze. Then he shrugged. "Guess it was obvious, huh?"

"Pathetic, more like," said Mara.

"Good thing I didn't have to stall very long," said Jay—and at once he dove aside, closing his eyes. "Hana!" he shouted.

There was a *crackle*, then a BLAM! and a flash so bright he could see it behind his eyelids. Mara howled; Jay opened his eyes, seeing the aftermath of Hana's alchemy. Mara was snarling and covering her eyes. There were scorch marks near her feet and traces of acrid smoke in the air.

No time to waste. "Andi!" Jay shouted.

Andi, hidden beyond the Morning Star's hull, gave a few sharp whistle commands—and then Hotah was off in a flash. The lycalcyon leapt with her powerful legs and latched onto Mara's arm, growling and snarling. Mara screamed, dropping the fiddle. Hotah sank her teeth deeper.

"Rye!" shouted Jay. "Now!"

Andi whistled again, and Hotah immediately let go of Mara, jumping out of the way. Mara stared at her bloody arm, then glanced up—just as Rye wrenched off the braces from the Morning Star's wing-sail with her bare hands. The wing mast groaned. Mara didn't even have the chance to cry out.

WHOMPH!

The entire wing-sail, mast and canvas alike, came flopping down on top of her. Jay swooped in and snatched up the fiddle, cradling it in his arms.

"Ark!" he yelled. "Finish it!"

Now that Mara no longer had the fiddle as a shield, Ark didn't have to hold back. He bellowed with his full voice:

"*Resisstardanndo!*"

At his song, one of the most bizarre muses Jay had ever seen emerged from the ground. It looked like a cluster of translucent seaweed vines, their leafy veins glittering. The seaweed rippled in an invisible current, weaving a tight barrier around Mara. Mara screeched in outrage.

"Can you take her out?" said Jay, jogging up to Ark.

Ark sank to one knee, his face shining with sweat. "Gimme a minute."

"Take your time," said Jay.

He'd barely said it when they all felt a tremor beneath their feet. Through the muse's translucent leaves, Jay could see a black substance smoldering around Mara, pushing the fallen wing-sail off her shoulders. Mara rose.

Jay gulped. "I mean, maybe not *too* much time."

Ark still looked in no shape to stand up, much less use music. He coughed to clear his throat, then turned to Andi, Hana, and Rye.

"I can't take her alone," said Ark, his voice hoarse. "Go find help. We'll hold Mara off as long as we can."

The three of them frowned.

"We can't keep this up forever," Ark insisted. "And no one is coming—not unless you bring them here. This is the only option."

They looked even less convinced at that. Jay shot them all a thumbs-up.

"Don't worry," he said, smiling. "Me 'n' Ark, we got this. Just hurry!"

The three of them exchanged a worried look, then dashed off through the snow. Just like that, Ark and Jay were alone with Mara.

Jay's smile faded. "We're gonna die, aren't we?"

Ark stared at him. "What happened to 'We got this'?"

"That's what ex-outlaws like me call *faking it*."

"No use faking it now," said Ark. "My barrier's failing."

Another tremor shuddered beneath their feet. The smoldering blackness around Mara grew denser and darker. She was throwing out a clawed hand, sending the blackness against the muse imprisoning her. The seaweed muse quailed with each blow, growing weaker every second.

"I'm going to release it," said Ark. "Otherwise Mara might hurt the muse." He glanced at Jay, looking down at the fiddle in his arms before meeting his gaze. "Get going."

Jay blinked. Huh?

"You're the Crafter's heir," Ark reminded him. "Get out of here and let me slow her down."

Jay blinked again. Then he shook his head with a dramatic sigh.

"You still think you can tell me what to do?" said Jay, more bravely than he felt. "Like I said, I'm not letting you have all the fun by yourself."

Ark shook his head. "Moron."

"Bum-wipe," Jay muttered back.

They shared a look for just a second. Then Ark turned to Mara, his face bent in concentration.

"*Caessurra!*"

The seaweed muse released its hold, its scored, wounded leaves vanishing back into the ground. At the same time, Ark whistled, summoning an antlered stag from the trees. He whistled again and again, differently each time, and two other muses came to his side: a silver-winged albatross and a furious-looking bear. Jay staggered away, clutching the fiddle.

Mara, free from her cage, hollered something raucous and guttural, firing off black, shrieking arrows from her hands.

"*Attaccacciacatura!*" Ark hollered. The muses shot forward.

Harmony and discord clashed, nearly knocking Jay off his feet. Ark chanted and Mara screeched, their voices colliding in an outrage of music and dissonance. The muses put up a fight, stomping, swooping, and charging against Mara. Mara deflected and dodged, the dischord's power within her now pouring from her hands in vicious, spear-like bursts.

Jay had never seen anything so fantastic, or terrifying. Ark wasn't giving Mara any advantage—but it was clear that controlling three muses at once was draining his energy at an alarming rate. Ark's voice grew rougher with each song, and he could barely hold up his arms.

Jay stared down at the fiddle, begging in his mind: *Help!*

The fiddle didn't respond. It remained mute and hollow in his hands.

Jay didn't waste more time trying. He tucked the fiddle under his arm and scooped up snow at his feet. He might not know how to fight a Dischordian or get the fiddle to work again—but causing trouble was still his specialty.

While Mara began to hiss another attack, Jay wound up his arm, aimed, and threw a snowball right in her face. Mara squawked, furiously wiping slush from her eyes.

Jay whooped—but beside him, Ark fell to his knees, gasping for breath, his whole body shaking like mad. Jay swallowed. Not a good sign.

Mara screeched in outrage. Oily darkness dripped from her like dirty dishwater wrung from a rag. Her serpentine face was haggard, and her breaths came in wheezy gasps. But her eyes were sharp, cold, determined.

"Our mission is clear," she said to Jay, black mist creeping from the sides of her mouth. "We must stop the Crafter's return. No matter what."

Jay found himself transfixed by Mara's yellow eyes, which she'd locked onto him the moment she spoke. Jay found himself unable to look away, even though he wanted to—he couldn't move his feet as she lifted her hands before her, gathering a crackling ball of dark, deadly lightning between her palms.

Ark shouted in warning, though Jay couldn't hear it above the siren of panic in his head. He was paralyzed by Mara's gaze, even as she prepared to fire that black lightning at him.

"*No!*" Ark yelled, slamming into Jay's side and shoving him out of the way. Jay tumbled into the snow, his trance broken.

"Ark—!" Jay cried out.

The next two seconds played out before Jay's eyes in slow motion. Mara shot her arms forward, the black lightning howling and sizzling over him.

It struck Ark square in the chest, enveloping him in a crackle of deadly black sparks. Ark screamed as the dissonant lightning sank into his chest. His back arched as his eyes popped from their sockets—

And then he collapsed to the ground.

Chapter Thirty-Four

BRIO

*J*ay stared numbly as Ark fell, then fought past his shock.

"Ark!" he shouted, ignoring Mara. Jay dropped the fiddle and stumbled through the snow, crashing on his knees. "Ark! Snap out of it!"

Ark remained still. So very still.

Ten thousand thoughts raced through Jay's brain. What should he do? Raise Ark's head? Check his pulse? Jay held a hand to Ark's nose. Was he breathing? Jay put his ear to Ark's chest. Was that a heartbeat? Ark's eyes wouldn't open. Why wouldn't his eyes open?

"It's pointless," said Mara. "He's dead."

The thoughts screaming through Jay's mind fell silent. He slumped backward.

Dead.

The world tilted sideways. Jay shook his head, over and over, unable to stop. His chest burned as if Mara's dissonant lightning had struck him, blowing a hole clean through.

Not possible. Not Ark.

But even as Jay watched, the color in Ark's face seemed to drain away, turning an unnatural gray sheen. The burning in Jay's chest grew into a searing pain, blazing through him like a firestorm, anger and guilt feeding the flames. He clenched his teeth against the pain, trembling as memories from just minutes before rewound before his eyes:

Ark, knocking him aside to save him—Ark, fighting Mara with three muses at once—Ark, sending their friends to safety—Ark, smiling at him in acceptance, even after Jay admitted what he'd done.

Dead.

Jay was so lost in the chaos that he didn't notice Mara approach. She stuck out her foot and nudged Ark's limp body, a strange look on her face.

"What a waste," she muttered.

"*Get away from him!*" Jay hollered, taking a swipe at her leg.

Mara responded by kicking him square in the face with her heel. WHAM!

Jay flew backwards. Every tooth in his mouth rattled with the blow.

"You deserved that," hissed Mara. With uncanny strength, she reached down and lifted Jay right off the ground with one hand. She wound up her other arm and threw her fist into his face, again and again.

"You've wasted our time," she snarled between punches. "You shouldn't have come back." *Bam!* "You could have had a nice, easy life." *Thwap!* "But you just had to play the hero, didn't you?" *Whack!*

She finally let go. Jay fell to his hands and knees with a gasp, his head throbbing in agony. One of his eyes swelled shut. He spat out a thick blob from his mouth, staining the snow red.

"And look where it got you," said Mara, her yellow eyes narrowed. "You crossed us. You reneged on our deal. And you'll suffer for it." She glanced at Ark, lying lifeless in the snow. "Like you made him suffer."

She spat on Ark's body.

The scorching pain in Jay's chest flared to life. Anger smoldered inside him, growing hot. With a yell, Jay stumbled up and threw his hand at Mara in a wild punch.

Mara caught his fist, stopping it in its tracks. Jay tried to pull out of her grasp, but she held him tight.

And then she *squeezed.*

Jay howled as the bones in his hand cracked, breaking in her grip.

"Have some self-respect," Mara spat, dropping Jay's hand at last.

Jay stumbled away and collapsed to his knees, cradling his crushed hand. It felt like a jumble of broken twigs.

"It's over. You've lost," said Mara. A sneer grew over her face. She raised her hands, oily black smoke screeching between her palms.

Jay doubled over and closed his eyes. The silence of the snowy lawn rang in his ears, and his heart pounded faster as the inevitable end came rushing for him, like an out-of-control train.

He thought back to his prayer in the cathedral, how he'd begged for a chance to set things right. But what did that mean anymore? Ark was gone. His friends hadn't returned in time. Nobody was left to stop Mara taking back the fiddle and turning the Royal Conservatory to ash—

The fiddle.

Jay's unswollen eye snapped open. He saw the fiddle lying where he'd dropped it, nestled in the snow drift just an arm's reach away. A tiny flicker of hope blinked to life inside him.

A heartbeat later, Jay lunged for the fiddle, snatching it up with his uninjured hand. He held it before himself like a shield.

Mara rolled her eyes.

"Do you think that pathetic lump of wood will stop us?" she asked, letting the smoky blackness between her hands grow. "We'll just pulverize Brio's instrument along with you."

Jay said nothing, trying not to lose his nerve. He focused all his attention on the fiddle instead, his body trembling.

He'd been running for so long. Running from his past. Running from his debt with the Capo. Running from his musical gifts. And there was one thing he'd been running from since the moment he'd first held this fiddle 'til right now, a truth he'd been too scared to face.

But not anymore. No more running from it.

He ran toward it instead.

Dredging up the last bit of nerves he had, Jay took up the fiddle with his left hand and set it under his chin. He positioned his fingers on the strings.

Mara shook her head.

"This is too pitiful to watch," she said. "Brio won't answer. You rejected him, remember?" She snickered. "Besides, how were you planning on playing without a bow? And just look at your hand!"

Her snicker grew to a cackle.

Jay ignored her. He glanced to the side, where Ark lay in the snow. He swallowed a knot in his throat. He wouldn't let Ark down.

It hurt worse than anything Jay had ever felt—but he clenched his teeth and lifted his busted hand. His hand shook as he raised it above the fiddle's strings, as if he were holding an invisible bow in position.

He closed his eyes and reached inward, trying to remember the perfect music:

Come.

"I've come," Jay told the fiddle. "I won't run anymore. I trust you."

As he spoke, Jay heard Mara approach through the snow. He could smell a rank odor emanating from her—could hear the foul, sizzling crackle between her hands. He pictured her taking aim, ready to send another bolt of deadly lightning through his skull.

"Farewell, Julian!" Mara hissed, gloating in triumph.

Jay didn't flinch or open his eyes. A peculiar energy pulsed through him as he drew in a deep breath, tuning out everything else.

"Come, Brio," he breathed aloud—then he drew his shaking hand above the strings, pulling the imaginary bow across them.

It wasn't possible for him to play it. Jay knew that.

But Brio didn't care about impossible.

A beautiful, incomprehensible sound poured from the heart of the fiddle, filling the snowy lawn with the purest harmony Jay had ever known.

Jay's eyes snapped open in shock. His hand had been empty a second ago—yet now he was holding a fiddle bow, one that looked like it was made of pure light. A golden glow shone from within the fiddle, coming from somewhere inexplicably far yet intimately close. Warmth pulsed from the fiddle's scuffed wood, pouring into Jay, soothing his aches and bruises. Even his hand didn't hurt now, though Jay could see it was still broken.

Mara turned to stone, staring with unblinking eyes. Then her face morphed in wild rage.

"No!" she howled in madness, trying to snatch the fiddle from his hands. Jay reeled away, pushing the bow of light against the strings.

FWOOOOSH!

The perfect music sang out through the fiddle like a siren in a storm, and a harmonic pressure wave burst from its strings, expanding out in a shining golden dome. The dome blew Mara away from Jay, sending her toppling head over heels. It stretched higher and higher, golden light sweeping over the lawn, the surrounding trees, the whole island. In a blink, the snaky dischord shadows slithering overhead were gone.

"Stop!" Mara shrieked, staring in horror. "Stop it!"

Jay didn't stop. He let the perfect music take the lead, guiding his hands and fingers. The fiddle quivered in his hands like a living, wild creature, ready to jump out of his grasp. Jay held on with all his might as it swept him into a new song, one both universal and personal, powerful yet gentle.

"I'll kill you!" Mara roared. She rose to her feet, flying toward him on a boiling cloud of black dischord.

But she couldn't get close. Jay played on, and the perfect music pushed her back, the cloud of dischord around her slowly shrinking.

The perfect music flowed from the fiddle as a sea of melody, reaching high and low like roaring waves—then new phrases of harmony joined in like streams flowing into a mighty river, each note spilling into the next in a swift current of sound. As the melodies and harmonies took shape, Jay could hear the perfect music telling its story through the song: a story of joy and pain, of love and rage, of life and loss. The song's current surrounded him, pulsing with such a familiar cadence that Jay wondered if the story was really his own—as if the perfect music was actually a part of him, and always had been.

Julian.

Jay laughed out loud, joy and relief rising in his chest. The perfect music was calling his name. Jay could sense its presence reaching for him from the heart of the fiddle, awake and alert and alive.

Jay reached back—and as he played, something in the deepest, most secret part of himself sparked to life. He felt a rush of energy explode from the fiddle, rippling out in a brilliant golden ribbon of light.

"*No, no, no!*" howled Mara.

Jay gasped, sweating and shivering. The song was over. The bow of light dissolved in his hand. He panted for breath, glancing up.

His mouth dropped open.

All around, countless muses had rallied together, each one focused on a single being standing before Jay. The being was unlike any muse Jay had ever seen. The muse looked like a person, more or less—except for the pair of great golden wings sprouting from its back. Shining robes cascaded over the muse, around its lustrous wings. It was hard to tell whether the muse was a guy or girl, like it was beyond such distinctions. The muse's face was more masculine, though, with sharp features and a bright, intimidating stare. His golden eyes were ancient—as deep as the night sky, as wise as the woods, as innocent as baby birds.

Jay couldn't breathe. His heart stopped.

Brio.

The muse turned, locking eyes with him. Jay's knees buckled.

Do not be afraid.

Brio didn't speak aloud; he spoke with the perfect music. At once Jay could breathe again. Brio turned to Mara.

Release her, forsaken one.

Mara screamed in fury. Jay stared in morbid fascination as she thrashed on the ground, throwing an almighty tantrum.

"*Never!*" she howled—though not aloud. She answered with the voice of a dozen spitting, shrieking snakes, all garbled together. It took Jay an awful second to realize it was the dischord itself speaking from inside Mara.

"*She gave me this vessel freely!*" the dischord continued, while Mara rose clumsily to her feet, like a marionette pulled by tangled strings. "*I am Dubito the Deceiver! I am of the Wretched, Din's first generation! For centuries I have scoured this realm. You cannot cast me out!*"

At that, Mara let loose an inhuman wail, bellowing like a beast. From her hands she shot a bolt of deadly dischord lightning, aimed right at Brio.

Brio didn't even blink. Before it got within a few strides of him, the lightning rebounded, crackling off in a shower of shrieking black sparks.

Release her! Brio repeated fiercely.

Brio's words were powerful and dreadful, so loud that Jay felt his entire body shake to his bones. Mara cried out in terror. She turned to run.

She didn't get far. Brio stretched his wings wide. Then, with a move that was too swift for Jay's eyes to follow, the muse transformed from a winged man to an enormous golden bird. The bird pumped its wings and shot forward with a piercing cry, aiming for Mara's back—then it flew straight *into* her, right through her heart.

And as Brio flew out the other side, he pulled *something else* out with him, pinched in his beak. It was like a sticky shadow with dozens of stretchy arms, all struggling to cling to Mara's body—but as Brio pulled, the shadow's arms snapped off one by one, releasing their hold on her.

Mara shrieked as Brio pulled the dischord out. For a moment, she was lifted clear off the ground, feet twitching and kicking above the snow—then, as the last shadowy arm broke loose, her voice died in a cry of agony. Her yellow snakelike eyes changed back to dull human ones. Her reptilian scales vanished. She hung suspended in the air for one last, eternal second —then she fell in a crumpled heap to the snow, unconscious.

A wave of light and pressure rolled from where Mara had fallen toward Jay. The wave passed over him, sweeping him into a strange place.

A young woman, dressed in clothes that looked like the height of fashion hundreds of years ago—she sat in a room lined with cots, so many cots, all occupied by the diseased and desolate—she was locked away with the dying, the last to be infected with the fatal plague, waiting for her inevitable end—no one cared what happened to her now, no one—she would be the last to go, all alone, left to darkness and starvation and death—

Jay watched as the scene played out. Right. This same thing happened when he'd played the fiddle in Lower Grimsborough. Back then, he'd seen Nanny's memories—which meant these were Mara's.

A stranger appeared to her, his face obscured by bandages, his clothes all castoff scraps of various fraying garments—the stranger whispered, "Do you want to escape death, my morsel?"—Mara, terrified of being the last to die, nodded—"Become my host, and death will never touch you!" he told her—the ritual was performed in the presence of the dead—the stranger vanished, and Mara's eyes became yellow—

Jay winced as the vision sped up. Entire centuries of memories flew past in flashes of color, lifetimes upon lifetimes.

Mara remained hidden in obscurity, unattractive, uninteresting, keeping herself to herself—and so no one learned of her true power, her endless life, her command over discord—over hundreds of years she carried out her master's will, hunting for the Crafter candidates, turning them away—as decades piled on, she grew numb to life, longing for death's release—but Dubito would not let death come for her, feeding on the immortal spirit inside her, overtaking her mind, her personality, her will. . . .

The vision ended. Jay shook himself from his trance, blinking as the present moment returned to his eyes. He looked over at Mara, not sure how to respond to all he'd just seen—then he stared, open-mouthed.

For the first time, he saw Dubito's true form.

Hovering near Mara's body was a writhing, screeching, hissing mass of tangled shadows, all twisted around each other like snakes tied in one impossible knot. The thing's countless heads stretched and snapped in all directions, searching for something to devour. Its hundreds of tails whipped this way and that, trying to wriggle away. But more than what it looked like, Jay realized what the thing *felt* like, out in the open: the dark embodiment of every doubt, eager to paralyze, to manipulate, to consume.

Brio had shifted back to his winged human form when Jay wasn't looking. The muse stood over Mara, shielding her so the nasty knot of snaky shadows couldn't possess her again. The dischord snarled at Brio—and then Jay felt the thing turn to look at him, its many snake heads facing him as one.

Think you've won? said Dubito, speaking in dissonant shrieks, its heads bobbing and spitting. *I will be summoned again. My brethren are everywhere, even on this island. You can never hide!*

Enough, said Brio, speaking in perfect music. He spread his wings wide, his form glowing brighter. *Be gone, forsaken one.*

Dubito screeched and snarled in agony. Bathed in Brio's golden light, the dischord began to smoke and smolder—then each tangled snake broke apart like fibers of unwinding rope, turning to dust. What was left of the Unraveling Man was unraveling before Jay's eyes.

And you, mighty Brio, terror of dischords! Dubito snarled sarcastically, even as his form dissolved. *The Wretched will rise. Your new Crafter will fall. The Magnum Opus will be rewritten.*

Jay felt like Dubito's eyes had settled on him again, though it was hard to tell with more than half of his form already gone.

And when the Voice of Din speaks at last, said Dubito with finality, *you will realize just how wrong you are. About everything.*

Before Jay could wonder what Dubito was talking about, the dischord evaporated until only the last snake head remained. Dubito sang out one last time, his voice sounding very far away:

Blood of blood and bone of bone,
Sorrow's Children stand alone.
Tooth for tooth and eye for eye,
One lives to see the other die.

The words burned into Jay's brain. Jay blinked—and Dubito was gone. It was over.

Jay knew he should've felt happy, or relieved, or something. But he only felt exhausted, overwhelmed by everything that'd happened. His whole body throbbed.

His eyes turned to Ark, lying in the same place he'd fallen. Jay shuffled through the snow and knelt next to him, feeling the weight of all that'd just happened come over him again. Ark's face was so still, like he was sleeping. Jay felt something inside himself splinter.

"I'm sorry," he said huskily. "Y'know, you were the closest thing to a best friend I've ever had. I'm sorry I never said it." His eyes started to sting. "You saved my life."

Jay wiped his eyes with the back of his sleeve, then took a deep breath.

"I promise I'll be the Crafter you said I was. I'm gonna be the best Crafter anybody's ever seen. Just watch."

He didn't know what else to say, so he simply knelt with his eyes closed, silently reciting the prayer Brother Elfenbein had taught him long ago: *Dust and ashes, yield to earth . . .*

". . . you'd better be."

Jay's eyes snapped open. The words had been so quiet that Jay swore he'd imagined them—but then he saw Ark's eyelids flutter. His chest rose with a breath, and then another.

And then Ark opened his eyes. He winced, groaning as he sat upright.

"How . . . ?" Jay squeaked. "You were dead!"

Ark looked down and studied the blackened hole in his coat, tracing his fingers along the scored edge. "Apparently not," he said. He reached inside the front of his coat and pulled out his notebook. The back cover had been obliterated, and half the pages were charred.

Jay blinked, beyond confused. "Did that save you?"

Ark slipped his fingers inside the cover, removing the sketch of his mom, which was thankfully unharmed. "I wish I knew," he said, folding the sketch and slipping it inside a different pocket. "But I won't question a miracle."

Jay wasn't about to, either. He and Ark exchanged a look.

"You look terrible," they said at the same time.

Then they began to laugh—soft chuckles that built into loud, stupid giggles of relief. Jay's bruised face hurt from grinning.

"What happened to Dubito?" Ark asked. He glanced beyond Jay—and his eyes popped out behind his spectacles.

"Great gavotte," he breathed aloud as Brio approached them, his wings stretched wide.

One last thing, he said to Jay, wearing the same kind smile.

Without another word, Brio morphed again into a giant golden bird, blazing like the sunrise. Brio flapped his wings and flew higher, higher still—straight to the highest point of the Royal Conservatory, where the two giant statues of Harmony Monument stood staring at the horizon.

Brio flew toward the statues so fast that the muse was just a blur of light, like a shooting star. Then, with a majestic cry of victory, Brio dove straight into the stone lantern the statues were holding.

There was an incredible burst of light, so bright that Jay and Ark both flinched. Jay blinked the afterimages from his eyes. The stone lantern was lit, burning with a white-gold flame that sang out a single, pure note of music before falling silent, flickering serenely.

Jay watched Brio's fire blaze from the lantern, stupefied. Huh. So *that's* how he was supposed to light it.

Brio flew from the stone lantern in a wide arc, swooping upside down. Directly above him, the giant golden bird angled into a dive. Jay cringed, bracing for impact.

But Brio didn't strike him dead on. Jay looked up in time to see Brio hovering, his feathers glinting like molten gold. A shimmering light shone from the muse, covering Jay like glittering fire falling from the sky. Jay felt the fire seep into him, almost too hot to bear.

Then, with a golden flash, Brio vanished—but a warmth Jay couldn't describe remained in his chest. A peculiar energy thrummed through him, tingling from his head to the tips of his fingers and toes.

"Jay?" Ark finally spoke up. "Are you—?"

Before Ark could finish, Jay's body rebelled. He slumped in the snow, more exhausted than he'd ever been.

"Jay!" said Ark, alarmed. "*Jay!*"

I'm fine, Jay wanted to answer, but his voice wouldn't work. He closed his eyes, drifting along the edge of a long, deep chasm he longed to fall into.

Next thing he knew—a few seconds later, or maybe hours—he heard more voices. He forced his eyes open. A bunch of people were suddenly all around him. Ark was standing to the side, holding Brio's fiddle in his arms and speaking rapidly with Grand Maestran Luthier. Dulcian, Callie, and several strangers Jay didn't recognize were gently lifting him off the ground. Jay thought he saw Andi, Rye, and Hana too, wearing fearful looks.

Jay tried to tell them not to worry, but his mouth couldn't form the words. A fresh wave of exhaustion rose like a tidal wave. Just before the wave crashed down, Jay looked up, seeing the stone lantern between the statues blazing like a beacon against the dark.

Let us begin, Brio's voice whispered within him.

Jay had no idea what Brio meant, but he was too tired to think.

At long last, the wave of pain and tiredness crashed over him, and Jay plunged into the void beyond.

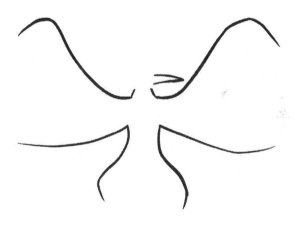

Chapter Thirty-Five

AN ASSIGNMENT

As he walked across the Royal Conservatory grounds, Ark touched his chest, his fingers tracing the spot where Mara's dissonant attack had struck. The damage to his talaris had been excellently mended, but the memory of the dischord lightning hadn't faded so easily.

He should have been dead. Why wasn't he?

Don't question a miracle.

The words echoed in his mind, a gentle reminder for him to leave it alone. Still, that wasn't easy to do. Besides, Ark didn't believe in miracles.

He shook the thoughts from his head and focused instead on the summons envelope in his hand. The envelope bore the purple seal of the Grand Maestran; the note inside ordered him to report to Captain Sharpe's office at eleven o'clock. He didn't know why the Grand Maestran wanted to see him, much less why he was being summoned to the Gray Wolf headquarters, of all places—but Ark sensed something was about to happen.

He came to the stolid, gray-stone building that housed the Gray Wolves exactly on time. Captain Sharpe met him at the entrance.

"Where is His Excellency?" asked Ark.

Instead of answering, Captain Sharpe ushered Ark inside without a word, guiding him down several corridors to a set of stairs. Down, down, down; Ark followed the silent captain deep underground. The stairs finally ended at the opening of a subterranean tunnel, lit by dim sonoluminous lamps.

"Where are we going?" asked Ark again.

Captain Sharpe still said nothing; he stepped off into the tunnel, and Ark had no choice but to follow. They passed several closed doors spaced evenly along either side of the tunnel, finally coming to a stop at the door at the tunnel's far end. The captain knocked crisply.

"Come in," Grand Maestran Luthier's voice greeted from within.

Captain Sharpe opened the door. Ark entered, peering around.

It was a barren cell, with thick iron bars dividing the room in half. The cell itself looked vacant. On the near side of the bars close to the door stood the Grand Maestran, looking grim.

"Thank you for coming, Sir Encore," he said.

Ark nodded, realizing just then that he wasn't the only one who'd been summoned. Dulcian and Callie were here too.

When they faced him, Ark felt his heart drop to his stomach. He hadn't seen them since the whole ordeal with Dubito. At once he lowered his head. "I am so, so sorry I wrongly accused you both—"

"It's okay, Arkalin," interrupted Dulcian, smiling. "You were tricked. It was an elaborate scheme on Dubito's part. I forgive you."

He turned toward Callie, arching his brow. Callie huffed.

"Fine. I forgive you too," she said in less-than-convincing agreement.

The Grand Maestran coughed, getting their attention.

Ark straightened, wondering again what they were all doing here—but then he took a closer look into the room's cell. Huddled in the darkest corner was a small, miserable figure curled up tight. The person was so still and small that Ark missed them at first glance.

"Miss Fipple," the Grand Maestran called.

The hunched figure twitched—then Mara turned. She was a pale, fragile shell of the woman she had once been. Her eyes were too wide, too bright. Her face looked haunted. Her hair was a knotted mess. Ark fought to keep his pity off his face, but it was difficult to look at her now.

"There are questions I hope you can answer," asked the Grand Maestran in a reassuring voice. "I asked Sir Mandore, Lady Vielle, and Mr. Encore here to provide context, as needed. Please know we are all here as friends."

Mara half-turned to face him, her too-wide eyes not blinking.

"We must know," said Grand Maestran Luthier. "Mis Fipple, while you were possessed, you claimed to be a Dischordian, an enemy of Musicians.

But you may not have been speaking for yourself at the time. Were you cooperating with the dischord Dubito while you were possessed, or were you being controlled against your will?"

Mara made no effort to answer. She started swaying in her cell.

"According to Julian's report," the Grand Maestran continued, changing tack, "Dubito made a claim that there were other Dischordians among us, right here at the Royal Conservatory. Is that true?"

Mara hummed softly, neither confirming nor denying it.

The Grand Maestran sighed in frustration. "Mara, I don't think you understand why we are here," he said. "This is your one chance to help yourself. Your sentence is still being determined by the Maestrans Council. The severity of your punishment is fully dependent upon just how freely you acted while you were held in thrall by Dubito—*and* how much information you can give us about other Dischordians you know." He frowned. "Have you nothing to say to me?"

Mara bit her lip, rocking back and forth, back and forth. Grand Maestran Luthier shook his head.

"So be it," he said sadly. "Good-bye, Miss Fipple."

He shuffled toward the cell's exit. Dulcian and Callie started off with cheerless faces and silent footsteps. Ark knew he was supposed to follow them, but his feet wouldn't move yet.

"The codes," he blurted.

Mara stopped rocking. Callie, Dulcian, and the Grand Maestran paused.

"All those messages you wrote me," Ark went on. "Were you trying to trick me, Mara—or were you trying to warn me?"

Mara's eyes widened. She gave Ark a long, steady stare, then scrambled up to the bars, reaching out to him.

"Notebook," she hissed, snapping her fingers. "And pencil."

Bewildered, Ark reached into his talaris and pulled out the sorry remains of what had once been his notebook. Only half of it was still intact; the other half had been charred so badly that Ark's only option was to tear it out and throw it away. He passed the half-notebook to her with his pencil nub.

Mara flipped through the pages impatiently before finding what she was looking for. She made a few scribbles, then passed the notebook back to him.

Ark studied the page she'd written on. It was the same page with the subtractive formula from a few days ago. Ark stared hard at the revised code with the Grand Maestran, Dulcian, and Callie reading over his shoulder:

$$34 - 33 = A$$

29
30 19 20 19 14 14 16 13 15 14 21 ~~28~~

DO NOT TRUST ME

Understanding blossomed in Ark's mind.

"*That's* why you told me not to go on my jury mission," he murmured. "That's what you were trying to tell me all along. You weren't helping him. You were fighting him."

Mara's face crumpled.

"Dubito finally figured it out," she whispered. "He forced me to change the last number. I had no choice. No choice, no choice, no choice."

Her words drifted off, and she started rocking again. After centuries of being held captive in her own body by a soul-sucking dischord, Ark wondered how fragile her mind was—and if she would ever recover.

The Grand Maestran exhaled. "That certainly casts a new light on your circumstances. Thank you."

Mara said nothing, muttering incoherently. Without another word, the Grand Maestran ushered Ark and the others outside of the cell.

"What will happen to Mara, Your Excellency?" asked Ark once they were back in the tunnel.

The Grand Maestran frowned. "That is up for the Council to decide. But we have other matters to discuss. I have new assignments for you three."

Ark straightened up. An assignment?

"The beacon at Harmony Monument has been lit," the man went on. "The world knows we have a new Crafter. Our priority must now be the Crafter's safety." He sent all three of them a steady look. "While he has proven his bond with Brio by defeating Dubito, I understand he has no musical training at all. He will need to master music if he is to stand on his own and defend Sedrinel from dischords." He spread out his hands.

"We have one option. Julian must be trained fully in musical arts, though for now his identity must be kept secret. I recommend he be sent to a remote location for study, somewhere far from the Royal Conservatory."

Dulcian and Callie shared a furtive glance.

"But where would Julian go?" asked Dulcian.

"Echostrait," the Grand Maestran replied without missing a beat. "I have already contacted the school's chancellor. Maestran Antonia Pandoura is more than capable of assisting us in this matter. And Echostrait has a proven track record for excellent graduates," he added, winking at Ark.

Ark didn't think to blush at the compliment. "What do you want us to do, Your Excellency?" he asked.

At that, the Grand Maestran turned to Callie and Dulcian. "Lady Vielle, Sir Mandore—your assignment is to accompany the Crafter to Echostrait as his personal guardians. To protect Julian's identity, however, you will also serve undercover. Otherwise, people may be suspicious. We don't want anyone looking too closely at Julian."

"Yes, sir," both Dulcian and Callie answered at once.

Ark couldn't help himself. "Will I be going with them?"

He tried not to feel disappointed when the Grand Maestran shook his head.

"You won't be going back to Echostrait. However, I want to offer you a different position."

Ark's ears perked at that.

"Until Julian is prepared to come out publicly as the Crafter, the Maestrans Council will function as it always has. I will continue to lead the Council in Merideyin's music-related matters. Of course, in the meantime, the Crafter's wishes must be respected, and we will need someone—a liaison—who would be willing to speak on his behalf and protect his interests."

Ark still wasn't sure what the Grand Maestran was getting at. The man's gaze settled on Ark.

"This liaison should be a peer who has already spent time with His Eminence and has developed a personal rapport with him. This person must be willing to travel to Echostrait on routine visits with His Eminence and share the latest decisions by the Council." The man smiled. "The assignment is yours, if you want it."

Ark blinked behind his spectacles, stunned by the offer. Only a few weeks ago, he was just an Adept trying to prove himself. Now he was being asked to become a peer liaison. For the *Crafter*.

"Do you accept?" asked the Grand Maestran.

Dulcian smiled encouragingly. Callie sent him a reassuring smirk.

"I—yes," Ark sputtered, still overcoming his shock. "Yes, of course, Your Excellency, I would be honored—"

"Wonderful," said the Grand Maestran, cutting him off. "Perhaps you would be so good as to pass the word along to our Crafter?"

"Yes, Your Excellency," said Ark. He bowed to them all and slipped out of the room—then he practically ran, his talaris flapping behind him.

Chapter Thirty-Six

A PROMISE

By the time Ark reached the right room, he was practically wheezing from running from the Gray Wolf headquarters. He took a moment to catch his breath, brushed his talaris, and raised his hand to knock on the door. Before his knuckles reached the wood, a voice called out from inside.

"That you out there, Ark?"

Ark smiled. No point in knocking, then.

"Thought so," said Andi, grinning from the far side of the room as Ark entered. Hotah barked a greeting, her tail wagging.

"Ark!" cheered Rye, bouncing up to give him a hug.

"Welcome back," said Hana, smiling.

Ark looked past his three friends to the solitary bed in the room. Jay was lying there, propped up on pillows. A mild grin spread across his face. He sent Ark a little wave. "Hey."

Ark smiled back at him. He saw that the worst of Jay's bruises were starting to fade, though his broken hand was still bandaged tight. But despite having the beating of his life just a week ago, Jay looked fine. More than fine. He seemed different somehow, though Ark couldn't put his finger on it. A new kind of light shone in Jay's eyes, glowing with resolve.

"We just finished lunch, though we saved some for you," said Hana, handing him a full plate. "What did the Grand Maestran want?"

Ark sat with them on the edge of Jay's bed. Between bites, he told them about Mara, then everything the Grand Maestran had told him about Jay going to Echostrait and Ark serving at the Royal Conservatory as the Crafter liaison.

"Congratulations, Ark!" said Rye, clapping and bouncing on the bed.

"Thanks," said Ark, feeling himself blush this time. "I wasn't expecting it. Living at the Royal Conservatory is going to take some getting used to."

"Don't worry," said Andi. "I'll be staying here, too."

Ark turned to him, surprised.

"The Grand Maestran offered," explained Andi. "He said I was welcome to stay on as a guest while I look for Hoku in the city. He said it was the least they could do after we'd helped fight Dubito."

"He told us the same thing," said Hana, gesturing between herself and Rye. "But the salvaged parts of the Morning Star are going to be sent back to Cindertown soon, and we need to travel back with them." She shared a glance with Rye. "The Cartwright sisters know where we are, but we *did* disappear on them during the whole Mount Vakra episode. I'm sure they want to see that we're okay."

"But when we're back in Cindertown, Jay will be all the way down in Echostrait, while Andi and Ark stay behind here," said Rye. Her face fell. "We won't see much of each other anymore, will we?"

The realization settled over them, and soon everyone was somber.

"Don't worry," said Jay, speaking for the first time. He waved in Ark's direction, smirking. "As lousy as Ark's luck is, we're all bound to get caught up in some new mess of trouble real soon."

They all laughed. But even while Ark chuckled along, he saw a worried look flash across Jay's face, like he wasn't reassured by his own joke.

The little clock on the wall chimed. Hana stood up.

"Time for your medicine," she said, making her way to the door. "I'll go get it."

As she left, Andi stood too, stretching. "I need some air. So does Hotah. I'm going to take her to run around outside." He tilted his head in Rye's direction. "Wanna come with, Rye?"

"Love to!" said Rye with a beaming grin, taking his elbow. They led each other out of the room.

Soon it was just him and Jay alone. Jay was staring out the balcony windows, his mind somewhere else. Ark set aside his empty plate; his eyes caught sight of the black Crafter talaris that hung on the frame of a wardrobe, carrying the promise of Jay's future. *Crafter Julian*.

Ark was so preoccupied studying the black talaris that he didn't even notice when Jay slid out of bed. He glanced over in time to see Jay step out onto the balcony, shuffling stiffly toward the banister.

A few moments later, Ark followed, shutting the balcony door behind them. When Jay glanced his way, Ark tossed the black talaris at him.

"It's cold out here, moron," he said. Jay obediently slipped the talaris on, careful of his injured hand.

"Feeling all right?" Ark asked him.

Jay's brow bent in thought, seriously considering the question.

"I feel different," he finally answered. "Like . . . I don't know how to say it. It sounds crazy, but it's like there's another heartbeat inside me now. Right here." He rested a hand on his chest.

"Brio's presence?" suggested Ark. "Or maybe one of Brio's gifts."

Jay shrugged. They both stood against the banister, not sure what to say.

"So . . . the Quickstep Kid, huh?" said Ark. "Want to tell me more?"

A sad smile came to Jay's face. "Someday, maybe."

Ark nodded, understanding. They settled into silence again. Below them, Ark could see Andi and Rye chatting together while Hotah ran through the trees, weaving this way and that—unaware that she was being followed by a flurry of muses who were chasing her, enjoying the run.

"Something's bothering me," said Jay out of the blue.

Ark glanced at him. Jay reached absently into his pocket and pulled out the beaded bracelet.

"Dubito said something weird to me before he disappeared," Jay went on, spinning the beads on their string. "Something I've had nightmares about."

Ark frowned. He understood nightmares. "What was it?"

Jay stared blankly out across the Royal Conservatory grounds, looking at a distant point on the horizon.

"Dubito said, '*The Wretched will rise. Your new Crafter will fall. The Magnum Opus will be rewritten. And when the Voice of Din speaks at last, you will realize just how wrong you are.*'" Jay glanced at Ark with a worried look. "Then he said one more thing at the very end."

He recited a strange verse in a quiet, rhythmic voice:

Blood of blood and bone of bone,
Sorrow's Children stand alone.
Tooth for tooth and eye for eye,
One lives to see the other die.

"Could you repeat that?" asked Ark. Jay did.

"I have no idea what it's all about," said Jay, frowning to himself.

Ark silently digested everything Jay said. He wasn't sure what to think, either. What was the Wretched? And the Voice of Din? And he'd never heard of the Magnum Opus before. But Dubito had been willing to burn the entire Royal Conservatory to the ground to get its hands on just one piece of it . . . and no matter what the Grand Maestran had said about the Magnum Opus being a fairy tale, there was more to it than the man would admit aloud.

The poem was even more disturbing. Sorrow's Children? Blood and bone? Tooth and eye? No clue what that meant. And what did it mean, *One lives to see the other die?*

It sounded like an omen. He doubted it was prophesy, at least. Prophesy was a thing of folklore and fantasy stories, like Darcy Harper. Ark didn't believe in prophesy.

But it *was* poetry, which was worse. Poetry always spoke the truth.

"I'm going to figure it all out," Jay declared. He straightened up, resting both hands gently on the banister. "I'll go study in Echostrait, and then I'll get to the bottom of it. The Magnum Opus, the Wretched—everything."

Ark stared at him. Jay was serious. He was gazing out over the treetops of the Royal Conservatory, his eyes holding the same determined light Ark had noticed before. It reminded him of Brio's eyes, which he'd glimpsed for just a moment before the ancient muse had vanished from sight.

For the first time, it really sunk in:

Jay was the Crafter. Brio's power was with him.

The Crafter had truly returned.

As that awesome epiphany settled through Ark, Jay turned to him.

"So, buddy—wanna help?" he asked, grinning.

Ark blinked, caught off guard. The Crafter was asking him to help fight a struggle they could barely grasp. But it was more than that. A few weeks ago, the two of them couldn't stand each other—and now Jay was standing by his side, asking for him to come along. As a friend.

Ark had no idea what the future held. But he was looking forward to it.

"Yes," he replied. "I'll help—*if* you promise to stop acting like a cretin."

Jay reared up. "Oh yeah? Then you can help, but only if *you* promise to stop being Mr. Stiff-Neck all the time."

"That's Sir Encore to you."

"That's Your Blazin' Eminence to *you*."

"Idiot."

"Jerk."

"Moron."

"Bum-wipe."

After running out of insults, they both fell silent, staring out across the Royal Conservatory. Despite his best efforts, Ark couldn't stop grinning.

CODA

It had been a long time since Inspector Argentine had seen so many news criers at once. He stood at the back of the swarming crowd, listening to various renditions of the most popular headline:

"The Crafter returns!"

"Harmony Monument beacon shines on Wintertide Day!"

"Sedrinel enters a new musical age!"

Argentine hummed. None of the reports mentioned any name besides "the Crafter"—but Argentine had his suspicions. Of course, it may have been a coincidence, both the attack on Cindertown a few weeks ago followed by the sudden return of the Crafter. But Argentine privately wondered whether one of them, Jay or Ark, could have been the Crafter's heir all along.

"Inspector!" someone barked. "Look alive!"

Captain Wallace Russ was at his side. Argentine straightened up.

"Sir," he answered, saluting.

"Been searching high and low for you!" said the Walrus, his mustache curling with a scowl. "Come on."

"What's the situation, sir?" asked Argentine, hurrying to keep pace with his superior. "Any more trouble with Mount Vakra?"

"What? No!" barked the Walrus. "Who said anything about a volcano? No, it's this blasted case!"

Argentine frowned. "To which case are you referring, sir?"

"The painting stolen from the mayor's house!" the Walrus snapped. "The chief has closed the books on it—but I *know* there's something fishy about that burglary. There were muses involved, I tell you!"

Argentine said nothing. The Walrus wasn't a terribly clever man, but his instincts about muses were sharper than most. "What did you tell the chief?"

"He told me to keep my nose out of it," the Walrus grumbled. "He said there wasn't enough evidence to justify reopening the investigation."

Argentine could sense where this conversation was going. "What's my assignment, sir?"

The Walrus turned a chubby smile toward him. "New project, Argentine," he beamed, thwapping Argentine on the arm. "I've put you in charge of Cindertown's music census. You'll be visiting every house to count anybody who could qualify as having musical potential. You'll also inspect homes to see whether you can spot traces of muses hanging about and identify areas where they may have been summoned for illegal use." He sent Argentine a meaningful glance. "Start with the mayor's house. Understood?"

Argentine smirked. "Understood, sir."

"Good." The Walrus bounded ahead. "You're absolutely indefensible!"

"*Indispensable*, sir."

"Whatever!"

∞

"Extra!" Lina cried, waving her family's latest bulletin in the air. "*Crafter returns to Sedrinel!*"

Even before she'd finished shouting, another villager came up to her, buying a copy. Lina counted through the short stack of bulletins she had left, grinning. She'd have to send Colton back to the shop soon so Ma could make another printing. Everybody in Hazeldenn wanted to buy the latest edition.

Lina skimmed the text of the article her mother had reprinted, sighing. If only she could get a sketch of him, or something. None of the articles her mother had gleaned from other presses had included any pictures of the new Crafter, though—so Lina could only imagine what he must be like.

He was probably tall. Cute, too. With a nice smile. Just her type.

She shook the thought from her head. She wouldn't get to meet somebody as important as the Crafter, not ever.

"Sis!" a familiar voice shouted.

Lina whirled around. "Colton, good timing. Tell Ma—"

"You've got mail!" said Colton, interrupting. He held up a brown paper envelope in both hands. "Who do you know from the capital?"

Lina was confused. She didn't know anybody from Fairdown Falls. But the postmark on the envelope was from the capital, sure enough.

"Who's it from?" she asked.

Colton looked the envelope over. "Dunno. But it says here: 'Miss Cecilina Kindle, Kindle's Paper Works, Hazeldenn.'"

Lina's curiosity outgrew her confusion. She accepted the envelope from Colton, pulling out the contents.

"What is it?" said Colton, bouncing along the bulletin stand.

Lina stared. There was a brief note inside. She read the scrawled, misspelled words in stunned silence:

> im sorry for wat i said on harvestide and for not saying goodby. plese tell mr. douse im sorry too.
> ps. this is still for you (in the onvelop)

Puzzled, Lina turned the envelope over. From the very bottom, something tumbled out and landed on the ground. It was her bead bracelet, the one he'd given her for Harvestide. Lina bent down to pick it up.

"Jay," she sighed with a frown, sliding the bracelet on. "You idiot."

∞

Hundreds of miles away, Klaste, Lord of the Wretched, was listening.

The cursed temple in which he dwelled was an ancient place, weathered by the storms of centuries. Its columns were cracked. Its roof had long since crumbled to dust. Curtains of cobwebs hung everywhere, tapestries that had been abandoned by their weavers long ago. Shattered statues and broken altars littered the floor. What had once been a magnificent place of worship now stood as an empty, decrepit shell.

But despite the many cracks in the stones along the floor, no natural growth had touched the barren earth around it. The place was too tainted by malevolence for any life to grow.

All was silent. It wasn't the sleepy silence of night, nor the peaceful silence of the wilderness. It wasn't even the sacred silence of death. It was the silence of terror. The silence of the abyss. The silence of despair.

And in that silence, Klaste listened. For the first time in centuries, he could hear the dischords that possessed this place beginning to stir. An unknown, unnamed presence had disturbed their prowl, filling the atmosphere with a sense of dread. They wouldn't dare speak its name.

Klaste knew what had caused his brethren such disquiet. He stepped onto the high altar and stared out through the decrepit columns across the ocean. Far, far, far in the distance, he could see the beacon of light glinting from Harmony Monument, shining in defiance at Din's place of defeat.

"The Crafter has returned," Klaste spoke aloud—and the mere sound of his voice against that forsaken silence was enough to send the nearest dischords hissing away, trembling at his presence.

"Dubito finally met his match." A smile broke across his face. "And the Age of the Disciple has begun."

He turned away from the ocean and crossed the barren stone floor, pausing at the centermost point of the temple. He lay his hand in the middle of the circle drawn there, a malignant spell scoring the ground.

"Come, Wretched," he said, invoking the arcane summons. "*Come.*"

From the darkest shadows, his brethren emerged. Odium, then Caligo, then Miseria, Malefás, and finally Despera. Dubito did not appear.

"What is your will, my lord?" they asked as one.

Klaste glanced toward the far-off Harmony Monument, where the beacon shone like a sore in his eye.

"The enemy has made his move," said Klaste. "He is preparing for the final battle, the fight for the Magnum Opus. And we must be ready."

He turned toward his fellow Wretched ones, his arms spread wide.

"Come," he hissed. "Let us begin."

ACKNOWLEDGMENTS

The greatest music requires an ensemble effort to achieve true harmony. The same is true with crafting a novel.

First, a shout-out to the awesome ladies at Hadleigh House Publishing and their team of editors, designers, and fellow authors. Thank you for being the ones to believe in *Brio* and for bringing Jay, Ark, and their story to print.

My thanks goes to Cindy Calder (hello, my teacher!) for encouraging me to write; I hope someday I can live up to your mighty green pen. Thanks also to Marilyn Kopperud, who spent countless hours sitting beside me at the piano to help me encounter the beauty of music.

Another shout-out goes to Sarah, Laurissa, and Michelle for being the greatest writers group west of the Mississippi. You ladies gave me the perfect balance of meticulous feedback and warm encouragement from the outset to help push this novel to the finish line.

Mom, Dad—saying "thank you" hardly seems sufficient. Thanks for every single thing you've done for me, including driving me around to music lessons, never missing a performance, and reading me stories every night.

My thanks also goes to Jessee and Apolline for sharing their expertise of the beautiful French language (and making sure I didn't butcher it).

My appreciation also goes to Dale and Christina Sanders, who reviewed the finished manuscript—and most especially to Cat, who read through *every single version* of *every single chapter* of this novel and who believed in me most when I didn't believe in myself.

A very special thanks to my daughter, Eleanor, my son, Joseph, and my dear husband, Tyler. You are the music of my life, the spark to my words, and the reason everything is worthwhile.

Finally, I'd like to acknowledge you, the one who chose to read this book. I'm grateful we had the chance to connect through these pages and share this story together.

ABOUT THE AUTHOR

Chris Cross (Christina Eberle) is a Colorado native who, to the chagrin of her friends and family, can ramble on about stories (especially children's books) for hours on end. She took her love of kid lit a little too seriously and earned her Master of Arts in children's literature from Kansas State University in 2010. *Brio* is her first novel, and when she's not too busy playing the piano, chasing after her kiddos, or tasting her husband's delicious cooking, she'll hopefully find time to continue Jay and Ark's story in future books.

Chris lives with her family in Northglenn, Colorado. You can geek out with her anytime at chriscrossauthor.com.

Made in the USA
Middletown, DE
16 March 2022